Mikhail Sholokhov was born in 1905 on a farm near the River Don in what is now the Rostov Region of Southern Russia. A former soldier in the Red Army, he won the Stalin Prize in 1941 and has twice been awarded the Order of Lenin. Best known for his three novels set in the Don Valley, *And Quiet Flows the Don*, *The Don Flows Home to the Sea* and *Virgin Soil Upturned*, Sholokhov's other works include *Fierce and Gentle Warriors*, *At the Bidding of the Heart* and *Fate of Man*. Mikhail Sholokhov was awarded the Nobel Prize for Literature in 1965.

Mikhail Sholokhov

TALES FROM THE DON

Translated from the Russian
by H. C. Stevens

First published in Great Britain by
Putnam and Company Ltd, 1961
Published in Abacus 1983 by
Sphere Books Ltd
30–32 Gray's Inn Road, London WC1X 8JL
Copyright © Putnam and Company Limited 1961

Reproduced, printed and bound in Great Britain by
Hazell Watson & Viney Limited,
Member of the BPCC Group,
Aylesbury, Bucks

CONTENTS

TALES FROM THE DON

THE BIRTHMARK

THE table is littered with cartridge cases smelling of burnt gunpowder, a mutton bone, a military map, a report, a filigreed bridle giving off a smell of horse's sweat, and a crust of bread. All these are on the table, but against the wall is a roughly hewn bench, mildewy with damp from the wall; Nikolka Koshevoi, the squadron commander, is sitting on the bench with his back pressed right against the window sill. There is a pencil in his stiff, frozen fingers. In front of him, side by side with some ancient posters opened out on the table, is a half-completed questionary. The rough, unglazed paper so far contains the dry information: Koshevoi, Nikolka, Squadron Commander; Landworker; Member of the Russian Young Communist Party.

In the column headed 'age' the pencil slowly enters: 18 years.

Nikolka is broad in the shoulder, and he looks older than his years. Heavily lined at the corners, his eyes look old, and his back is bent like an old man's.

"True, he's only a kid, a little rat, a green reed," the men of the squadron joke about him; "but you find another commander who has liquidated two bandit groups almost without loss; for six months and more he has led the squadron in fights and skirmishes as well as any older commander."

Nikolka is ashamed of his eighteen years. Whenever he has to fill in the hateful column headed 'age' his fingers slip and slow down, and his cheeks flush with chagrin. Nikolka's father was a cossack, and through his father he's a cossack too. He still has a half dream, half memory of how his father took and seated him on his service horse, when Nikolka was five or six years old.

"Hold on to the mane, sonny," he shouted, and Nikolka's mother, standing at the door of the summer kitchen, smiled at her boy. But she turned pale as with wide, staring eyes she gazed at the little feet tucked along the horse's bony back, and at her husband holding the rein.

That was ages ago. In the German war Nikolka's father had

disappeared without trace, as though he had fallen into a deep pool. Not a word was heard of him, not a smell. Then his mother died. From his father the boy inherited his love of horses, incomparable courage, and a birthmark the size of a pigeon's egg on the left leg above the ankle, just like his father's. Until he was fifteen he wandered around working in the towns, but then he wheedled a long military greatcoat out of a Red regiment passing through his district village, and went off to fight Wrangel. One day during the past summer he had been bathing in the Don with his military commissar. The commissar had suffered contusions, and he stuttered and twitched his head as he said, smacking Nikolka on his bowed, sunburnt back:

"You . . . you . . . you're lucky . . . lucky. . . . You are . . . you know . . . lucky. They say a birthmark's lucky."

Nikolka bared his dazzling white teeth, dived in and, snorting to clear the water from his nostrils, shouted back:

"That's all lies, you twister. I've been an orphan ever since I was a kid; all my life has gone in work, and you tell me I'm lucky!"

And he swam off to a yellow sandbank which embraced the river.

2

The hut in which Nikolka had his quarters stood on a bluff above the Don. From the windows he could see the green overflowing Don valley and the raven-black steel of the water. When the night was stormy the waves beat heavily at the foot of the bluff, the window shutters moaned and sobbed, and Nikolka imagined the waters stealthily creeping through the cracks in the floorboards, rising till they carried off the hut.

He would have liked to shift to other quarters, but somehow he never managed it, and remained there till the autumn. One frosty morning he went out to the veranda, shattering the brittle silence with the ring of his iron-shod boots. He went down into the little cherry orchard and stretched himself out on the tear-stained and dewily grey grass. He heard the housewife in the cowshed trying to get the cow to stand quietly; a calf lowed in a deep, imperative tone, and a stream of milk tinkled against the side of the iron bucket.

The yard wicket gate creaked, the dog started barking. He heard a troop commander's voice:

"Commander at home?"

Nikolka raised himself on his elbows:

"I'm out here. Well, what's your news?"

"An urgent courier arrived from the district village. He says a bandit force has broken through from Salsk district and occupied Grushinsky collective farm."

"Bring him here."

The courier was dragging a horse covered with hot foam towards the stable by the rein. In the middle of the yard it went down on its forelegs, then rolled over, breathed heavily, spasmodically for a moment, then died, staring with glazing eyes at the chained dog which was howling mournfully. It died because three crosses were marked on the packet the courier had brought; the three crosses indicated that the packet was most urgent, and with it the courier had galloped twenty-five miles without drawing rein.

Nikolka read the note in which the chairman asked him to bring his squadron to their aid; then he went back into the house, belting his sabre round him as he went, and thinking wearily: "I'd like to go and study somewhere; but now this further lot of bandits has turned up. . . . The military commissar's ashamed of me: you're a squadron commander, he says, but you can't write a single word properly. . . . Was it my fault that I failed to go right through the village school? He's nuts. And now another bandit group has come along. . . . More blood; but I'm worn out and fed up with living like this. . . . I've just about had enough."

He went out into the yard, loading his carbine as he went; but his thoughts were speeding like a horse along a well-used high-road: "How I'd like to go to a town to study . . . just to study. . . ."

As he went to the stable past the dead horse, he glanced at the black ribbon of blood oozing from the dusty nostrils, and turned away.

3

Along the summer track, over the windlicked ruts, curls the mouse-coloured knotweed; the goosefoot and catstails spread thickly and rampantly. At one time hay had been carted along the summer track to the threshing floors, which now were marked out in the steppe by amber sprinkles; but the beaten road was marked by the mounds at the foot of the telegraph poles. The poles run off into the white autumnal haze, stride across the hollows and ravines, and along the velvety track past the poles the ataman leads his band, half a company of Don and Kuban cossacks discontented with the Soviet régime. For three days now it has been retreating along roads and across the pathless virgin waste, like a hungry wolf forced away from a flock of sheep; for Nikolka Koshevoi's squadron is hard on its heels.

The men led by the ataman are a desperate lot, former service men, experienced, but even so the ataman is sunk deep in thought; he stands in his stirrups, sends his gaze roving far over the steppe, and reckons the miles to the bluish fringe of forest that stretches on the farther side of the Don.

And he is slipping off like a wolf, but behind him Nikolka Koshevoi's force follows closely.

During those pleasant summer days in the Donside steppes, under the deep and translucent sky, the ears of corn sway and tinkle with a silvery ring. It is the eve of the harvest, when the beard of the granular wheat blackens in the ears like the stubble of a seventeen-year-old lad, and the rye shoots up and tries to outgrow a man.

Bearded cossacks are sowing rye in little wedges of soil along the sandy clayey ground, over the sandy rises, around the edges of the village orchards. This soil has never been fruitful, for years and years the two-and-a-half acres have never yielded more than thirty measures; but they are sowing on this ground because illicit vodka, clearer than a maiden's tears, can be distilled from the rye; because it had always been so; their grandfathers and great-grandfathers sowed and drank. It was not for nothing that the arms of the Don Cossack Army depicted a drunken cossack straddling a wine barrel. In the autumn the villages and district centres wade through a heavy and deep intoxication, the crimson crowns of the cossacks' fur caps nod tipsily above the osier wattle fences.

And for the same reason the ataman also is rarely sober in the daytime, and for the same reason all the drivers and machine-gunners sit drunkenly askew on their springed carts.

The ataman had not seen his native village for seven years. Prison in Germany, then Wrangel, Constantinople dissolving in the sunlight, a prison camp surrounded with barbed wire, a Turkish felucca with salty, tarry wing, the plumy reeds of the Kuban, and then command of this bandit group.

That had been the ataman's life as he saw it if he glanced back over his shoulder. His soul had become worm-eaten, just as the marks of the bullocks' cloven hoofs by the steppe road go worm-eaten in the summer heat. A strange, incomprehensible pain gnawed at his inside, his muscles felt nauseatingly weary, and he felt sure he would never forget it, nor would his recurring fever ever be assuaged by any illicit spirit. Yet he went on drinking, he was never sober in the daytime, for the rye flowers sweetly and scentedly in the Don steppes, which lie extended under the sun like a thirsty, earthy belly; and the swarthy-cheeked hussies in the villages cook up such a fine home-concocted vodka that it is not to be distinguished from the water of a gushing spring.

4

At sunset there was the first slight frost. It sprinkled a silvery grizzle over the spreading leaves of the water-lilies, and in the early morning next day Lukich noticed thin, vari-coloured plates of ice, like mica, on the wheel of the water-mill.

Lukich got up feeling seedy; he had a burning pain in the loins, and with this gnawing pain his feet felt like cast iron, they clung to the ground. He shuffled about the mill, finding it difficult to move his absurd body, like a bag of bones. A reconnaissance sent out by the mice darted from the bran bin; he looked up with rheumy eyes; from the rafter high up under the roof a pigeon grumbled away in a rapid, businesslike patter. With nostrils that looked as though they had been moulded from clay, the old man drew in the clinging smell of watery mildew and the scent of fine-ground rye, listened as the sobbing water sucked unpleasantly around and licked the wooden piles, and fingered his wispy beard thoughtfully.

He lay down on the ground to rest, by the beehive. He slept under his sheepskin greatcoat, his mouth wide open; a warm and sticky spittle dribbled from the corners of his lips over his beard. The twilight shadows smudged out the old man's little hut, the mill was lost in milky shreds of mist.

But when he woke up he saw two horsemen riding out from the forest. One of them shouted to Lukich as he went through the beehive enclosure :

"Hi, old man, come here !"

Lukich stared suspiciously, and stopped. During the mournful years he had seen many armed men like this couple, they had taken food and flour without asking permission, and he had taken a strong dislike to all of them without distinction.

"Hurry up, you old radish !"

He made his way between the beehives made of hollowed tree trunks, began to mumble silently with his faded lips, and halted some distance away from the riders, looking at them with lowering gaze.

"We're Reds, daddy. . . . You needn't be afraid of us . . ." the ataman croaked in a conciliatory tone. "We're hunting a bandit group, and we've lost touch with our men. You may have seen a force come this way yesterday?"

"There was something of the sort."

"Where did they go to, daddy?"

"The devil only knows."

"And didn't any of them remain behind with you in the mill?"

"Not here," Lukich said curtly, and turned his back on them.

"Wait a bit, old man." The ataman sprang out of the saddle, swayed drunkenly on his bandy legs, and said with breath smelling strongly of home-made vodka : "We're liquidating the communists, daddy. Get that? And who we are is nothing to do with you." He stumbled, and the rein fell from his hand. "Your job is to get grain ready for seventy horses and to keep a still tongue in your head. And get that grain ready in two-twos. Get that? Where do you keep your grain?"

"I haven't any," Lukich said, looking away.

"Then what's in the granary?"

"All sorts of rubbish. There's no grain here."

"All right, come along."

He seized the old man by the collar and dragged him towards the lop-sided granary with its walls sinking into the ground. He flung the doors open. The corn bins contained millet and oats.

"What's that if it isn't grain, you old dog?"

"It's grain, it's my food. . . . It's what I've earned from the grinding. I've collected it a whole year, grain by grain. And now you want to feed it to your horses. . . ."

"So in your view our horses can die of hunger, can they? Tell me straight, are you on the side of the Reds, is it death you're asking for?"

"Have mercy, have pity on me. . . . What have you picked on me for?" Lukich snatched off his cap, flopped down on his knees and, seizing the ataman's hairy hands, started to kiss them.

"Tell me, are you fond of the Reds?"

"Forgive me. . . . Excuse my stupid remark. Oh, forgive me, don't kill me," the old man howled, putting his arms round the ataman's legs.

"Swear that you are not on the side of the Reds. . . . But don't cross yourself; you eat some earth."

With his toothless gums the old man chewed away at the soil he had collected in his palm, watering it with his tears.

"All right, now I believe you. Get up, old man."

The ataman laughed as he watched the old fellow unable to stand upright on his stiff legs. Meanwhile more horsemen had ridden up; they dragged out the oats and wheat from the bins, poured the food under their horses' hoofs and carpeted the yard with the golden grain.

5

The sun set in haze, in a humid mist.

Lukich slipped past the sentry and set off for the village, not taking the high road, but a forest path known only to him. Across the ravines he went, and through the forest, disturbed from its sensitive doze in the last hour before dawn.

He got as far as the windmill and was about to strike across the pasturage road into a side alley, when before him the vague outlines of horsemen suddenly loomed.

"Who's there?" came a cautious challenge through the silence.

"I'm the . . ." Lukich mumbled and went quite limp; he was shaking with terror.

"Who is it? Where's your pass? What are you wandering about for?"

"I'm the miller . . . from the water-mill hereby. I need to go to the village. . . ."

"What's the need? Here, you come along to the commander. Walk in front," one of the horsemen cried, riding his horse at him.

Lukich felt the horse's steaming lips against his neck. Limping, he ambled off to the village.

They halted on the square, outside a tile-roofed hut. The guard slipped with a grunt down from his saddle, tethered his horse to the fence, and with a clatter of his sabre went up the steps to the veranda.

"You follow me."

In the windows was a glimmering light. They went in.

The tobacco smoke made Lukich sneeze. He took off his cap and hurriedly crossed himself towards the ikon corner.

"We've caught this old fellow. He was making his way into the village."

Nikolka raised his tousled head, matted with down and feathers, and asked sleepily but sternly:

"Where were you making for?"

Choking with joy, Lukich stepped forward:

"My own lad. So you are ours. But I thought it was our enemies again. . . . I felt too shy, I didn't like to ask. I'm the miller. When you came through Mitrokhin forest and rode up to my mill I gave you milk to drink, my dear. . . . Surely you remember?"

"Well, what have you got to tell us?"

"I'll tell you this, dear lad: yesterday evening as dusk was falling that same band rode up to my mill and fed all my corn to their horses. They laughed at me. . . . Their commander said: swear to me this minute, and he made me eat earth."

"But where are they now?"

"They're still there. They've brought vodka with them; they're lapping it up, the unclean spirits, in my room. But I ran all the way here to report to your kindness; maybe you'd like to do justice on them."

"Order the horses to be saddled." Smiling at the old man, Nikolka rose from the bench and wearily drew on his greatcoat by the sleeves.

6

Dawn came on.

Green in the face with sleepless nights, Nikolka galloped up to the two-wheeled cart carrying the machine-gun.

"When we go into the attack open fire at their right flank. We've got to smash their wing."

Then he galloped back to the squadron advancing in open formation.

Round a straggling clump of dwarf oaks the horsemen emerged on to the high road, riding four to a rank, the carts in the middle of the column.

"At the gallop!" Nikolka shouted. Feeling the growing thunder of hoofs behind him, he brought his whip down over his stallion.

A machine-gun began to chatter desperately from the edge of the forest, and the men on the highroad swiftly opened out into a long, extended line, as though on the parade ground.

A wolf, its coat matted with burrs, dashed out from some fallen trees on the hillside. It stood listening, its head thrust forward. Not far away shots rang out, and the various noises of battle swayed back and forth in a heavy wave.

A shot spat out, 'tuk,' from a clump of alders, and somewhere beyond the hill, beyond the ploughlands, an echo hurriedly muttered 'tak'.

Then, again, a repeated 'tuk, tuk, tuk!' And from beyond the hill came the reply: 'Tak, tak, tak!'

The wolf stood listening for a moment or two longer, then it unhurriedly trotted into a hollow, into the undergrowth of yellow, unmown rushes.

"Hold on! Don't abandon the carts. Make for the coppice. Make for the coppice, damn you all!" the ataman shouted, standing in his stirrups.

But his drivers and machine-gunners were already bustling round the carts, cutting the traces; and the file of horsemen, shattered by machine-gun fire, broke into uncontrollable flight.

The ataman turned his horse round, and saw a rider flying towards him, waving his sabre. By his cloak and the field-glasses dangling from his neck, the ataman guessed that this horseman was no rank-and-file Red Army man, and he reined in his horse. Across the intervening distance he saw a youthful, whiskerless face distorted with fury, and eyes screwed up against the wind. The horse under the ataman began to prance, falling back on its haunches. Tugging the Mauser from his belt, he shouted:

"You white-faced whelp! Wave away, wave away, but I'll wave at you!"

He fired at the increasing expanse of black cloak. The other man's horse galloped some twenty feet further, then it dropped. Nikolka threw off his cloak and ran towards the ataman, firing as he went, drawing closer, closer. . . .

Beyond the coppice someone howled like an animal and broke off abruptly. The sun was hidden behind a cloud, and floating shadows fell over the steppe, the highroad, the forest ragged with winds and autumn.

"The infant, the titty-sucker, he's hot-blooded, and death will catch him here as the result," the ataman thought. Waiting till his adversary had fired all his bullets, he shook out the reins and flew at him like a kite.

Leaning out of the saddle, he swung his sabre and brought it down. He at once felt the body go limp beneath the blow and obediently slip to the ground. The ataman jumped off his horse, tore the field-glasses from the dead man, glanced at the legs still twitching with a fine shiver, looked about him, and squatted down to remove the chrome leather boots his victim was wearing. With one leg pressing down on the cracking knee, he drew off the first leg boot swiftly and dexterously. But evidently the sock had rucked up under the foot in the other boot, for he could not pull it off. Cursing furiously, he tugged and tugged, tore off the boot together with the sock, and just above the ankle noticed a birthmark the size of a pigeon's egg. Slowly, as though afraid of awakening the dead man, he turned the chilling head face upward, smearing his hands in the blood oozing in a broad bubbling stream from the mouth, and stared at the lad's features. Then he awkwardly put his arms round the bony shoulders and said huskily:

"Little son! My little Nikolka! My very own blood."

A shadow darkened his face, and he cried aloud:

"But do speak to me, say just one word. My dear! However could this have happened, ah?"

He dropped down and, raising the lids flooded with blood, gazed into the glazing eyes. He shook the helpless, yielding body. But Nikolka had gripped the bluish tip of his tongue firmly between his teeth, as though afraid he might say something terribly big and important.

The ataman pressed his son's rigid hands to his chest; then he kissed them. Gripping the sweating steel of his Mauser between his teeth, he shot himself in the mouth.

*   *   *

In the evening, when horsemen appeared and disappeared beyond the coppice, when the sound of voices, the snorting of horses and the clatter of stirrups were borne on the wind, the carrion kite reluctantly started up from the ataman's tousled head. It flew up and dissolved into the grey, autumnally colourless sky.

1924.

THE HERDSMAN

For sixteen days a burning wind had been blowing across the steppe, brown and scorched with sunlight, from the white, cracking saltmarshes, from the east.

The earth charred, the grass was shrivelled yellow, the runnels feeding the wells plentifully scattered along the highroad dried up, and the corn went a sickly white even before it emerged from the sheath, the stalks bent down towards the ground, bowed like old men.

At midday the coppery jangle of the church bell sounded over the dozing village.

Sultry heat. Silence. The only sound to be heard was the shuffling of feet along by the wattle fences, stirring up the dust, and the tapping of old men's sticks over the hummocks as they felt for the road.

The bell was ringing to summon a village meeting. The business before the meeting was the hiring of a herdsman.

A hum of voices in the Executive Committee office. Tobacco smoke.

The chairman tapped a pencil stump on the table.

"Citizens, the old herdsman refuses to mind the herd any longer, he says the pay isn't sufficient. We, the Executive Committee, propose to hire Gregory Frolov. He's one of us, he's an orphan, and a Young Communist. His father, as you know, was a cobbler. He lives with his sister, and he's got no one to feed him. I think, citizens, you'll understand his position and hire him to look after the herd."

Old Nestiorov couldn't stand for that, he began to wriggle and fidget on his lopsided bottom:

"We can't agree to that. The herd's healthy, but what sort of herdsman would he make? The herd has got to be driven out to the common land, for there's no food for them nearer, and he's not used to the job. By the autumn we shall be missing half our calves."

20

Ignat the miller, a sage old fellow, snuffled in a spitefully honied tone:

"We'll find a herdsman without the help of the executive committee; it's our concern, not theirs. . . . We've got to choose an old, reliable man, and one gentle with the cattle. . . ."

"Quite right, daddy. . . ."

"Hire an old man, citizens, and you'll lose your calves all the quicker. These days aren't like in the past, there's a lot of thieving going on everywhere. . . ." The chairman put his point insistently and expectantly, and he won support from the back:

"An old man's no use at all. . . . Remember these aren't cows, but summer calves. That calls for dogs' legs. Let the herd go rampaging mad with the clegs and then you try to round them up. An old man would start running around and shake out all his guts."

The laughter came in gusts, but old Ignat stuck to his view, grumbling in an undertone:

"The communists have got nothing to do with this. This has got to be tackled with prayer, and not so that . . ." The malevolent old man stroked his bald head.

But the chairman answered him with all due severity:

"I must ask you, citizen, to keep those remarks to yourself. For that . . . that sort of thing . . . I'll have you put out of the meeting."

*   *   *

In the reddening sunrise, when the smoke crawls out of the chimneys in clumps of greasy cottonwool and spreads low over the square, Grigory collected the herd of 150 cattle and drove them through the village, out to the grey and unfriendly hillside.

The steppe was speckled with the brown pimples of marmot mounds; the marmots sounded their long drawn out, anxious whistles; the little bustards flew up out of the low-growing grass of the hollows, their silvery plumage glistening.

The herd was quiet. The calves' cloven hoofs pattered over the furrowed skin of the ground like a fine rain.

Duniatka, Grigory's sister and assistant, strode along at his side. Her sunburnt, freckled cheeks were dimpled with a smile, her eyes, her lips, were all smiles, for she had only known seventeen springs, and at the age of seventeen everything seems vastly amusing: her brother's knitted brows, and the flop-eared calves chewing the steppe scrub as they went. She even found it amusing that for two days they hadn't had a bite to eat.

But Grigory was not smiling. Under his weather-stained cap his forehead was lined with furrows and his eyes looked tired, as though he had seen far more than his nineteen years.

Quietly the herd wandered along the roadside, drifting in a speckled streak.

Grigory whistled to the lagging calves, and turned to Duniatka:

"Dunia, we'll have earned some grain by the autumn, and then we'll go off to the town. I'll enter the Workers' University, and fix you up somewhere or other. Possibly at a school, too. In the towns, Duniatka, there are lots of books, and they eat clean bread with no grass in it, not like ours."

"But where shall we get the money from to go there?"

"You're a funny one. They'll pay us 700 pounds of grain, and there's your money. We'll sell it at a rouble for 36 pounds, then we'll sell the millet, and dung fuel bricks. . . ."

He halted in the middle of the road, stopping to write something in the dust with his knout, and calculating.

"Grisha, what are we going to eat today? We haven't a scrap of bread."

"I've got a piece of stale griddle cake in my bag."

"That's all right for today, but how about tomorrow?"

"Tomorrow they'll come out from the village and bring us some flour. The chairman promised. . . ."

The noonday sun scorched down. Grigory's baggy shirt was wet with sweat, it clung to his shoulders.

Now the herd was fidgeting restlessly, the clegs and flies were stinging the calves; the bellowing of the cattle and the buzzing of the clegs hung in the blazing hot air.

Late in the afternoon, just before sunset, they drove the herd into its night quarters. Not far off was a pond and a shanty made of straw rotted with rain.

Grigory rounded up the herd at a trot. He ran heavily to the stockyard and opened the small wattle gate.

Then he counted the calves, letting them pass one by one through the black oblong of the gateway.

2

On a mound, which stuck up like a succulent pea beyond the pond, they made themselves a new shanty. They daubed the walls with dung, and Grigory covered it in at the top with scrub.

Next day the chairman rode out to see them. He brought with him eighteen pounds of flour and a small bag of millet.

He sat down and had a smoke in the cool.

"You're a good lad, Grigory. You look after the herd, and then in the autumn you and I'll drive to the regional town. Maybe from there we'll find some way of arranging for you to go and study. I know someone in the Education Department there; he'll help. . . ."

Grigory flushed with joy, and, when he saw the chairman off, he held his stirrup and squeezed his hand firmly. He stood for quite a time gazing after the curly wisps of dust that streamed from under the horse's hoofs.

At midday the dried-up steppe, flushed consumptively, panted under the oppressive heat. Grigory lay on his back and gazed at the hill half lost in a melting bluish haze, and had the feeling that the steppe was a living thing and was finding life difficult under the burden of the innumerable settlements, villages, and towns. The ground seemed to be rocking with a spasmodic breathing, and somewhere beneath the surface, under the thick layers of strata, another, unknown, life was pulsing and throbbing.

And in the midst of the day he was filled with awe.

With his eyes he measured the immeasurable lines of hills, gazed at the streaming haze, at the herd speckling the tawny grass, and thought he was completely cut off from the world, like a crust of bread from the loaf.

On the Saturday evening he drove the cattle into the stockyard. Duniatka was lighting a fire by the shanty to cook some millet gruel and some tastily smelling sorrel.

Grigory squatted down by the fire and, stirring up the scented dung fuel with his knout handle, remarked:

"Grishak's calf's not well. We ought to tell him. . . ."

"Perhaps I ought to go to the village?" Duniatka asked, trying to appear unconcerned.

"No need. I can't mind the herd on my own." He smiled. "So you're longing for company, eh?"

"Yes, I am, Grisha, my dear. We've been living a whole month in the steppe now and we've only once seen a human being. Why, if we spend all the summer out here we'll even forget how to talk."

"Stick it out, Dunia. In the autumn we'll go off to the town. You and I'll study, and then, when we've finished studying, we'll come back here. We'll start to work the land scientifically, for we're an ignorant lot here, the people are asleep. None of them's educated, we haven't any books. . . ."

"Then they won't take you or me into the school. We're ignorant too."

"Yes, they will. When I went to the district in the winter I read a book by Lenin in the secretary's group. In that book it says the power belongs to the proletariat, and about learning it says those who're poor ought to learn."

Grisha slipped down on his knees, coppery reflections from the fire danced over his cheeks.

"We've got to learn in order to know how to run our republic. The workers are in power in the towns, but the chairman of our district's a kulak and the chairmen in the villages are all rich peasants. . . ."

"Grisha, I'd scrub floors, I'd do washing, and earn money while you studied. . . ."

The dung-fuel bricks smouldered away, smoking and breaking into little flames. The steppe was drowsily still.

3

The party secretary, Politov, sent Grigory a message by a militia-man going to the regional town, to the effect that he was to go to the district centre.

He left the herd before dawn, and by dinner-time he could see from a rise the village belfry, and tiny houses roofed with straw and sheet iron.

Dragging his weary feet, he struggled into the square.

The club was in the house formerly belonging to the priest. Over new paths smelling of fresh straw he entered a large room.

The room was in twilight, for the shutters were closed. Close to a window Politov was planing some wood to make a window frame.

"I've heard all about it, brother, I've heard," he smiled as he gave Grigory his sweaty hand. "Well, why don't you write something? I inquired in the regional town, and heard lads were wanted in the oilmill there; but it turns out they've already got a dozen more than they need. . . . So you go on looking after the herd, and in the autumn we'll send you to school."

"If only this job was . . . The village kulaks were all against my being made herdsman. . . . They said I was a Young Communist, and godless. You can guard the herd without praying," Grigory laughed wearily.

Politov swept away the shavings with his sleeve and sat down on the window sill, scrutinising Grigory from under his knitted and sweatily moist brows.

"You've gone quite thin, Grisha. . . . How do you manage for food?"

"We manage."

They were silent for a while.

"Well, come along to my place. I'll let you have some new books; we've received newspapers and books from the town."

They walked along the street running down to the graveyard. Chickens were bathing in grey heaps of ash, a well-crane cracked, and the oppressive silence rang in the ears.

"You spend the night here. We're going to have a meeting. The lads have already been asking after you. 'Where's Grisha, why and what for?' You'll meet the lads again. I'm giving a lecture this evening on the international situation. . . . Spend the night with me, and walk back tomorrow morning. Right?"

"I can't spend the night here. Duniatka can't look after the herd on her own. I'll stay to the meeting, but as soon as it's over I'll set out to walk through the night."

It was cool in the passage-way of Politov's house.

It had a sweetish smell of dried apples, and the collars and reins hanging on the walls gave off the scent of horses' sweat.

There was a barrel of kvass in one corner, with a rickety bedstead beside it.

"That's my corner; it's too hot in the hut."

Politov stooped down, and carefully drew out a back number of *Pravda* and a couple of books from under the sheet.

He thrust them into Grigory's hands, then opened the mouth of a patched linen sack.

"Here, hold this."

Grigory held the sack by the ears, but he was already running his eyes along the lines of the newspaper print.

Politov scooped up flour by the handful, shook down the half-filled sack, then flew into the other room.

He brought back two hunks of pork fat, wrapped them in a rusty cabbage leaf, put the package into the sack, and barked:

"When you go back home take this with you."

"I'm not taking it," Grigory flared up.

"Why not?"

"Because I'm not. . . ."

"What game are you playing, you serpent?" Politov shouted, going white and boring into Grigory with his eyes. "And you're a comrade! You'll die of hunger and not say a word. Take it or you're no longer a friend of mine. . . ."

"I don't want to take your last . . ."

"The priest's last wife!" Politov said more gently, watching as Grigory angrily tied up the mouth of the sack.

The meeting lasted almost till dawn.

Then Grisha strode off into the steppe. His back was burdened with the sack of flour, his burning feet were raw and bleeding, but he walked along bravely and cheerfully towards the flickering sunrise.

4

At daybreak Duniatka left the shanty to gather dry dung for fuel. Grigory came running from the stockyard. She guessed something unpleasant had happened.

"What's the matter?"

"Grishak's calf has died. And three others are sick." He stopped for breath, then added: "Run to the village, Dunia. Tell Grishak and the others to come out here today. Tell them the calves are falling ill."

Dunia hurriedly dressed for the walk back. Then she strode off across the rise with her back to the sun creeping up over the ridge.

Grigory stood watching her go, then slowly went back to the stockyard.

The herd had wandered off into a hollow, but three calves were lying by the wattle fence. By midday all three were dead.

Grigory rushed from the herd to the yard: two more calves were sick.

One had dropped on the damp slime around the pond; it turned its head towards Grisha and lowed mournfully; its bulging eyes were glassy with tears, and salty tears rolled down over Grisha's own sunburnt cheeks.

At sunset Dunia returned, bringing the owners of the calves with her.

Touching the motionless body of a calf with his stick, old Artiomich said:

"It's the steppe murrain, that's what it is. . . . Now all the herd will catch it and drop."

They flayed the hides and buried the carcasses not far from the pond. Over them they heaped the dry black earth into a mound.

But next day Duniatka again had to take the road to the village. Seven more calves had fallen sick.

The days passed in gloomy succession. The yard grew desolate. And Grisha's soul grew desolate too. Out of the 150 head only 50 were left. The owners drove up in their waggons and flayed the dead calves, dug shallow pits in the hollow, heaped earth over the bleeding carcasses and rode off. But the herd entered the yard reluctantly: the calves bellowed as they scented blood and death invisibly creeping among them.

Each dawn, when yellow-featured Grisha opened the creaking gate of the yard, the herd came out to graze, invariably making its way across the dry grave mounds.

The stench of decaying flesh, the dust kicked up by the frenzied cattle, a long drawn out and helpless lowing, and the sun, as hot as ever, marching in a slow procession over the steppe.

Hunters rode out from the village. They fired their guns round the wattle stockyard to scare the raging pest away. But the calves went on dying, and with every day the herd grew smaller and smaller.

Grisha began to notice that the graves had been roughly dug up and opened; gnawed bones were lying not far from the spot, and the herd grew restless and fearful at night.

In the silence of the night a savage howl suddenly broke out, and the herd tore about the yard.

Smashing down the fencing, the calves made their way in little groups to the shanty. They slept close to the fire, breathing heavily and chewing the cud.

Grisha had no idea what was troubling them until one night he was awakened by the barking of the dogs. Pulling on his sheepskin coat as he went, he dashed out of the shanty. The calves rubbed their dewy wet backs against him.

He stood for a moment at the entrance, whistled to the dogs, and heard a broken varied howling of wolves in reply. From the blackthorns crowning the hill another wolf answered in deep tones.

He went into the shanty and lit the wick floating in a saucer of oil.

"D'you hear that, Dunia?"

The howling faded away only together with the stars fading in the dawn.

5

Next morning Ignat the miller and Mikhei Nestiorov drove out to see them. Grigory was in the shanty patching his boots. The two old men came in. Ignat took off his cap and, half closing his eyes to shield them from the slanting rays of sunlight creeping over the earthen floor, raised his hand to cross himself before the small portrait of Lenin which hung in one corner. But he realized his mistake and halted his hand halfway up to his chest, thrust it hurriedly behind his back, and spat indignantly :

"So . . . So you haven't got a godly ikon?"

"No. . . ."

"But who's that hanging in the sacred corner?"

"Lenin."

"That's the cause of all our troubles. God isn't here, and so there's bound to be disease. . . . And that's why the calves have died. . . . Ah, our merciful Creator . . ,"

"Daddy, the calves died because you didn't send for the veterinary surgeon."

"We lived quite well before without your vet. . . . You're too educated. . . . You should cross your heathen brow more often, and then a vet. wouldn't be necessary."

Rolling his eyes, Nestiorov shouted:

"Take that anti-Christ down from the sacred corner. It's all through you, you heathen, you blasphemer, that the herd is dying off."

Grisha turned rather pale.

"You should put your own house in order. There's no need to shout. He's the leader of the proletariat."

Mikhei Nestiorov bridled up, turned livid, and bawled:

"You work for the community. You do as we want. We know the likes of you. . . . You look out, or we'll be settling accounts with you before long."

Clapping on their caps, they went out without saying goodbye.

Duniatka looked at her brother in alarm.

But next day the smith, Tikhon, came out from the village to see how his calf was getting on.

Squatting on his heels outside the shanty, he smoked a cigarette and remarked, smiling bitterly and wryly:

"Ours is a rotten life. . . . They've sacked the old chairman, and now Mikhei Nestiorov's son-in-law is running the show. And they're doing things their own way. Yesterday they parcelled out the land: as soon as any of the poor peasants gets a good strip they arrange a fresh share-out. The rich are sitting on our backs again. . . . They've taken all the good land, Grisha, my boy. And we're left with the clay. That's the song they're singing now."

Grigory sat on by the fire till midnight, writing painfully on the broad saffron leaves of Indian corn. He wrote about the unjust division of the land, he wrote that instead of calling a veterinary surgeon they had fought the cattle disease with rifle fire. Handing the packet of dry, scribbled Indian corn leaves to Tikhon, he said:

"If you happen to go to the regional town, ask where the paper *Red Truth* is printed. And hand them these. I've written it all out clearly, but don't crush the packet, or you'll rub out the charcoal."

With his blackened fingers, burnt with coal, the smith carefully took the rustling sheets and put them under his shirt, next to his heart. As he said goodbye he said with the same smile:

"I'll take a walk to the regional town; maybe I'll find the Soviet authorities there. It's a hundred miles and I'll get there in three days. When I get back in a week's time I'll come and see you again."

6

The autumn came on with rain, with cloudy mugginess.

Duniatka had gone off early in the morning to get food.

The calves were grazing on the hillside. Drawing on his home-woven coat, Grigory followed them, kneading a head of faded roadside burdock thoughtfully in his hands. Just before the autumnally brief dusk two horsemen rode down the hill.

Their horses' hoofs drumming, they galloped up to Grigory.

Grigory recognized one of them as the village Soviet chairman, Mikhei Nestiorov's son-in-law. The other was Ignat, the miller's son.

The horses were lathered with sweat.

"Hallo, herdsman."

"Hallo."

"We've come to see you."

Bending over in the saddle, with frozen fingers the chairman unbuttoned his greatcoat, taking a long time over it. Then he took out a yellowing sheet of newspaper. He opened it out against the wind.

"Did you write this?"

The words he had written on the sheets of maize leaves danced before Grigory's eyes: concerning the unjust share-out of the land and the deaths of the cattle."

"Now come along with us."

"Where to?"

"Why, just across there, to the hollow. We've got to have a talk with you. . . ." The chairman's bluish lips were twitching, his eyes shifted heavily and slowly.

Grigory smiled.

"We can talk here."

"We can talk here, too, if you wish."

He pulled a pistol out of his pocket, and said hoarsely as he held in his restless horse:

"Are you going to write any more in the papers, you snake?"

"What's it to do with you?"

"It's this to do with me, that because of you I'm having to face a trial. Are you going to do any more intriguing? Speak up, you communizing mongrel."

Without waiting for an answer he shot Grigory in his tight-lipped mouth.

The lad fell under the rearing horse's hoofs, groaned, tore up a clump of damp, rusty grass with crooked fingers, then was still.

Ignat, the miller's son, sprang off his horse, clawed up a handful of black earth, and thrust it into the dead lad's mouth, which was beginning to foam with bubbling blood.

*   *   *

Broad is the steppe and no man has measured it. Many are the roads and human settlements scattered over it. Darker than dark was the autumnal night, and the rain washed the traces of horse hoofs clean away.

A light frost. Twilight. The road running off into the steppe.

If a man has a little bag with a crust of barley bread over his back, and a stick in his hands, it is not hard for him to go.

Duniatka walked along at the side of the road. The wind tore at the edges of her ragged blouse and drove in gusts against her back.

All around, the steppe lay unwelcoming, gloomy. Night was falling.

A little off the road a mound loomed up, on it a shanty with locks of tossing scrub.

She approached it with a wavering step, as though drunk, and lay face downward on the settling grave.

Night. . . .

Duniatka made her way along the well-worn track which runs straight to the railway station.

It was easy for her to go, for in the bag on her back was a crust of barley bread, a well-worn book with pages smelling of the pungent steppe dust, and her brother Grigory's linen shirt.

When the heart swells with grief, when tears scald the eyes, then somewhere, far from inquisitive gaze, she takes an unwashed linen shirt out of her bag. She presses it to her face, and is conscious of the smell of sweat, the sweat of her own blood brother. She lay a long time on the mound, without stirring.

Now the miles are retreating behind her. From the steppe ravines comes the howl of wolves furious with life; but Duniatka strides along at the roadside, for she is going to the town where the Soviet government rules, where the proletariat study in order to know how to run their republic in the future.

So it is said in the book Lenin wrote.

1925.

"YOU'RE an educated woman, you wear glasses, and yet you can't get this into your head. . . . What am I to do with him?

"Our detachment is quartered some twenty-five miles away. I've come here on foot, carrying him in my arms. You can see the skin's all rubbed off my feet. If you're the head of this children's home, take in the child. You say there's no room? But what am I to do with him? I've suffered enough through him already. I've supped of bitterness right up to my front teeth. Why, yes, he's my little son, he's my family. He's in his second year, but he hasn't any mother. There was something quite special about his mother. Oh, yes, I can tell you all about it, if you'd like to listen. The year before last I was in a company organized for special assignments. At that time we were hunting the Ignatiev bandit group through the upper districts of the Don. To be exact, I was a machine-gunner. One day we rode out of a village, the steppe all around was as bare as a baldheaded man, and the heat was unbelievable. We rode over a rise and began to drop down the hill into a little wood. I was in front on a two-wheeled cart. Suddenly I look and think I can see a woman lying on a mound close by. I touch up the horses and make for her. She was just an ordinary sort of woman, but there she was lying mug upwards, and the edge of her skirt dragged right up to her head. I get down and could see she was alive, but breathing hard. I thrust the point of my sabre between her teeth and forced her mouth open, splashed her with water from my flask, and she came right back to life. Then the cossacks of the company galloped up and questioned her:

"'Who are you, and why are you lying so close to the road exposing yourself indecently?'

"She gave tongue as though wailing for the dead, and after a lot of hard work we got out of her that a band from the Astrakhan area had taken her on their waggon, had raped her on the spot and, as usual, flung her out on the road. I say to my fellow-cossacks:

"'Brothers, allow me to take her on my cart, seeing as she's suffered from bandits.'

"And all the company cried out:

"'Take her on your cart, Shibalok. Women are living things, the carrion; let her get a bit better and then we'll see.'

"Well, and what would you expect? Although I'm not the sort to be fond of sniffing at a woman's petticoats I felt sorry for her, and I took her on, to my own sin. She survived and grew quite used to us; she started washing the cossacks' rags, and then you'd notice that she'd patched somebody's trousers, and she did all the woman's work for the company. But we began to feel that it was a bit of a scandal to keep a woman with the company. The captain swore:

"'Take her by the tail, the hen, and turn her back to the wind.'

"But I felt sorry for her, and that to the highest and greatest degree. So I told her:

"'Clear out for your own good, Daria, or some idiotic bullet will get wedded to you, and then you'll be crying. . . .'

"She burst into tears, and stormed back at me:

"'Shoot me on the spot, dear cossacks, but I'm not going to leave you.'

"Soon after that my driver was killed off, and she tries the following trick on me:

"'Take me as your driver, ah? You see, I can manage horses just a well as anyone else. . . .'

"I hand her the reins.

"'If,' I tell her, 'we get into a fight and you can't manage to turn the cart round back to front in two shakes, lie down in the middle of the road and die: in any case, I'll flog you to death.'

"She drove to the amazement of all the serving cossacks. Even though she was a female she knew as much about horses as any cossack. There were times during a fight when she would swing the cart round so fast that the horses reared on their hind legs. And the longer we went on the more she did. And we began to get involved with her. Well, as you could expect, she got a belly.

Women have to put up with a lot from the likes of us. And so for some eight months longer we hunted that bandit group. The cossacks in our company lashed out at me:

"'Shibalok, look how fat your driver's got on government rations: she's too big for the driver's seat now.'

"And then we got into a bit of a mess: we'd used up all our ammunition and supplies hadn't come up. The bandit force was holding one end of a village, we the other. We kept it a very deep secret from the villagers that we hadn't any bullets left. And then there was a spot of treachery. In the middle of the night—I was on sentry duty—I hear the ground groaning. They came streaming round the village and had in mind to encircle us. They tore into the attack, and clearly hadn't the least fear of us; they even went so far as to shout to us:

"'Surrender, you darling red cossacks, you bulletless ones. Otherwise, dear brothers, we'll finish off the lot of you.'

"Well, they hunted after us. They twisted our tail so hard that we had to run races over the rises to see who had the best horse. Next morning we reassembled in a forest some ten miles outside the village, and a good half of us failed to answer the roll-call. Some had cleared off, and those left behind were cut down. I was pretty miserable, not a house anywhere near, and Daria now fell ill. She'd galloped on horseback all night and she was changed completely, black shadows under her eyes. I see her trying to get away from us, and she goes off into the forest, into a thicket. I guessed what was up and went after her. She plunged into a ravine, among fallen logs, found a clear spot washed clean with rain, and, just like a she-wolf, scraped fallen leaves together and lay at first face downward, then turned over on to her back. She starts groaning, her labour began, but I squatted down behind a bush and didn't stir, watching her through the branches. And she groaned and groaned, then she began to scream, her tears ran down her cheeks, she went green all over, her eyes goggled, she strained until a spasm bent her double. It wasn't fitting for a cossack to do what I did, but I watched and saw that if she didn't drop the baby she'd die. I ran out from behind the bush and over to her; I could see I'd got to help her. I stooped down, rolled up my sleeve, and I felt so fearful and helpless I went all wet with sweat. I've had to kill people in my time, and I've never felt any fear then, but now what was I like? I go fussing round her, she stops howling and fires this blast at me:

" 'Yasha, do you know who told the bandits we hadn't any ammunition?' And she looked at me kind of serious.

" 'Well, who was it?' I asked her.

" 'It was me.'

" 'You fool, have you got rabies? This isn't the time for chatter; you lie quiet.'

"But she stuck to her point:

" 'Death's standing at my head, I must confess to you, Yasha. You don't know what a snake you've been warming under your shirt. . . .'

" 'Well, confess away,' I said. 'The devil's in you.'

"And she told me all, beating her head against the ground; she told me:

" 'I,' she says, 'was in the bandit group of my own free will and I went around with their leader, Ignatiev. . . . A year ago they sent me to your company to get them any news I could, and I made up the story that I'd been raped, just for show. I shall die now, but otherwise I'd have given away the whole company sooner or later. . . .'

"At that my heart went mad with fury and I couldn't stand it. I kicked her with my boot and made her mouth all bloody. But then her labour set in again, and I see the child coming between her legs. There it lay all wet, and twittering like a little hare in a fox's teeth. . . . But now Daria was crying and laughing, she crawls to my feet and tries to put her arms round my knees. I turned away and went off to the company. And I told the cossacks how it had all been.

"And there was a fine row. At first they wanted to sabre me on the spot, but then they tell me:

" 'You took her on, Shibalok, now you must finish her off complete with the new-born babe; for if you don't we'll shred you like cabbage.'

"I went down on my knees and said:

" 'Brothers! I shall kill her not because I'm afraid of your threats but for conscience' sake, because of those brothers and comrades of ours who've lost their heads through her treachery. But have pity on the child. In it she and I have got half shares;

it's my family, so let it live. You've got wives and children, but I haven't a soul except this baby.'

"I pleaded with the company and kissed the ground. And they had pity on me and said:

" 'Well, all right. Let your family grow up, and may it grow up to be as fine a machine-gunner as you, Shibalok. But finish off the woman!'

"I ran back to Daria. She was sitting up; she'd come round and was holding the child in her arms.

"And I say to her:

" 'I won't let you put the child to your breast. Since it's been born in a bitter year may it never taste mother's milk; and as for you, Daria, I've got to kill you because you're against our Soviet government. Stand up with your back to the ravine.'

" 'Yasha, but how about the child? He's your flesh. If you kill me he'll die without milk. Let me feed him, and then kill me: I don't mind. . . .'

" 'No,' I say to her, 'the company's given me strict orders. I can't let you live, but don't worry about the child. I'll feed it on mare's milk; I won't let it die.'

"I stepped back a couple of paces and slipped my rifle off my shoulder. But she put her arms round my legs and kissed my boots. . . .

"And afterwards I went back without looking round, my hands trembling, my knees sagging, and the child, slippery, naked, slipping out of my hands.

"Some five days later we rode back past the same spot. In the dell above the forest was a cloud of crows. . . . I've known much bitterness through this child.

" 'Take it by the feet and smash it against the cartwheel. What are you suffering with it for, Shibalok?' the cossacks used to ask.

"But I was sorry beyond anything I can tell for the little scamp. I would think: 'Let him grow up, he'll take on my job, my son will defend the Soviet régime. And Yakov Shibalok will leave a memory behind, I shan't die like scrub in the steppe, I shall leave my child.' You see, believe me, good woman citizen, I'd wept tears over him, though I hadn't known tears for ages. One of our mares had a foal, we shot the foal, and so I made use of its mother's milk. Sometimes the babe wouldn't take the teat, it was a real pest; but then he grew used to it and sucked away at the teat as well as any other child at its mother's titty.

"I made him a shirt out of my old underpants. Now he's grown rather too big for it, but that doesn't matter, we'll manage.

"And now get it all clear in your head: what am I to do with him? He's too small, you say? He's intelligent and he can chew. Take him and chance it. You'll take him? Well, and thank you, citizeness. As soon as we smash the Fomin bandits I'll ride over and visit him.

"Goodbye, little son, Shibalok's family. Grow up . . . Sh, you son of a bitch! What are you tugging at your daddy's beard for? Haven't I nannied you? Haven't I looked after you, and now you're trying to fight me, are you? Well, before we part, let's kiss the top of your noddle.

"Don't worry, good citizeness. D'you think he'll start screaming? Not he! He's got a little of the bolshevik in him: he can bite all right, there's no point in denying it, but you won't get any tears out of him!"

1925.

THE FOOD COMMISSAR

The regional food commissar arrived in the district.

Tugging at his spiteful-looking lips, which were shaven till they were blue, he said hurriedly:

"According to our statistics it's absolutely necessary to draw 150,000 poods of grain from the district entrusted to you. Comrade Bodyagin, I've appointed you to this district as local food commissar because you're an energetic, enterprising worker. I hope you'll prove so. Time, one month. The tribunal will arrive in a day or two. The grain is needed by the army and the centre like this"—he smacked his protruding, scrubby Adam's apple with his palm and clenched his teeth hard: "If anyone out of malice tries to conceal their grain, shoot them."

He nodded his bald, shaven head, and drove off.

2

The telegraph poles, hopping like sparrows all over the district, passed on the words: grain requisition.

In the villages and hamlets the cossacks with large sowings drew their richly ornamental belts tighter round their bellies, and decided at once without thinking twice about it:

"Give up our grain for nothing? Not us!"

And, in the night, inquisitive eyes peering around would have seen holes being filled to the brim with the finest corn; it was buried by the hundredweight. Every man knew where his neighbour had hidden his store of grain, and how.

But they held their tongues.

Bodyagin and his food requisitioning detachment went merry-go-rounding over the district. The snow swished and squeaked under the cart wheels, the hoar-frosted wattle fences sped past. The evening shadows drew down. The district village was just like any other district village, but to Bodyagin it was home. Six years had not made it seem any older.

That was how he remembered it: a sultry July, the foaming yellow camomile along the field bounds, harvesting time. Ignat Bodyagin was fourteen. He was scything the corn together with his father and a hired labourer. His father struck the labourer because he broke a tine of the fork; Ignat went straight up to his father and said through clenched teeth:

"Father, you're a swine."

"Me?"

"Yes, you."

A blow from his father's fist sent Ignat flying; he beat the boy across the loins till the blood came. When they returned home from the fields that evening his father cut a cherry stick in the orchard, trimmed it, and, stroking his beard, thrust it into Ignat's hand:

"Go, sonny; you go off into the world and get some wisdom into your head. Then you can come back." And he smirked sarcastically.

Thus it had been six years ago, and now his cart was rustling past the hoar-frosted fences, the straw-thatched roofs sped away behind him, the painted shutters. Bodyagin glanced at the garden behind his father's paling fence, at the tinplate cock on the roof, its wings spread in a voiceless crow; he felt a lump rise in his throat and he caught his breath. That evening he asked the master of the house where he was staying:

'Is old Bodyagin still alive?"

The man, who was mending some harness, twisted the thread into a waxed end with his stained fingers, and knitted his brows:

"He gets richer and richer. He's brought home a new woman; his old woman died long ago, his son's disappeared somewhere. But he still goes running after the soldiers' grass widows, the old radish."

Adopting a more serious tone, he added:

"But he's a good husbandman, he has an eye for everything. You don't happen to know him, do you then?"

At breakfast next morning the chairman of the travelling revolutionary tribunal remarked:

"At the meeting yesterday two kulaks tried to persuade the

cossacks not to hand over their grain. During the search they put up resistance, and beat up two Red Army men. We're organizing a summary trial; we'll deal with them."

3

The tribunal chairman, a former cooper, announced from the low stage of the People's House as simply as though he were fixing a new band round a barrel:

"To be shot!"

The two men were escorted to the door. Bodyagin recognized the second cossack as his father. The old man's red beard had gone silvery grey only at the edges. He watched the retreating sunburnt, furrowed neck, and followed him out.

On the veranda he said to the commander of the guard:

"Send that fellow, that old man, over to me."

His father strode up with back bowed moodily. He recognized his son, and a flame blazed up in his eyes, then died down. He concealed his eyes under the tousled corn of his eyebrows.

"So you're with the Reds now, sonny?"

"Yes, father."

"Hm-m-m!" His father looked away.

They went silent for some moments.

"It's six years since we last saw each other, father; haven't we anything to say to each other?"

The old man malevolently and obstinately knitted his brows:

"Hardly anything. . . . Our paths happen to have been different. I've got to be shot for my property; because I won't let go of my granary I'm a counter-revolutionary. But if someone rummages in someone else's corn bins, is that lawful? But steal away, you've got the power."

The skin on the sutures of the food commissar's skull went a dull grey.

"We're not stealing from the poor; but from those who've grown rich on other men's sweat we'll take the lot. You've been the first to suck the blood of the labourers all your life."

"I myself worked day and night. I didn't go wandering about the wide world like you."

"Those who work sympathize with the government of the workers and peasants; but you welcomed it with a cudgel. You wouldn't let it come near your fence. And so you're to be smashed to bits."

The old man started to pant hoarsely. He said huskily, as though he had just snapped the thin thread that had joined them hitherto:

"You're no son of mine, and I'm not your father. . . . For using such language to your father may you be thrice accursed, anathema. . . ." He spat and strode away without another word. But he turned sharply round and shouted with undisguised fervour: "Now, Ignat, my boy. If we don't happen to see each other again, then damn you. The cossacks are coming from Khopersk to slit up the throats of your government. If I should live, if the Mother of God protects me, I'll squeeze the soul out of you with my own hands."

That evening a little group of men marched past the windmill outside the district village. They went to the claypit where dead cattle are thrown. Teslenko, the commander, knocked out his pipe and said curtly:

"Stand close up to the hole. . . ."

Bodyagin glanced at the sledge cutting the violet-hued snow of the roadside with its runners, and said in a shaking voice:

"Don't be angry, father. . . ."

He waited for an answer.

Not a sound.

"One . . . two . . . three. . . ."

The horse on the farther side of the windmill started, the sledge wriggled in alarm over the rutty road, and the painted shaft bow, glimmering above the bluish shroud of the autumnal snow, went on nodding up and down for some time.

4

The telegraph poles, hopping like sparrows all over the district, passed on the news: 'Rising in Khopersk.' Executive Committee offices burnt down.' 'Many of the Soviet workers have been killed off, others have fled.'

The food-requisitioning detachment retired into the heart of the district. Bodyagin and the tribunal commandant, Teslenko, remained in the village a further twenty-four hours. They stayed on to despatch the last waggon loads of grain to the receiving point. In the early morning a storm blew up. It raged, it smoked, it lashed the village with a white mist of snow. Late in the afternoon a dozen or so horsemen galloped into the square. The alarm bell went rattling out over the village, sunk in snowdrifts. Horses' neighing, dogs' howling, the strained, hoarse cry of the bells. . . .

A rising.

Over the hill, across the flattened bald patch of a mound, two riders urged on their horses. Below the hill, across the bridge, came the clatter of horse hoofs. A handful of horsemen. The leader, wearing an officer's fur cap, drove on his long-legged blood mare with his whip.

"Don't let the communists get away."

Beyond the mound, Teslenko, a lop-eared Ukrainian, touched up his Kirghiz trotting horse with the reins.

"By hell, they'll overtake us."

They rode their horses steadily. They knew that these rolling hills continued for some twenty miles.

Behind them the pursuit extended in a long line. In the west, on the edge of the world, night stooped and hunched down. Some two miles outside the village, in a shaggy drift in a hollow, Bodyagin noticed a human being. He galloped up and shouted hoarsely :

"What the devil are you doing, sitting there?"

The boy, his face waxily blue, swayed on his feet. Bodyagin swung his whip, his horse threw up its muzzle and pranced right up to the boy.

"D'you want to freeze to death, you devil's progeny? How did you come to be here?"

He sprang out of the saddle, bent down, and listened to the incoherent whisper :

"I . . . daddy . . . I'll freeze. . . . I'm an orphan. . . . I'm wandering about the world." With a chilly gesture he drew the edge of the woman's ragged blouse he was wearing over his head, and was still.

Bodyagin, without speaking, unbuttoned his short sheepskin jacket, wrapped the thin little body in it, and slowly climbed back on to his restive horse.

They galloped off. The boy snuggled up under the sheepskin, thawed out, and clung firmly to Bodyagin's leather belt. The horses were perceptibly slowing down, they snorted and neighed spasmodically, sensing the rising thunder of hoofs behind them.

Seizing Bodyagin's horse by the mane, Teslenko shouted through the biting wind:

"Abandon the kid. D'you hear, you son of all the devils? Abandon him, or they'll catch you." He swore furiously by God and the devil's dam, and lashed Bodyagin's blue hands with his whip. "They'll overtake us and finish us off. May you burn in a clear flame with your kid."

The horses' foaming muzzles drew level. Teslenko's whip had drawn blood on Bodyagin's hands. Bodyagin hung the reins over his saddle bow, squeezed the lad's feeble little body with his stiff fingers, and felt for his pistol.

"I'm not abandoning the boy, he'll freeze to death. Get away, you old carrion, or I'll shoot you."

Drawing on the reins, the grey-haired Ukrainian sobbed:

"We can't get away. We're done for."

Bodyagin's fingers seemed not to be his own, they were so disobedient to his orders. He ground his teeth as he tied the boy with a leather thong across his saddle. He tested the strap to make sure it would hold, and smiled.

"Cling tight to the mane, big-head."

He struck the horse's sweating crupper with his sabre scabbard. Teslenko thrust two fingers under his drooping whiskers and gave a piercing, brigand whistle. They stood watching the horses as they tore away at an easier gallop. Then they lay down side by side. They greeted the furcaps coming up the rise with a dry, distinct volley.

They lay in that spot for three days. Teslenko, in dirty cotton drawers, exhibited to heaven a bubbly clot of frozen blood that protruded from the gash of his mouth running from ear to ear. Crested steppe birds hopped fearlessly over Bodyagin's bare chest; they unhurriedly pecked black-awned barley from the ripped-up belly and empty eye sockets.

1925.

THE CHAIRMAN OF THE REPUBLIC
REVOLUTIONARY MILITARY SOVIET

"OUR republic isn't particularly large; it numbers only a hundred or so houses altogether, and it is situated some twenty-five miles from the district centre along the Swampy Ravine.

"It became a republic this way: In the early spring I come back to my native village from comrade Budionny's army, and the citizens elect me chairman of the village, because I have two Orders of the Red Banner for my glorious bravery against Wrangel, which comrade Budionny personally pinned on me and squeezed my hand very respectfully.

"So I took over the job, and we in our village would have lived in a state of peace like everybody else. But quite soon a bandit force turned up in our parts and set to work to ruin our village to the last grain. They'd ride in and take our horses, flinging a dead nag at us in exchange, and they'd eat our last scrap of food.

"The people in the neighbourhood of our village are a poor lot, they showed respect for the bandits and welcomed them with bread and salt. Seeing that that was how the neighbouring villages were treating the bandits, I called a meeting of our village and said to the citizens:

" 'Have you made me chairman?'

" 'We have.'

" 'Well, then, in the name of all the proletariat in the village I ask you to observe your autonomy and to stop going to the neighbouring villages, because they're counter-revs and it's very shameful indeed for us to go the same road as them. But in future our village will be known not as a village but as a republic, and I, having been elected by you, appoint myself chairman of the republic revolutionary military Soviet and declare a state of siege all round.'

"Some of them, who weren't class conscious, kept their mouths shut; but the young cossacks who'd spent some time in the Red Army said:

" 'And about time too! No need to vote. . . .'

"So I started to make them a speech:

" 'Come on, comrades, let's help our Soviet government and start to fight the bandits to the last drop of our blood, because they're a hydra and the scum are gnawing at the roots of universal socialism.'

"The old men standing at the back opposed this at first, but I used my tongue to good purpose to propagand them, and they all agreed with me that the Soviet government's our nursing mother and we must all cling categorically to her skirts.

"The meeting sent a document to the District Executive Committee, asking them to issue us rifles and cartridges, and appointed me and the secretary Nikon to ride to the district centre.

"In the early dawn I harness up my little mare, and we drive off. We cover some seven miles, drive down into a hollow, and then I see the wind sending the road dust up, and behind the dust five horsemen galloping towards us.

"At the sight I felt a funny feeling in my middle. I guessed they were wicked enemies from that same bandit group galloping up to us.

"We and the secretary couldn't think of any initiative, nor was any possible: for it was steppe all around, stripped naked to shame; not one little bush, not one ravine or even a gulley, and we halted the mare in the middle of the road. . . .

"We hadn't any weapons, and we were as innocent as swaddled babes, and it would have been very stupid to try to gallop away from those horsemen.

"My secretary was terrified at the sight of these wicked enemies, and he began to feel very bad. I could see he was planning to jump out of the cart and run But where to run to, he himself had no idea. I say to him:

" 'Nikon, you tuck in your tail and don't make a sound. I'm the chairman of the revolutionary soviet, and you're my secretary, and so you and I have got to accept death together.' But, not being class conscious, he jumped out of the cart and set out to click his heels over the steppe, running so fast you'd have thought not even bloodhounds could have caught up with him. But, in reality, seeing this suspicious-looking citizen fleeing over the steppe, the horsemen set off after him and quickly caught up with him just by a small mound.

"I honourably slipped down off the cart, swallowed all the necessary papers and documents, and watched to see what would happen next. All I saw was that they didn't waste much time talking to him, but, gathering together in a ring, began to slash at him with their sabres crisscross fashion. He fell to the ground, and they rummaged through his pockets, fussed around him a bit and then remounted their horses and came galloping over to me.

"All right, a joke's a joke, but it was time I got away. However, there was nothing I could do about it, so I waited. They galloped up.

"At their head was their ataman, Fomin by nickname. A ragged, shaggy fellow, all red beard, his mug covered with dust, but a beast to look at, and goggling his eyes.

" 'Are you Bogatiriov, the chairman?'

" 'I am.'

" 'Haven't I sent you orders that you're to give up your chairmanship?'

" 'I've heard something about it.'

" 'Then why don't you?'

"He asks me several other filthy questions like that, but he doesn't give any sign that he's angry.

"And I began to feel desperate, for I could see that in any case I wouldn't get away from such company with my head on my shoulders.

" 'Because,' I told him, 'I stand firmly by the platform of the Soviet government, I observe all the programmes to the last dot, and you categorically won't push me off that platform.'

"He swore at me, using a lot of unnecessary words, and zealously brought his knout down on my head. At once a tender bump rose across my forehead; by its calibre it must have come from a mother cucumber, the sort women set aside for seeds.

"I feel that bump between my fingers and say to him:

" 'You behave so rottenly because of your lack of class consciousness, but I myself broke the civil war and ruthlessly destroyed men of the Wrangel type; I've received two orders from the Soviet government, and, as for you, I regard you as just empty nothingness, and I tell you I just don't see you.'

"At that he raged and stormed more than ever, he tried to make his horse ride me down, and he lashed away with his knout. But I remained unshakable in my positions, like all our proletarian government, though the horse smashed my knee with its hoof and under his blows I had an unpleasant jangle of bells in my ears.

" 'Go on in front.'

"They drove me to the little mound, and my Nikon was lying there beside the mound, all swimming in blood. One of them slipped out of his saddle and turned Nikon belly upward.

" 'Look,' he said to me, 'we'll get you up in a moment just like your secretary if you don't renounce the Soviet goverment. . . .'

"Nikon's trousers and drawers had been taken down and his sexual question mark had been slashed beyond recognition with their sabres. As I looked at this filthy treatment I felt queer; I turned away, but Fomin bared his teeth.

" 'Don't turn your nose away. We'll fit you up exactly like him and we'll set fire to your stubborn communistic village with fire at all the four corners. . . .'

"I'm hot of speech; I couldn't stand any more of that, and I answered him rather roughly:

" 'Let the cuckoo weep for me in the orchard; but, as for our village, it's not alone, there are more than a thousand like it all over Russia.'

"I took out my tobacco pouch, struck fire with my flint, and lit a cigarette. But Fomin touches up his horse with the reins, rides at me, and says:

" 'Give me a smoke, brother. You've got some good tobacco there, but we've gone without for two weeks now; we're smoking horse dung. And in exchange we shan't execute you, we'll just cut you down as if in honest battle, and we'll let your family know so they can come and collect your body to bury. But hurry up, for we haven't much time.'

"I held my pouch in my hand, and I was bitterly upset to think that tobacco I'd grown in my own garden, and the scented clover grown on our beloved Soviet soil, would be smoked by such spiteful parasites. I looked at them, and they were all terribly afraid

I'd scatter the tobacco to the winds. Fomin stretched out his hand to take the pouch as he sat in the saddle, and his hand started to tremble.

"But what I did was to shake out the tobacco into the air and say:

"'Kill me as you think best among yourselves. I shall die from a cossack sabre; but as for you, my little pigeons, you'll certainly dance from the end of a well-crane, that being the fashion.'

"They started to slash at me very cold-bloodedly, and I fell to the damp ground. Fomin fired his pistol twice and shot me through the chest and leg. But then I heard coming from the high-road:

"'Bang bang!'

"The bullets whistled all around us, and made the scrub rustle. My murderers were quick to get moving. I see the district militia raising the dust along the road. I jumped up smart, ran some hundred yards or so, then the blood closed my eyes and the ground began to sway under my feet.

"I remember I shouted:

"'Brothers, comrades, don't leave me to perish.'

"And then the wide world faded from my sight.

"Two months I lay like a block; I lost my speech, my memory went. When I came to have some feeling again I groped and found my left leg was missing. It had been cut off because gangrene had set in.

"I returned home from the hospital, hobbling along somehow with a stick to reach the ledge round the hut, and one day the district military commissar rides into the yard and demands without saying one word of greeting:

"'You, what made you call yourself chairman of the revolutionary military Soviet and proclaim your village a republic? Don't you know we've only got one republic? On what ground did you introduce autonomy?'

"But I answered him straight out, and very straight:

"'I ask you, comrade, not to start getting so serious, but in regard to the republic I can explain: it was because of the bandits. But now peace has come our village is called Topchansk. But, bear in mind, if the white hydras and other scum make any more attacks on the Soviet government we'll turn every village into a fortress and a republic, we'll set old men and children on horses, and, although I've lost a leg, I'll categorically be the first to go and shed blood.'

"He had nothing to answer to that; and, squeezing my hand very hard, he rode off the way he had come."

1925.

THE WATCHMAN IN THE VEGETABLE
PLOTS

WHEN father came back from seeing the district ataman he was cheerful, something or other had pleased him mightily. A laugh had got stranded under his bushy eyebrows, his lips were furrowed with a restrained smile; Mitka hadn't seen his father like that for many a long day. Ever since his return from the front he had been harsh and gloomy; he was always hitting his fourteen-year-old son Mitka, and he tousled his red beard thoughtfully. But today he was like the sun peering through clouds; he even pushed Mitka jokingly off the steps when the boy got in the way, and laughed:

"Now, clumsy! Run along to the orchard and call your mother in to dinner."

At dinner the whole family was assembled: the father under the ikons, the mother squeezed on the very edge of the bench, closer to the stove, and Mitka next to Fiodor, his older brother. Towards the end of the meal, when they had finished their thin Lenten soup, the father combed his beard into two bushy halves and smiled again, wrinkling his purplish lips.

"The family should be delighted to congratulate me: today I have been appointed commandant to the district field court martial." He was silent for a moment or two, then added: "The medals I earned during the German war haven't been wasted, the command haven't forgotten my officer's rank and distinctions for valour."

Turning livid as his face flushed heavily with blood, he flashed his eyes at Fiodor.

"What are you sitting there with your head hanging for, you scum? Aren't you glad to see your father happy? Ah? You watch out, Fiodka! D'you think I don't see how you're hobnobbing with the peasants? Through you, you worthless dog, the ataman looked me straight in the eye and said: 'You, Anisim Piotrovich,' he told me, 'do genuinely guard our cossack honour; but your precious son Fiodor's hobnobbing with the bolsheviks. It's a pity, the lad's twenty, he may suffer for it. . . .' Tell me, you son of a bitch, do you go visiting the peasants?"

"I do."

Mitka's heart quivered; he thought his father would strike Fiodor. But he only leaned across the table, clenched his fists, and snarled:

"But do you know, you Red Army chitterlings, that we're arresting your friends tomorrow? Do you know the tailor Yegorka and the smith Gromov are to be shot tomorrow?"

And Mitka heard his brother again say firmly, though pale of face:

"No, I didn't know, but now I do."

Before his mother had time to place herself in front of Fiodor or Mitka had time to cry out, with a great swing of the hand his father flung a heavy copper mug. The jagged edge of the broken handle caught Fiodor above the eye. The blood spurted in a fine stream. Without saying a word Fiodor covered his eyes, which were blinded with blood. His mother groaned and put her hands round his head; but his father sent the bench flying with a crash and went out of the hut, slamming the door behind him.

The mother was busy in the kitchen all that afternoon. She took out some dried fish plaited in a braid from the family chest, poured a quantity of dried rusk bread into a bag, then sat down at the window to patch Fiodor's underwear. As he passed her, Mitka saw his mother sitting motionless, her head on the pile of garments, but her shoulders were heaving spasmodically.

Their father came home from the district administration office after dark and did not bother to have any supper. He lay down on the bed without undressing. Trying to avoid making the floorboards creak, Fiodor tiptoed into the store-room, brought out a saddle and bridle, then went into the yard.

"Mitka, come here."

Mitka, who was driving in the calves, threw away his switch and went over to his brother. He had a vague suspicion that Fiodor was intending to ride beyond the Don to the bolsheviks, to where the sky was lit up with lurid flashes and whence the muffled sound of gunfire rolled over the district centre. Fiodor asked him, without looking at him :

"You don't know whether the stable's locked, do you, Mitka?"

"It is. . . . But what d'you want to know for?"

"I just need to, that's all." Fiodor was silent for a moment, whistling through his teeth, then unexpectedly he began to whisper : "The stable keys are under father's pillow . . . at his head . . . go and get them for me . . . I want to ride. . . ."

"Where to?"

"To go and serve with the Red Guards. You're small yet, you'll understand later which side is fighting for the right. . . . Well, I'm riding away to fight for the land, for the poor people, and so that everybody shall be equal, so that there won't be any rich and poor any longer, but everybody will be equal."

Fiodor let go of Mitka's head, which he had been holding between his palms, and asked sternly :

"Will you get the keys?"

The boy answered without hesitation :

"I'll get them." He turned his back on Fiodor and went into the hut without looking round.

The best room was in semi-darkness, the flies scattered over the ceiling were buzzing noisily. At the door Mitka kicked off his shoes, and, holding the door firmly by the handle to prevent it creaking, opened it and softly shuffled in his bare feet towards the bed.

His father was lying stretched out with his head to the window, one hand in his pocket, the other hanging over the edge of the bed, with one fingernail, large and tobacco stained, resting on the floorboard. Holding his breath, Mitka went up close to the bed and halted, listening to his father's gurgling snore. A silence, heavy and still. . . . There were breadcrumbs and eggshell on his father's red beard, a horrible, strong smell of spirits came from his gaping mouth, and from somewhere at the bottom of his throat a stranded cough rattled and escaped.

Mitka stretched out his hand to the pillow, his heart beating violently.

The blood rushing to his head rang in his ears like a deafening triple peal. First he pushed one finger under the greasy pillow, then another. He felt the slippery thong and the cold bunch of keys, and drew them out very gently. But suddenly his father grabbed him by the collar with one hand.

"What are you thieving for, you scum? For two pins I'd tear all the hair off your head."

"Daddy! Dear daddy, I came for the stable keys. . . . I didn't want to disturb you. . . ."

His father squinted with his swollen, bile-tinged eyes at Mitka.

"And what d'you want the keys for?"

"The horses seem a bit restless. . . ."

"Why didn't you say so at first?" His father threw the bunch of keys on the floor and, turning his face to the wall, sighed, and in a moment was snoring again.

Mitka flew out of the house into the yard, to Fiodor, who was waiting in the shadow of the shed's overhanging roof. He thrust the keys into his brother's hand, and asked:

"But which horse will you take?"

"The little stallion."

Mitka sighed as he followed his brother, and said in an undertone:

"Fiodya, but supposing daddy beats me?"

Fiodor did not answer. He silently led the stallion out of the stable, saddled it, and seemed a long time hooking his foot into the refractory stirrup. It was only as he rode out of the gate that he whispered, bending down from the saddle:

"You stick it, Mitka. We shan't sup of misery for ever. But you tell our father, Anisim Piotrovich, what I say: if he lifts so much as a little finger against you or mother I'll take a savage vengeance on him."

He rode through the gateway, settling the stallion down for a long journey, while Mitka squatted on his haunches by the wattle fence, anxious to watch Fiodor go. But his eyes were filmed over with salty tears, and a choking sob clutched his throat.

2

His father was half choking with his gurgling snore. Mitka got up earlier than ever next morning, bridled the bay, and rode down to the Don, to water the working horse and give it a bathe. The dried-out chalk rustled and scattered in dusty powder under the bay's hoofs; he rode down a gulley to the water's edge, unbridled the horse, and threw off his clothes; his skin bristled with the misty early morning rawness. He listened to the groaning howl coming across the water from far, far off, and then, rolling down the bank, slipped into the river. As he went in head first, stung all over with the prickly morning chill, he smiled and thought: "Fiodor ought to be with the bolsheviks by now; he's doing his service with the Red Guards."

His thoughts shifted to his home, to his father, and his feeling of joy faded at once, like a spark in the wind. He rode back huddled up on the horse's back, a dull look in his eyes.

As he rode up to the house he was thinking: "I could make a getaway over to them, to the bolsheviks. . . . They've got the right on their side, Fiodor says. I ought to join up with him. Father will flay me, he'll give me a bloody nose."

He removed the horse's bridle at the steps, and slowly went into the hut. His father shouted from the best room:

"Why didn't you take the stallion down to bathe?"

Mitka glanced at his mother, who was standing frozen still by the stove, and felt the blood rushing back to his heart.

"The stallion isn't in the stable."

"Where is it, then?"

"I don't know."

There was a shuffling sound in the best room as his father drew on his legboots. The old man passed through the kitchen and went to the store cupboard, his glittering eyes swollen with sleep.

"Where's the saddle?" he thundered from the entrance passage.

Mitka drew closer to his mother and, as in the old days, when he had been a child, clung to her arm. His father came back into the kitchen, clutching a leather strap in his hand.

"Who did you give the keys to?"

His wife placed herself in front of Mitka.

"Don't touch him, Anisim Piotrovich, for Christ's sake; don't beat him. . . . Haven't you any pity on your son?"

"Let go, you devilish bitch. D'you hear me or don't you?" He pushed his wife aside, flung Mitka to the floor, and kicked him systematically and brutally for a long time, until the dull, groaning cries stopped coming from Mitka's throat.

3

The gunfire grew louder and louder. Each morning, after the herd was driven out to pasturage, Mitka would sit under the old windmill on the field road. The windmill roof whistled and the sheet-iron grated under the wind, the sails rattled away with a long, drawn-out and boring noise, and, covering all these more timid sounds, from somewhere beyond the rise came a deep-toned 'boom'.

The deep, modulating roar of the gunfire slowly died away beyond the district village, and was lost in the ravines hidden in the fine bluish haze of the moment before dawn. Every morning waggons loaded with shells, cartridges, and barbed wire dragged through the village towards the Don.

On their return journey they brought back the wounded, lice-infested cossacks and unloaded them on the square, outside the district administration office. The inquisitive chickens fussily pecked over the cigarette butts, the bloodstained bandages, the cotton-wool with its clots of blood, and listened attentively to the groans, and tears, and husky swearing of the wounded men.

Mitka tried to keep out of his father's sight.

After breakfast he would go off with hooks and lines to the Don; sitting on the bank, he watched as cavalry rode across the bridge, two-wheeled carts thundered past, infantry combed the frosty dust. He returned home at nightfall. One evening a bunch of Red Guard prisoners was driven into the village. They walked in a compact group, downcast, barefoot, in poor-quality, ragged great-coats. The cossack women ran out into the street, spat into their grey, dusty faces, and swore at them foully, to the thunderous laughter of the cossacks and the escort. Mitka followed behind, swallowing the pungent dust kicked up by the prisoners' feet; his heart, clenched with anxiety, quivered unevenly. He looked into the eyes with their bluish black rings, shifted his gaze from one whiskerless face to another, and expected at any moment to recognize his brother Fiodor in one of these grey-coated men.

The prisoners were halted on the square, by the communal granary, which in former times had been used for storing the district grain. Mitka saw his father come out on to the administration

veranda, his left hand clutching his sabre knot. He barked:
"Caps off!"

Slowly, slowly, the Red Guards removed their caps, and stood
with their shaggy heads bowed, only occasionally exchanging whispered remarks. Again that familiar, ominous voice:

"Fall in in two lines. And be quick about it, you Red scum!"

The bare feet shuffled as the men obeyed. The grey line of
haggard faces extended right to the steps of the administration.

"By the right, number."

Husky voices. The trained, swift turn of the head. But Mitka
felt a lump in his throat, pity for these men who were treated as
aliens, pity to the point of burning pain, of sickening nausea.
And for the first time in his life he felt a bitter hatred for his
father, for his self-satisfied smile, his red bushy beard.

"Into the shed . . . quick . . . march."

One by one they passed into the yawning gap of the door. The
last man, short and staggering on his feet, had a bloodstained rag
wound round his head. Mitka's father struck him on the head with
his sabre scabbard; stumbling and swaying, the man broke into
a run, ran some five paces or so and fell heavily face downward
on the rough, beaten ground. A roar of laughter arose on the
square, a howl of voices, eyes wrinkled with laughter, women's
mouths gurgling with spittly laugh. But Mitka gave a hoarse,
broken cry and covered his face with his suddenly chilly hands;
jostling against the crowd, he ran off down a street.

4

His mother was busy at the stove, finishing her cooking. Mitka
sidled up to her, and said without looking at her:

"Mummy, bake some pastry. I'll take it along to the men in the
shed . . . the prisoners. . . ."

His mother's eyes went suddenly wet.

"Yes, take some along, sonny; may be our Fiodka too is suffering
somewhere. Even the prisoners have got mothers, and I expect
their pillows are wet with tears each night, like mine."

"But supposing father finds out?"

"God forbid! You take it along in the evening, Mitka, my boy.

If there are cossacks on guard, give it to them and tell them to
hand it in. . . ."

As though in spite, the sun slowed down and crept over the
village, indifferent to Mitka's impatience, imperturbable. He
forced himself to do nothing till darkness had fallen, then went
into the square, crawled like a lizard between the barbed wire
and up to the door, pressing the little packet of food close to his
chest with one hand.

"Who goes there? Halt, or I'll fire."

"It's me. . . . I've brought some food for the prisoners."

"Who are you? Come out here before I try my butt-end on you.
The devil must have sent you wandering around here at night.
Isn't the day long enough for you to bring food in?"

"Wait a bit, Prokhorich, isn't this the commandant's boy,
surely?"

"Are you Anisim Piotrovich's son?"

"Yes. . . ."

"But who sent you with the food? Your father?"

"No-o. I brought it myself."

The two cossacks went right up to Mitka. The older man, a
bearded fellow, seized him by the ear.

"Who's taught you to take food to the prisoners? Don't you
understand they're our most dangerous enemies? Supposing I
report what you're up to to your father? What will he say to
you?"

"Drop it, Prokhorich. D'you grudge another man a bit of food?
You haven't got two throats to eat with, after all. Take the food
and we'll hand it in."

"But supposing Anisim Piotrovich finds out about it? It's all
right for you to open the floodgates, you're single; but I've got a
family. They send you to the front for this sort of thing, and give
you a good hiding into the bargain."

"Oh, go to the devil, you sniveller. Hey, sonny, where are you
off to? Give me your food, we'll hand it in, don't worry."

Mitka handed the younger man the bundle; the cossack stooped
down and whispered in his ear:

"I'm always on duty on Wednesdays and Fridays. Bring it
then. . . ."

Every Wednesday and Friday evening Mitka went to the square.

Trying to avoid getting hooked up in the barbed wire, he crawled under the barrier, handed the packet of food over to the guard, and went back home, bent double along by the wattle fences and keeping a sharp look-out.

5

Each day, as soon as the night opened its speckled golden canopy, little groups of Red Guard prisoners were led out of the shed and escorted into the steppe, to the misty ravines. The wind carried the echoes of a rattling volley and single rifle shots to the village. When more than twenty prisoners were taken out, a machine-gun followed them on a cart with creaking wheels. The gunners dozed on the wide bench seats, a cigarette glowed between the driver's lips. He sluggishly shook out the reins, the horses moved reluctantly and at an uneven pace, and the uncovered gun gleamed dully with its gaping muzzle, as though it were drowsily chewing. Half an hour later, the machine-gun would sound in dry bursts in some ravine, the driver lashed the foaming, snorting horses with his knout, the gunners shook about as they bumped up and down on the seats, and the troika of horses dashed up to the commandant's headquarters, which gazed out with its three lighted windows onto the sleepy street.

One Wednesday evening Mitka's father said to him:

"What are you always idling around for? Take the bay out for exercise tonight, only see you don't let him get into the grain. If you let him tread down anyone's grain, I'll beat you to death."

Mitka got the bay ready, and managed to whisper to his mother:

"You take the food yourself, mummy. Hand it over to the guard."

He drove off with the other village lads to the waste land beyond the ataman's fields. He returned next morning before sunrise. He opened the wicket gate, unbridled the bay, clapped him on his belly, swollen with green fodder, and went into the hut. As he walked into the kitchen he saw blood on the floor and the walls. There was something white and bloodstained in the corner by the stove. From the best room came a gurgling, a moaning . . . Mitka went in. His mother was lying on the floor, her hair hanging in bloody icicles, her face swollen and purple. She saw Mitka and began to moan again, her body twitched, but she did not speak. Her bluish tongue flickered between her swollen lips, her eyes laughed wildly and senselessly, a rose-coloured, bubbling spittle dribbled from her slashed mouth.

"Mi . . . mi . . . tya . . . tya . . . tya. . . ."

And a hollow, groaning laugh.

Mitka dropped to his knees and kissed his mother's hands, her eyes flooded with black blood. He embraced her head, and his fingers were imbrued with blood and white, slippery clots. . . . On the floor beside her was his father's pistol, the butt smeared with blood.

He had no idea how he ran out. At the wattle fence he fell over, but from the next yard the neighbour shouted to him:

"Hey, you! Clear out, my boy, wherever you can get to. Your father's found out that your mother was taking the prisoners food; he's shot her to death and swears he'll do the same to you."

6

A month had passed since the day Mitka hired himself out to work as a watchman guarding the vegetable plots outside the village. He lived in a shanty on the crown of a hill. From there he could see the milky-white ribbon of the Don, the village frozen still below the hill, and the cemetery with the brown mounds of its graves. When he asked to be taken on as a watchman the cossacks made a fuss.

"He's Anisim's son. We don't want the likes of him. He's got a brother in the Red Guards, and his bitch of a mother was feeding the prisoners. He ought to be strung up on an aspen, not taken on as a watchman."

"He isn't asking for payment, good old men. He says he'll watch over the vegetable plots for the love of Christ. If you feel like it you can give him a crust of bread, but if you don't he'll die in any case."

"We won't give him any; let him die."

None the less, they listened to the ataman's advice. They took him on. And why shouldn't they take on a labourer for the community? He didn't ask for any wages and he would guard the village vegetable plots all the summer just for the love of Christ. Pure gain. . . .

The yellow melons and the speckled and striped water melons swelled and ripened under the sun. Mitka wandered moodily among the rows of field vegetables and melons, scared off the crows with his shouting and his noisy rattle. Each morning he crawled out of the shanty, lay down on rotted scrub beside the wall, and listened to the sound of gunfire across the Don, gazing long, with misted eyes, in that direction.

Up the hill, past the vegetable plots, past the steep sides of the chalky ravines, the rutted summer road winds like a serpent's tail. In summer-time it is used by the cossacks for the carting of hay, and along it they now drove the Red Guard prisoners to the ravines, to shoot them. Night after night Mitka was awakened by the sounds of hoarse shouting and rifle shots below, beyond the orchards, beyond the thick wall of willows. After each burst of shots the dogs set up a howl, and then the summer road would echo to the thunder of footsteps, a military cart would sometimes rattle past, little sparks of cigarettes faded in the darkness, a restrained hum of talk reached Mitka's ears. One day he went along the road to where the winding ravines tie tangled knots, and saw dried blood on the slope; while below, on the stony bottom, where flood water had washed out a shallow grave, a bare foot was sticking out; the sole was dry and wrinkled, and the steppe wind rustling through the ravines carried up the stench of corpses. After that he didn't go again.

One day a crowd marched earlier than usual along the summer road from the village; on each side were the cossacks acting as escort, in the middle were the Red Guards in greatcoats flung anyhow around their shoulders. The sun sank into the glittering whiteness of the Don slowly, as though it wanted to wait and see the thing that was not done in daylight. In the orchards and trees crows dropped in a black cloud to the height of the willows. A spidery web of silence was woven over the vegetable plots. Mitka stood by his shanty, his eyes following the men marching along the summer road until they reached the turn. Suddenly he heard a shout, then firing, again, and yet again. . . .

He rushed from the shanty to the top of the rise, and saw the

Red Guards running down the road to the ravines. The cossacks had dropped on one knee and were firing hurriedly, while two more, waving sabres, ran after the prisoners.

The shots disturbed the frozen silence like a bell. Tik-tak; tuk-tak; ta-ta-tak.

One of the prisoners stumbled, dropped on to his hands, jumped up, and ran on again. . . . The cossack following him drew closer, closer. . . .

Now. . . . The sabre flashed in a half-circle, and was brought down on the man's head. . . . The cossack slashed away at the man as he lay.

The world went dark before Mitka's eyes and his mouth was filled with the taste of nausea.

7

At midnight three horsemen galloped up to the shanty.

"Hey, watchman! Come out for a minute."

Mitka went out.

"You didn't see which way three men in military greatcoats ran this evening, did you?"

"No, I didn't."

"Don't you dare lie to us. You'll answer strictly for it if you are."

"I didn't see them. . . . I don't know. . . ."

"Well, we're wasting our time here. We must ride along the ravines to the Filinov wood. We'll surround the wood and catch them there, the snakes."

"Touch up your horse, Bagachev."

Mitka couldn't sleep all night. Thunder roared in the east, the sky was draped heavily with shaggy leaden clouds, lightning dazzled the eyes. Rain came on.

Just before dawn he heard something stirring and groaning just outside the shanty.

He listened, trying not to move. His body was paralysed with fear. Another rustle, then a protracted groan.

"Who's there?"

"Good man, come out, for God's sake. . . ."

Mitka went out, walking unsteadily on his trembling legs. By the back wall of the shanty he saw a man lying.

"Who are you?"

"Don't give me away . . . don't let me perish. . . . I got away from the firing party yesterday . . . the cossacks are hunting for me. . . . My leg's shot through. . . ."

Mitka tried to say something, but his throat went tight; he dropped to his knees, crawled on all fours and embraced the legs in the ragged puttees.

"Fiodya. My own dear brother. . . . My dear . . ."

He cut down a heap of dried sunflower stalks, and dragged it all into the shanty, got Fiodor in and laid him on the heap in one corner, piled scrub and sunflower stalks on top, then went off to the vegetable plots.

All the morning he drove the impudent crows out of the green, curly strips of cultivation, anxious all the time to get back to the shanty, to gaze into his brother's dear eyes, to listen again and again to his story of the sufferings and joys he had known. They had already come to a firm decision: as soon as dusk fell they would bandage Fiodor's wounded leg more tightly, and by familiar forest paths would take a roundabout route down to the Don, swim over to the other side, to where the people were fighting for the right, to those who were fighting the cossacks for the land and for the sake of the poor people. All the morning, cossacks went galloping along the summer track from the village, twice they turned aside to have a drink of water in the shanty. Just as evening was drawing on, Mitka saw a group of eight horsemen ride down from the gleaming white, bare summit of the sandy mound, letting their weary, stumbling horses take their own pace down the hill. Mitka was sitting by the shanty; he watched the horsemen's huddled forms, and, without turning his head, said in an undertone to Fiodor:

"Lie still and don't move, Fiodor. One horseman is riding across the vegetable plots to the shanty."

From under the pile of scrub Fiodor's voice sounded muffled:

"But are the others waiting for him, or have they ridden on to the village?"

"They've gone off at a trot, they're just disappearing below the hill. Now, keep still."

The cossack rode standing and swaying in his stirrups, waving his knout; his horse was wet with sweat.

Mitka turned pale, and whispered:

"Fiodor, it's father galloping here."

His father's red beard was soaked with sweat, his face was a livid blue under the suntan. He reined in his horse right by the shanty, climbed out of the saddle, and went up to Mitka.

"Tell me, where's Fiodor?"

He fixed his bloodflecked eyes on Mitka's white face. His blue cossack uniform stank of sweat and naphthaline.

"Was he with you during the night?"

"No."

"Then whose blood is that down there, by the shanty?"

He bent down to the ground; his crimson neck rolled out of his collar in folds of fat.

"Get into the shanty."

They went in, Mitka's father first and the boy, with gloomy face, coming behind.

"You watch out, you little snake. . . . If you're hiding Fiodka here I'll make mincemeat of both of you."

"He's not here. . . . I don't know. . . ."

"What's that you've got under the scrub in the corner?"

"That's where I sleep."

"We'll see." He strode over to the corner, squatted down on his heels, and slowly pulled away the rotten, rustling scrub and sunflower stalks.

Mitka was behind him. He saw the blue uniform drawn tight across his father's back, rising and falling in smooth lines.

After a moment or two his father exclaimed hoarsely:

"Aha! What's this?"

Fiodor's bare foot protruded among the brown stalks. With his right hand their father seized the butt of the pistol at his side. Mitka swayed, leaped, and snatched up the axe standing against the wall, groaned with a suddenly rising feeling of sickness, and, swinging the axe with all his strength, brought it down on his father's nape.

They covered the chilling body with scrub and went out. Along the ravines, between the windfallen trees, through dense thickets of thorns they went, they crawled, they forced their way. Some five miles from the village, at a point where the Don takes a sharp turn and thrusts up against the grey hills, they dropped down to the river. They swam out to a sandbank; the water, chilly with the night, carried them down swiftly. Fiodor, groaning, clung to Mitka's shoulder.

They reached their goal, and lay a long time on the damp, granular sand.

"Well, time we were moving, Fiodya. The rest shouldn't be quite so wide."

They entered the water. Once more the Don lapped round their faces and necks, their rested arms ploughed the water more confidently.

They felt land under their feet. The forest beyond was held in the darkness of the night. They set off in a hurry.

It grew lighter; somewhere quite close a gun thundered out. In the east the dawn came on, faintly extending its crimson fringe.

1925.

THE FAMILY MAN

THE sun was caught fast among the feeble green brush of the undergrowth beyond the outskirts of the village. I was walking down from the village to the Don, to the ferry. The damp sand smelt rotten underfoot, like a tree rotted and swollen with water. The road slipped in a tangled hare-track through the undergrowth. Straining and livid, the sun plunged down behind the village graveyard, and along my tracks through the undergrowth the dusk gathered in a greyish mist.

The ferry boat was tethered to the bank, the lilac-hued water gurgled under its keel; dancing and swinging sideways, the oars groaned in the rowlocks.

The ferryman was scraping the fusty bottom with a bailer, bailing out water. Raising his head, he looked at me sideways with his almond-shaped, yellowish eyes, and barked reluctantly :

"You want to get to the other side? We'll be going in a minute; untie the rope."

"D'you want me to row, too?"

"You'll have to. Night's coming on, and I don't know whether anyone else will be arriving or not."

As he turned down his trouser legs he looked at me again, and asked :

"I can see you're not a local, not from our parts, are you? Where has God brought you from?"

"I'm going home from the army."

The ferryman threw off his cap, flung his hair back with a toss of the head (the hair looked like spun cossack annealed silver, all silver and black) and winked at me, baring his decayed teeth.

"How are you going, on a pass or just on the hop?"

"Demobilized. My year has been demobilized."

"All right, then, no need to worry."

We sat down to the oars. The Don playfully dragged us towards the young underwater growth of the bankside forest. The water rubbed with a dry sound against the rough bottom of the boat.

The ferryman's bare feet, streaked with blue veins, swelled with bunched muscles; the bluish soles pressed stickily against the slippery footboard. His hands were long and bony, the fingers had knotted knuckles. He was tall, and narrow in the shoulders; he rowed awkwardly, hunched up; but the oar rested obediently on the ridge of the wave and clove the water deeply.

I listened to his even, regular breathing; his knitted woollen shirt stank of pungent sweat, tobacco, and the musty smell of water. He dropped his oar and turned to face me.

"It looks like we shall be carried into the forest. It's stupid, but there's nothing we can do about it, my lad."

In the middle the current was strong. The boat was carried away, it capriciously threw up its stern, and floated sideways on towards the forest. Within half an hour we were driven into the sunken willows. The oars snapped. The splintered fragments fidgeted offendedly in the rowlocks. Water leaked with a sucking noise through a hole in the bottom. We transferred to a tree to spend the night. The ferryman, tucking his legs round a branch, sat at my side, sucking at a clay pipe, and remarked as he listened to the whistle of geese's wings cutting the clinging darkness above us:

"So you're going home, to your family. . . . I suppose your mother's waiting for you; the son, the breadwinner, is returning, he'll cheer her old age. But I suppose you don't worry overmuch that she, your mother, is pining for you by day and shedding motherly tears by night. . . . You sons are all the same. . . . So long as you haven't had children of your own you haven't any feeling in your soul for your parents' sufferings. But what a lot every one of them has to bear!

"Sometimes when a woman is cutting open a fish she crushes the spleen; you try the roe and it tastes terribly bitter. And that's just like me: I go on living, but I've only bitterness to taste. There are times when you stick it and stick it, but then you say: 'Life, life, when will you get still worse? . . .'

"You're not one of us, you're from other parts, so you can judge with a free mind: into which noose am I to thrust my head?

"I've a daughter, Natasha; this year she's in her seventeenth spring. And she says to me:

"'It's quite unpleasant for me to sit at the same table with you, father. When I look at your hands I remember that with those very hands you killed my brothers; and I feel like heaving my soul out.'

"But, the little bitch, she doesn't understand who was the cause of it all. It was all through them themselves, through the children.

"I married young; my wife proved to be fruitful, and dropped eight empty-bellies; but with the ninth she came a cropper. She brought it to birth all right, but, the fifth day after, she was carried off with a fever. I was left all on my own, like a snipe in a marsh, but God didn't take away a single one of my little ones, no matter how hard I pleaded. . . . Ivan was the oldest. Swarthy like me, and with a good-looking face. . . . He was a handsome cossack and conscientious in his work. My second child was a son four years younger than Ivan. He was born like his mother: stocky, plump, fair hair rather bleached, and black eyes; and he was the one I was fondest of, my best beloved. We called him Danilo. The other seven mouths were little boys and girls. I gave Ivan in marriage to a girl in our own village, and before long he had a child. Danilo was on the point of getting married, too, but then the mournful times came. Then there was a rising in the district against the Soviet government. Next day Ivan comes running to me.

" 'Father,' he says, 'let's go over to the Reds. In the name of Christ the God I ask you. We ought to support their side because their government is just to the extreme.'

"Danilo also said we should. They tried a long time to get me to agree, but I said to them:

" 'I shan't try to stop you; you go, but I'm not going anywhere. Besides you, I've got seven more sitting on the benches, and every mouth asking for food.'

"So they vanished from the village, but our district took up whatever arms they could lay their hands on, and me, too, they carried off with bare hands to the front.

"At the village meeting I said:

" 'Good elders of the village, you all know I'm a family man. I've got seven little children. And, if I get shot, who's going to justify my children then?'

"I said one thing and I said another, but it didn't make any difference. They paid no attention, they just took me and sent me to the front.

"At that time the positions ran right below our village. And so, it happened just about Eastertime, nine prisoners were driven into the village, and among them was Danilo, the pride of my heart. They marched them across the square to the company commander. The cossacks poured out into the street, shouting:

" 'Kill them off, the snakes! When they're brought out after examination just leave them to us.'

"I stood among them, my knees shaking, but I gave no sign that I felt sorry for my son, my own Danilo. I look around and see the cossacks whispering together and nodding in my direction, Arkashka, the sergeant, comes up to me and asks:

" 'Tell me, Mikishar, will you fight the communes?'

" 'I will, the bloody this-and-that thieves. . . .'

" 'Well, here's a bayonet for you; go and stand on the veranda.' He gives me a bayonet, and snarls through his bared teeth: 'We're keeping an eye on you, Mikishar. . . . Look out, or it'll be the worse for you.'

"I stood by the steps, thinking: 'Most Holy Mother, surely I haven't got to kill my own son?'

"I heard the captain shout. The prisoners were brought out, and my Danilo was the very first. I looked at him, and my blood ran cold. His head was all swollen, like a bucket, kind of scalped. . . . The blood was caked in clots, he had fur gloves on his head so that they shouldn't beat him on the bare spots. . . . The gloves had got soaked with blood and had dried to the hair. They'd beaten up the prisoners on the way to the village. He comes staggering down the steps. He looked at me, held out his hands to me. . . . He tried to smile, but his eyes were all blue with bruises, and one was filled with blood. . . .

"Then I realized that if I didn't hit him my own villagers would kill me, and my little children would be left bitter orphans. He drew level with me.

" 'Father,' he says; 'my own father, goodbye.'

"The tears washed away the blood off his cheeks, but I . . . I forced myself to raise my hand . . . it seemed to have gone like stone . . . I had the bayonet clutched in my fist. I struck at him with the end that fits on to the rifle. I struck at this spot here, just above the ear. . . . How he cried out 'Oi! Oi!' and covered his face with his hands and fell down the steps. The cossacks roared:

" 'Make the blood flow, Mikishar. We can see you're being easy on your Danilo. Beat him up, or we'll let the blood out of you.'

"The captain came out on to the veranda. He was swearing, but there was laughter in his eyes. . . . When they began to slash the prisoners with bayonets my soul was troubled. I turned and ran down the street; but I looked back and saw them rolling my Danilo over the ground. The sergeant thrust a bayonet into his throat, but he only groaned."

Below us the ferry boat's planks grated under the pressure of the water, I could hear the water slapping, but the willow quivered and creaked oppressively. Mikishar touched the bow with his feet as it rose, and said, knocking a yellow snowstorm of sparks out of his pipe:

"Our boat will sink; we shall have to sit on the lookout till mid-day tomorrow on this willow. To think that this had to happen."

He sat silent for a long time, then, lowering his voice, he said huskily:

"For that business they made me a senior sergeant.

"Much water has flowed down the Don since then, but to this day I sometimes hear of a night as though someone's crying out, sobbing. . . . Just as I heard my own Danilo's deep groan as I ran. . . . But there it is, it's conscience, and it hurts. . . .

"We held the front against the Reds until the following spring; then General Sekretov joined his forces with us, and we drove the Reds across the Don, into Saratov province. I'm a family man, but they wouldn't let me have any relief from service, because my sons had joined the bolsheviks. We reached the town of Balashov. I hadn't heard a word or even a smell of my oldest son, Ivan. Then the cossacks found out—may the plague take them—that Ivan had come over from the Reds and was serving in the 36th Cossack battery. Our villagers threatened that if they came across him anywhere they'd squeeze the soul out of him.

"We occupied a certain village, and the 36th was there. . . .

"They found my Ivan, tied him up, and brought him in to the company. There the cossacks beat him without mercy and said to me:

" 'Drive him over to the regimental staff.'

"The staff headquarters was some eight miles from this place.

The captain gives me a paper and says—but he wouldn't look me straight in the eye:

" 'Here's your document, Mikishar. Drive your son to the staff; it'll be more reliable if you do it, he won't run away from his father.'

"And then the Lord gave me wisdom. I guessed they had made me the escort thinking I'd let my son go free, and then they'd catch him and kill me. . . .

"I go to the hut where Ivan was held and tell the guard:

" 'Hand over the prisoner, I'm driving him to the staff.'

" 'Take him,' they said, 'we haven't any objection.'

"Ivan flung his greatcoat round his shoulders; but he twisted and twisted his cap in his hands and finally threw it down on the bench. He and I went out of the village and up the rise; he was silent, and I was silent. I looked back once or twice; I wanted to see if they were following us. We'd only just got halfway, we'd just passed a wayside shrine, but there was not a soul to be seen behind us. Then Ivan turned to me and said in a pitiful voice:

" 'Father, all the same they'll kill me in the staff; you're driving me to my death. Is your conscience really still asleep?'

" 'No, Vania,' I say, 'my conscience isn't asleep.'

" 'But don't you feel sorry for me?'

" 'I'm sorry, little son; my heart is mortally sorry. . . .'

" 'But if you're sorry, let me go. I haven't had much of a life so far in this world.'

"He dropped in the middle of the road and bowed down to the ground before me three times. And I say to him:

" 'When we get to the ravines, little son, you run; but I'll fire after you once or twice just for show.'

"Well, I expect you'll think I was a poor lot, and you can't always get out a kindly word; but he flung himself on me and kissed my hands. We went on together a couple of miles; he was silent, and I was silent. We drew near to the ravines; he halted.

" 'Well, father, let's say goodbye. If I should get through alive I'll look after you to the day of your death; you'll never hear an angry word from me.'

"He embraced me, but my heart was full to overflowing with blood.

" 'Run now, sonny,' I said to him.

"He started to run towards the ravines, continually looking back and waving to me.

"I let him go possibly a hundred yards, then I slipped my rifle off my shoulder, went down on one knee, so that my hand shouldn't shake, and fired into his . . . back."

Mikishar spent quite a long time pulling out his pouch, still longer striking fire with his flint; then he smoked, smacking his lips. The tinder glowed in his cupped palms, his cheekbones worked in his face, but from under his swollen lids his slanting eyes gazed sternly and remorselessly.

"Well, then he struggled to his feet, ran on another forty yards, clutched at his belly with both hands, and turned towards me.

" 'Father, what's this for?' He fell again, and his legs began to jerk uncontrollably.

"I run to him and bend over him; but he rolled his eyes right up and there were bubbles of blood on his lips. I thought he was dying, but he got up suddenly on to his knees and said, seizing my hand in his :

" 'Father, but I've got a wife and child. . . .'

"His head slipped sideways, he fell over again. He pressed the wound together with his fingers, but what was the good? The blood spurted even through his fingers . . . He began to groan and cough, lay over on his back, and gazed at me sternly, but his tongue was already stiffening. . . . He tried to say something, but all he could get out was 'fa . . . fa . . . fa . . . ther.' The tears rolled down from my eyes, and I said to him :

" 'Dear Ivan, take on my behalf the crown of the martyr. You've got a wife and a child, but I've got seven sitting on the benches. If I was to let you go the cossacks would kill me, and my children would have to go begging about the world in the name of Christ. . . .'

"He lay a little longer and then died, but he held my hand in his hand. I took off his greatcoat and boots, covered his face with a rag and walked back to the village.

"Well, and now judge us, good man. I've suffered so much sorrow because of my children, my grey hairs have swept all the others away. I earn a bit of food for them, I get no peace day or night, but they . . . there's my daughter, Natasha, for instance, she says : 'It's unpleasant for us to sit at the same table as you, father.'

"How d'you think I can bear that now?"

The boatman Mikishar hung his head, and looked up at me with a fixed, heavy stare; the vague dawn curled up behind his back. On the right bank, amid the black mass of shaggy willows, the ducks' quacking was broken by a chilled and sleepy shout:

"Mi . . . ki . . . sha . . . . r! You de . . . vil! Bring the ferry over!"

1925.

THE SHAME-CHILD

MISHKA dreamt his grandfather had cut down a healthy cherry switch and was coming after him, waving the switch and saying sternly:

"Now you, come here, Mikhail Fomich; I'll warm you up in the place your legs grow out of."

"What for, grand-dad?" Mishka asked.

"Because you've stolen all the eggs from the nest of the crested hen in the henroost, and taken them off to have a ride on the roundabout, you damnation."

"Grand-dad, I haven't had one ride on the roundabout this year," Mishka shouted in alarm.

"Lie down, you little devil, and pull down your trousers."

Mishka cried out and woke up. His heart was beating as if he really had suffered from the switch. He opened his left eye the tiniest bit—it was daylight in the hut. Outside the window the morning dawn was warming up. Mishka raised his head and heard voices in the passage: his mother was squealing away, chattering without stop, sobbing with laughter; his grandfather was coughing; but a strange voice was saying: 'Bu-bu-bu.'

Mishka rubbed his eyes as he saw the door opened then slammed shut again; then his grandfather ran into the best room and stood dancing up and down, his spectacles bounced about on his nose. At first Mishka thought the priest had come with the singers (his grandfather danced about just like that when he came at Easter-time). But an enormous unknown soldier in a black greatcoat and a cap with ribbons, but no peak, pushed his way into the best room after grandfather, while Mishka's mother hung round this big fellow's neck and howled like mad.

In the middle of the hut the stranger pushed her off his neck and barked:

"But where's my son and heir?"

Mishka took fright and retreated under the blanket.

"Mishka, sonny, what are you fast asleep for? Your daddy's arrived home from service," his mother cried.

Before Mishka had time to blink the soldier picked him up, threw him up to the ceiling, and then pressed him to his chest and —it was anything but a joke—with his ginger whiskers he pricked Mishka's lips, his cheeks, his eyes. The whiskers were wet and salty for some reason. The boy tried to tear himself away, but it was hopeless.

"What a fine bolshevik my boy has grown into. He'll be taller than his daddy before long. Ho-ho-ho!" his father shouted, and began to dandle Mishka in real earnest, first setting him on his palm and twisting him round, then throwing him right up to the ceiling crossbeam.

Mishka stuck it as long as he could, but then he drew his brows down just like his grandfather, put on a stern look and seized his father's whiskers:

"Let go, daddy!"

"No, I won't let go."

"Let me go. I'm big now, and you're nursing me like a little baby."

His father seated the boy on his knee, and asked with a smile:

"How old are you, my little pistol?"

"I'm getting on for eight," Mishka barked, scowling up at his father.

"But d'you remember, sonny, how I made steamers for you two years ago? D'you remember how we sailed them in the pond?"

"I remember," Mishka cried, and timidly put his arms round his father's neck.

And then the fun really began. His father put Mishka on his shoulders, held him by the legs and went dancing round and round the best room, bucking and neighing just like a horse until Mishka was screaming with rapture. His mother tugged at his sleeve and bawled:

"Go outside and play. Go outside, I tell you, you screamer." And she asked her husband: "Put him down, Foma Akimich. Please put him down. He isn't giving me a chance to get a look at you, my bright eagle. We haven't seen each other for two years, and now he's all you're concerned about."

His father set Mishka down on the floor and said:

"Run and play with the boys; come back later and I'll give you some presents."

Mishka closed the door behind him, and thought at first he would stand and listen in the passage to what the grown-ups had to say. But then he remembered that none of the other boys knew his father had come home and he flew through the yard, over the garden, treading down the holes prepared for the potatoes, and dashed to the pond.

He bathed in the stinking, standing water, rolled over and over in the sand, had one last dive and then, hopping on one foot, drew on his drawers. He was all ready to go back home when Vitka, the priest's son, came up to him.

"Don't go, Mitka. Let's have a bathe and then you come along to our place to play. Your mummy's given you permission to come to us."

Mishka held up his slipping drawers with his left hand, adjusted the braces over his shoulders, and said reluctantly:

"I don't want to play with you. There's too much stink comes from your ears."

Vitka screwed up his left eye spitefully, and said as he drew the knitted shirt off his bony shoulders:

"That's because of scrofula; but you're a peasant and your mother had you under the garden fence."

"Why, did you see her?"

"I heard our cook telling my mummy."

Mishka dug at the sand with his foot and looked Mitka up and down.

"Your mummy's lying. My daddy fought in the war, but your daddy's a bloodsucker and he eats other people's dumplings."

"You bastard," the priest's son shouted, curling his lips.

Mishka snatched up a stone rubbed smooth by the action of water. But the priest's son held back his tears and smiled very graciously:

"Don't fight, Mishka; don't be angry. If you like I'll give you my dagger: it's made of iron."

"My daddy's brought me one back from the war better than yours."

"That's a lie!" Vitka drawled distrustfully.

"You're lying yourself. When I say he's brought me one I mean he's brought me one. And a real gun. . . ."

"Just imagine, haven't you grown rich!" Vitka sneered enviously.

"And he's got a cap too, and there are ribbons hanging from the cap and on them words are written in gold, like you've got in your books."

Vitka pondered for some time over some way of astonishing Mishka; he knitted his brows and scratched his white belly.

"But my daddy will be a bishop soon, and yours was a shepherd. What d'you say to that?"

Mishka was fed up with standing there; he turned and started back towards the orchard. The priest's son called after him:

"Misha, Misha: I'll tell you something."

"Tell me then."

"Come closer."

Mishka went closer and looked at the priest's son suspiciously.

"Well, tell me."

Vitka danced over the sand on his thin, crooked legs, and smiled as he shouted malevolently:

"Your father's a communar. And as soon as you die your soul flies up to heaven; but God will say: 'Because your father was a communist you go off to hell.' And there the devils will start to roast you in a frying-pan."

"But how about you? Don't you think they'll roast you too?"

"My daddy's a priest. But you're an uneducated fool and you don't understand a thing. . . ."

Mishka felt frightened. He turned and silently began to run home.

But by the orchard fence he stopped and shouted, threatening the priest's son with his fist:

"I'll ask my grand-dad. If you're lying, don't you dare come past our yard."

He climbed over the fence and ran off home; but all his eyes saw was a frying-pan, and on it he, Mishka, was boiling and foaming in bubbles. He felt a shiver run up and down his back; he simply must run quick to his grand-dad and ask him. . . .

As though to spite him, a pig had got stuck in the wicket gate, its head outside, its body inside, its feet planted firmly on the ground, wriggling its tail and squealing to wake the dead. Mishka rushed to its rescue: he tried to open the gate wider, but the pig began to groan and pant. He seated himself astride on its back, it strained and strained, pushed over the wicket gate, gave one gasp and dashed across the yard towards the threshing-floor. Mishka's heels banged against its side and it went so fast that the wind flung his hair back. At the threshing-floor he jumped off, looked round, and saw his grandfather standing on the veranda and beckoning with his finger.

"Come here, my dear boy."

Mishka had no idea why his grandfather was shouting, but he happened to remember the hellish frying-pan again and trotted up to the house.

"Grand-dad, grand-dad, are there devils in heaven too?"

"I'll give you devils in a moment. I'll spit well on certain parts of you and then dry them off with a switch. Ah, you wicked child, what were you riding that pig for?"

He seized Mishka by his forelock, and called his mother out from the best room.

"Come and admire your precious son!"

She came running out.

"What are you doing that to him for?"

"What d'you mean, what for? I saw him riding a pig round the yard so fast the wind sent the dust flying up."

"Was he riding the sow that's about to farrow?" his mother groaned.

Before Mishka could open his mouth to explain, his grand-dad removed the leather thong from his waist, and, holding up his trousers with his left hand to keep them from falling down, thrust Mishka's head between his knees with his right. He whacked away, saying very sternly between each whack:

"You're not to ride on the pig. You're not to ride . . ."

Mishka tried to shout out, but his grand-dad added:

"So, you cat of a bitch, haven't you any pity for your daddy? He was tired out with his journey and lay down to get some sleep. But now you'd start hollering, would you?"

So Mishka had to keep quiet. He tried to kick his grandfather, but couldn't reach him. His mother seized him and pushed him into the house.

"You sit there, you son of a hundred devils. I'll deal with you in a moment. I shan't flay you like your grandfather!"

His grandfather sat on the bench in the kitchen, occasionally taking a look at Mishka's back.

Mishka turned round to him, wiped the last tear away with his fist, and said, with his back leaning against the door:

"Well, grand-dad, you mark my words . . ."

"What, you wicked child, threatening your grand-dad now?"

Mishka saw his grandfather unfastening the thong again, and hastily opened the door a little way.

"So you are threatening me?" the old man queried.

Mishka vanished altogether through the door. Peering through the chink, he closely watched every movement his grandfather made, and announced:

"You wait, you wait, dear grand-dad. Your teeth can fall out but I won't do the chewing for you. Even if you ask me to."

His grandfather walked out on to the veranda, and saw Mishka's head dancing up and down through the garden, over the shaggy green hemp plants; his blue trousers flashed along. The old man stood threatening him with his stick for some time, but there was a smile lurking under his beard.

* * *

To his father he was Minka. To his mother, little Minka. To his grandfather, in his kindly moments, he was a wicked little rascal; at other times, when his eyebrows hung in grey tufts over his eyes, it was: "Hey, Mikhail Fomich, come here; I'll warm your ears for you."

But to everybody else—to the gossiping neighbours, to the other boys, to all the village—he was Mishka and 'the shame-child'.

His mother had given birth to him out of wedlock. And though she married the herdsman, Foma, by whom she had had the boy, a month later, the nickname 'shame-child' had stuck to him like a scab, and had remained with him all his life.

Mishka was of slender build; from spring right through the summer his hair was the colour of the straps of a sunflower head; in June the sun burnt his hair with its heat, it went shaggy and skewbald in the wind; his cheeks were sprinkled with freckles like a sparrow's egg with speckles. But with constant bathing in the pond and the sun his nose peeled and peeled, till it cracked and scabbed. There was one good feature about bow-legged Mishka: his eyes. They gazed out through their narrow slits, blue and saucy, looking like unmelting chips of river ice.

And it was because of his eyes and his exuberant inability to sit still that his father was fond of him. He had brought his son back from military service a present of a very ancient, very hard gingerbread in the form of a monogram, and some well-worn boots. Mishka's mother wrapped up the boots in a towel and stowed them away in the family chest; but Mishka broke up the gingerbread into crumbs with a hammer the same evening and ate them to the very last crumb.

Next day Mishka woke up at sunrise. He gathered up a palmful of warmish water from the iron pot, smeared yesterday's dirt over his cheeks, and ran out into the yard to get dry.

His mother was busy with the cow, his grandfather was sitting on the earthen ledge of the hut wall. He called Mishka over to him:

"Crawl under the granary, you rascal. A hen was clucking away there just now; I expect she's dropped an egg."

Mishka was always ready to do his grandfather a good turn: he dived on all fours under the granary, crawled through to the farther side, and came out in such a state! He galloped through the garden and ran to the pond, looking back to see whether his grandfather was watching. As he ran to the fence he brushed the burrs off his legs. But his grandfather was waiting, grunting as old men do. At last he couldn't wait any longer and himself crawled under the granary. He got smothered with chicken dung, screwed up his eyes to protect them against the steamy heat, knocked his head painfully against the floor joists, but he crawled right through.

"You're a little idiot, Mishka, that's as true as I'm here. I look and look but I can't find you. Is a hen going to lay her eggs here? Not under that stone . . . there ought to be an egg there. But where have you crawled to, you little rascal?"

Silence was the only answer. Brushing off the bits of dung clinging to his trousers, he gazed towards the pond, saw Mishka, and waved his hand in a hopeless gesture.

At the pond the other boys surrounded Mishka and asked:

"Has your daddy been to the war?"

"Yes."

"And what did he do there?"

"You know what: he fought."

"That's a lie. He killed lice there and gnawed a bone outside the kitchen."

The boys roared with laughter, pointed their fingers at Mishka, and danced round him. In his bitter shame the tears started to his eyes, and to make matters worse, Vitka, the priest's son, gave him a painful knock.

"But is your father a communist?" he asked.

"I don't know. . . ."

"I know he is. This morning my daddy said he's sold his soul to the devil. And he also said all the communists will be hung before long."

The other lads said nothing, but Mishka's heart constricted painfully. They'd hang his daddy: but what for? He gritted his teeth and said:

"My daddy's got a magic gun, and he'll kill off all the bourgeois."

Vitka thrust one foot forward and said triumphantly:

"He's got short arms. My daddy won't give him a holy blessing, and without that he won't be able to do a thing."

Dilating his nostrils, Proshka, the shopkeeper's son, pushed Mishka in the chest and shouted:

"But don't you try it on too much with your daddy. He took things from my father when the revolution started, and father said: "Well, if this government is ever overthrown, I'll kill Foma, the herdsman, first of all. . . .""

Natasha, Proshka's sister, stamped her foot.

"Give him one, boys; what are you standing and looking for?"

"Beat the communar's son."

"The bastard."

"Make him see stars, Proshka."

Proshka swung a switch and struck Mishka on the shoulder. Vitka, the priest's son, stuck out one foot and Mishka went flying headlong, striking the sand heavily.

The lads set up a roar and flung themselves on him. Natasha

squealed away in a thin voice and scratched his neck with her nails. Someone kicked him painfully in the belly.

Shaking Proshka off, Mishka jumped up and, wriggling across the sand like a hare eluding the hunt, tore off home. They whistled after him and flung stones, but didn't run to overtake him.

He took breath only when he plunged into the green, prickly growth of hemp rising right over his head. He squatted down on the damp, scented earth, wiped the blood off his scratched cheeks, and burst into tears; overhead, forcing its way through the foliage, the sun tried to look him in the eyes, dried the tears on his cheeks and kindly, like his mummy, kissed him on his tousled ginger mop.

He sat there a long time, until his eyes were dry; then he rose and quietly wandered back to the yard.

Under the overhang of the shed his father was smearing the wheels of the cart with grease. His cap had travelled back on to his nape, the ribbons were dangling, and he was wearing the blue shirt with white stripes. Mishka approached him sideways on and stood by the cart. For a long time he said nothing. At last, growing bolder, he touched his father's hand and asked in a whisper :

"Daddy, what did you do at the war?"

His father smiled in his ginger whiskers, and said :

"I fought, sonny."

"But the boys, the other boys say you only killed lice there."

The tears rose again in Mishka's throat. His father laughed and picked him up in his arms.

"They're telling lies, my son. I sailed on a steamer. A big steamer sails over the sea, and that's what I sailed on. And then I went off to fight."

"Who did you fight with?"

"I fought the gentry, my boy. You're still quite small, so I had to go to war in your place. There's a song we sing about that."

His father smiled and, gazing at Mishka, tapping the time with his feet, began to sing softly :

> "O, Mikhail, Mikhail, my dear little Mikhail,
> Don't you go to war, just let your daddy go.
> Your daddy's getting old, he's seen a lot of the world,
> But you're still young, you haven't got married yet."

Mishka forgot the other boys' insults, and laughed, for his father's ginger whiskers stuck out like a bunch of the twigs his mother tied together to make besoms, while below the whiskers his lips made a funny, smacking noise and his open mouth was like a round, black hole.

"But don't come bothering me now, Mishka," his father said. "I'll finish repairing the cart, and when you go to bed this evening I'll tell you all about the war."

*   *   *

The day dragged on and on like a long empty road across the steppe. The sun set, the herd came home through the village, the dust settled, and the first little star peered bashfully down from the darkened sky.

Mishka was possessed with impatience, but his mother seemed almost out of spite to spend a long time fussing around the cow, a long time straining the milk; then she climbed down into the cellar and remained buried there a good hour. Mishka twined around her like bindweed.

"Shall we be having supper soon?"

"You'll have it all in good time, you fidget, you starveling."

But Mishka wouldn't move one step from her side: his mother in the cellar, he after her; his mother in the kitchen, he followed her. He stuck to her like a leech, clung to her skirt, trailed after her.

"Mum . . . my! Will we be having supper soon?"

"Oh, get away, you clinging mange. If you want something to eat take a piece of bread and get that down you."

But Mishka didn't give up. Even the smack which his mother gave him on the cheek made no difference.

At supper-time he managed somehow to swallow his soup while it was still hot, and dashed into the best room. He flung his trousers far beyond the family chest, dived at a run into the bed and under his mother's patchwork quilt. He lay quietly and waited for his father to come and tell him all about the war.

His grandfather went down on his knees before the ikons, whispering a prayer, bowing his forehead right to the floor. Mishka raised his head; bending his back with difficulty, his grandfather supported himself with the fingers of his left hand on the floor and beat his forehead against the board : bang. So Mishka knocked his elbow against the wall : bang.

His grandfather whispered again, whispered and banged his head in an obeisance. Mishka banged his elbow against the wall. The old man grew annoyed, and turned to the boy.

"I'll show you, you wicked child, the Lord forgive me. You knock after me and I'll knock you."

There would have been a bit of a tussle, but Mishka's father came into the room.

"What have you got into bed in here for, Mishka?" he asked.

"I sleep with mummy."

His father sat down on the bed and silently began to twist his whiskers. After a moment's thought he said :

"But I've made up your bed with grand-dad."

"I won't sleep with grand-dad."

"Why ever not?"

"His whiskers stink too much of tobacco."

His father twisted his whiskers again, and sighed.

"No, sonny, you go and sleep with grand-dad."

Mishka drew the quilt over his head and, peering out with one eye, said in an offended tone :

"You lay in my place yesterday, daddy; and tonight. . . . You go and sleep with grand-dad."

He sat up in bed and, clutching his father's head between his hands, whispered :

"You go and lie with grand-dad, for I don't suppose mummy will want to sleep with you. You stink of tobacco too."

His father got up and went into the kitchen.

"Daddy !"

"Well?"

"You lie down here," Mishka said with a sigh and got up. "But you'll tell me all about the war, won't you?"

"I will."

His grand-dad took the wall side, and Mishka lay down on the edge. A little later his father came in. He shifted the bench over to their bed, sat down and lit a stinking cigarette.

"You see, it was like this. You remember how the shopkeeper used to sow his corn right behind our threshing-floor?"

Mishka recalled how in the old days he had gone running

through the scented, high-standing wheat. He could climb over the stone barrier of the threshing-floor and dive into the corn. It covered him right over his head, the heavy, black-whiskered ears tickled his face. It smelt of dust, camomile, and the steppe wind. His mother used to say to him:

"Don't go far into the corn, Misha, dear, or you'll get lost."

His father was silent for a moment, then said, stroking Mishka on the head:

"But do you remember how you drove with me to the Sandy Mound? Our grain was right out there. . . ."

And Mishka again recalled that along the roadside beyond the Sandy Mound there had been a narrow, winding strip of corn. One day Mishka drove there with his father, and they found the corn had been trodden down and ruined by cattle. The ears lay in filthy bunches trodden right into the ground, the bare stalks were swaying in the wind. Mishka remembered that his father, so big and strong as he was, pulled a terrible face, and a few tears ran down his dusty cheeks. Mishka cried too as he looked at him.

On the way back his father had asked the watchman minding the vegetable plots:

"Tell me, Fiodot, who trampled down my grain?"

The watchman spat down at his feet and answered:

"The shopkeeper drove some cattle to the market and let them go into your strip on purpose. . . ."

Now his father shifted the bench still closer, and began to talk:

"The shopkeeper and the other people occupied all the land, and the poor people had nowhere to sow. And it was like that everywhere, not only in our village. They treated us terribly in those days. It grew really hard to live, I hired myself out as a herdsman, and then I was taken off to do my military service. I had a bad time in the army, the officers punched you in the face for the least thing. But then the bolsheviks turned up, and the head of them is called Lenin. In himself he didn't seem all that clever, but he had a very learned mind, though he came of our peasant stock. The bolsheviks talked to us to such good purpose that we stood gaping. 'What are you standing catching flies for, peasants and workers?' they said. 'Drive out the masters and bosses in a couple of shakes and with a filthy broom. It's all yours. . . .'

"And with those words they really put it across us. We started to use our minds, and it was true. We took the land and their properties away from the masters; but they longed for their filthy life, they got upset and made war on the peasants and workers. . . . Get that, sonny?

"But that same Lenin, the head of the bolsheviks, turned over the people just like a ploughman turns over the ground with his plough. He collected the soldiers and workers and really shook up the masters until the down and feathers began to fly off them. The soldiers and workers came to be known as the Red Guard. And I was in the Red Guard. We lived in a very large house, it was called Smolny. The corridors in it are very, very long, sonny, and it has so many best rooms you could get lost quite easily.

"I was standing on guard at the entrance one night. It was cold outside, and I had only my greatcoat on. And the wind pierced right through you. Two men came out of this house and walked towards me. They came up quite close, and I guessed one of them was Lenin. He came up to me and asked kindly:

" 'Aren't you cold, comrade?'

"But I answer him:

" 'No, comrade Lenin; it isn't all that cold, but no enemies whatever will break us. We didn't take the power into our hands in order to hand it over to the bourgeois.'

"He laughed and shook my hand hard. And then he walked quietly to the gate."

Mishka's father was silent a while; he took the tobacco pouch out of his pocket, struck a match, and on his ginger whisker Mishka noticed a bright and shining little tear, just like the drops of dew which hang on the ends of the nettles of a morning.

"That's the sort he was. He thought of everybody. His heart felt sorry for every soldier. After that I saw him quite a lot. He'd come walking past me, and would notice me when still quite a long way off; he'd smile and ask:

" 'So the bourgeoisie won't break us?'

" 'They aren't all that clever, comrade Lenin,' I used to reply.

"And it all came about as he said, sonny. We took over the land and the factories and kicked out the rich, our bloodsuckers. When you grow up, never forget that your daddy was once a sailor and shed his blood four years for the commune. I shall be dead by then, and Lenin too, but our work will live on through the centuries,

When you grow up you'll fight for the Soviet government like your father fought, won't you?"

"I will!" Mishka shouted, and jumped out of the bed, intending to fling himself round his father's neck. But he forgot his grandfather lying at his side, and he set his foot on the old man's belly.

Grandfather groaned violently, and stretched out his hand to seize Mishka by the forelock. But Mishka's father picked him up in his arms and carried him into the best room.

And in his arms Mishka fell asleep. But before dropping off he thought a long time about that extraordinary man named Lenin, about the bolsheviks, the war, and steamers. At first he heard a restrained hum of talk through his doze, he was conscious of the pleasant smell of sweat and home-grown tobacco. Then his eyelids stuck together, it was as though someone had pressed them down with his palms.

Almost as soon as he fell asleep he dreamed he saw the city: wide streets, chickens bathing in the scattered ash; there was a great number of chickens in the village, but there were far, far more in the town. The houses were exactly as his father had said: an enormous hut covered with fresh reeds; on its chimney stood another hut, and on that one's chimney yet another; and the chimney of the one right at the top stuck into the sky.

As Mishka walked along the street, craning his head, looking around him, suddenly, he had no idea where from, a rather tall man in a red shirt came striding towards him.

"Here you, Mishka, what are you wandering around for, doing nothing?" he asked very kindly.

"My grand-dad's sent me out to play," the boy replied.

"But do you know who I am?"

"No, I don't. . . ."

"I'm comrade Lenin."

Mishka's knees sagged under him with fear. He felt like taking to his heels, but the man in the red shirt took him by the sleeve and said:

"You haven't got a conscience worth a brass farthing, Mishka. You know very well I'm fighting for the poor people, so why don't you join up in my army?"

"My grand dad won't let me go," Mishka pleaded.

"Well, it's as you wish," comrade Lenin said, "but I can't manage without you. You ought to come and join my army, that's all there is to it."

Mishka took him by the hand and said very resolutely:

"Oh, all right, I'll join your army without permission and I'll fight for the poor people. But if my grand-dad tries to whip me with a switch because of it you must take my part."

"Of course I shall," comrade Lenin said, and went off down the street. But Mishka felt he had lost his breath with joy, he couldn't breathe, he tried to shout something but his tongue was too dry.

He trembled violently in bed, kicked his grandfather with both feet and went right off to sleep.

His grandfather grunted and chewed his lips in his sleep; but through the little window the sky beyond the pond turned softly pale, and the clouds floating up from the east were embroidered with a rose-coloured edging.

*　　　*　　　*

After that, every evening Mishka's father told him about the war, about Lenin, and the countries he had seen.

On the Saturday evening, the Executive Committee watchman brought a short, stocky man in a greatcoat and with a document case under his arm to the hut. He called Mishka's grandfather, and said:

"I've brought a Soviet worker comrade to stay with you. He's come from the town and he'll spend the night with you. Give him some supper, old man."

"Oh, of course, we don't mind," grand-dad said. "But have you any mandates, Mister comrade?"

Mishka was amazed at his grandfather's learning and, poking one finger in his mouth, hung around to hear what it was all about.

"I have, daddy; I've got everything," the man with the document case smiled, as he went into the best room.

Grandfather followed him, and Mishka followed his grandfather.

"What business has brought you to us?" the old man asked as they went in.

"I've come to hold fresh elections. We shall elect a chairman and members of the Soviet."

A little later Mishka's father arrived home from the threshing-floor. He greeted the stranger and told his wife to get some supper ready. After supper the father and the stranger sat side by side on the bench; the stranger unfastened his leather document case, took out a packet of papers and began showing them to the father. Mishka couldn't control his curiosity; he hung around trying to get a peep at them. His father picked up one document and showed it to him.

"Look, Mishka, this is Lenin himself."

The boy tore the small card from his father's hand, fixed his eyes on it and gaped in astonishment: on the card was a picture of a man full length, not at all tall, and not even wearing a red shirt, but a jacket. One hand thrust in his trouser pocket, the other pointing to something. Mishka fixed his eyes on him, and took all the picture in in a single second: once for all, for ever, the knitted brows, the smile lurking on the face and in the corners of the lips were registered in his memory: he memorized every little detail of the features.

The stranger took the picture from Mishka, snapped the lock of the document case and went off to bed. He undressed, lay down and covered himself with his greatcoat, and was just dozing off when he heard the door creak. He raised his head.

"Who's there?"

He heard bare feet slapping over the floor.

"Who's there?" he asked again, then, unexpectedly, he saw Mishka standing by his bed.

"What d'you want, little boy?"

Mishka stood for a moment without speaking, then, growing bolder, whispered:

"Man, I'll tell you what . . . give me Lenin."

The stranger did not answer, but hung his head over the side of the bed and stared at the boy.

Mishka was seized with fear: supposing the man was a miser and wouldn't give him the picture? Trying to control the quiver in his voice, hurrying and panting, he whispered:

"You give it me for keeps, and I'll give you . . . I'll give you a good tin box and I'll give you all the conkers I've got and . . ." In his desperation he waved his hand and said: "And I'll give you the boots daddy brought me home."

"But what d'you want Lenin for?" the stranger asked with a smile.

"He won't give it me." The thought flashed through the boy's mind. He hung his head so that the man shouldn't see his tears, and said thickly:

"I just need it."

The stranger laughed, took out his document case from under the pillow and handed Mishka the card. The boy hid it under his shirt, pressed it to his chest, to his heart, very hard, and trotted out of the best room. His grandfather woke up and asked:

"What are you wandering around for, you nightbird? I told you not to drink milk at night, but now you've had to get up. . . . Go and piss in the slop-pail; I don't see why I should take you out into the yard."

The boy lay down without saying a word, clutching the card with both hands. He was afraid to turn over in case he creased it. And thus he fell asleep.

He woke up before dawn. His mother had just milked the cow and driven it out to join the herd. She saw Mishka, and clapped her hands.

"Now what fever is tormenting you? What have you got up so early for?"

He pressed the picture under his shirt and hurried past his mother to the threshing-floor. He dived under the granary.

Docks were growing around the granary walls, and the nettles rose in a green, impenetrable wall. He crawled underneath the granary, scraped aside the dust and chicken droppings with his hand, tore off a dock-leaf going yellow with age, wrapped the picture in it, and put a small stone on top of it so that the wind shouldn't blow it away.

Rain fell all day. The sky was covered with a grey canopy, the puddles foamed in the yard, little streams chased one another down the street.

Mishka had to spend the day indoors. Dusk was falling when his grandfather and father got ready and went off to the meeting in the Executive Committee building. The Committee was accommodated in the former church lodge. Mishka put on his grandfather's peaked cap and ran off after them. Panting, he climbed up the creaking, filthy steps on to the veranda and went into the room. Tobacco smoke was floating high up under the ceiling, the place was filled with people. The stranger was sitting at a table by the window, saying something to the assembled cossacks.

The boy quietly slipped in right at the back and sat down on a bench.

"Comrades, who's in favour of Foma Korshunov being chairman? Please hold up your hands."

Prokhor Lisenkov, the shopkeeper's son-in-law, who was sitting just in front of Mishka, shouted:

"Citizens . . . I propose you turn him down. His behaviour's indecent. We saw that plainly enough even when he used to mind our herd as the herdsman."

Mishka saw Fiodor, the cobbler, rise from his seat on the window sill and shout, waving his arms about:

"Comrades, the rich people don't want a herdsman to be chairman; but because he's a proletariat and on the side of the Soviet government . . ."

The rich cossacks, standing in a bunch by the door, stamped their feet and whistled. There was a hubbub of shouting.

"We don't want the herdsman."

"He's just come back from military service; let him become the community herdsman again. . . ."

"To hell with Foma Korshunov."

Mishka glanced at the pale face of his father, who was standing by a bench, and he in turn went white with fear for him.

"Not so much noise, comrades . . . I'll have you put out of the meeting," the stranger bawled, banging his fist on the table.

"We'll elect one of our men from among the cossacks."

"We don't want him."

"We won't have him, damn and blast him," the cossacks stormed, but Prokhor, the shopkeeper's son-in-law, most of all.

A brawny, red-bearded cossack in a ragged, patched jacket, and with an earring in one ear, jumped on to a bench.

"Brothers! You can see how things are going. The rich intend to put their man in as chairman by force. And then once more . . ."

Through the uproar Mishka caught only some of the words the cossack with the earring was shouting:

"When the land's . . . shared out . . . the poor get the clay . . . they take the black earth for themselves."

"Prokhor for chairman," a yell came from close by the door.

"Pro- . . . khor. . . . Ho-ho-ho! Ha-ha-ha!"

The stranger struggled energetically with the hubbub, knitting his brows, dribbling spittle and shouting again and again.

"I expect he's swearing," Mishka thought.

At last the stranger asked in a loud voice:

"Who's for Foma Korshunov?"

Many hands were raised above the benches. Mishka raised his hand too. Someone jumped from bench to bench, counting aloud.

"Sixty-three . . . sixty-four. . . ." He pointed to the boy's raised hand without looking at him, and cried: "Sixty-five."

The stranger wrote something down on a paper, and shouted:

"Those in favour of Prokhor Lisenkov, raise their hands."

Twenty-seven rich cossacks and Yegor, the miller, swiftly put up their hands. Mishka looked about him, and put up his hand too. The man counting the votes came to him, looked him up and down, and seized him painfully by the ear.

"Ah, you ragamuffin! Clear out or I'll throw you out. You voting too!"

A laugh arose from the people around, but the man took Mishka to the door and pushed him in the back. The boy recalled what his father had said when quarrelling with grand-dad, and as he slipped down the dirty, slippery steps he shouted back:

"You haven't any right . . ."

"I'll show you my right."

The insult, like all insults, was very bitter.

When he reached home he wept a little and complained to his mother. But she only told him angrily:

"Well, don't go where you oughtn't to. Sticking your nose into every hole. . . . You're nothing but a plague to me, that's what you are."

Next morning, while sitting at breakfast, they heard a quiet music, subdued by distance. Mishka's father put down his spoon and said, wiping his whiskers:

"But that's a military band."

Mishka flew off the bench as though blown by the wind. The door of the passage slammed, a rapid scuttling of feet sounded outside the window.

His father and grandfather followed him into the yard, and his mother leaned half out of the window.

At the end of the streets ranks of Red Army men were marching in a green, swaying wave. At their head, musicians were blowing into enormous trumpets, and the sounds hung over all the village.

Mishka's eyes started out of his head. He danced up and down uncertainly, then tore off and ran up to the band. He had a pleasantly tight feeling in his chest, and it rose to his throat. He glanced at the Red Army men's cheerful, dusty faces, at the musicians importantly puffing out their cheeks, and at once, as though struck down, decided: 'I'll go and fight with them.'

He remembered his dream, and gained fresh courage from somewhere. He hitched himself on to the knapsack of a man on the outside file, and asked:

"Where are you going? To fight?"

"Why, of course. What do you think?"

"But who are you fighting for?"

"For the Soviet government, idiot! Here, get into the middle."

He pushed Mishka into the middle of the rank, where someone laughed and clipped him on his bristly nape. Another took a dirty piece of sugar out of his pocket as he marched along and pushed it into the boy's mouth. When they reached the square a voice shouted from somewhere in front:

"Halt!"

The Red Army men came to a halt, then scattered over the square, lying down in little groups in the cool, in the shadow of the school fence. A tall, clean-shaven Red Army man with a sword at his side came up to Mishka and asked, curling his lips into a smile:

"And how did you get tacked on to us?"

Mishka assumed an air of importance, and tugged up his slipping trousers.

"I'm going off with you to fight."

"Comrade Combat (Battalion Commander), take him on as your assistant," one of the Red Army men shouted.

The others burst into a roar of laughter. The boy blinked rapidly, but the man with the strange title of Combat frowned, and shouted sternly:

"Now, what are you sniggering at, you dolts? Of course we'll take him with us, but on condition. . . ." Combat turned back to Mishka and said: "You've only got one brace to your trousers; you can't go about like that, you'd bring disgrace on us looking like that. Look at me: I've got two braces; and all the others have got two. Run and get your mother to sew on another brace for you and we'll wait for you here." He turned to the men and shouted, winking: "Tereshchenko, go and bring the new Red Army man a greatcoat and gun."

One of the men lying under the fence got up, put his hand to the peak of his cap, and answered:

"Very good!" He went off swiftly along by the fence.

"Now, hurry up! Get your mother to sew on a second brace, quick!"

Mishka gave Combat an old-fashioned look.

"You watch out, don't try any games on me!"

"What makes you think I would? How could I?"

It was some distance from the square to his home. By the time he had run all the way to the gate he was out of breath. He flung off his trousers as he ran through the gate, and, his bare legs twinkling, he burst like a storm into the hut.

"Mummy . . . my trousers. . . . Sew on another brace."

There was not a sound to be heard in the hut. The flies were buzzing in a black swarm above the stove. He ran all through the yard, the threshing-floor, the garden, but couldn't find his mother, nor his father, nor his grandfather. He dashed back into the best room, and a sack caught his eyes. He cut off a long strip with a knife; he hadn't time to sew it on, even if he had known how to. He hurriedly tied it to his trousers, flung it across his shoulder, tied it down once more in front and dashed out and under the granary.

He tore away the stone, took a swift glance at Lenin's hand pointing at him, Mishka, and whispered, taking deep breaths:

"Well, you see; I've joined your army now."

He wrapped the picture carefully in the dock-leaf, pushed it into the opening of his shirt at the breast and ran out into the street. With one hand he pressed the picture to his chest; with the other he held up his trousers. As he ran past his neighbour's fence he shouted to her:

"Anisimovna!"

"Well?"

"Tell my folk to have dinner without me."

"Where are you flying off to, crazy?"

He dismissed the question with a wave of the hand.

"I'm going off to do my military service."

He ran all the way to the square, and there halted as though rooted to the ground. There wasn't a soul to be seen. Cigarette ends were scattered under the fence, together with conserve cans, and someone's torn leg-rags. From the very far end of the village came a muffled thunder of music, he could hear the tramp of the marching soldiers' feet echoing on the hard-beaten road.

A sob burst from his throat, he cried out, and rushed to overtake them as fast as his legs could carry him. And he would have overtaken them, without fail he would have done. But outside the tanner's yard a yellow, long-tailed bitch was lying right across the road, baring its teeth. While he was running round through another street he lost all track of the sounds of music and the tramp of feet.

*　　　*　　　*

Two days later a force of some forty men arrived in the village. The soldiers were wearing grey felt boots and workmen's jackets. Mishka's father came home from the Executive Committee for dinner, and told grandfather:

"Get the grain in the granary ready, grand-dad. A food requisitioning detachment's arrived. They've started carrying out a search for grain."

The soldiers went from yard to yard, probing the ground in the sheds with their bayonets, digging up the buried grain and carrying it on waggons to the communal granary.

They called on the chairman, too. The leader, sucking a pipe, asked grandfather:

"Have you buried your grain, old man? Come on, own up to it."

Grand-dad stroked his beard and said proudly:

"But my son's a communist!"

They went into the granary. The soldier with the pipe took in the bins with one glance and smiled.

"Bring out the grain from this bin, daddy, and the rest you can keep for food and seed."

Grand-dad harnessed up the old horse into the cart, grunted and groaned as he filled eight sacks, waved his hand miserably, and carried it all off to the communal granary. Mishka's mother cried a little out of regret for the grain, but he helped his grandfather to pour it into the sacks and then went off to play with Vitka, the priest's son.

They had only just sat down on the kitchen floor and spread out horses cut from paper when the same soldiers came in. The priest, half tripping over his cassock, ran out to meet them, fussed over them and invited them to come into the room. But the soldier with the pipe said sternly:

"We'll go to the granary. Where do you keep your grain?"

The dishevelled priest's wife ran out of the best room, and smiled craftily.

"Just imagine, gentlemen, we haven't got any grain at all here. My husband hasn't driven round to collect his tithes yet. . . ."

"But have you any cellar in the house?"

"No, we haven't. We used to keep the grain in the granary."

Mishka remembered that he and Vitka had crawled down into a spacious cellar once, and he said, turning to look at the priest's wife:

"But Vitka and I climbed down into the cellar from the kitchen. Have you forgotten?"

She turned pale, but laughed aloud.

"You've got it all wrong, my child. Vitka, I think you could go out into the garden to play."

The soldier with the pipe narrowed his eyes and smiled at Mishka.

"How do you get down there, sonny?"

The priest's wife cracked her finger joints and said:

"Surely you don't believe a silly little boy? I assure you, gentlemen, we haven't any cellar."

Waving the edges of his cassock, the priest added:

"Wouldn't you like a bite to eat, comrades? Let's go into the other room."

As the priest's wife went past Mishka she gave him a painful pinch on the hand and smiled graciously.

"Go into the garden, children; don't get in the way in here."

The soldiers winked at one another and went into the kitchen;

they knocked on the floor with their rifle butts. They shifted the table standing by the wall, and tugged at some sacking. The soldier with the pipe lifted a floorboard, glanced into the cellar, and shook his head.

"Aren't you ashamed of yourselves? Saying you haven't any grain when your cellar's filled to the top with wheat."

The priest's wife gave Mishka such a look that he took alarm and thought he had better get back home as quickly as possible. He got up and went into the yard. Sobbing, she rushed out into the passage after him and, seizing him by the hair, began to drag him to and fro.

He wrenched himself away by sheer force, and tore back home without looking back. Choking with his tears, he told his mother everything; but she only clutched her head.

"Whatever shall I do with you? Get out of my sight before I give you one."

From that time on, after every affront Mishka crawled under the granary, shifted the stone, unwrapped the dock-leaf and, wetting the paper with his tears, told Lenin about his troubles and complained of the person who had upset him.

A week passed. He began to be bored. He had no one to play with. The neighbours' children wouldn't have anything to do with him, and to the nickname 'shame-child' was added another the children had picked up from their elders. They called after him:

"Hey you, communar! You communar's abortion, you watch out."

One day Mishka came back from the pond late in the afternoon. As he went into the hut he heard his father talking in sharp tones, while his mother was howling and lamenting as if over the dead. He slipped through the door and saw his father rolling his greatcoat and pulling on his legboots.

"Where are you going, daddy?"

His father laughed as he answered:

"You look after your mother, sonny. She's making me sick with her bellowing. I'm going off to the war, but she won't let me go."

"And I'm going with you, daddy."

His father belted himself with a strap and put on his cap with the ribbons.

"You're a queer boy, straight you are. We can't both of us go off together. When I come back then you'll go, but otherwise, when the grain ripens, who's going to harvest it? Your mother's got the house to look after, and grandfather's old. . . ."

As he said goodbye to his father Mishka held back his tears, and even managed to smile. As on the day of her husband's home-coming his wife hung round his neck, and he had to force her to let go. But grandfather only grunted and whispered into the soldier's ear as he kissed him :

"Foma lad, my own son. Perhaps you needn't go after all? Perhaps they can manage without you somehow? Maybe you'll be killed, and then what will happen to us?"

"Drop it, father. That's not the way to talk. Who's going to defend our government if every man crawls under the woman's petticoat to hide?"

"Oh, all right; go then, if your cause is right."

The old man turned away and unnoticed wiped away a tear. They all went as far as the Executive Committee office to see the soldier off. In the yard some twenty men with rifles were crowded. The father also obtained a rifle and, giving Mishka one last kiss, marched off with the others down the street to the outskirts of the village.

Mishka and his grandfather walked home together, with the mother staggering and dragging behind them. In the village a dog howled from time to time, rare lights shone out. The village was lost in the nocturnal darkness, like an old woman in a black shawl. A fine rain began to sprinkle down; somewhere over the steppe outside the village lightning flickered, and thunder rolled with muffled, prolonged peals.

As they drew near the house Mishka, who had not spoken before, asked his grandfather :

"Grand-dad, but who has daddy gone off to fight?"

"Get away !"

"Grand-dad !"

"Well?"

"Who is daddy going to fight?"

As the old man thrust home the gate bolt he answered :

"Wicked men have turned up not far from our village. The people call them a band, but I think they're just bandits. And your father's gone off to fight them."

"Are there a lot of them, grand-dad?"

"They say about two hundred. Well, off to bed with you, naughty one; you've been hanging around long enough."

During the night Mishka was awakened by the sound of voices. He stirred and felt over the bed : his grandfather wasn't there.

"Grand-dad, where are you?"

"Shut up! Go to sleep, you fidgety child."

Mishka got up and groped in the darkness to the window. His grand-dad was sitting on the bench, in only his underpants, with his head thrust through the open window. He was listening. Mishka strained his ears, and in the dead silence clearly heard shots rattling out beyond the village, then the measured burst of volley after volley.

Trak . . . tra-ra-trak. Ta-trak.

Just as though someone were driving nails into wood.

The boy was filled with terror. He huddled against his grand-father and began to wail :

"Is that daddy firing?"

His grandfather ignored the question, but his mother broke again into tears and lamentations.

The firing outside the village went on till dawn came, then died away. Mishka curled himself up like a little loaf on the bench and dropped off into a heavy, joyless sleep. At daybreak a group of horsemen galloped along the street on their way to the Executive Committee office. His grandfather woke him up, and they ran out into the yard.

Smoke was rising in a black column from the Executive Committee yard, the fire leaped across to the surrounding buildings. More horsemen cantered along the street. One of them rode up to the yard and shouted to grandfather :

"Have you got a horse, old man?"

"Yes."

"Harness it up and go and fetch your communists, they're lying in the scrub outside the village. Pile then on your cart and bring them in; their families can bury them."

The old man hurriedly harnessed up the bay to a cart, and drove out of the yard at a trot.

There was a hubbub of shouts in the village; dismounted bandits were dragging hay out from the threshing-floors, and slaughtering

sheep. One of them leaped off his horse outside Anisimovna's yard
and ran into her hut. Mishka heard her howling at the top of her
voice. But the bandit ran out on to the veranda, his sabre clattering; he sat down, pulled off his boots, tore Mrs. Anisimovna's
flowered holiday shawl in half, tore off his filthy leg-rags, and
wrapped each leg in half the shawl.

Mishka went into the best room and lay down on the bed, pressing his head into the pillow. He got up only when he heard the
gate creak. He ran out on to the veranda and saw his grandfather
leading the horse into the yard. His beard was wet with tears.

On the cart a naked man was lying with his arms flung out; his
head bounced up and down on the back, and thick black blood was
oozing over the bottom boards.

Swaying as he went, the boy went up to the cart and glanced at
the face; it was carved up with sabre slashes, and he could see the
bared teeth, the cheeks hanging, cut away to the bone, and on one
bulging eye, floating and swaying in blood, was a large green fly.

Still he did not guess who the man was, but he shivered all over
with horror, shifted his eyes to the body and, seeing the blue and
white stripes of the bloodstained sailor shirt, crumpled as though
someone had struck him behind the knees; with dilated eyes he
looked again into that rigid face, and jumped on to the cart.

"Daddy, dear, get up. My dear daddy!" He fell off the cart and
tried to run away; but his legs sagged under him, he crawled on
all fours to the veranda steps and thrust his head into the sand.

*   *   *

His grandfather's eyes were deeply sunken, his head shook and
danced, his lips whispered something without making a sound.

He sat stroking Mishka on the head, saying not a word for a
very long time; then, looking at his daughter-in-law lying stretched
out on the bed, whispered :

"Let's go outside, little grandson."

He took the boy by the hand and led him out on to the veranda.
As Mishka went past the best room he screwed up his eyes, and
trembled; on the table in that room his daddy was lying, silent and
serious. They had washed the blood off him, but Mishka could still
see his father's bloody glazed eye with the green fly on it.

Grandfather went to the well, and fumbled with the rope for a long time, untying it. Then he went into the stable, led out the bay, for some reason wiped its frothy lips with his sleeve, then bridled it, listening all the while: the village echoed with shouts and laughter. Two men rode past the yard, their cigarettes glowed in the darkness, and their voices floated clearly to Mishka's ears.

"Now we've carried out a grain requisition on them! In the next world they'll remember how to take grain from the people."

The sounds of horse hoofs died away; grandfather bent down to Mishka's ear and whispered:

"I'm old . . . I can't get on to the horse . . . I'll put you on it, sonny, and you ride with God to Pronin village . . . I'll tell you the way to go. . . . That Red force that came through our village with music ought to be there, by all accounts. . . . Tell them to come back to the village: the band is here. Understand?"

Mishka nodded without speaking. His grandfather seated him on the horse, tied his legs with the rope to the saddle so that he couldn't fall off, then led the bay through the threshing-floor, past the pond, past the bandit guard into the steppe.

"Up on the rise you'll find a ravine running into the hill; ride along above it, don't turn to right or left. It'll take you straight to Pronin. Now, off with you, my dear boy."

The old man kissed him and gave the bay a gentle smack with his hand.

The night was moonlit, and clear. With a snort the bay set off at a gentle trot; but, feeling the burden light on its back, it began to move faster. Mishka touched it up with the reins, and smacked his hand on its neck as he shook and bounced on the saddle.

A quail rattled away boldly in the green thicket of ripening grain. A spring tinkled at the bottom of the ravine, the wind brought a breath of cool.

Mishka was frightened to find himself all alone in the steppe; he put his arms round the bay's neck and pressed close to the animal in a little chilly bundle.

The ravine crawled upward, dropped again, then rose once more. Mishka was too frightened to look back, and he whispered to himself, trying to avoid thinking of anything. The silence froze in his ears, he kept his eyes closed.

The bay tossed its head, snorted, and quickened its pace. The boy opened his eyes just the tiniest bit, and saw little pale yellow fires below him, under the hill. The wind brought the sound of a howling dog to his ears.

For a moment his breast was warmed with joy. He touched up the bay with his heels and shouted :

"Get . . . on !"

The dog's howling sounded closer, now the vague outline of a windmill was visible on the rise.

"Who goes there?" Someone shouted from the windmill.

Mishka silently urged on the bay. Cocks began to crow over the drowsy village.

"Halt! Who goes there? Halt or I fire!"

In his alarm Mishka tugged on the reins, but the bay scented the proximity of other horses, and with a whinny broke into a gallop, taking no heed of the reins.

"Halt!"

Shots rang out from the windmill. Mishka's shout was drowned in the thud of horse hoofs. The bay groaned, reared up and fell heavily on its right flank.

For one moment Mishka felt a terrible, unbearable pain in his right foot; the shout died on his lips. The bay pressed more and more heavily on his foot.

The sound of horse hoofs drew closer. Two men galloped up with clattering sabres; they leaped off their horses and bent over the boy.

"Holy Mother—why, it's that little boy!"

"Surely we haven't killed him?"

Someone thrust a hand into the opening of Mishka's shirt and breathed the smell of tobacco into his face. Someone's voice said in a tone of delight :

"He's all right. But it looks as though the horse has crushed his foot."

As he lost consciousness, Mishka whispered :

"The band are in our village. They've killed my daddy. They've burnt down the executive committee, and grand-dad told me to ride here as fast as I could."

Circles of light floated before his fading eyes. . . . His daddy went past, twisting his ginger whiskers, and laughing; but a great green fly was swaying on his eye. Grand-dad walked by, reproachfully shaking his head, and then mummy, then a small, big-browed man with outstretched hand. And that hand was pointing straight at him, at Mishka.

"Comrade Lenin!" Mishka cried in a thin, choking voice; with a struggle he raised his head, and smiled, stretching both hands out before him.

1925.

THE DIEHARD

IGNAT returned from the district centre at sunset.

He pushed open the wattle gates and broke down the peaked snow drift, led the rime-coated horse into the yard and, not stopping to unharness it from the waggon, ran up the steps. Then there was the sound of frozen boards creaking in the passage, and the besom hurriedly used to sweep the snow off the felt boots. Pakhomich, who was sitting on the stove, shaping an axe handle, brushed the shavings off his knees and said to his younger son, Grigory:

"Grisha, go and unharness the mare; I've put down hay in the stable."

Throwing the door wide open, Ignat slipped in, greeted the others, and fumbled a long time, trying to unfasten the strings of his cowl with his frozen fingers. He pulled the melting icicles off his whiskers, knitting his brows with pain, and smiled, not attempting to conceal his joy.

"I've heard a rumour that the Red Guards are marching on the region."

Pakhomich dropped his legs over the side of the stove, and asked with restrained curiosity:

"Going to the war or what?"

"I've heard various stories. But there's a lot of unrest in the district village; the people are all worked up, there's a tremendous crowd in the commune office."

"You haven't heard anything being said about the land?"

"They say the bolsheviks are putting the landowners' land under the rake."

"So-o-o!" Pakhomich grunted, and jumped down from the stove like a young man.

The old woman cooking at the stove plate rattled the spoons; as she poured out cabbage soup into the bowls she said:

"Call Grisha in for supper."

Twilight fell outside. A fine snow was sifting down and then stopping, and the night was dark with grey-blue cloud. Pakhomich put down his spoon, wiped his beard with an embroidered hand towel, and asked:

"Did you find out anything about the steam mill? When will they be starting it up?"

"The mill's already working; we can take ours along."

"Well, finish your supper, then let's go to the granary. We'll have to winnow the grain again, and tomorrow, if the weather's fine, I'll drive over to get it ground. What's the road like: well beaten down?"

"The track's never at rest, people driving along it day and night. But it's difficult for anything to pass. The snow at the roadside is more than waist deep."

2

Grigory went out of the gate to see his father off.

Pakhomich drew on his gloves and settled down in the driver's seat.

"Look after the cow, Grisha. Her udder's filling, she'll be calving any moment now."

"All right, father; off with you."

The sledge runners crunched the half-melting icing of the snow. Pakhomich gently played the hairy reins, drove round the ashes scattered in the street. If he went over a bare patch of road the runners would stick to it. Straining and arching their backs, the horses pulled hard. Though the harness was in good order and the animals well fed, from time to time Pakhomich had to climb out of the sledge, grunting, and walk: the sledge was loaded too heavily with sacks.

He drove up the hill, gave the sweating horses a breather, then sent them off again at a long, striding trot. Here and there the thaw had eaten into the snow and had rutted and pitted the road monstrously. The first warmth of early spring. The soil was melting in the noonday.

He was about to drive past the forest when a troika came dashing towards him. But the snow at the roadside was heaped into great mounds. Only a narrow track had been gnawed through the yard-deep drifts; there was no possibility of the two sledges passing on the road.

"Well, here's a fine thing; my goodness! Whoa!"

He halted his horses, got out, and took off his cap. The wind licked his grey, sweaty head. He took off his old cap because in the troika coming towards him he recognized Colonel Boris Alexandrovich Chornoyarov. And he had rented land from the colonel for eight years in succession.

The troika drew closer. The sleighbells carried on a conversation with one another in undertones. Pakhomich could see the foam flying in flecks from the side horses, and the shaft-horse was swaying heavily, heavily. The driver half rose in his seat and waved his knout.

"Turn aside, you grey-headed raven. Have you taken over all the road?"

He drew up and halted the horses right in front of Pakhomich's pair. The old man, tangling his legs in his short sheepskin coat, ran bareheaded up to the sleigh and made a low bow.

The man in the sleigh, wrapped to the ears in a bearskin, stared with two unwinking, goggling eyes. The furrowed lips, shaven clean and blue, were curled.

"Why don't you get out of the way, scum? Have you got a whiff of the bolshevik freedom? Equality?"

"Your excellency! For Christ's sake drive round me. You're empty, but I've got a full load. If I turn off the road I'll never get out again."

"Am I to choke my horses in the snow for your benefit? Ah, you swine! I'll teach you to have respect for officers' epaulettes and to yield the road."

He threw the rug off his legs and flung his kid gloves on the seat.

"Artiom, give me the knout."

The colonel jumped out of the sleigh and brought the knout down with a swinging blow between the old man's eyes.

Pakhomich groaned and staggered; he covered his face with his hands, and blood seeped between his fingers.

"Take that, you scoundrel, and that!"

The colonel tugged at the old man's grey beard, and roared hoarsely, dribbling with saliva:

"I'll knock the Red Guard spirit out of you. You'll remember Colonel Chornoyarov, you cur!"

A moment later a dove blue shaft-bow gleamed above the thawing crust of snow at the roadside. Pakhomich's horses were struggling and tearing at the traces; the sledge lay over turned, humbly and helplessly, with snapped centre-shaft. But Pakhomich stood watching the troika with unwinking gaze. He would stand gazing until the back, shaped like a swan neck, disappeared into a dip in the road.

He would never forget Colonel Boris Alexandrovich Chornoyarov.

3

Pakhomich's old wife came back with full buckets from the spring.

The rooks were raging in the shamefully bare willows. Beyond the yard the sun was setting for the night over the rise, between the sails of the red-capped windmill. In the ditches the water was gurgling painfully, shaking the wattle fences. But the sky was like a fading cherry flower.

When she reached the yard she saw a cart at the gate, postal horses with tails twisted and tied up very short; the chickens were pecking at the steaming dung between their mudspattered, chilly hoofs. Gathering up the folds of his officer's greatcoat, a tall, thin man in a caracoul fur hat clambered out of the tarantass. He turned his frozen face to look at the old woman.

"Misha! My own son! So unexpected."

She dropped the yoke with the two buckets, and flung her arms round his neck; her withered lips could not reach his, she writhed against his chest and kissed the bright buttons and grey cloth.

Her ragged blouse smelt of cow dung. He pushed her away a little, smiled, and, as one might say, splashed tar in his mother's face.

"It's not seemly in the street, mamma. You show me where to stable my horses, and then carry my trunk into the room. Drive into the yard, d'you hear, coachman?"

4

A cornet, With white, new-looking epaulettes. A neatly clipped row of little hairs on the upper lip. This son was his own, flesh of his flesh, yet Pakhomich felt as embarrassed as if the man were a stranger.

"Come home for long, sonny?"

Mikhail was sitting by the window, his white fingers, obviously not used to work, drummed on the table.

"I'm commanded from Novocherkassk with a special commission from the military ataman. I shall stay for a time, of course. . . . Mamma! Wipe the milk off the table, you ought to be more tidy. I shall be staying here a couple of months."

Ignat came in from the yard, leaving marks on the floor from his dirty boots.

"Hallo, brother! Welcome home!"

"Greetings."

Ignat held out his hand and was about to embrace his brother; but somehow they missed each other, and only their fingers met in a cold and unfriendly clasp.

Smiling a restrained smile, Ignat said:

"So you're still wearing epaulettes, brother; but we cut them off long ago and threw them to the devil."

Mikhail frowned.

"I haven't sold my cossack honour yet."

They lapsed into a tedious silence.

"How are you getting on?" Mikhail asked at last, bending down to take off his boots.

Pakhomich got off the bench and rushed to his son.

"Let me take them off, Misha; you'll get your hands dirty." The old man went down on his knees, and replied as he carefully drew off the boots: "We manage, and we have bread to eat. Our way of life is well known. What's the latest news from you people in the town?"

"Well, we're organizing the cossacks to drive out the Red Guards."

Ignat asked, with his eyes fixed on the earthen floor.

"And what need is there to drive them out?"

Mikhail smiled wryly.

"Don't you know? The bolsheviks are taking our cossack life away from us, they want to set up a commune, so that everything should be in common, the land and the women. . . ."

"You're telling old wives' tales. The bolsheviks are following our line."

"And what's your line?"

"They're taking the land from the gentry and giving it to the people; that's where their line is leading."

"Why, Ignat, are you on the side of the bolsheviks?"

"Well, and whose side are you on?"

Mikhail did not answer. He sat turned to the tear-stained window and, a smile on his face, drew faint designs on the glass.

5

Beyond the ravine, beyond the tops of the oak saplings, a burial mound extends along the Hetman highway.

On the mound is a woman carved from stone, eaten away and porous with the centuries, and of a morning the sun shines across her weed-grown head, then climbs higher, and through the misty coverlet of dust diligently licks the steppe, the gardens, the tiled roofs of the houses with its clinging burning rays, like a bitch licking her whelps.

At dawn Pakhomich turned his bullocks and plough off the highway. With legs feeble with age he paced out ten acres, cracked his knout at the bullocks, and began to comb the black earth with his ploughshare.

Grisha put all his weight on the handles, and turned the soil over almost knee deep; but Pakhomich hobbled along the velvety furrow waving his knout and rejoicing as he watched his son: the lad was only nineteen, but he could stand his ground with any cossack.

They ploughed three furrows and then had a rest. The sun was rising. The stone woman, sunk deep into the soil of the mound, stared at the ploughmen with unseeing eyes, and turned crimson in the sunlight as though enveloped in flame. Along the highway the wind sent the mealy dust flying up in a whirling column.

Grisha stood gazing for a moment: a horseman was galloping along.

"Father, is that our Mikhail coming on horseback?"

"It looks like him. . . ."

Mikhail galloped up, left his foaming horse by the cart, and ran towards the ploughmen, stumbling over the furrows. When he reached them he could hardly get his breath. He was panting like an overdriven horse.

"Whose land are you ploughing?"

"Ours."

"But this is Colonel Chornoyarov's land."

Pakhomich blew his nose and wiped it on the edge of his canvas shirt, then said weightily and slowly:

"It was theirs once; but now, son, it's ours, the people's."

Going white in the face, Mikhail shouted.

"Father! I know who's responsible for this. Grisha and Ignat are leading you into bad ways. You'll answer for it, taking over other people's property."

Pakhomich thrust his head out testily.

"It's our land now. There's no law that anyone can have more than two thousand acres. That's that. . . . It's equality. . . ."

"You've no right to plough up other people's land."

"And he hasn't been given the right to rule the steppe. We have had to sow on the salt marshes, but he took over all the black earth, and now the land has lain barren for three years. Is that right?"

"Stop ploughing, father, or I'll order the ataman to arrest you."

Pakhomich turned right round and shouted, going livid and his head twitching spasmodically:

"Through your own kith and kin you were brought up, and educated. You're a scoundrel, you son of a bitch."

Mikhail went green and grated his teeth.

"I'll show you, you old. . . ." He strode towards his father with clenched fists. But he saw Grisha snatch up an iron pole and come running with great leaps across the furrows, and, drawing his head down between his shoulders, not looking back, he went off to the village.

6

Pakhomich had a hut thatched with straw. The palisade round the yard stuck up like the ribs of a horse's skeleton.

Grigory drove back from the ploughing with his father. Ignat was mending the cattle-yard fence with brushwood. He came up to them, and his hands gave off the bitter scent of long-lying leaves.

"They've sent for us to go to the administration, Grigory. A village meeting has been called in the market square."

"What for?"

"Mobilization, so they say. The Red Guards have occupied the village of Kalinov."

Beyond the threshing-floor grain-dryers, the evening sunset faded and died away. One ray of sunlight got stranded in the threshing-floor on a pile of reddish husks; the easterly wind stirred up the husks, and the ray faded.

Grisha groomed his horse, and gave it oats. On the veranda Ignat, a widower, was fussing over his small six-year-old son. As Grisha went past he looked his brother in his laughing eyes and whispered :

"We must ride to Kalinov tonight, or we'll be mobilized here."

To his mother, who was driving a calf out of the passage, he said :

"Get underwear ready for me and Ignat, mother, and some dried bread."

"Where the devil are you going, then?"

"To the 'Who-Knows-Where' fields."

Till late in the night the hum of voices sounded in the village square. Pakhomich returned from the meeting after dark. By the door of the granary where Grisha was sleeping he halted. He stood awhile, then sat down helplessly on the stone threshold. A sickening weariness flooded through his body, his heart fluttered with feeble beats, and a prickling, prolonged ringing sounded in his ears. He sat there, spitting from time to time at the moon's faint reflection in a half-frozen puddle, and felt painfully that all his well-arranged, normal way of living was passing without looking back, and most likely would never return.

Somewhere, in the gardens down by the Don, dogs were barking vociferously, a quail beat regularly and distinctly in the meadow. The night unfolded its wings over the steppe and a milky haze enveloped the yards. Pakhomich coughed gently, the door creaked.

"Are you asleep, Grisha?"

The smell of silence and long-lying grain came from the granary. He stepped inside, and groped to feel his son's sheepskin coat.

"Grisha, are you asleep?"

"No."

The old man sat down on the edge of the sheepskin. Grisha heard his father's hands doing a fine, incessant, trembling tattoo. Pakhomich said thickly:

"I shall go with you . . . to serve . . . with the bolsheviks."

"What are you saying, father? How about our home? And besides, you're old. . . ."

"Well, and what if I am? I can serve in the camp, and, if not, I can sit a saddle. . . . Mikhail can look after the home. We're strangers to him, and the land's strange too. . . . Let him live: God will be his judge, but we'll go and win back our breadwinner, mother earth."

The first cocks began to crow in their various voices. The dawn began to flicker across the Don, beyond the ragged palisade of the forest. The melting shadows crawled away fearfully, cautiously.

Pakhomich led out three horses, watered them, examined the saddle-cloths carefully, and saddled the animals. His old woman sobbed, and the gate sobbed, too, with her; the horse hoofs squelched juicily over the salt marsh.

"We must take the summer road, father; we might fall in with someone on the highroad," Ignat said in an undertone.

The sky turned pale. The grass sweated with a honied, chilly dew. From beyond the Don, from the granular, lemon-coloured sands the dawn strode on.

7

Little stars were modestly sketched in with copying ink pencil on Colonel Chornoyarov's military khaki tunic. His cheeks were fleshy and netted with blue veins. His courtly, burring baritone beat against the spider-webbed walls of the village meeting room.

His puffy, rosy, hairless fingers gesticulated with restraint and perfect decorum.

But the cossacks crowded round him in a sweating ring, breathing out hot fumes of home-grown tobacco and slightly sour wheaten bread. Fur caps with crimson crowns, colourful beards. Mouths gaping greedily and dribbling, drinking in the words which came in a burring, hissing baritone, from lips scabby with syphilis.

"Dear fellow villagers. From time immemorial you have been the firm support of our father the tsar and the country. Now, in this great, sorrowful country, all Russia is looking to you. Save her from the filthy bolsheviks. Save your own possessions, your wives and daughters. As an example of how to perform your civic duty take your fellow villager, Ensign Mikhail Kramskov: he was the first to inform us that his father and two brothers had gone over to the bolsheviks. And he is the first, as a true son of the Quiet Don, to stand to its defence."

"Resolved:

"The cossacks of our village, Piotr Pakhomich Kramskov, and his sons, Ignat and Grigory, having gone over to the enemies of the Quiet Don, are hereby deprived of their title as cossacks, and also all their shares in land and allotments, and when captured they are to be handed over to the Vieshenska district Field Court Martial."

8

The detachment halted by a stack of hay to feed the horses. In the village a machine-gun could be heard beyond the threshing-floor fences.

The commissar, a bullet hole through his cheek, galloped up on a stallion white with sweat to the two-wheeled cart, and shouted in a heartrending, nasal voice:

"All is lost. They'll smash us, that's certain."

He brought his whip down between his stallion's ears and, hawking and choking up black clots of blood, hissed into the detachment commander's ear:

"If we don't break through to the Don we may be done for. The cossacks will cut us off and make chaff of us. Call on your men to go into the attack."

The commander, a former engineer in an iron foundry, as slow as the first turns of a flywheel, lifted his clean-shaven head and shouted, without taking the pipe out of his mouth:

"To horse!"

The commissar rode off, but when he had gone some twenty paces he turned and asked:

"What do you think? Will they liquidate us?" He galloped off without waiting for an answer.

The bullets sent up a floury dust under the horses' hoofs; they hissed as they bored through the hay. One bullet sent a tarry splinter flying from the cart and then in its flight it kissed the machine-gunner. He dropped the oily leg-rag he was holding, squatted down, cocking his head on one side like a bird, bristled up and so died, one foot in his boot, the other bootless. The wind brought the straining hoot of a locomotive from the railway track. On the platform waggon a snub-nosed muzzle turned and spat into the steppe, towards the stack, towards the group of men scurrying about. Then, with couplings clattering, Armoured Train 'Kornilov No. 8' set off. But its spittle fell to the right of the stack. With a screech it let loose a puff of oily smoke and tangled braids of water-melon flesh from the previous year's harvest.

Under the unusual weight the rusty rails went on sobbing for some time, the sleepers groaned and rang; but by the stack in the steppe, Pakhomich's pregnant mare, its legs broken by shrapnel, struggled long to get up; it flung up its head with a snort, the half-worn horseshoes glittered on its hoofs. The sandy spot greedily drank in the rosy foam and blood.

Pakhomich's heart was pierced with pain, and he whispered:

"A blood mare. . . . Ah, I wouldn't have brought her if I'd known."

"Don't be stupid, father," Ignat shouted as he galloped past. "Run and get on the britchka; can't you see we're going into the attack?"

The old man watched him go unconcernedly.

A machine-gun rattled as though a linen towel were being torn to shreds. Pakhomich lay on the cartridge chest, swallowing a

bitter, unpleasant spittle. But the pleasant scent of earthy rust, the
tickling odour of last-year grass rotting down to the roots, floated
in a smoky, streaming haze over the ground softened with the
spring rains, with the sunlight and the steppe winds scented with
thyme and wormwood.

The horned, azure fringe of the forest on the horizon danced in
the mirage, and above it, through the golden canopy of dust spread
over the steppe, a skylark accompanied the machine-guns with a
beady trill. Grigory came running up for more cartridges.

"Don't grieve, father. The mare's expendable."

Grisha's brown lips were splitting with the heat, his eyes were
swollen with sleepless nights. He picked up two cases of cartridges
in his arms and tore off again, sweaty and smiling.

By the evening they were drawing near to the Don. A battery
raked them from a hollow until dusk fell; cossack reconnaissances
appeared and disappeared on the rise. During the night the auda-
cious yellow eye of a searchlight groped through the thorny undergrowth, feeling for the tetherposts, the men's tents. For a whole
minute it picked them out clearly, flooding them with dead light,
then it went out.

With the dawn, line after line came on in solid waves down the
rise. The bristling thorn replied with volleys, taking careful aim,
at intervals. At noon the detachment commander knocked out his
pipe on the patched sole of his boot, and ran a heavy, indifferent
gaze over all his force.

"We can't hold them back, comrades. Swim across the river;
seven miles on the other side is the village of Gromov. Our people
are there . . ." he ended wearily.

As Grisha unsaddled his horse he shouted to his father:

"What's the matter with you?"

"It's all rubbish!" Pakhomich answered sternly; but his lower
jaw was quivering. "You swim across, Grisha. Unbridle the horse.
But as for me . . . I'm too old. . . ."

"Goodbye, father."

"God go with you, my son."

"Now, come on, baldy. What, you devil, frightened?"

Grisha waded in up to his waist, up to his chest, and then only
his head with its frowning brows and the horse's pointed ears were
visible above the dove-grey water.

Pakhomich drove home the cartridge with a crooked finger, took the figures of running men into his sights, then ejected the last smoking cartridge case and raised his hairy hands.

"We're done for, Ignat."

Ignat fired pointblank at a horse's muzzle, sat down, spreading his legs wide apart, spat on the raw, wave-kissed shingle and tore the collar of his khaki shirt open down to the waist.

9

At breakfast he sat twisting his waxed flaxen moustaches self-satisfiedly.

"Mother, I've been made a company commander now, because I'm cutting down bolshevism at its roots. There's no playing about with me; the least thing and I put them up against a wall."

She sighed.

"But how about our folk, Misha? Supposing they should happen to come. . . ."

"Mother, as an officer and a faithful son of the Quiet Don I must not take any family ties into account. Not even my father, not even my own brothers. . . . All the same, I'll hand them over to be court-martialled."

"My little son! My darling Misha! But how about me? I fed you all from the same breast, I'm sorry for all of you alike."

"There's no need to be sorry." He turned his eyes sternly on Ignat's little son. "And remove that brat from the table, or I'll twist his head off, the communar abortion. Pah, he looks at me like a wolf cub. When he grows up, the snake, he'll be a bolshevik too, like his father."

10

The orchard down by the Don was scented with flood-water and the swelling poplar buds. The crested waves rocked the mallards, licked the orchard fence, sucking at it.

Pakhomich's old wife was setting potatoes; she shifted painfully along between the rows. When she bent down the blood flowed into her head, and made it swim till she felt sick. She stood still for a moment, then sat down. She gazed silently at the black veins making an intricate pattern on her hands. She mumbled tonelessly with her lips.

On the farther side of the fence Ignat's son was playing with the sand.

"Grannie!"

"Well, little grandson?"

"Look, grannie, what the water has brought up."

"What has it brought up, my dear?"

The old woman scrambled up, thrust her spade unhurriedly into the earth, and opened the creaking gate. On the shoal a dead horse was lying, its coat gleaming with water, its hoofs turned to the ground. The belly was split right across, and the breeze blew up a smell of decay.

She went up closer.

A dead man's arms were twined inseparably round the horse's neck; the rein was twisted firmly round the left wrist; the head was flung backward, and the hair hung over the face. She looked without blinking at the lips, gnawed by fish, grinning and laying bare the dead rows of teeth. Then she fell. . . .

Tossing her grey locks, she crawled on all fours down to the water, clutched the head with its black hair, and moaned :

"Gri-sha! My dear son!"

———————

Extract from Order No. 186.

"For his self-sacrificial and incessant labours to root out bolshevism within the bounds of the Upper Don Region, company commander Mikhail Kramskov is raised to the rank of first lieutenant and is appointed commandant to the N— Field Court-Martial."

Commander of the Northern Front :
Major-General Ivanov.
Adjutant : (signature illegible).

II

The road scorched. Escorts on horses, and two men on foot. Their soles in festering wounds. In their underwear, stiff with blood. Through the villages, through the streets, taunted by the people as they passed, under a crossfire of blows. On the evening of the second day they came to their own village. The Don and the low, bluish ridge of chalky hills, like a crowded flock of sheep. Pakhomich stooped and tore up a clump of green wheat; he had difficulty in moving his lips.

"Can you guess, Ignat? This is our land. Grisha and I ploughed it. . . ."

Behind them the whistle of a curling whiplash.

"No talking!"

Speechless, with bowed heads, they went through the village. Their feet like lead. Past the palisade, past the straw-thatched hut. Pakhomich glanced into the yard densely overgrown with rampant scrub, and rubbed his breast where his heart was thumping with a painful, awkward beat.

"Father! Look, there's mother in the threshing-floor."

"She hasn't seen us."

From behind them :

"Silence, you scum!"

The square overgrown with curly chickweed. The village administration. A crowd gathered below the veranda.

"Hallo, Pakhomich! I thought you went off to win back the land?"

"He's already won back seven feet . . . in the cemetery."

"That'll teach the old hound."

Pakhomich raised one finger, with its swollen nail looking like tortoiseshell, and choked out, panting for breath:

"Now, now, you lot of yes-men. Even if we die, even if the good goes to the ground, they'll raise a memorial to you too; you're not in the right."

His neighbour, Anisim Makeyev, sidled up to him, baring his teeth between his red beard, and, losing control of himself, struck Pakhomich on the head.

"Beat them up!" A shout came from the back of the crowd.

With a groaning roar, like wild beasts the human wave closed round them, seething with crimson-crowned fur caps, concentrated in a frenzied din. The blows sounded heavy and resonant to the accompaniment of a rapid stamping. But Mikishar flew down like a hawk from the veranda, and drove a wedge to split the swaying crowd in two. He burst into them in his ragged shirt, white and with writhing lips, and bawled:

"Brothers! Front-line men! Don't allow murder to be done!" He tore his sabre out of its scabbard and waved the gleaming steel fanwise above his head. "You don't see these blasted scum at the front, so why should they be allowed to kill here?"

"Beat up Mikishar! He's sold himself to the bolshies."

Mikishar and eight front-line men home on furlough ranged themselves in a solid line and barred Pakhomich and Ignat off from the crowd.

The old men stood around for some time, yelling and muttering, then they wandered off from the square in ones and twos. Dusk fell.

*　　　　*　　　　*

"I would like to hear your deciding voice, lieutenant. Of course, we've got to shoot them, but all the same they are your father and brother. . . . Perhaps you'll undertake the task of interceding for them with the ataman of the punitive force?"

"I, your excellency, have served in faith and truth, and I shall continue to serve the tsar and the all-powerful Don Army. . . ."

The colonel, with a tragic gesture:

"Lieutenant, you have a magnanimous soul and a valiant heart. Allow me to kiss you in the Russian fashion for your self-sacrifice in the task of serving the throne and your own nation."

A smack of kisses, thrice repeated, then a pause.

"What do you think, my dear lieutenant? If we shoot them aren't we likely to arouse indignation among the poorer strata of the cossackry?"

Lieutenant Mikhail Kramskov was silent for some time; then, without raising his head, he said thickly:

"We have some reliable lads in the escort command. . . . We can send the prisoners under their escort to the Novocherkassk prison. The lads won't talk. And sometimes prisoners try to escape. . . ."

"I understand, lieutenant. You can count on the rank of captain. Permit me to shake your hand."

12

The shed accommodating the prisoners of war was enveloped in barbed wire like a spider's nest with web. Inside it were Ignat and Pakhomich, their faces swollen and like cast iron; on the street side was Ignat's small son, wearing his father's peaked cap, and Pakhomich's old wife, with hands like stone, frozen with yearning to the wire: she blinked her bloodshot eyelids, her mouth writhed, but she shed no tears; she had wept them all away long since.

Pakhomich had difficulty in shifting his split tongue.

"Ask Lukich to harvest the wheat; you'll pay him: give him the yearling calf."

He chewed his lips and coughed a dry cough.

"Don't grieve for us, old woman. We've had our day. We'll all be there. Afterwards, read the funeral service for us. And remember: don't write 'Red Guard Piotr,' but put it straight: shot soldiers Piotr, Ignat, Grigory. Otherwise the priest won't take us. . . . But now, goodbye, old lady. Keep going, look after our grandson. Forgive me if I've ever done you any wrong. . . ."

Ignat picked up his son in his arms: the guard turned away as though he hadn't noticed. With quivering fingers Ignat fashioned a windmill from reeds for his son.

"Daddy, what have you got blood on your head for?"

"I knocked it, little son."

"But why did that man hit you with his gun when you came out of the shed?"

"You're a funny boy! He did it deliberately, just for fun."

They were silent. The reed stalks crackled under Ignat's nails.

"Let's go home, daddy. You can make me a windmill there."

"You go home with grannie, little son." Ignat's lips quivered a little, and twisted. "I'll come along later."

Ignat strode round the confines of the yard like a tethered wolf, dragging one leg wounded by a rifle butt; he pressed the thin little body to his chest, he pressed and pressed. . . .

"Daddy, why are your eyes all wet?"

Ignat was silent.

The twilight shadows gathered. From the meadows, from the wooded riverside marshes, from the alders and the mudflats the mist crawled and descended on the gardens in a dewy, silvery sediment. It pressed the grass down to the chilled, damp ground.

They came out of the shed in a little bunch. The officer with lieutenant's epaulettes, wearing a caracoul fur cap, tall and thin, said in an undertone, breathing out a smell of home-distilled vodka :

"Don't take them far. Just outside the village, in the brushwood."

Hollow steps and the clatter of rifle bolts echoed in the strained silence.

The night was starless, wolfish. Beyond the Don the lilac-hued steppe was lost in shadows. On the rise, beyond the luxuriant shoots of the wheat, in a ravine washed with spring water, in a lair made under the heady scent of long-lying dead leaves, a wolf bitch was whelping; she groaned like a woman in labour, gnawed at the sand under her saturated with her blood, and as she licked the first wet, shaggy whelp, she pricked up her ears as in the scrubby undergrowth not far from her lair she heard two muffled rifle shots and a human cry.

She strained her ears anxiously, and in answer to the short, groaning cry she howled hoarsely and brokenly.

1925.

THE WAY AND THE ROAD

Part One

I

THE Hetman's highway runs along beside the Don, through the steppe right to the sea. On its left side is the rolling sandy Don basin, the green, stunted mirage of water meadows, with the occasional whitish gleam of nameless lakes; on the right are the beetling, frowning hills, and beyond them, beyond the smoky fringe of the Hetman's highway, beyond the chain of low, guardian tumuli, are little rivers, the great steppe and the small cossack villages and district centres, and a grey, bristling sea of feathergrass.

*   *   *

Autumn that year came on early, the steppe was left bare, and sparkled with touches of burning frost.

One morning, as Piotr's father was sorting over the wool in the felt-maker's hut, he said to his son:

"Well, sonny, we'll be having more work than we want now! The frosts have arrived, the cossack women are combing the wool, and our job will be to stroke the string and roll our sleeves up higher, otherwise we'll have wet backs."

The father raised his head and smiled, narrowing his faded grey eyes; dark, deeply carved furrows ran down his cheeks, which were shaggy with a grey scrub.

Piotr was sitting at the table fashioning a small block of wood; he noticed the smile fade on his father's face, but said nothing. It was sickeningly stifling in the hut, a measured drip fell from the ceiling, flies were crawling over the small, fly-blown mica window. Through the window the rimy wattle fence, the willows, the well-crane all seemed pallidly rainbow hued or covered with rusty green. Piotr took one swift glance outside, shifted his gaze to his father's hunched, bare back, counted the knobs on the backbone, moving his lips as he counted, and sat watching as the shoulderblades rose and fell and the withered skin gathered in furrows on his father's shoulders.

With accustomed dexterity the gnarled fingers picked the burrs, the thorns and straw out of the wool; and the shaggy head, and the shadow of that head on the wall, rocked in time with the movements of his fingers. The steamed sheep's wool had a cloying and sour stink. The sweat rolled down Piotr's face in little beads, the hair hung dankly over his eyes. He wiped his brow with his palm and put the block on the window sill.

"Let's have our mid-day break, father. Look where the sun's climbed to : it's dinner-time almost."

"Mid-day break? Wait a bit. For goodness sake, the burrs there are in this wool! I've been bent over it a good hour."

Piotr jumped up from the table and glanced into the stove. His sweaty cheeks were greedily licked by the glow from the fire.

"I'll get the cabbage soup, father. I've gone hungry long enough; I'm all ready to eat."

"Well, go on then; the work'll wait."

They sat down at the table without putting on their shirts. They sipped their soup slowly, enjoying the garnishing of vegetable oil.

Piotr glanced sidelong at his father, and said with a yawn :

"You've gone quite thin, just as though you were being eaten by some disease. It's not you who eats the bread, the bread eats you."

His father smiled, and his cheekbones worked up and down.

"You're a queer lad. You compare yourself with your father. By the Blessed Virgin's Day I shall be going on for fifty-seven, and you're seventeen or so. It's old age that's eating at me, not disease." He sighed. "Your dead mother ought to see you. . . ."

They sat silent for a time, listening to the deep buzz of the flies. In the yard a dog began to bark furiously. There was a clatter of feet past the window. The door was flung open, it banged against the tub of steeping fleeces. Sidor, the smith, sidled into the mud-daub hut. He did not take off his cap, and spat down at his feet.

"Well, it's a fine dog you keep. The damned animal isn't content to bite just anywhere, he always aims above the legs."

"He realizes that you've come for your felt boots, and they're not ready, and so he tries to stop you."

"I haven't come for my felt boots."

"Well, if you haven't, sit down for a little while on that barrel, and be our guest."

"I drop in as a guest at my time of life, and you seat me on a wet barrel. Piotr, my boy, don't you be such a dangerous sort as your father."

Laughing in his little bushy beard, Sidor squatted down by the door, and spent a long time rolling a cigarette with his stiff fingers. As he smoked with a smacking of lips he barked:

"Haven't you heard anything, daddy Foma?"

Rolling a fleece into a sack, Piotr's father shook his head and smiled. But he noticed little sparks of joy in Sidor's eyes, and grew anxious.

"Why, what's happened?"

Through the haze of tobacco smoke Sidor's face bloomed, his lips twisted harelike into a smile, his eyes shifted joyfully and anxiously under his bleached eyebrows.

"The Reds are pressing on, they're getting close to the other bank of the Don. There's talk of retreat here in our village. This morning at dawn I was working in my forge, and I heard horsemen galloping along the street. I looked out, and they ran into my forge. "Is the smith here?" they ask. "Yes, I'm here," I answer. "Get that mare shod in two twos, if you spoil her I'll whip you." I go out of the smithy, all black with coal as usual. I could see by his epaulettes he was a colonel, and he had an adjutant with him. "Excuse me, your excellency," I said. "I know my job perfectly." I shod the mare on the forefeet, knocking away with my hammer but listening as I worked. And then I realized that their cause isn't worth a pinch of snuff."

He spat and crushed out his cigarette with his foot.

"Well, so long for now. When we've got our freedom I'll come along for another chat."

The door slammed, the steam curled over the sweating walls of the felt-boot maker's hut. The old man sat silent for a long time; then, rubbing his hands, he went over to Piotr.

"Well, Piotr, my boy; so we've lived to see our day. The cossacks won't be lording it over us for much longer."

"I'm afraid Sidor's talking rubbish, father. Again and again he brings us the news that this and that are coming, but we never get a smell of them close up."

"Give it time and it'll smell so strong that the cossacks won't even have the chance to sniff."

The old man clenched his knotted fist firmly, a flush showed faintly under the skin drawn tightly over his cheekbones.

"We, my son, have worked for the rich ever since we were little. They've lived in houses built by other men's hands, they've eaten bread grown by other men's sweat; but now they can get out."

An asthmatic coughing burst from his throat. He waved his hand without speaking, huddled up and, pressing one hand to his chest, stood a long time by the tub in the corner. Then he wiped the rose-coloured spittle from his lips with his apron, and smiled.

"You can't walk along two roads at once, sonny. Only one way has fallen to us to walk, and along it you go without turning till you die. We've been born workers, fleece curers, so we've got to support our workers' government."

The yarn began to sing under the old man's fingers, it quivered with a yearning twang. The dust entangled the window in a curtain of spider webs. The sun glanced through the little window for a minute; then, hurrying on, rolled down towards the west.

2

Next day an officer called, and with him a freckled, stupid-looking cossack who was on duty in the district administration. Smacking his horsewhip against his new leggings, the young, bloated-faced ensign asked :

"Are you Foma Kremniev?"

"Yes."

"By order of the district ataman and the chief of the intendancy administration I have to collect from you all the stocks of felt boots you have ready. Where do you keep them?"

"Your excellency, my son and I have worked a whole year. If you take them we'll die of starvation."

"That's nothing to do with me. I've got to confiscate the felt boots. Our cossacks at the front have nothing to wear on their feet. I ask you : where do you keep them?"

"Mr. ensign! Why, it wasn't sweat, it's blood we've shed over them. They're our daily bread."

A spiteful smiled crawled like a snail over the ensign's pimply face. His gold teeth gleamed under his moustaches.

"I hear you're a bolshevik, aren't you? So what's the worry? When the Reds come they'll pay you for your boots."

Puffing at a cigarette, with spurs clattering he strode to a corner and with his whip handle dragged away a canvas sheet.

"Aha, there are the very boots we need. Shustrov, take and carry them outside; the waggon will be driving up any moment."

The father and son ranged themselves shoulder to shoulder, guarding with their bodies the felt boots piled in the corner.

The ensign went livid with fury : dribbling warm sprinkles of saliva from his quivering lips, but retaining some degree of self-control, he cried hoarsely :

"I shall talk with you in a different fashion tomorrow, when you're hauled off by your collar to a field court-martial, you old dog."

He tugged the old felter away, and used his feet to push the smoothed and shaped, dried felt boots to the door. Pair after pair the pile of boots diminished in the corner. The old man held his tongue, but when the cossack picked up his own worn, grey felt boots from by the stove he strode across to him and with unexpected strength pressed him up against the stove wall. The cossack started forward, the old man's worn shirt tore easily at the collar; and then he struck the felter in the face with a short arm jab.

Piotr cried out and rushed to help his father, but before he could reach him he received a violent blow from a pistol butt; he threw out his arms and dropped to the floor.

The ensign goggled his stupid, bloodshot eyes, ran over to the old man, and gave him a resounding smack on the cheek.

"Sabre him down, Shustrov! I'll answer for it. Go on, beat him up, damn you!"

Without letting go of the felt boots in his left hand, the cossack reached with his right for his sabre. The old man went down on his knees and bent his head; the shoulder-blades heaved in his brown, withered back. The cossack looked at the grey head bent down to the floor, at the old man's wrinkled skin, drawn tight over the bony ribs, and fell back; glancing at the officer, he turned and went out.

The ensign beat up the old workman with his whip, swearing hoarsely, violently. The blows sounded hollowly on the hunched back, livid weals rose on the flesh, the skin was broken, blood began to ooze in thin streaks, and without a groan the old man's bloodstained head sank lower, lower, down to the earthen floor.

*   *   *

When Piotr came round and staggered to his feet he found no one else in the hut. The chilly wind was strewing the faded leaves of the poplars plentifully through the wide open door, and was stirring up the dust; at the threshold their neighbour's bitch was hurriedly licking up the last thick little pool of congealed black blood.

<h1 style="text-align:center">3</h1>

The great highway runs right through the district centre.

In the pasturage, by a wayside shrine, roads from the surrounding villages, from the Tauride settlements[1] and the neighbouring hamlets come together. The cossack regiments, the baggage trains, the punitive detachments all marched through the district centre on their way to the northern front. The square was always crowded with people. Outside the administration building, couriers' foam-flecked horses stood nibbling at the rain-stained palisade. The district stables housed the intendancy and artillery stores of the Second Don Corps.

The sentries fed the fat swine on conserves gone bad. The square smelt of laurel leaves and disinfectant. And on the square, too, was the prison, hurriedly covered with rusty netting. Outside the gate was the guard, an overturned field kitchen, and a telephone box.

The autumn wind blew through the village, along the beaten tracks of the alleys, past the wattle fences, scattering the russet gold of maple leaves, tousling the fringes of the reeds under the shed roofs.

[1] Taurides: the name given in the Don region to Ukrainians whose forebears were transferred by order of Catherine 2nd from southern districts adjacent to the Crimea (Tauria).

Piotr made his way to the prison. The sentry was at the gate.

"Hey you, sonny, don't come too close. Halt, I tell you. Who do you want?"

"I want to see my father. . . . His name's Foma Kremniev."

"He's here. Wait and I'll ask the chief."

The sentry went into the telephone box, rolled a water melon from under the bench, slowly cut it up with his sabre, and ate it, smacking his lips and spitting the brown seeds out at Piotr's feet.

The lad gazed at his face with its protruding cheekbones and bronzed with sunburn, and waited for him to finish eating. The man flung the water melon rind at a pig waddling past, stared after it long, with a serious look, and then, with a yawn, picked up the telephone mouthpiece.

"A young fellow has come along here to see Kremniev. Am I to let him in, your excellency?"

Piotr heard someone's roaring bass sound hoarsely from the ear-piece, but he could not distinguish the words.

"Wait here; they'll come and search you."

A minute later two cossacks came out through the wicket gate.

"Who's come to see Kremniev? You? Put your hands above your head."

They rummaged in Piotr's pockets, felt his ragged cap, the lining of his jacket.

"Take your trousers off. What, you scum, too shy? Who d'you think you are, a beautiful maiden?"

Behind Piotr the wicket gate slammed, the bolt clattered home; past the barred windows they went to the commandant's office, and from every chink eyes of all colours stared at Piotr.

The long corridors stank of human excrement, of mustiness. The stone walls had a bloom of damp green moss and rotten fungus. The oil lamps glimmered faintly. At the far end the guard halted, tugged back the bolt, and kicked a door wide open.

"In you go!"

Groping over the pitted floor with his feet, stretching his hands out in front of him, Piotr went towards the wall. The bluish light of the autumnal day seeped into the cell through a very tiny window carved out right under the ceiling.

"Piotka, my boy! Is it really you?"

The voice came in gasps, like that of a man who has been long ill. Piotr started forward; with his bare feet he groped for the felting on the floor, squatted down, and silently took his father's bandaged head in both hands.

The guard stood leaning against the open door, playing with his sabre strap, singing a rollicking soldiers' song.

Under the vaulted ceiling the echoes rattled fearfully. Piotr's father turned on an encouraging little laugh as he coughed; but as Piotr squatted on the floor, through the round eye of the window he could see the brown clouds curling past in freedom, and below them two flocks of copper-voiced cranes clove the sky.

"Twice I've been taken out for questioning. . . . The investigating officer kicked me, tried to make me sign depositions such as I've never given in all my life. But no, Piotka, you can't knock words out of Foma Kremniev like that. Let them kill me, they'll pay for it; but I'm not turning off the way and the road which have been laid down for me from birth."

Piotr caught the well-known, rather hoarse little chuckle and gazed with a quiet joy at the earthily dark face swollen with blows.

"Well, but now what? Will you be in here long, father?"

"No. They'll let me out today or tomorrow. . . . They'd shoot me, the sons of bitches, just for the fun of it; but they're afraid the foreign[1] peasant settlers would start a strike. And that wouldn't suit them at all."

"Will they let you out for good?"

"No. To put a good show on it they'll fix up a court from the elders of our village to try me. The village assembly will judge. But then we'll see whose side is the strongest. We'll see what we shall see."

The guard at the door clicked his fingers and stamped his feet, shouting:

"Hey, you, you cheerful blighter, turn out your son. Your visit's finished for today."

4

Late in the afternoon their neighbour's youngster came running to Piotr in his hut.

"Piotr !"

---

[1] The cossacks regarded the Ukrainians among them as foreigners.

"Well?"

"Run to the meeting at once. They're killing your father on the square outside the administration office."

Piotr didn't stop to put on his cap, he flew to the square.

He ran at full speed along the crooked little alley that huddled down by the river. Ahead of him, along the wattle fence, the rose-coloured shirt of his neighbour's son flickered: the wind flung back the yellow, sunbleached strands of hair over his head; outside every yard he squealed in a shrill, heartrending voice:

"Run to the square, Foma, the felter, is being killed by the cossacks."

Little groups of lads ran out through the gates and the wicket gates, their bare feet pattered rapidly along the alley.

By the time Piotr reached the administration there was no one to be seen on the square: the streets and alleys had sucked in the departing people.

Outside the gate of her house the priest's corpulent wife, cupping her hand to her eyes, stared at Piotr as he ran up. She was wearing a shawl flung over her cotton dress; a little, astonished smile was fixed on her thin, sarcastic lips. She stopped for a moment, gazing at Piotr, scratched one fat calf, quivering with the cold, with her other foot, then turned to go indoors.

"Fekliushka," she called, "where are they beating up the felter?"

"By the true Cross! With my own little eyes I saw them beating him so hard, mother." Piotr heard footsteps slapping down the veranda steps. The hunchbacked cook hobbled right up to the priest's wife, waving her arms and panting. She whined: "I look, mother, and see him led out of the prison to the assembly. The cossacks started to shout, but he took no notice. He walks along grinning, the old dog, but he was fearfully black all over. The gentlemen officers had already beaten him up before. . . . They led him to the steps, and when they started to hit him all I could hear was crunch, crunch, but he bellowed fit to make the heart ache. Well, and there they finished him off, some with sticks, others with crowbars, but mostly with their feet."

The district secretary came down the steps of the administration building, his fat bottom waggling.

"Ivan Arsionovich, come here a minute."

The secretary hitched up his broad riding breeches and minced up to the priest's wife, admiring the polished toes of his boots as he went. When some eight paces away from her he bent his curved spine backward and, trying to imitate the colonel intendant, negligently put two fingers to the peak of his cap.

"Good day, Anna Sergeevna."

"Good evening, Ivan Arsionovich. What's this murder that's just taken place outside your administration office?"

The secretary pouted his lower lip contemptuously.

"The cossacks have killed the felter Foma for belonging to bolshevism."

The woman shrugged her fat shoulders and groaned:

"Oh, how horrible! And did you really have a hand in this murder?"

"Yes . . . the truth is . . . You know, when they began to beat him, the scoundrel, and he shouted as he lay on the ground, 'Kill me, I'll never go back on the Soviet régime,' then of course I gave him a kick; and I regret to say I got involved in it. It was quite unpleasant: my boot and breeches were smeared with blood."

"But I never imagined you were such a brutal man."

The priest's wife narrowed her little eyes and smiled at the spruce-looking secretary. But Piotr sat down on the wet, bloodstained sand by the administration steps and, surrounded by a horde of children, stared at the shapeless, bloodstained heap in front of him.

5

The cranes went flying over the village, sending their challenging calls down to the frosty earth. Piotr sat staring through the little window for hours on end, unable to tear his eyes away.

Sidor, the smith, came along to the hut, saw Piotr grinding grains of Indian corn between two bricks, and sighed:

"Ah, you poor kid, the misery you've had to put up with. But, all right, don't let it get you down, our people will be arriving soon, and then life'll be easier. But come along to my place tomorrow; I'll give you a couple of measures of flour."

He sat on for a little while, sent an azure ribbon of tobacco smoke through his stained teeth, spat down by the stove, and went off, sighing and not saying goodbye.

But he was not allowed to see any easier life. Late next afternoon Piotr walked across the square, and saw two cossacks ride
out through the prison gate. Between them Sidor was walking in
a long canvas shirt reaching below the knees. The shirt was rent
down to the waist; his chest, with its growth of coarse, curly hair,
was visible in the opening.

As, stumbling with weariness, he drew level with Piotr, he
turned his head to look at the boy.

"They're taking me off to do me in, Piotka, my boy; goodbye,
sonny."

He waved his hand wretchedly and broke into tears.

The time melted past for Piotr as though he were in a heavy,
stifling doze. He grew lousy, his yellow cheeks were overgrown
with down, he looked older than his seventeen years. The days
flowed, and flowed: they flowed away in a dumb yearning. With
every day that departed from the district together with the setting
sun, the Reds drew nearer the village; in the hearts of the cossacks
fear swelled like dropsy.

Of a morning, when the women drove out the cows to the pasturage, they could hear the guns firing some distance away. A dull
roar flew over the yards dozing in the greenish morning haze; it
beat against the reed walls of Piotr's hut and set the mica window
shivering. He slipped off the stove, flung on his coarse coat, went
outside, lay down beside an ancient, gnarled willow, and listened
to the ground groaning and grunting like an old man under the
gunfire. Beyond a clump of huddled poplars machine-guns stuttered and rattled, mingling with the cries of the rooks.

One day he went out earlier than ever and pressed his ear to
the freezing earth, scorching his flesh with the clinging cold. He
lay listening. The guns fired sluggishly, but the machine-guns
boldly, youthfully beat out a dull rat-a-tat in the frosty air:

"Ta-ta-ta-ta-ta. . . ."

At first rarely, then more frequently: a minute's pause, then
again, hardly audible:

"Ta-ta-ta-ta-ta. . . ."

To avoid getting his knees frozen Piotr tucked the edges of his
coat under his legs and arranged himself more comfortably. But
a thin, frozen voice floated over the wattle fence:

"Listening to the music, sonny? Interesting, isn't it?"

Piotr started up and slipped into a squatting position; across the fence aged eyes were boring him from under tufty brows; a smile lurked in the yellowish beard.

Piotr guessed by the voice that it was daddy Alexander. The fourth of that name. He replied angrily, trying to keep his voice from quivering:

"You go your way, daddy. It's nothing to do with you."

"It's nothing to do with me; but I can see it's to do with you, isn't it?"

"Don't ask questions, daddy, or I'll bash you with this stone here, and then you'll be sorry."

"You're too sharp. Too sharp, I say. You can pipe all right, but I'll stroke you with my stick for showing such respect to an old man!"

"I'm not touching you, and don't you touch me."

"You're only a green snot, if the truth must be told; but how you flare up!"

The old man took hold of the wattle stake and lightly hoisted his dry, shrivelled body over the low fence. He went up to Piotr, adjusting his torn, striped trousers as he walked, and squatted down beside him.

"Can you hear the machine-guns?"

"Some can hear, and some not."

"But you and me now, we can hear!"

Piotr took a long, stealthy look at the old man lying stretched out at his side, then said irresolutely:

"If you lie down the other side of the willow you can hear much better."

"Let's go and listen the other side of the willow."

The old fellow crawled on all fours beyond the willow, clutched the bare, brown roots with his hands, which themselves looked like roots, and lay still and silent for a good two minutes.

"Interesting!" He half rose, brushed the shaggy moss off his knees, and turned his face to look at Piotr. "My boy, you listen to me. I can see everything right through the earth, and I see at once what you're thinking. We can listen to that music to all eternity, but we and our son haven't any mind to do that. . . . D'you know my Yashka? The one our dear, kind cossacks whipped for bolshevism?"

"Yes."

"Well, we and he have decided to go and meet the Reds, and not wait till they call on us."

The old man leaned across to Piotr, his beard tickling the lad's ear, and he breathed in a sour-smelling whisper:

"I'm sorry for you, my boy. You don't know how sorry. You come with us away from here, let's spit and part with the Almighty Don Army. Agreed?"

"But you're not lying, are you, daddy?"

"You're young to accuse me of lying. I ought to give you a proper whipping for that sort of remark. Only a bitch lies, but I'm telling the truth. There's no need for me to argue with you, you can stay here if you want to."

And he walked off to the fence, his striped trousers twinkling.

Piotr ran after him and seized his sleeve.

"Wait, daddy."

"There's nothing to wait for. If you want to come with us, all well and good; but if you don't, well, like a woman off the cart, it's lighter for the mare."

"I'll come, daddy. But when?"

"We'll talk over that later. You come along to us this evening; Yasha and I'll be in the threshing-floor."

6

Alexander the Fourth had been notorious for his garrulity since time out of mind; in his cups he was foolish, but when sober he was a fine man. Nobody could remember his surname. Long, long before, when he came home from doing his military service at Ivanovo-Voznesensk, where a cossack company was always stationed, in his drunken fit he told the old men of the village assembly:

"You've got Tsar Alexander the Third; well, I'm not a tsar, but all the same I'm Alexander the Fourth, and I spit on your tsar."

By the decision of the assembly he was deprived of his cossack title and his allocation of land, was given fifty lashes in the district market place for disrespect to the Supreme Name, and the affair was regarded as closed. But as he pulled up his trousers

Alexander the Fourth made a low bow in all four directions to the cossack villagers, and declared as he buttoned up the last button :

"I thank you most gratefully, gentlemen elders, but I'm not in the least frightened by all that."

The district ataman knocked with his ataman's staff.

"Seeing he's not frightened, give him some more."

After the additional lashes Alexander the Fourth did not open his mouth. He was carried home, but the nickname 'Alexander the Fourth' remained with him till the day of his death.

Piotr went along to Alexander the Fourth in the late afternoon. The hut was empty. A bridled goat was nibbling at cabbage stumps. He went through the yard to the threshing-floor gates : they were wide open. The old man's frozen, thin voice came from the chaff shed :

"Come here, my boy."

He went in and greeted him, but the old man didn't look at him. He was fashioning a pestle from stone, knocking out chips. Chips of grey stone and greenish sparks flew off from under the hammer. By the winnowing machine his son Yakov did not turn his head from his work : he was hammering and banging, nailing the sheet iron back in its place on the side of the machine.

"What are they doing all this for, with winter coming on?" Piotr wondered. But the old man tapped away with his hammer, and said, without turning his head to look at him :

"We want to leave my old woman all the farm in good order. She's a pain in my neck; the least thing and you can't stop her bawling. I might have left everything just as it is, but I'm afraid there'd be no end to her reproaches. She'd say the old so-and-so went off and left not even a blade of grass growing at home."

His eyes smiled. He got up, clapped Piotr on the back, and said to Yakov :

"Stop the banging, Yasha. Let's talk with the felter's son about other things."

Yakov spat the small nails with which he had been fastening the sheet iron out of his mouth into his palm, came over to Piotr, and extended his lips in a smile.

"Hallo, my little Red."

"Hallo, Yakov Alexandrovich "

"Well, d'you think you'd like to come with us?"

"I told daddy Alexander yesterday I would."

"That's not sufficient. You can be stupid enough to get ready at night and, goodbye, village! But you've got to leave some memento of yourself behind. We've known so much good from our villagers! They beat my father, and then me, because I wouldn't agree to go to the front. And they beat your father to death. . . . But why talk about it?"

Yakov bent down quite close to Piotr, and muttered, his hanging, bushy eyebrows rising and falling as he spoke:

"D'you know, sonny, that they, the Cadets, I mean, have set up an artillery store in the village stables? Have you seen them taking shells and such like in there?"

"Yes."

"And if they're set fire to, for instance, what will happen?"

Old Alexander nudged Piotr in the side with his elbow, and smiled:

"Ter-ror!"

"Now, my father says it's terror, and so on; but I think differently. The Reds are close to Shchegolsk district, aren't they?"

"They occupied Krutenky hamlet yesterday," Piotr said.

"Well, then, but supposing, to put it this way, there's an explosion here and the cossacks are robbed of their food as well as their military stores, then they'll retreat all the way to the Donietz river without looking back. So there!"

Old Alexander stroked his beard, and said:

"Tomorrow, as soon as it's getting dark, you come to this same spot. And wait here for us. Bring with you whatever you need for the road, but don't worry about food, we'll get that ready."

Piotr went to the threshing-floor gate, but the old man called him back.

"Don't go through the yard; there are people wandering about in the street. Climb over the fence into the steppe. Caution's always necessary."

Piotr climbed over the fence, jumped across a ditch filmed with speckled ice, and made his way home past the village threshing-floors, past the haystacks gloomy and grey with hoarfrost.

7

During the night a wind sprang up from the east, and heavy, wet snow fell. The darkness huddled into every yard, every little alley. Wrapping himself in his father's coat Piotr went out, stood a moment or two by the wicket gate, listening to the willows howling above the little stream and bending under the pressure of the rushing wind, then slowly walked along the street to Alexander the Fourth's yard.

Through the darkness a voice came from the granary.

"Is that you, Piotr?"

"Yes."

"Come in here. Keep more to the left, or you'll fall over the harrow."

They prepared for the road. The old man crossed himself, sighed, and went towards the gate.

They reached the church. Coughing hoarsely, Yakov whispered:

"Piotka, my boy, you can't be seen so easily and you're nimbler than us . . . they won't notice you. . . . You crawl across the square to the stores. Have you noticed where the cartridge chests are piled close to the wall?"

"Yes."

"Here's flint and tinder, and this is hemp soaked in paraffin. Crawl right up, cover yourself with your coat and strike fire. When the hemp begins to burn, push it between the chests and get back to us quick. Well, off with you. And don't be afraid. We'll wait for you here."

The old man and his son squatted down by the church wall, and Piotr crawled towards the stores, wriggling on his chest along the ground with its coating of shaggy, fluffy rime.

The wind tugged at his coat, the cold crawled up his back like little burning wires, and pricked his legs. His hands froze on the ice-bound ground. He groped his way to the stores; some fifteen paces away the guard's cigarette shone out in a tiny red glow. The wind howled under the boarded roof, a loose board banged and clattered. The wind brought faint voices from the direction of the cigarette glow.

Piotr squatted down on his heels and wrapped his coat round him right over his head. The flint trembled in his hand, the tinder dribbled out of his frozen fingers.

Chk, chk! The steel clinked almost inaudibly against the edge of the flint; but Piotr felt sure that the noise must have been heard all over the square, and fear wound itself round his throat like a clinging snake. The tinder had got damp in his moist fingers, and wouldn't catch. Another, and yet another strike, a little purplish spark began to smoke, and suddenly the bunch of hemp burned up brightly. With trembling hand he thrust it under a chest, momentarily caught the smell of charring wood and, as he rose to his feet, heard the thud of boots and hoarse voices in the darkness.

"By God! Fire! Oh, look!"

Recovering his wits, Piotr tore off into the startled darkness. Shots rang out behind him, two bullets whistled protractedly over his head, a third in its humming flight furrowed the darkness far to his right. He had almost reached the wall. Behind him rose excited shouts.

"Fire! Fire!"

More shots rang out.

"If I can only get to the corner," the thought fluttered through his head.

He ran with all his strength. A prickling ring jangled in his ears. "Only get to the wall."

A burning pain seared his leg; he ran on, hobbling several more paces; a warm wetness crawled down his leg below his knee. He fell, but was up again in a moment, springing along on all fours, getting entangled in his long coat.

The old man and Yakov were a long time sitting by the wall. In the church enclosure the wing tugged at the rope tied to the great bell and, swinging the clappers of the smaller bells, rang them quietly in their various tones.

Through the darkness round the stores piled in heaps in the middle of the square they caught snatches of muffled voices carried away by the wind. Then fire licked away the darkness with a ruddy flame, a shot rang out, a second, a third . . . then, close to the wall they heard a quiet movement, broken breathing, a stifled voice:

"Daddy, help me! My leg. . . ."

The old man and his son picked up Piotr between them and ran off into the dark alley, stumbling over tussocks and falling. They had got past two blocks of houses before the alarm sounded from the church belfry; its ringing lashed the silence and rolled over the sleeping village.

At Piotr's side old Alexander breathed heavily and flung out his feet fussily. His flying beard tickled the lad's cheeks.

"Father, into the orchards. . . . Make for the orchards."

They jumped across a ditch and halted to get their breath.

Above the village, above the square, it was as though the earth were split in two. The crimson columns of flame leaped higher than the belfry, the smoke billowed thickly. Another explosion, and yet another.

A moment's silence, then the dogs all over the village began to howl in concert. The alarm bell, which had stopped for a time, thundered out again; women's heartrending cries came from the houses. On the square a flickering yellow flame licked bare the crumbling walls of the warehouses and, long-armed, reached out towards the priest's house and its surrounding buildings.

Yakov sat down against a bare thorn bush and said very quietly:

"It's quite impossible to get away now. You could pick up needles anywhere in the village, look how it's flaming. And besides, we ought to see to our Piotka's leg."

"We must wait for daybreak, till the people are tired out, and then we'll make our way to the state forest."

"You're quite an old man, father, yet you think like a child. How can we hang about in the village when they're searching for us everywhere? And if we turn up at home they'll get us at once. We're the first people in the village they'll suspect."

"That's true. You're talking sense, Yasha."

"We might be able to get through the day in our yard, in the shed?" Piotr asked, knitting his brows with the pain from his leg.

"Well, that's a possibility. Is there any lumber in there?"

"We've got dung fuel bricks piled up in it."

"Then let's set off, getting there by easy stages. Now, father, what are you going off in front for? You ought to follow very quietly in the rear."

8

By the morning Yakov and Piotr had dug a deep hole in the store of dung bricks; to make it warmer, they lined the bottom and sides with dry scrub; then they all dropped down inside, and covered the top above them with dry bindweed and water-melon stalks which Piotr had brought in for fuel from the vegetable plot.

Yakov tore up the tail of his shirt and bound Piotr's wounded leg. They sat in the hole all day, until evening came on. They heard someone come into the yard during the morning; the muffled sounds of conversation reached them, a lock was rattled, then a voice quite close to the shed remarked :

"The felter's lad must be working out in one of the hamlets. Stop rattling the padlock, brother. What's the point of doing that? All you'll find in that hut is lice and wool; you won't get very fat on them."

The footsteps died away somewhere behind the shed.

The night brought with it deep frost. After dusk they could hear the earth, swollen with moisture from the autumn rains, cracking in the alleyway. A lopsided moon fussed along on her nocturnal march over the cloud-speckled sky. Night peered into the shed through holes in its roof.

It was warm in the pit among the dung bricks. Old Alexander slept on and on, his chin thrust between his knees, snoring, fidgeting with his feet. Piotr and Yakov talked in undertones.

"Father, wake up. Will you never have had enough sleep? Time we were off."

"Ah? Time we were off? I'm ready. . . ."

They spent a long time over the task of cautiously removing the bricks. Then they opened the door gently : there was not a soul in the yard or the alley.

They stole past the last house in the village, and made their way across the pasturage into the steppe. They crawled two hundred yards over the snow to reach a ravine. Behind them the village stared fixedly out into the steppe with the yellow freckles of its lighted windows. They stole quietly down the ravine to the state forest, always moving cautiously, as though tracking an animal.

The icicles tinkled under their feet, the snow scrunched. Here and there the bare, stony bottom of the ravine was blocked with a drift; the blue pittings of hare tracks ran over the heaped snow.

One arm of the ravine thrust into the edge of the state forest. They made their way to the top, looked around them, and slowly filed in between the trees.

"It'll be dangerous to make our way to Shchegolsk without knowing what's happening. If we reach the front we might fall in with the Whites."

Yakov drew his head down between the spread edges of his sheepskin, and worked for some time before he succeeded in striking fire from the tinder. The fiery sparks went flying and the steel clinked drily against the stone. The tinder, rubbed with sunflower ash, at last turned red and began to give off a stinking smoke. Yakov lit his cigarette, took a couple of puffs, and then answered his father:

"This is what I suggest: we'll go along to Danila, the forester; he's a man we know well. We'll find out from him how to get through the lines, and it'll give us the chance to warm up Piotr a little, otherwise he'll be freezing to death on our hands."

"I'm not very cold, Yakov Alexandrovich."

"You shut up; don't tell lies, my boy. That coat of yours wasn't made to keep out the cold but the sun."

"Get on, Yasha; get on, my son. Look how high the Great Bear has climbed; it'll be midnight soon," the old man said.

They stopped about a hundred yards away from the forest lodge. There was a light in Danila the forester's window, they could see the smoke lazily rising from the chimney. The moon hung awkwardly on its side above the forest.

"It looks all quiet to me. Come on."

A dog under the shed began to bark. The frozen steps of the veranda scrunched beneath their feet. They knocked.

"Is the master at home?"

Someone's beard was pressed against the inside of the window.

"Yes. But who has God brought us?" came the answer.

"Friends, Danila Lukich; let us in to warm ourselves, for Christ's sake."

The door opening on to the passage creaked, the bolt was shot back. The forester stood on the threshold, staring at his visitors from under his right hand, holding a rifle hidden behind his back in his right.

"Surely it isn't you, daddy Alexander?"

"His very self. Would you let us spend the night with you?"

"Who knows? . . . Oh well, come in; I expect we'll find room."

The little room was very hot. Three men were lying on some felting spread out by the stove; they had saddles at their heads, and rifles piled in the corner. Yakov fell back to the door.

"Who have you got with you, master?"

A voice came from the felting.

"Why, don't you recognize your fellow villagers? But we've been waiting for you ever since yesterday. We felt sure you'd have to come through the state forest and visit Danila's hut. Well, take your coats off, dear guests; we'll spend the night here, but tomorrow we'll despatch you to the Tsar's swing. The rope's been weeping for you a long, long time."

The cossacks scrambled up from the felting and seized their rifles.

"Tie the incendiaries' arms together, Semion."

9

Two lay asleep on bedding, the third sat at the table, his head drooping; his rifle between his legs. The forester spread sacking on the floor.

"Lie down there, daddy Alexander; it'll be more comfortable for your old bones."

"You watch out you don't have to sleep on it yourself, you soft-hearted man. D'you hear, forester? Take up that sacking. They set fire to the stores, and for that it would be no sin to make them sleep outside in the frost with your watchdog."

Late in the night the old man asked to go outside.

"Let me go outside, son; I've got to for convenience. . . ."

"Don't worry, daddy; piss in your trousers or your felt boot. We'll hang you from a rafter tomorrow, and you'll soon dry out then."

The feeble winter dawn scratched at the window. The cossacks got up, washed, and sat down to breakfast. At a moment when they were occupied, Yakov whispered unnoticed to his father and Piotr:

"I wore through my rope during the night. When we get near the village we'll all scatter into the orchards, and from there up the hill into the warren where we used to dig out stone. They'll never catch us there."

Bound together by the arms with a hempen rope the three of them walked along; Piotr limped on his wounded leg, and ground his teeth with the nagging pain.

The village appeared below them, with the grey locks of its orchards scattered round its edges, like the hair of a woman in a fever. As they turned into the first alley Yakov, writhing his blenched lips, broke through the rope and, zigzagging over the snow, dashed into an orchard. Old Alexander and Piotr followed him. Each separately. From behind them came a shout:

"Stop, stop, damn you!"

Shots and the thud of horsehoofs. As he leaped across the ditch Piotr looked back: old Alexander had fallen, burying his head, pierced by a bullet, in a drift; he flung his legs high in the air.

The hill, its summit belted with snow, ran to meet Piotr. The holes from which the cossacks dug out stone showed up like black eye sockets. Yakov dived into one first, Piotr after him.

Wriggling, tearing their clothes, scratching their bodies into blood against the jagged edges of the stone, they crawled into the damp, oppressive darkness. At times Piotr suffered a painful kick from Yakov's boot. The warren divided into two: they took the left fork. Piotr's palm was smothered with freezing clay; water oozed from above and dripped behind his collar.

A hole under their feet. They dropped into it and squatted down side by side.

"Unhappy me! I think they've killed my father," Yakov whispered.

"He fell just by the ditch. . . ."

Their voices deafened them; they sounded as though they were not coming from them. The darkness clung to their eyelids.

"Well, Piotr, now they'll be able to starve us out. We shall be done for, like a polecat in its warren. But afer all, who knows? They'll be too afraid to come crawling in after us. Father and I dug out these galleries before the German war. I know all the passages. Let's crawl in further."

They crawled in. At times they found themselves in a blind alley. Then they turned back and sought another route.

*   *   *

They huddled together in the thick, clinging darkness for two days.

The silence rang in their ears. They hardly ever talked. They slept with one ear always cocked. Somewhere above them they could hear running water. They woke up, and dozed off again.

Then, groping along the wall like blind puppies, they crawled back to the entrance. They wandered along the passages for some time; then quite suddenly the bright light seared their eyes painfully.

At the entrance to the cave they found a heap of grey ashes, butt ends, cartridge cases, the traces of very many feet. And, when they looked out, they saw: along the road to the village, men were riding in file on horses with docked tails; infantry was following behind them in a grey cloud of dust; the wind fluttered a crimson banner and brought the sound of voices, laughter, commands, the squeaking scrunch of sledge runners.

They dashed out. They ran, they fell. Yakov waved his arms and shouted in a high-pitched, breaking voice:

"Brothers! Reds! Comrades!"

The horsemen drew their bay horses together into a clump on the road.

The mudstained infantry pressed on them from behind.

His head shaking, Yakov wept as he rushed to kiss the stirrups and ironshod boots of one Red Army man. But they caught Piotr up in their arms, swung him into a sledge, into a heap of scented steppe hay, and covered him with greatcoats.

The boy's head swam, he felt sick, but his heart blossomed with joy, like May rye after rain. A hand lifted the greatcoat off him, a whiskerless, weather-beaten face bent over him, a smile slipped over the soldier's lips.

"Alive, little friend? Would you like some bread?"

Half chewed, toasted bread was thrust into Piotr's unresponsive mouth. They chafed the lad's frozen hands with their rough mittens. He tried to say something, but he had a mash of rye bread in his mouth, and tears had got stranded in a lump in his throat.

He seized the rough, black hand and gave it a strong squeeze, pressing it to his chest.

PART TWO

I

A large house, roofed with sheet iron; six cheerful windows with blue shutters looking out on to the street. Formerly it was the district ataman's home, but now it was the club of the Young Communist League. Year 1920, a cloudy, freezing September, nocturnal darkness in the gardens and alleys.

A meeting was being held in the club, the atmosphere was thick, there was a hum of voices. At the table the group secretary, Piotr Kremniev, was sitting; beside him was Grigory Raskov, a member of the committee. An important question was being decided: how to turn the land which the Land Department had assigned to the group into a model farm.

Half an hour later one of the minutes of the meeting read:

"Comrade Raskov reported on the allocation of land in the Krutenky district.

"Resolved: to assign comrades Raskov and Kremniev to make an immediate survey and measurement of the land."

The lamps were put out. There was the sound of many feet quietly tapping down the steps. Piotr stood at the corner for a moment and, seeing Raskov's white shirt glimmering in the milky darkness, shouted into the hollow silence of the sleeping village:

"Grishka, d'you hear? The people are busy ploughing; don't try to get a village cart for us: forget it. We'll hoof it."

2

A consumptive dawn. A herd had recently passed along the firmly-beaten highway. Dust clung to the tips of the steppe wormwood. Ploughing was going on over the rise. People were crawling over it like worms; the oxen harnessed into the ploughs crept along. The wind carried away the shouts of the drivers, the whistle and crack of whips.

The two lads strode along without talking. The sun was in the zenith when they approached the district where their land was situated. A dozen or so Tauride houses and yards were scattered over a steppe ravine. Close to a dam a woman with skirts tucked up was beating linen clean with a board. On the farther side, the vari-coloured cows had entered the water up to their bellies. Raising their ears, they stood staring stupidly at the lads. Suddenly, taking fright at something, the leading cow raised its tail wildly and scrambled back on to the dam; the rest of the herd rushed after her. The grey-bearded herdsman gave his whip a hearty crack. His boy assistant ran kicking up his filthy heels to turn them back. In a threshing-floor, to the spasmodic knocking of a steam thresher, a girl cried in a singsong voice:

"Harpishka, come and look! Two handsome young fellows have come to see us."

All the afternoon the lads looked for the chairman of the village; they ate scented melons in his house, and finally decided to go out and survey the land next day. The housewife made up a bed in the passage for them. Grigory fell asleep at once, but Piotr turned and tossed for some time, hunted a flea under the sheepskin coat covering him, and thought: what land would this rascally chairman allocate to them?

At midnight, the master shot back the door bolt, glanced from the veranda up at the starry sky, and went off to the stable to fodder the horses. The well-crane creaked, a foal out in the steppe whinneyed challengingly, protractedly. The faint sound of voices drifted in from the yard. Piotr woke up.

Grigory ground his teeth in his sleep, turned over on to his other side, and muttered mournfully and distinctly:

"Death, brother, isn't a pound of currants."

The chairman came into the passage, stamping his feet.

"Boys, hey, boys! Are you awake?"

"Well?"

"Hell knows what. . . . One of our people has just ridden over from Viezhenka village, and he says Makhno, the bandit, has captured it. You'd better be getting away, boys."

Piotr mumbled sleepily:

"All right, but how about the land? Measure out our section tomorrow, and then we'll get away. But why should we wear out our feet for nothing?"

At dawn, Piotr was dreaming that he was at a meeting in the district committee office, but someone trod heavily on the roof and the sheet iron groaned, bending under the weight: 'Hoo-oo, haa-aa.'

He woke up and tumbled to the reality: gunfire. His heart cramped anxiously. They hurriedly dressed, snatched up the wooden measuring rod, and, beating off the frenzied dogs, went to their section.

"How far is it to Viezhenka?" Grigory asked.

He had been striding along without speaking, thoughtfully pulling the florets from the purple head of a wayside thistle.

"Eighteen miles perhaps."

"Then we'll have time."

Passing the vegetable plots, they mounted the rise. Piotr happened to drop his wallet of cartridges, turned to pick it up, and grunted: from the farther side of the valley, horsemen were coming down the hill in orderly columns. The leader was carrying a black banner, which the wind caught away and sent fluttering like the injured wing of a bird.

"Ah, by your mother!"

"God did love her!" Grigory finished the jesting phrase, but his lips were quivering and a grey shadow crossed his face.

The chairman dropped the measuring rod and groped in his pocket for his tobacco pouch, hardly knowing why. Piotr impetuously dashed into a ravine, Grigory after him.

The disobedient legs get strangely entangled with each other, they seem to be running like tortoises, while the heart thumps to pieces and there is a burning sensation in the mouth. At the bottom of the water-washed ravine the ground was damp. It smelt of slime, their feet stuck in it. Piotr kicked off his boots as he ran, and took a more convenient grip of his rifle; Grigory's face turned green, his lips stuck together, his breath came in gasps. He fell down and flung his rifle far from him.

"Throw yours away too, Piotka. If they catch you with it they'll kill us."

Piotr was appalled.

"Are you mad? Pick yours up quick, you cur!"

Grigory sluggishly took up his rifle by the strap. For a minute they glared at each other with heavy, hostile eyes.

They started running again. At the end of the ravine Grigory fell over on his back. Piotr gritted his teeth, caught his comrade's scraggy body under the armpits and dragged him along. The ravine forked; one branch, strewn with horses' bones and grey wormwood, led straight into ploughland. By a waggon an old man was harnessing horses to a plough.

"Your horses to drive to the district centre. The Makhno band will catch us."

Piotr seized a horse by the collar, the old man seized Piotr.

"You can't take it. The mare's in foal, where can you drive to with her?"

The strong old fellow took a firm grip of Piotr's rifle barrel, and the thought flashed through the lad's mind : if he wrests away the rifle he'll kill me for the sake of his mare in foal.

He took in the sight of those terrible, jabbing eyes fixed on him, the reddish brush on the cheeks, a fine quiver round the mouth, and tore the rifle away. The bolt clattered.

"Stand back."

The old man stooped down to pick up an axe lying by the waggon. But Piotr, feeling a sticky, sick feeling in his throat, struck out at the nape with the rifle butt. The legs in the furrowed boots kicked out shudderingly like spider's legs.

Grigory cut free the traces and jumped on to the mare. The dapple grey Tauride gelding danced under Piotr. They galloped over the ploughland to the road. The hoofs began a rapid chatter. Piotr glanced back : the wind was raising dust over the ravine. The pursuit was strung out over a distance, and was coming on at breakneck speed.

They galloped some three miles, the others drawing steadily

nearer. Now the two lads could see the foremost horse with raised
head throwing back the yards in great bounds; the rider's shaggy
black cloak streamed out behind him.

The mare under Grigory was perceptibly slowing down, it
snorted and gave a quick, convulsive neigh.

"She'll be dropping her foal . . . I'm done for, Piotka," Grigory
shouted through the cutting wind.

At a turn by a mound he jumped off in full flight, for the
horse dropped. Piotr galloped on several yards furiously, but recovered his control and turned sharply back.

"What are you playing at?" Grigory wailed, but Piotr jumped
off his horse, confidently and neatly drove a cartridge home,
went down on one knee, fired at the oncoming black cloak and, as
he ejected the cartridge case, he smiled.

"Death, brother, isn't a pound of currants."

He fired again. The horse reared, the black cloak slipped to the
ground, one foot remained fast in the stirrup, and the horse went
galloping over the roadless steppe in a cloud of dust.

Piotr watched it go with unseeing eyes, and sat down on the
road, spreading 'out his legs. Rubbing a scented head of thyme
between his palms, Grigory smiled wildly.

Piotr said seriously, quietly :

"Well, and now goodnight." He stretched himself out on the
ground, face downward.

3

In the executive committee yard the Soviet workers were burying
documents sewn up in sacks. The chairman, Yakov the Fourth,
was on the veranda, putting a rusty and wretched-looking machine-
gun in order. Since early morning they had been waiting for the
return of the militia men who had been sent out on reconnaissance.
At noon Yakov called to the young communist, Antosha Grachev,
as he ran past, and said, his eyes smiling :

"Take the best-looking horse in the stable and gallop towards
Krutenky. If you fall in with our reconnaissance tell them to return
here. Have you a rifle?"

His bare heels twinkling as he ran off, Antosha shouted :

"I've got a rifle and twenty cartridges."

"Well, shoot, and get a move on!"

Five minutes later Antosha tore out of the executive committee yard like a whirlwind, flashed his little mousey-grey eyes at the chairman and vanished in a cloud of dust.

From the executive committee veranda Yakov could see the horse's neck measuredly swinging, and Antosha's bare, curly head. He stood for a second on the steps, then went into the corridor festooned with spiders' webs. The Soviet workers and the communist group were assembled. He ran his tired eyes over them, and said:

"Antosha's galloped off to find the reconnaissance." He paused, then added, thoughtfully drumming his fingers: "But the lads out in Krutenky . . . will they get away from Makhno . . . or won't they?"

They wandered through the echoing, deserted rooms of the executive committee building, read Demian Biedny's doggerel rhymes on the fading posters for the thousandth time. Some two hours later the militia men who had been on reconnaissance came into the yard at a canter. Without stopping to tether their horses they ran on to the veranda. The leader, thickly covered with dust, shouted:

"Where's the chairman?"

"Here he is. Well, have you seen them? Is there a lot of them? Shall we sit it out in the belfry?"

The militia man waved his hand to indicate the hopelessness of the situation.

"We ran into their leading squadron. We got away by sheer speed. There are ten thousand of them altogether. They're coming on like black crows."

Knitting his brows, the chairman asked:

"Didn't you meet Antosha?"

"We saw a single rider making his way into the steppe beyond the Steep Ravine, but we didn't recognize who it was. He must have fallen into Makhno's hands."

They stood in a solid group, whispering among themselves. The chairman tugged at his ragged beard, and his voice came from somewhere deep inside him.

"The lads who went off to measure the land are lost, that's clear . . . Antosha too. . . . We'll have to take to hiding in the reeds. Against Makhno we can do nothing."

The official in charge of grain collection opened his mouth to say something, but a voice came anxiously, curtly from outside the door :

"Come on, comrades. There's cavalry coming over the rise."

The people blew away like the wind. They had been, and now they were not. The village died. The shutters were closed fast. Silence sank over the houses; only in the scrub by the executive committee's wattle fence a hen took alarm at something and cackled away in a strained tone.

4

The wind blew out the shirt on Antosha's back like a flapping balloon. Riding bareback is painful. The horse had a jerky gait; it had not been trained for riding. He held on to the reins, began to mount the hill from the Steep Ravine and unexpectedly, less than a mile away, saw a company of horsemen with two military waggons behind them. The thought flashed through his head : "Makhno men."

He reined in the horse, a prickly chill ran down his spine. He turned his mount round, but, as though in despite, it moved sluggishly; it was reluctant to pass from its tranquil trot into a gallop.

They saw him, began to whoop and holloa, let fly a hail of shot. The wind lashed his face, tears filled his eyes, he had a piercing whistle in his ears. It was fearful to look back. He glanced over his shoulder only as he galloped past the outlying houses of the district village. He jumped off his horse as it went, and, bending double, ran to the fence. He thought : "If I run across the square they'll see me and catch me up. I'll get into the church enclosure, to the belfry."

Gripping his rifle in his left hand, with his right he pushed open the wicket gate; his bare feet went rustling through the leaves scattered over the ground. The winding church stairs. The scent of incense and musty decay, pigeon droppings.

On the upper platform he stopped, lay down flat, and listened. Silence. Only cocks crowing in the village.

He put his rifle down at his side, took off his wallet, wiped the clinging sweat from his forehead. In his head his thoughts were

playing leapfrog. "They'll kill me in any case. I shall fire at them.
. . . Piotka Kremniev said once that Makhno's a bourgeois mer-
cenary."

He remembered how only the previous Sunday all the lads had
gone across the river and practised shooting at a cart a hundred
paces away, and he had hit it more often than anyone else. He had
a tickling pain in his throat, but his heart was beating more regularly.

Six horsemen rode cautiously into the square, dismounted, and
tied their horses to the school palisade.

Antosha's heart again started to beat faster. He clenched his teeth
firmly, controlling his trembling, and with dancing fingers slipped
a cartridge into his rifle.

From a second narrow alley another horseman tore out; he circled
round on his madly dancing horse and, bringing his whip down on
her, tore back as impetuously the way he had come. By his negli-
gent, dashing seat Antosha knew he was a cossack; his eyes followed the green tunic swaying above the horse's crupper, and he
sighed.

Carts rumbled up; he heard the thud of innumerable horse hoofs,
the thunder of cannon. The district village began to swarm with
infantry like carrion with worms; the streets were dammed with
military waggons, ammunition carts, machine-gun tripods.

Feeling a fine shiver all over him, Antosha touched the rifle lock
with cold, unfamiliar fingers, and listened. Among the rafters
above him a pigeon cooed.

"I'll wait a little. . . ."

Around the church enclosure dismounted Makhno men were
feeding their horses. Between the bunches of horses they lay in their
colourful, baggy trousers and brilliant sashes, like vari-coloured river
shingle. There was the sound of talk, bursts of laughter. But the
gun-carriages went rolling two by two along the road.

Making up his mind, Antosha took the grey fur cap of a gunner
in his sights. The shot rang out muffledly, the machine-gunner
dropped his head between his knees. Another shot; a driver
dropped the reins and gently slid under the wheels. Another, and
another. . . .

At the tetherposts the horses began to rage: they squealed and
kicked out at their riders. A wounded side-horse writhed in its

traces on the road; outside the school a machine-gun cart turned over at full pelt, and the machine-gun in its white cover helplessly buried its muzzle in the ground. Above the belfry horses' neighing, shouts, orders, irregular rifle shots, hung in a cloud.

A battery turned back with a clatter and rattle. They had spotted Antosha. From the wooden platform the bullet juicily found its mark. The square swiftly emptied. A Makhno sailor expertly set up a machine-gun on the school veranda, the bullets jingled mournfully as they slipped over the bell, green with verdigris. One ricochetted and hit Antosha on the hand. He crawled back and half stood up, clinging to the brick column: the sailor clapped his hands, spun round and fell chest downward on the sagging, crooked veranda steps.

Outside the village, by the graveyard, a six-inch gun sprang away from its limber, and gaped with its steel maw at the peeling walls of the church. The tensely waiting village was shaken by its roar.

The shell struck under the cupola, sprinkled a dusty heap of bricks over Antosha, and spurted against the bell with an indignant jangle.

5

Piotr lay face downward without moving, but keenly inhaling the spicy scent of the thyme and listening to the distinct thud of horsehoofs.

A horrible, sickening feeling arose within him, turning his soul inside out. He shook his head and, half rising, saw close to Grigory's canvas shirt a horse's foaming muzzle, a blue cossack coat, and slanting Kalmik eyes in a face brown with the sun.

Half a mile away others were circling round a horse which was dragging with it a broken human body in a torn cloak.

When Grigory began to cry, sobbing like a child and panting, then screamed in a heartrending tone, something living quivered below Piotr's heart. He watched without blinking as the Kalmik rose in his stirrups and, leaning over sideways, swung a white band of steel. Grigory squatted awkwardly upon his heels, clutched his head, cloven in two, with his hands, then rolled over with a hoarse groan; the blood bubbled in his throat and poured out in a stream.

Piotr's memory fixed for ever Grigory's twitching legs and the livid scar on the Kalmik's peeling cloak. The sharp spikes of horse-shoes piercing his chest robbed him of consciousness; a hairy lasso lashed round his neck, and everything went spinning in fiery sparks and a burning haze.

*   *   *

He came to, groaning with the terrible pain piercing his eye. He touched his face with one hand, and was filled with horror at the thick gelid mess slipping from under his eyelid on to his cheek. One eye had been knocked out, the other was swollen and bleary with tears. Through the narrow chink of the lid he had difficulty in recognizing the horses' muzzles and the men's faces above him. Someone bent down close to him and said:

"Get up, boy, or you won't be left alive. We're taking you to the staff of our group for questioning. Well, getting up? It's all the same to me, we can put you up against a wall without question-ing you first."

Piotr got up. He was surrounded by a colourful sea of heads, the hum of talk, horses' whinneying. His escort, wearing a grey lambs-wool hat, went in front. Piotr followed, swaying.

His neck burned from the hairy lasso, the wounds and scratches on his face had caked with blood. All his body was consumed with pain, as though he had suffered a long and ruthless beating up.

On his way to the staff he had a good look around him: wher-ever he looked: on the square, in the streets, in the beaten, crooked little alleys, he saw men, horses and carts.

The staff of the force was in the priest's house. The aged twang of guitars, the rattle of utensils, came into the street through the wide open windows; the priest's wife could be seen fussing about in the kitchen, receiving and regaling her welcome guests.

Piotr's escort sat down on the steps to smoke, and mumbled:

"Stand by the steps, they're busy in the staff."

Piotr leaned against the creaking balustrade; his mouth was parched, his tongue dry. He said, moving his split tongue with difficulty:

"I'd like a drink. . . ."

"They'll water you in the staff all right."

A freckled sailor came out on to the veranda. His blue jacket was belted with a red bunting sash, the fringes hung down to his knees; a sailor's round cap was on his head, the ribbon bore the faded words: "Black Sea Fleet". He was carrying a fine-looking, beribboned accordion. He looked down at Piotr with bored, greenish little eyes, put on an oily smile and sluggishly opened the bellows of the accordion.

> "Communist youngster,
>   Why get married?
> When our old man Makhno comes,
>   Where can you get to?"

His voice was tipsy, but melodious. Without opening his closed eyes, he repeated:

> "When our old man Makhno comes,
>   Where can you get to?"

The escort took a last draw at his cigarette, and said without turning his head:

"Hey you, crooked carrion, follow me."

Piotr climbed the steps and entered the house. In the entrance hall a black banner was unfurled over the wall. Broken by the folds were the words: "Staff of the Second Force," and, a little higher, "Long Live Free Ukraine".

6

In the priest's bedroom a typewriter was rattling away. Voices crawled through the open door. Piotr had to wait a long time; he hung about in the half-dark entrance hall. A dull, gnawing pain robbed him of will and judgment. He was thinking: the Makhno men had killed off the lads of his Young Communist Group, as well as the Soviet workers, and now, from the priest's bedroom, death was giving him a challenging wink. But he felt no chill of fear. His breath came evenly, not spasmodically, his eyes were closed, and only his blood-clotted cheek twitched.

From the bedroom came voices, the rattle of the typewriter, women's giggles and the fragile jingle of glasses.

The priest's wife trotted past Piotr into the passage; she was followed by a flaxen-whiskered, tight-waisted Makhno man jingling his spurs and twisting his moustaches. She was carrying a carafe; her little eyes were blossoming like an almond tree.

"It's a fruit liqueur six years old; I've kept it for celebrations. Ah, if you only knew how horrible it is to live under those barbarians. Continual persecution. The communists even ordered the piano to be taken from us. Just imagine: to take our own piano away from us. Ah?"

As she came past him she fixed her shiftily darting eyes on Piotr, frowned contemptuously and, recognizing him, whispered to the Makhno man:

"He's the chairman of the Young Communist Group here . . . a rabid communist. . . . You ought to do with him. . . ."

Through the rustle of her skirts Piotr didn't catch the end of her remark.

A minute later he was ordered:

"Go to the end room quick, may you be damned to hell. . . ."

At the table the flaxen-whiskered man in a silver caracoul fur cap was sitting.

"Are you a Young Communist?"

"Yes."

"Have you shot at our men?"

"Yes."

The Makhno man chewed the end of his whisker thoughtfully, and asked, gazing over Piotr's head:

"If we shoot you you won't take offence?"

With his hand the lad wiped away the blood which had oozed on to his lips, and said firmly:

"You won't shoot all of us."

The man turned swiftly in his chair, and shouted:

"Dolbishev, take this lad and hand him over to the second troop for a little walk."

Piotr was led out. On the veranda his escort tied his arms with a thong, asking as he pulled the knot tight:

"It doesn't hurt, does it?"

"Chuck it!" Piotr said, and went to the gate, waving his bound hands awkwardly.

The escort closed the gate behind him and slipped the rifle off his shoulder.

"Wait a bit! There's the troop commander."

Piotr stopped. He was fed up because his chin was itching intolerably, and he couldn't scratch it with his hands bound.

The stocky, bandylegged troop commander came up. His English legboots stank of tar. He asked the escort:

"Bringing him to me?"

"Yes. They said you're to be quick."

The troop commander looked at Piotr with sleepy eyes and said:

"A rum lot! Playing about with this kid, torturing him and they're tortured themselves."

Knitting his ginger eyebrows, he took another look at Piotr, swore foully, and shouted:

"Get to the shed, clod! Now! Get on, I tell you, and stand with your mug to the wall."

The flaxen-whiskered Makhno man from the staff came out on to the veranda. Leaning across the fretted balustrade, he said:

"Troop commander: d'you hear? Don't shoot the lad. Send him back to me."

Piotr went on to the veranda and stood leaning against the door. Flaxen whiskers came right up to him and said, trying to peer into the narrow, bloodstained slit of Piotr's one eye.

"You've got spunk, boy. I feel sorry for you; I'll enrol you in the Old Man's army. Will you serve?"

"I will," the lad answered, closing his one eye.

"But you won't run away?"

"Give me food and clothing and I shan't run away."

Flaxen whiskers laughed, wrinkling his nose.

"But even if you wanted to we shan't let you. . . . I'll keep my eye on you." Turning to the escort, he said: "Take the boy into your company, Dolbishev; supply him with whatever he needs out of the loot. He'll ride on your cart. Keep both eyes on him. Don't give him a rifle for the time being."

He slapped Piotr on the shoulder and, swaying, went back into the house.

They drove out of the village at noon next day. Piotr sat beside Dolbishev of the drooping whiskers, jogged about on the seat, and thought oppressive, tedious thoughts.

After the rains the mud kneaded on the road was swollen in hummocks. They made the cart shake, and sent it rocking from side to side. The telegraph poles strode past, the road wound along without end.

In every hamlet and outlying farm they were welcomed with hubbub, peasants eyeing them from under scowling brows, women's whining voices.

The Second Force had been detached from the main army and was marching in the direction of Millerovo. The main army was moving more to the left.

Late in the afternoon Dolbishev fished a mis-shapen loaf of bread from under the seat, and cut up a water melon. As he chewed he nodded to Piotr.

"Eat, brother; you're of our faith now."

Piotr greedily ate a section of the ripe water melon and a piece of bread which smelt of horse's urine.

Dolbishev carved off another piece with his cutlass, and held it out to Piotr.

"Though I don't trust you a bit. What I think is, you'll run away from us. We ought to shoot you, it would be far better that way."

"No, daddy, you mustn't think like that. What have I got to run away from you for? You may be fighting for the right. . . ."

"Well, yes, for the right. Why, what did you think?"

"But if you're fighting for the right why do you go around upsetting the people?"

"How are we upsetting them?"

"How? Why, in all sorts of ways. When we drove through the village where you took the last handfuls of oats from a peasant for your horse. And now his little children have got nothing to eat."

Dolbishev twisted a cigarette and lit it.

"That was the Old Man's order."

"But supposing he gave you the order to hang all the peasants?"

"Hm. . . . Now look where you've landed me."

He spread a canopy of smoke from his home-grown tobacco above his head, and was silent.

But when they halted for the night the company commander, the freckled sailor and accordeon player Kiriuka, sent for Piotr and said, waving his Mauser:

"You'll be in your grave, damn you, you so and so, if you stick your nose into politics again. I'll order a cart shaft to be raised and

have you hung from it upside down, you son of a bitch. . . . Get
that?"

"Yes," said Piotr.

"Well, clear off quick; and remember, you crooked bastard, the
least thing and I'll gut you and hang you."

Piotr realized that he would have to carry on his propaganda
more circumspectly. He spent two days trying to wipe out his mistake: he asked Dolbishev all kinds of questions concerning the
'Old Man', and the countries they had been in; but the troop commander maintained a stubborn silence, gave the boy suspicious
looks from under his brows, and said few words through set teeth.
However, Piotr's servility and respect for him (he was not any
common ranker but had come from Makhno's own village, Gulai-
Polya, and had been his near neighbour) thawed him out, and he
began to talk more freely. A day or so later he let him have a
carbine and eighty cartridges.

That same day, late in the afternoon, the company pitched camp
not far from Koshara settlement. Dolbishev unharnessed the horse
from the cart and, handing Piotr a bucket, told him:

"Ride to those willows, lad; there's a pond there, get some water
and we'll cook some gruel."

Trying to restrain his beating heart, Piotr mounted the horse and
gently trotted off to the pond.

"I'll ride to the pond, and then up the hill and away," the idea
flashed through his head.

He rode to the pond, round the narrow, crumbling dam, cautiously dropped the bucket and, kicking the horse with his heels,
galloped to the foot of the rise. As though in warning, a shot rang
out from the camp, a bullet whistled over his head. With his one
misty eye he measured the distance between him and the camp: it
was barely half a mile.

"If I gallop up the hill," he reflected, "a bullet is sure to reach
me." Reluctantly he turned the horse round and rode back.

As Dolbishev hung a billycan of potatoes from the end of the
shaft pole he glanced at Piotr and said:

"If you play about I'll kill you. Remember that."

7

In the early morning, Piotr was disturbed by a howling roar of voices. He woke up, and threw off the horsecloth which covered the cart for the night. In the thinning greyness of the autumnal dawn a shout came to his ears in gusts:

"Daddy, what's all that noise?"

Standing bolt upright on the seat, Dolbishev waved his shaggy fur cap and bawled, livid with the strain:

"We're welcoming the Old Man. Hurrah!"

Piotr half rose, and saw a cart drawn by four raven horses rolling along the road. White flecks of foam flew off the horses, the cart was surrounded by riders, and Makhno himself, who had been wounded near Chernishevsky, held a stick under his armpit and writhed his lips, either from the pain of the wound or in a smile. From the back of the cart a rug hung right to the ground, the dust sped in shaggy plumes from the back wheels.

The cart dashed past, and a minute later there was only dust to be seen swarming along the road in the distance; the roar of voices faded into silence.

8

Three days passed. The Second Force advanced towards the railway line. Nowhere along the road did it have to fight. The Red units retreated towards the Don. By now Piotr knew all the company: of the 150 men sixty or more were Red Army deserters, the rest were riffraff.

One night they gathered round the camp fire and began a Trepak dance to the strains of the accordion. The earth, gripped with a very slight frost, groaned dryly under their feet.

Dolbishev danced round the ring in the squatting position, slapped his dusty legboots with his hands and breathed heavily, like an overheated horse.

Then, spreading out their greatcoats and goatskins, they lay round the fire. Lighting his cigarette with a brand taken from the fire, Manzhulo, the machine-gunner, remarked:

"This is what some of us are saying : they say the Old Man will lead us through the mining district to the Rumanian frontier, and there he'll give the army the chuck and go over into Rumania on his own."

"That's a lot of lies," Dolbishev barked.

Manzhulo bristled up, swore at Dolbishev vigorously and, pointing one finger at him, shouted :

"There he is, the stupid nancy boy. You can have him for twenty roubles. But as for you, you pig's trotter, I suppose you thought he'd come and ask you to ride in his cart?"

"He can't give the army the chuck," Dolbishev shouted fierily.

"Blockhead! Dirty Dunia from birth! Why, the Rumanian tsar isn't going to let twenty thousand on to his land. . . ," the machine-gunner shouted back, going white with anger.

Others came to his support.

"You're right there."

"You've hit the bull's eye, Manzhulo."

"We're of use so long as we shed our blood for the Old Man and the paramours he carts around with him. . . ."

"Ho-ho-ho! Ha-ha-ha! Give it him, brother!" shouts arose round the fire.

Dolbishev got up and hurriedly went off to the company commander's cart. The others whistled piercingly and catcalled after him, while one man flung a burning brand.

"He's gone to squeal. All right, let him. . . . In the next fight we'll give him one in the back of the neck."

Piotr saw the company commander Kiriukha striding up to the fire, and shifted farther away from it.

"What's all this, lads? Which of you is so anxious for a noose? Who wants to swing from a telegraph pole? Come on, speak up."

Manzhulo got up from the ground, went right up to the commander, and said, breathing hard and spasmodically :

"Don't bend the stick too much, Kiriukha. A stick has two ends. Rein in your filthy tongue."

"Well, you come along to the staff."

Kiriukha seized the machine-gunner by the sleeve, but a deep roar of protest came from the others; they clambered up and closed behind the company commander in a wall of shaggy fur caps.

"Don't you touch him."

"We'll skin the soul out of you."

"We'll turn you upside down and the staff too."

Little by little they started to jostle Kiriukha; then someone gave him a resounding blow on the ear. The commander's blue caftan was split at the collar. Rifle locks rattled. Kiriukha broke away from the ring, his groaning cry hung in the air:

"Guards, sound the alarm! Treach . . ."

The machine-gunner closed his mouth with one hand, and whispered into his ear:

"Clear off and keep your mouth shut, or you'll get a bullet in your back."

Forcing a way through the Makhno men, he led the company commander to the nearest cart and then returned to the fire.

A rolling peal of laughter thundered out again, the accordion wheezed, the dancers drummed their heels. But close to a cart a small group flung Dolbishev to the ground, stuffed a sash into his mouth, and gave him a thorough beating with rifle butts and boots.

*   *   *

Next day an orderly galloped out from the Force staff and handed the company commander a greasy sheet torn from a note-pad. On the sheet were only nine words, scribbled in pencil: "I order the company to capture the Soviet Farm."

9

From the top of the hill they could see the Soviet Farm below them. Behind the winding white stone wall were brick buildings and the lofty chimney of a brick works.

Leaving the carts on the high road, the company advanced towards the farm in extended order across open country.

Company commander Kiriukha, his face wrapped in a woman's fleecy shawl, rode in front. The raven mare stumbled under him; he looked back again and again at the thin line of men silently marching behind him.

Piotr was the seventh man from the left flank. For some reason he felt sure that today, quite soon now, something big and important was going to happen. And this expectation brought him a growing feeling of joy.

When their advance brought them within rifle shot of the farm the commander leaped from his horse and shouted:

"Lie down."

Close to a ravine they scattered and lay down. They opened fire in a ragged volley at the stone wall. A machine-gun began to chatter hoarsely and uncertainly from one of the farm roofs. People were running about the yards. Bullets hit the ground behind the long line of Makhno men, raising little clouds of melting dust.

Three times the company went into the attack, and three times it retreated to the ravine. The last time, as Piotr ran back, he saw Dolbishev lying face downward close to a marmot mound; he bent over him and saw a little hole in the man's forehead, just below his fur cap. The boy realized that he had been shot by one of his own men, almost point-blank, in the face above the eye.

Yet a fourth time Kiriukha, the company commander, drew his curved Caucasian sabre from its scabbard and, running owlish eyes over the company, roared hoarsely:

"Forward, lads! Follow me!"

But the lads began to murmur, and didn't move. Manzhulo, the machine-gunner, flung the bolt out of his rifle and shouted:

"Leading us to the slaughter? We're not going."

Feeling his fingers going icy, his body breaking into a sticky sweat, Piotr shouted at the top of his voice:

"Brothers! What are you shedding blood for. What are you going to your death and killing workers like yourselves for?"

The voices died away. Piotr felt the rifle strap beginning to sweat under his hands.

"Brothers! Let's lay down our arms. Every one of you has a family of his own. Haven't you any pity on your wives and children? Have you stopped to think what will happen to them if you're killed off?"

The commander drew his Mauser out of its holster, but Piotr had anticipated the movement; throwing up his rifle, he fired at the blue caftan almost without taking aim. Kiriukha spun round like a wolf cub and fell flat, pressing both hands to his chest.

The others surrounded Piotr: one man struck him on the back

with a rifle butt; others seized him and flung him to the ground. But Manzhulo, spreading his arms wide, stood over him and roared in an ugly tone:

"Stop! Don't kill the boy. Let him say his say, and then we'll finish him off after."

He raised Piotr from the ground, shook him down, and said:

"Now speak."

The earth and the sky with its patches of tousled cloud floated before Piotr's eye. He concentrated all his will and answered:

"Kill me! You can only do it once."

From the back came a snarl:

"Louder. . . . We can't hear."

With his sleeve he wiped the blood running from his temple and went on, raising his voice:

"You think it over properly. Makhno will lead you to Rumania and then he'll abandon you. He only needs you now. Anyone who wants to be a slave will follow him; the others the Red Army will wipe out. But if we surrender now nothing will happen to us. . . ."

The air in the ravine was raw. Silence. They all found it difficult to breathe, as though there was a shortage of air.

The machine-gunner wiped his brow with his hand, and quietly asked:

"Well, what d'you think, lads?"

Hanging heads. On the ground a little way off, Kiriukha, the commander, tore open his shirt on his wounded chest, kicked out his legs a last time, then lay quietly, all his body gently twitching.

"Those for surrender, step to the right. Those against, to the left," Piotr shouted.

The machine-gunner waved his hand in a desperate gesture and stepped to the right, others followed him hurriedly and closely. Some eight men were left standing; they hesitated and hesitated, but finally joined the others.

Five minutes later they were advancing towards the Soviet Farm in a serried mass. Piotr and Manzhulo, the machine-gunner, in front. A piece of white rag torn from Piotr's shirt tail was flying from his rusty bayonet instead of a flag.

A group of men came streaming out of the Soviet Farm. Their rifles at the ready, they watched distrustfully.

When they had advanced to some three hundred paces from the

Soviet group the company halted. Piotr and Manzhulo went on walking towards the farm, leaving their rifles behind. Two Soviet farmers came to meet them. They met halfway. The talk was brief. A bearded Soviet farmer embraced Piotr. Wiping his whiskers, Manzhulo kissed the other man on both cheeks.

A roar of approval from both sides. The company piled their rifles with a clatter in a single heap, and went in ones and twos through the wide open gates of the Soviet Farm.

10

A Cheka plenipotentiary arrived at the farm from the regional town. He questioned Piotr, wrote down his statements in a book, and, after shaking both his hands, rode away.

Some of the Makhno men joined up, entering the Red Cavalry regiment which was pursuing Makhno; the others were transferred to the military commissariat in the regional capital. Piotr remained in the Soviet Farm.

After all he had gone through, how good it was to lie quietly in bed. Even the burning pain in his empty eye socket seemed to be easier then. It was just as though he had never been dragged along by a lasso, never been beaten almost to death. Somehow the recent past did not remind him of itself, and he had no desire to recall it.

But when he passed a cracked mirror hanging in the Soviet Farm, and had a momentary glimpse of his earthen, distorted face, bitterness compressed his lips and he found it more difficult to breathe.

Late one Tuesday afternoon the secretary of the farm's communist group came into his room. He sat down beside him on the bed, tucked up his long legs in their hunting boots, and cleared his throat :

"Come along in an hour's time to a general meeting in the club."

"All right, I'll come."

The secretary sat with him a moment or two longer, then went. An hour later Piotr went to the club. He listened to reports from the farm chairman, the agronomist, the brick works manager, the veterinary surgeon. Before him the reports unfolded an ordered, measured life, running like clockwork.

The minutes of the meeting. Resolutions. Suggestions.

When they reached 'any other business' the group secretary asked to be allowed to say a few words.

"Comrades, we have here among us in our Soviet Farm the young communist, Piotr Kremniev. You know we owe it to him that our Soviet Farm was saved from destruction. The communist group proposes we should send Kremniev to the regional town for treatment, and then enter him for the next free place in our works. Let's vote on it : all in favour. . . ."

Unanimous, *nem. con.* But Piotr rose from his seat, a thin, hasty tear ran down from his empty eye socket over his cheek. His lips were pressed together. He stood a moment, looking round the meeting with his one half-closed eye, and said, moving his reluctant tongue with difficulty :

"Thank you, but I can't stay with you . . . I'd be very glad to work with you. . . . But the point is . . . the point is that your life runs along as though on rails, but in the district village where I come from life hobbles, we had difficulty in getting anything organized, we started a Young Communist Group, but I expect many of them are no longer there. . . . The Makhno men have killed them off . . . and I want to go back . . . they've a much greater need of workers there. . . ."

The meeting was silent. They all agreed. There was not a sound to be heard in all the hall.

II

Almost the whole farm turned out to see him off. As he said goodbye and went up the hill dusk was falling. Darkness spread over the road, over the mute line of telegraph poles.

The Hetman highway runs along by the Don, above the beetling, frowning hills. Piotr strode along silently.

In the black, clinging darkness, in the empty silence of the sleeping night his footsteps sounded clearly. The frost scrunched under his boots. The holes left by horses' hoofs were filmed with a very thin sheet of ice which gave off a gentle tinkle as it broke. The freezing water beneath it splashed.

From beyond the mound guarding the road a moon livid with

strain climbed up. Uneven, slanting shadows floated over the steppe. The fading wayside wormwood exuded a bitter scent, a smell of bitter sweat.

Without end the way and the road winds along; but Piotr was striding resolutely along that road to meet the oncoming night, and from the azure floor of the sky a five-pointed star twinkled down to him with a pale greenish light.

1925.

THE FOAL

HE emerged from his mother's womb in broad daylight, head foremost, his little forelegs stretched out, by a heap of dung thickly plastered with emerald flies. And the first thing he saw right in front of him was the fine, dove-grey, melting cloud of a shrapnel explosion. A howling roar flung his little wet body under his mother's legs. Terror was the first feeling he experienced on this earth. A stinking hail of grapeshot rattled on the tiled roof of the stable and, sprinkling over the ground, forced the foal's mother —red-bearded Trofim's mare—to jump to her feet and then with a brief neigh to drop her sweating flank against the sheltering dung heap.

In the sultry silence that followed, the flies buzzed more distinctly; a cock, which because of the gunfire had not dared to jump to the top of the wattle fence, flapped its wings a time or two somewhere in the shadow of the burdocks and unconstrainedly but muffledly crowed. From the hut came the wailing groan of the machine-gunner. From time to time he cried out in a sharp yet hoarse voice, interspersing his cries with incredible oaths. Bees were humming among the silky purple heads of the poppies in the enclosure. In the meadow beyond the village a machine-gun finished off its belt, and while it cheerfully rattled away, in the interval between the last and the next gun fire, the sorrel mare lovingly licked its firstborn. And the foal, dropping down to her swollen udder, had its first realization of the fullness of life and the unforgettable sweetness of a mother's caresses.

After the second shell had smacked down somewhere behind the threshing-floor, Trofim came out of the hut, slammed the door, and went towards the stable. As he passed round the dung heap he shielded his eyes from the sun with his palm, and, noticing the foal quivering with the strain of sucking at his, Trofim's, sorrel mare, in his bewilderment he felt in his pocket. With trembling hands he searched for and found his tobacco pouch and, after lick-

ing the paper to roll himself a cigarette, recovered the gift of
speech :

"So-o-o! So you've foaled, have you? A fine time for that sort of
thing, I must say!" A bitter note of injury sounded in his last
remark.

Scrub stalks and dry dung were clinging to the mare's flanks,
which were shaggy with dried sweat. She looked indecently thin
and watery, but her eyes shone with a proud joy touched with
weariness, and her velvety upper lip curled back in a smile. So at
least Trofim imagined. He put the mare back in the stable; she
snorted as she rummaged in the bag of grain. Then he leaned
against the door post and, giving the foal an unfriendly look, asked
her dryly :

"So you've had your fun and got burnt?"

Without waiting for a reply he went on :

"I wouldn't have minded if you'd got it from Ignat's stallion;
but as it is the devil knows which was responsible. . . . And, besides, what can I do with him?"

Through the twilight silence of the stable came the sound of
grain being crunched, a crooked sunbeam sent a golden dust through
a chink in the door. The light fell on Trofim's left cheek; his ginger
whiskers and the brush of his beard were tinged with a reddish
hue; the furrows round his lips showed in deep, curving lines. The
foal stood on its thin, fluffy legs like a child's wooden horse.

"Kill him?" Trofim's forefinger, stained with tobacco juice,
crooked in the direction of the foal.

The mare rolled her bloodshot eye, blinked, and gave her master
a sidelong, humorous look.

*   *   *

In the best room, which the squadron commander occupied, that
same evening there was the following conversation :

"I could see my mare was in foal, she couldn't trot, I couldn't
force her into a canter, she started to pant at once. I took a good
look at her, and she turns out to be in foal. And she took such care
of it, such care. . . . The foal's a sort of bay colour. . . . That's
all. . . ." Trofim told his story.

The squadron commander clutched the copper mug of tea in his fist, clutched it as if it were his sabre hilt before going into an attack, and looked at the lamp with sleepy eyes. Above the little yellow flame, hairy moths were raging; they came flying through the window and burnt themselves against the glass one after another.

". . . It doesn't matter. Bay or raven, it's all the same. Shoot it. With a foal around we'd be sort of gypsies.

"What? That's just what I'm saying, just like gypsies. And supposing the commander comes along, what then? He'll arrive to review the regiment, and the foal will go prancing out in the front and up will go its tail. . . . We'll be shamed and disgraced in front of all the Red Army. I don't even understand how you could have allowed it, Trofim. At the very height of the civil war, and suddenly we get this debauchery. Why, it's positively shameful. Give the horsekeepers the strict order to keep the mares separate."

Next morning Trofim came out of the hut with his rifle. The sun hadn't yet fully risen. Dew was shining rosily on the grass. The meadow, pockmarked with the infantry's boots, criss-crossed with trenches, recalled a girl's tearstained, sorrow-lined face. The cooks were bustling around the field kitchen. On the veranda the squadron commander was sitting in an undershirt rotten with years of sweat. His fingers, accustomed to the encouraging chill of a revolver butt, awkwardly recalled the forgotten past, his native parts, as he bound a ladle for fishing out curd dumplings. As Trofim went past he asked with a show of interest :

"Making a dumpling ladle?"

The commander finished off the handle with a thin strip of wattle, and said through set teeth :

"That woman, our housewife, asked me to. . . . 'Do make me one. . . .' At one time I was expert at this sort of thing, but now somehow it doesn't come out right."

"Well, I think it's good," Trofim praised his handiwork.

The squadron commander brushed the chips off his knees and asked :

"Going to liquidate the foal?"

Trofim waved his hand and said nothing; he went on to the stable.

With head bent, the commander waited for the shot. A minute passed, then another, but he heard no shot. Trofim reappeared round the corner of the stable; he looked worried by something.

"Well?"

"The hammer must have gone wrong. It won't strike the percussion cap."

"Well, let me have a look at it."

Trofim reluctantly handed over the rifle. The squadron commander pulled the bolt back and forth, and screwed up his eyes.

"Why, you haven't got any cartridges in it."

"I don't believe it," Trofim exclaimed heatedly.

"I tell you you haven't."

"Then I must have dropped them there, behind the stable."

The commander laid the rifle aside and spent some time turning over the new ladle in his hands. The fresh wattle was honiedly scented and sticky, his nostrils inhaled the scent of flowering alders, of the soil, of past toil long forgotten in the vast conflagration of war.

"Listen! Damn him! Let him live with his mother. For the time being and so forth. He may come in useful when the war ends . . . for ploughing. And if anything happens the commander will understand that the foal's a suckling and he's got to suck. The commander has sucked at the titty, and we've sucked too, and since that's the regular custom, that's all there is to it. But as for your rifle, it's in perfect order."

*　　　*　　　*

It so happened that a month later, not far from the district town of Ust-Khopersk, Trofim's squadron was involved in a fight with a company of cossacks. They opened fire on one another late in the afternoon. As they went into the attack the sky was darkening. Halfway to the enemy, Trofim was left hopelessly behind his troop. Neither the whip, nor the bit, pulling the mare's mouth to pieces, could persuade her to break into a gallop. Tossing her head high, she whinneyed hoarsely and trod the ground in one spot until the foal, waving his tail, caught up with her. Trofim leapt out of his saddle, thrust his sabre into its scabbard and, his face distorted with fury, tore the rifle from his shoulder. The men on the right flank were already at handgrips with the Whites. Close to a ravine a group of men was swaying back and forth as though before a gusty wind. They wielded their sabres without uttering a sound. The ground echoed dully under their horses' hoofs. Trofim glanced in their direction for a second, then took the foal's slender head in his sights. His hand may have trembled in his agitation, or possibly there was some other reason to account for his missing. Anyway, at the shot the foal kicked up its heels idiotically, whinneyed in a thin voice and, throwing up clumps of grey dust with its hoofs, circled round and came to a stand a little way off. Trofim fired a clip of cartridges, but not the ordinary sort, but armour-piercing ones, at the little red devil. Then, realizing that these special cartridges (which had come to his hand quite by chance as he groped in his wallet) had brought neither injury nor death to his mare's progeny, he leapt on to her back and, swearing foully, rode off at a jogtrot to where bearded crimson-faced Old Believers were pressing hard on the squadron commander and three other Red Army men, driving them towards a ravine.

The squadron spent that night in the steppe not far from a shallow gulley. They smoked but little. They did not unsaddle the horses. A reconnaissance returning from the Don reported that considerable enemy forces were deployed to prevent the Reds crossing the river.

Wrapping his bare feet in the folds of his mackintosh, Trofim lay dozing and recalling the events of the past day. Before his eyes passed pictures of the squadron commander jumping into the ravine, the gap-toothed Old Believer who signed the cross with his sabre on the political commissar, the skinny little cossack who was sabred into mincemeat, someone's saddle washed with black blood, the little foal. . . .

In the early dawn the squadron commander came up and squatted down beside him in the darkness:

"Are you asleep, Trofim?"

"Just dozing."

Gazing at the fading stars, the commander said:

"Annihilate your foal. It's causing panic in battle. When I look at him my hand trembles. . . . I can't use my sabre. And all because he looks so homelike, and that sort of thing isn't desirable in war. . . . It turns the heart from stone into water. And besides, when the horses went into the attack they wouldn't tread him down, he got between their legs, the blighter." He was silent a

moment, then smiled dreamily, only Trofim didn't see the smile:
"You follow, Trofim? His tail, well, you know, he folds it over his
back, kicks up his heels, and the tail's just like a fox's. . . . It's a
really remarkable tail."

Trofim made no comment. He drew his greatcoat over his head
and, shivering in the dewy dampness, fell asleep with amazing
speed.

Opposite a certain ancient monastery the Don is forced against
cliffs and dashes along beneath them with reckless impetuosity.
At the turn the water spins in little whirlpools, and the green,
white-maned waves fling themselves on the sandy shoals scattered
amid the river by the spring landslides.

The cossacks had occupied the bend where the current was
weaker and the Don broader and more peaceable, and had started
raking the foothills with fire from their vantage point; otherwise
the squadron commander would never have decided to send the
squadron across the river by swimming opposite the monastery.

They began the crossing at noonday. A small dugout boat took
on board the machine-gun with its team and three horses. When, in
the middle, the boat swung right round athwart the current and
gently careened to one side, the left side-horse, which had never
seen a river before, took fright. The men under the cliff, where the
dismounted squadron were unsaddling their horses, clearly heard
its anxious snorting and the stamp of its hoofs on the boat's
wooden bottom.

"It'll sink the boat," Trofim barked, frowning, and his raised
hand intended for the sweating back of his mare was suspended in
mid-air: on the boat the side-horse snorted wildly, backing on to
the guncart shaft and rearing on its hind legs.

"Shoot it!" the commander bawled, his hand clutching and un-
clutching his whip.

Trofim saw the gunlayer hang on the horse's neck and thrust
his pistol into its ear. The shot sounded like a child's popgun; the
shaft horse and the right side-horse huddled closer to each other.
Fearing for the boat, the machine-gunners pushed the dead horse
to the back of the cart. Its forelegs slowly bent, its head hung
down. . . .

Some ten minutes later the squadron commander rode down
from the spit of land beneath the cliff and led the way into the

water with his dun horse; the rest of the squadron followed him with a thunderous splash, one hundred and eight half naked swimmers, and the same number of horses of various colours. The saddles were taken across on three canoes. Trofim was steering one of them; he had handed over his mare to the troop commander Nechuperenko. From the middle of the river Trofim watched the leading horses wading up to their knees, reluctantly gulping in water. Their riders urged them on in undertones. In less than a minute, some 150 feet from the bank the water was speckled with horses' heads, snorting in all kinds of tones. The Red Army men swam at their sides, clinging to the manes, their clothes and wallets tied to their rifles held above their heads.

Flinging his oar into the boat, Trofim rose to his full height and, screwing up his eyes against the sun, looked anxiously for his mare's red head among the swimming horses. The squadron looked like a gaggle of wild geese scattered over the sky by hunters' shots. Right in front was the squadron commander's dun, his velvety back rising high out of the water; close to its tail appeared the silvery white ears of the horse which had belonged to the political commissar; behind it was a dark bunch of animals and, last of all, as Trofim could see, came troop commander Nechuperenko's bristling head, with the pointed ears of Trofim's mare on his left hand. Straining his eyes, Trofim caught sight of the foal too. He was swimming in a series of spurts, now rising high out of the water, then sinking till his nostrils were hardly visible.

And then the wind gusting over the Don brought a challenging neigh, as thin as a spider's thread, to Trofim's ears.

The cry sounded over the water as ringing and keen as the point of a sabre. It struck right at Trofim's heart, and something remarkable happened to him : he had gone through five years of war, death had gazed like a maiden into his eyes again and again, and God knows what else; but now he went white under his red, bushy beard, went as white as ash. Snatching up the oar, he sent the boat back against the current towards the spot where the helpless foal was spinning in a whirlpool. And some sixty feet away Nechuperenko was struggling with, but could not hold back, the mother from swimming towards that whirlpool, whinneying hoarsely. Trofim's friend, Steshka Yefremov, who was sitting on a pile of saddles in the boat, shouted sternly :

"Don't play the fool. Make for the bank. Don't you see, there they are : cossacks."

"I'll shoot it," Trofim sighed, and tugged at his rifle-strap.

The current had carried the foal far from the spot where the squadron was crossing. The small whirlpool smoothly swung him round and round, licking him with its green, foam-capped waves. Trofim worked his oar desperately, the boat moved in a succession of spurts. On the right bank cossacks came rushing out of a ravine. The rapid bass of a Maxim gun began to drum. The bullets hissed as they smacked into the water. An officer in a ragged canvas shirt shouted something, waving his pistol.

The foal whinneyed more and more rarely, the short, cutting cry grew fainter and fainter. And that cry sent a chill of horror through all who heard it, for it was exactly like the cry of a baby. Nechuperenko abandoned the mare and easily swam across to the left bank. Trembling, Trofim snatched up his rifle and fired, aiming just below the head sucked down by the whirlpool. Then he kicked his boots off and, stretching out his hands, with a dull bellowing moan dived into the water.

On the right bank the officer in the canvas shirt barked :

"Cease fire !"

In five minutes Trofim was right beside the foal; with his left hand he clutched him under his chilling body, and, panting and hiccuping in spasms, made for the left bank. Not one shot was fired from the right bank.

Sky, forest, sand : all brilliantly green, transparent. With one last stupendous effort Trofim's feet scraped the ground. He dragged the foal's slippery little body on to the sand and, sobbing, vomited into the green water, scrabbling over the sand with his hands. . . . From the forest came the muffled voices of the squadron, somewhere beyond the spit of land rifle shots rang out. The ginger mare stood at Trofim's side, shaking herself and licking the foal. A rainbow stream dripped down from her hanging tail and pitted the sand.

Swaying, Trofim clambered to his feet, took a couple of steps along the sand, then sprang into the air and dropped on his side. It was as though a hot prick had pierced his chest. He heard the shot as he fell. A single shot in the back, from the right bank. On that bank the officer in the ragged canvas shirt unconcernedly rattled his carbine lock, ejecting the smoking cartridge case, while on the sand, two paces from the foal, Trofim twitched and jerked, and his rough blue lips, which for five years had never kissed a child, smiled as they foamed with blood.

1926.

THE AZURE STEPPE

OLD Zakhar and I are lying under a bush of wild thorn above the Don, on a mound bald with scorching sunlight. A brown kite is wandering under the scaly ridge of a cloud. The thorn leaves, decorated with bird droppings, afford us no shade at all. The sultry heat sets up a ringing in the ears; when you look down at the curling, speckled surface of the Don or under your feet at the furrowed water-melon rinds, a sticky saliva runs into your mouth and you're just too lazy to spit it out.

Down in the hollow, close to a pond drying out, sheep are huddled together in a serried bunch. Wearily presenting their haunches to the world, they wag their bedraggled tails and sneeze painfully with the dust. By the dam a healthy young lamb, its hind feet thrust firmly against the ground, is sucking at a dirty yellow ewe. Occasionally, it thrusts its head hard against its mother's udder: the ewe groans and hunches her back, letting the milk flow. And I get the impression that there is a look of suffering in her eyes.

Old Zakhar is sitting sideways on to me. Throwing off his knitted woollen shirt, he wrinkles up his eyes half blindly and gropes for something in the folds and seams. He is seventy all but a twelve-month. His bare back is intricately furrowed with lines, his angular shoulder-blades stick through his skin; but his eyes are blue and youthful, the glance under his grey brows is alert and keen.

He holds the louse he has caught in his trembling, gnarled fingers with difficulty; he holds it carefully, tenderly, then puts it down on the ground as far away from himself as possible, signs the air with a tiny cross and thickly mumbles:

"You crawl, off, insect. So you want to live, do you? That's just it. . . . But you've sucked enough . . . you landowner. . . ."

With a grunt he pulls on his shirt and, throwing back his head, takes a long pull at the tepid water in his wooden jug. With every gulp his Adam's apple slips upward; two soaked folds of skin hang from his chin to his throat, the drops of water flow over his beard, the sun shines redly through his closed, saffron lids.

Replacing the lid on the jug, he looks sidelong at me and, catching my glance, chews his lips drily and stares out into the steppe. Beyond the hollow a haze is rising smokily, the wind blowing over the sun-scorched earth smells of thyme honey. After a moment or so the old man pushes away his shepherd's crook and points past me with one tobacco-stained finger.

"D'you see the crowns of the poplars beyond that ravine? That's the property of the Tomalin gentry: Poplarovka. And close by it is the peasants' settlement of Poplarovka; in the old days they were serfs. My father was the gentleman's coachman all his life. He used to tell me, his poor kid, how Mr. Yevgraf Tomilin exchanged him for a tame crane with a neighbouring landowner. After my father's death I became the coachman in his place. The gentleman himself was nigh on sixty then. He was a stout man, full blooded. In his youth he had served in the tsar's guards, but when he finished his service he came to live out his life on the Don. The cossacks took away his land on the Don, but the treasury carved him out seven thousand acres in Saratov province. He rented them out to the Saratov peasants, and he himself lived in Poplarovka.

"He was a wild sort. He always went about in a long Georgian coat of fine cloth, with a dagger. He used to drive around visiting friends; we'd drive out of Poplarovka, and he'd order me:

"'Whip them up! You little scum!'

"I'd whip up the horses. We'd gallop along, the wind didn't have time to dry our tears. We'd come to a little runnel across the road, the spring floods used to carve them deep across the road. Not a sound from the front wheels, but the back wheels went 'Clack!' We'd drive on half a mile or so, and then the gentleman would roar: 'Turn back!' I'd turn back and drive up to this runnel again at top speed. Up to three times we'd bounce across that damned hole, until we broke a spring, or we'd pull a wheel right off the carriage. Then my master would grunt, get out and set off on foot, while I followed him, leading the horses by the reins. He had another way of amusing himself too: we'd drive out of the estate, and he'd be sitting beside me on the driver's seat. And he'd tear the knout out of my hands. 'Tickle up the shaft-horse.' I'd get the shaft-horse galloping at full stretch, the shaft-bow would be dead level the whole time, while he slashed away at a side-horse. We always drove a troika, we had Don horses of the purest blood stock as side-horses : like snakes, with heads turned sideways, they'd gnaw at the ground.

"And he'd lash away at one of them, the poor creature would be larded with foam. Then he'd pull out his dagger, bend forward and, snip : he'd cut the trace like a hair with a razor. The horse would go flying head over heels for five or six feet, then he'd crash down on the earth, blood pouring from his nostrils. And that was that. And the same with the other side-horse. He'd go on lashing at the shaft-horse till it was broken-winded, but he didn't care what happened so long as he could have his bit of fun, and the blood would glow in his cheeks.

"We rarely drove all the way to the place we set out for : either the carriage was smashed, or the horses were driven to death, and we'd finish the journey on foot. He was a gay spark. But it's all past now, may God judge us. He made up to my wife; she worked as a housemaid. He'd come running into the servants' room, his shirt in rags, and roaring like a sturgeon. I'd see her breasts had been all bitten, the skin hanging in ribbons. One night he sent me off to fetch the quack. I knew there was no need for him to come, I guessed what was up, so I hung about in the steppe for a bit in the night and then went back. I drove into the estate through the threshing-floor, left the horses in the orchard, took my knout and went to the servants' quarters, to my own room. I made the door creak, I deliberately didn't strike a light, and I heard a noise on the bed. And when my master got up I went for him with the knout, and it had a bit of lead in the end of its lash. I heard him climbing up to the window, and in the darkness I gave him an-other lash across the forehead. He jumped out of the window, I whipped my wife a bit and went to bed. Five days later we had to drive to the district village. I started to button the rug over the seat, but he picked up my knout and examined the lash end. He turned it over and over in his hands, felt the lead, and asked :

" 'You, dog's blood, what have you fastened this lead into your knout for?'

" 'You yourself were good enough to order me to,' I answered.

"He said no more, and all the way as far as the first runnel he whistled through his teeth. But I turned round gently in my seat and saw he had his hair combed down over his forehead, and his cap drawn down over his eyes.

"Some two years later he was struck paralytic. We took him in his carriage to Ust-Medveditsa and sent for doctors, but he lay all black on the floor. He took packet after packet of roubles from his pocket, flung them on the floor, and bawled hoarsely: 'Cure me, you snakes! I'll give you everything.'

"May he rest in peace, he died with his money. His son, an officer, was his heir. When he was quite small he used to skin puppies alive, he'd flay them and then let them go. He went to the bad like his father. But when he grew up he stopped playing about. He was tall, thin, and always had black rings under his eyes just like a woman. He wore gold pince-nez, with a string to them. In the German war he was commander of a camp for prisoners of war in Siberia, but after the revolution he turned up in our parts. By that time I had grandsons of full age through my dead son. The older, Semion, was married, but Anikei was still a lad. And I lived with them. I had the ends of my life all tied up in a neat little knot. In the spring there was another revolution. Our peasants drove the young gentleman out of his estate, and the very same day Semion persuaded them in the assembly to divide up the gentleman's land and to take his personal property home. And so they did: they dragged out all the personal things and shared out the land and set to work to plough it. A week later, or possibly less, the rumour reached us that the gentleman was coming with cossacks to wipe out our settlement. So we sent two waggons to the station for weapons. In Holy Week they brought back weapons from the Red Guards, and we dug trenches round Poplarovka. They stretched right up to the gentleman's pond.

"D'you see, over there where the thyme grows in rings? Beyond that ravine was where the men of Poplarovka lay in their trenches. My boys were there too, Semion and Anikei. The women took them out food first thing in the morning, but when the sun was right overhead horsemen appeared over the hill. They spread out in a long line, their sabres gleamed blue. From the threshing-floor I could see the leader on a white horse, waving a sword, and the horsemen swept like peas down the hill. By his gait I recognized the gentleman's white riding horse, and by the horse I recognized the rider. Twice our people beat them off, but the third time the

cossacks came round to them from the rear, they resorted to cunning, and that began the slaughter. The fight was over by nightfall. I go out of my hut into the street and see the cossacks driving
a group of men towards the estate house. I picked up my stick
and hurried there.

"Our Poplarovka peasants were huddled in a group in the yard,
just like those sheep over there. There were cossacks everywhere.
I went up and asked:

" 'Tell me, brothers, where are my grandsons?'

"I heard both of them call out from the middle of the group.
We had a little talk among ourselves, then I see the gentleman
come out on to the veranda. He saw me, and roared:

" 'Is that you, daddy Zakhar?'

" 'Yes, it's me, your excellency.'

" 'What do you want here?'

"I go up to the veranda and drop down on my knees:

" 'I've come to rescue my grandsons from woe. Have mercy,
sir. I served your papa, may he rest in peace, all my life. Remember my zeal, sir, have pity on my old age.'

"But he says:

" 'Now listen, daddy Zakhar: I greatly respect your services to
my papa, but I cannot release your grandsons. They're thorough
mischief-makers. You must be reconciled in your soul, old man.'

"I embraced his legs, and crawled over the veranda.

" 'Have mercy, sir. My own dearest master, remember how
daddy Zakhar served you, don't finish me off. My Semion has a
baby at the breast.'

"He lit a scented cigarette, sent the smoke up and said:

" 'Go and tell them, the scoundrels, to come to see me in my
room. If they plead for forgiveness, then so be it. For the sake of
my papa's memory I'll have them whipped and enrol them in my
detachment. Maybe by zeal they'll cancel out their shameful guilt.'

"I ran out into the yard and told my grandsons, I tugged at their
sleeves:

" 'Go along, you fools, and don't get up from the ground till he
forgives you.'

"If only Semion had raised his head! But he remained squatting
on his heels and pecking at the ground with a twig. Anikei stared
and stared at me and burst out:

" 'Go to your master,' he says, 'and tell him : old Zakhar has crawled on his knees all his life, and his son crawled too, but his grandsons don't intend to. You can tell him that.'

" 'So you won't go, you son of a bitch?'

" 'No, I won't.'

" 'You scoundrel, you don't care a brass farthing whether you live or die, but where are you dragging Semion to? Who are you throwing his wife and her baby on to?'

"I notice Semion's hands starting to tremble, he dug at the ground with the twig, seeking God knows what there. But he said nothing. He was as silent as a bull.

" 'Go away, grand-dad, don't keep on at us,' Anikei asks.

" 'I shan't go away, you reptile mug. If anything happens Semion's Anisia will lay hands on herself. . . .'

"The twig snapped in Semion's hands and was broken in two.

"I go on waiting. He still said nothing.

" 'Semion, my boy. Do come to your senses, my breadwinner. Come along to the gentleman.'

" 'We've come to our senses. We aren't going. You go and crawl,' Anikei stormed.

"But I answered :

" 'Do you reproach me with going down on my knees to the gentleman? What if I do? I'm an old man; instead of my mother's titty I tasted the gentleman's knout. And I'm not ashamed to go down on my knees to my own grandsons either.'

"I went down on my knees, I bowed down to the ground, I pleaded with them. The other peasants turned their backs, pretending they didn't see what was going on.

" 'Go away, grand-dad. Go away, or I'll kill you,' Anikei roared. There was foam on his lips and his eyes were as wild as those of a lassoed wolf.

"I turned round and went back to the gentleman. I pressed his feet to my chest; he didn't push me away; my hands went like stone, and I couldn't get out a single word. He asked :

" 'But where are your grandsons?'

" 'They're afraid. . . .'

" 'Ah, so they're afraid.' And he said no more. He kicked me right in the mouth with his boot and went out on to the veranda."

Old Zakhar breathed rapidly and spasmodically; for a full

minute his face was furrowed, it went white. With a terrible effort
he mastered his sobs, the sobs of an old man; he wiped his dry lips
with his hand, and turned away. The kite, dipping his wide-spread
wings, dropped down into the grass and lifted a white-breasted
little bustard from the ground. The feathers fell in a miniature
snowstorm, their gleam was unbearably keen and prickling as they
touched the grass. Old Zakhar blew his nose and, wiping his
fingers on the edge of his knitted shirt, began to speak again :

"I went out on to the veranda after him, and saw Semion's
wife Aniska come running with her child. Just like that kite she
flew up to her husband and froze in his arms. . . .

"The gentleman called the sergeant, and pointed to Semion and
Anikei. The sergeant took six cossacks and led the two brothers
into the gentleman's orchard. I followed them; but Aniska abandoned the child in the middle of the yard and dragged after the
gentleman. Semion went in front of them all, walking very fast.
When he reached the stable he sat down.

" 'What have you sat down for?' the gentleman asked.

" 'My boots are squeezing my feet, I can't stand any more of it.'
And he smiled.

"He took off his boots and handed them to me.

" 'Here, grand dad, take and wear them for your health's sake.
They're good ones, they've got double soles.'

"I picked up the boots, and we went on again. They drew level
with the garden fence, and the cossacks set them against the wattle.
They loaded their guns, the gentleman stood close by, trimming
his finger-nails with small scissors, and his hand was very white. I
said to him :

" 'Sir, allow them to take off their clothes. They've got good
clothes, they'll be of use to us in our poverty, we'll wear them.'

" 'They can take them off.'

"Anikei took off his trousers, turned them inside out and hung
them on the fence post. He took his tobacco pouch out of his
pocket, lit a cigarette, and stood with his legs straddled, sending
out the smoke in little rings, then spitting over the fence. Semion
stripped himself naked, he even took off his linen drawers, but
somehow he forgot to take off his cap, it was quite clear he forgot.
One moment I was shivering with the frost, the next burning with
heat. I clutched my head, and for some reason my sweat was cold,

as cold as spring water. I look and see them standing there, side by side. Semion's chest was all overgrown with hair, he was naked, but he had his cap on his head. Anisia, just like a woman, looked and saw her husband standing naked and in his cap. She rushed to him and wound herself round him like hops round an oak. He pushed her away:

" 'Get off, crazy! Think what you're doing in front of everybody. Rushing at me like that, can't you see I'm naked . . . it's shameful. . . .'

"But she tore her hair and cried at the top of her voice:

" 'Shoot both of us.'

"The gentleman put his scissors in his pocket, and asked:

" 'Shoot you too?'

" 'Shoot, curse you.'

"She said that to the gentleman.

" 'Tie her to her husband,' he ordered.

"She came to her senses and fell back; but it was too late. The cossacks laughed as they tied her to Semion with a halter rope. She fell down, the fool, and dragged her husband down to the ground with her. The gentleman went up to them and asked through his teeth:

" 'Perhaps for the sake of the child you're leaving behind you'll ask for pardon.'

" 'I ask,' Semion groaned.

" 'Well, then ask, but it's God you'll have to ask; it's too late to ask me.'

"And as they lay on the ground, so they killed them. After the first shots Anikei swayed on his feet, but he didn't fall at once. First he dropped to his knees, then he turned over suddenly and lay face downward. The gentleman went up to him and asked in a very kindly voice:

" 'Would you like to live? If you would, then ask for pardon. And then fifty lashes, and off to the front you go.'

"Anikei worked up a mouthful of spittle; but he hadn't the strength to shoot it at the gentleman, it ran down over his beard. He went quite white with rage, but what was the good? Three bullets had bored holes in him.

" 'Drag him on to the road,' the gentleman ordered.

"The cossacks dragged him away and flung him over the fence,

into the road. Meanwhile a company of cossacks rode into the
village from Poplarovka, and they had two guns with them. The
gentleman hopped like a cock on to the fence and cried in a loud
voice :

" 'Drivers! Drive at the trot. Don't drive round him.'

"My hair stood on end. I was holding Semion's clothes and boots
in my hands, but my legs wouldn't hold me up, they bent beneath
me. The horses, they have a spark of the divine in them, not one
of them trod on Anikei, they all jumped across him. I fell against
the fence, I couldn't close my eyes, my mouth was dry. . . . The
gun wheels went over Anikei's legs. They scrunched like a rye rusk
in the mouth, and were crushed into thin little sticks. I thought
he'd be sure to die in mortal agony, but he didn't even cry out, he
didn't even groan. . . . He lay with his head drawn in to his body,
thrusting road dust into his mouth in handfuls. He chewed at the
earth and gazed at the gentleman, his eyes didn't blink, and his
eyes were bright and as serene as the sky. . . .

"Thirty-two men Mr. Tomilin shot that day. Only Anikei was
left alive because of his pride."

Old Zakhar took a long and thirsty drink from his jug. Wiping
his faded lips, he ended reluctantly :

"Time has overgrown all that. All that's left are the trenches in
which our peasants fought and won the land for themselves. The
grass grows in them and the steppe mugwort. . . . They amputated
Anikei's legs, he goes about on his hands now, dragging his carcass
over the ground. He looks cheerful enough, every day he and
Semion's little son measure each other against the door post. The
boy's outgrowing him fast. . . . In the winter he used to crawl out
into the alley, and when the people drove the cattle down to the
river to water them he'd raise his hands and sit in the road. In
their terror the bullocks would dash on to the ice and all but tear
themselves to pieces on the slippery surface; but he'd just laugh.
But one day I happened to notice something. . . . In the spring our
commune tractor was ploughing up along by the cossack boundary,
and he had himself tied on to it and rode out there. I was minding
the sheep not far off. I saw them lay my Anikei down on the
ploughed land. I wondered what he was up to. And I saw him look
all around him, see there was no one at all near, and then he turned
over with his face to the earth, to the clods the share had turned

over, and embraced them, pressed them to himself, stroked them with his hands, kissed them. . . . He's twenty-five now, but he'll never be able to plough the soil. . . . And he feels bad about it."

The azure steppe was dozing in the smoky bluish twilight, the bees were gathering their last harvest for the day from the round caps of fading thyme. The feather grass, fair haired and all fluffed up, swung its plume tresses haughtily. A flock of sheep came slowly down the hill towards Poplarovka. Old Zakhar walked away without saying another word, leaning on his stick. In the intricately designed towelling of dust lying on the road I could see tracks : one like a wolf's, step after step, rare and widespread; the other shredding the road with slanting stripes : the tracks of the Poplarovka tractor.

Where the summer track joins the forgotten, plantain-grown Hetman's highway the two tracks separated. The wolf-like track turned off to one side, into a ravine shaggy with green impenetrable thicket of scrub and thorn, leaving behind on the road the one track smelling of close and heavy paraffin fumes.

1926.

ALIEN BLOOD

THE first snow fell on St. Philip's day, after the fast. During the night a wind blew up across the Don; it made the faded mugwort rustle in the steppe, wove the shaggy snowdrifts into tresses, and licked the hummocky ridges of the roads quite bare.

Night enfolded the village in a greenish, dusky silence. Beyond the houses the steppe dozed, unploughed, overgrown with scrub.

At midnight a wolf howled faintly in a ravine, the dogs in the village replied, and old Gavrila woke up. Dropping his legs down over the side of the stove, clinging to the chimney breast, he sat coughing and coughing, then he spat out and felt for his tobacco pouch.

Every night the old man wakes up after the first cocks, sits and smokes and coughs, clearing his lungs of phlegm with a grunt; and in the intervals between his attacks of coughing his thoughts pass through his head along their customary, well-trodden path. Of one thing alone the old man thinks : of his son, vanished without trace in the war.

He had had only the one, the first and the last. He had worked for him without ever folding his arms. Then the time came to see him off to the front, to fight the Reds. The old man led two pairs of bullocks to the market, and with the proceeds bought a service horse from a Kalmik. It wasn't a horse, it was a flying steppe storm. He took a saddle out of the family chest, and his grandfather's bridle with its silver ornamentation. At the parting he said :

"Well, Piotr, I've done you proud : even an officer wouldn't be ashamed to have such horse harness. Serve as your father served, don't bring shame on the Cossack Army and the Quiet Don. Your grandfathers and great-grandfathers served the tsars, and so should you."

Now he gazed out of the window sprinkled with the green reflections of moonlight, listened to the wind rummaging about outside, seeking the unimaginable; he listened as he recalled the days that would never come back nor return.

To see the service man off, the cossacks thundered out the ancient cossack song under the reed-thatched roof of Gavrila's hut:

"But we fight, we never break our fighting order,
    We obey one command alone;
    And what our father-commanders have commanded us
    We follow, we sabre, we thrust, and we fight."

Piotr sat at the table, tipsy, with a bluish pallor on his cheeks; he drank his last glass, the 'stirrup cup,' with eyes screwed up wearily. But he sat his horse firmly. He adjusted his sabre and, bending down out of the saddle, picked up a handful of earth from his native yard. But where now does he lie, and whose earth in a strange land warms his breast?

The old man coughs long and painfully, the bellows in his chest creak and wheeze in various keys; but in the intervals, when he has finished coughing, he leans his crooked back against the chimney breast, and the thoughts pass through his head along their familiar, well-worn path.

*   *   *

He saw his son off, and a month later the Reds arrived. They burst into the ancient cossack way of life as enemies, turned the old man's normal existence inside out as if it were an empty pocket. Piotr was on the other side of the front; down by the Donietz River he had won non-commissioned officer's stripes through his zeal in battle; but away back in the village old Gavrila nursed, tended and developed a feeling for the Muscovites and the Reds just as he had once for his fair-haired little son Piotr; only now the feeling was an old man's dull and heavy hatred.

To spite them he wore his cossack striped trousers with the traditional crimson band of cossack freedom stitched with black stitches down the outer seams of the trouser legs. He dressed in his long cossack coat with its orange galloons denoting a guards regiment, and still showing the traces of the sergeant's stripes and shoulder straps he had worn in the old days. Across his chest he pinned the medals and crosses awarded him for serving the monarch in faith and truth; and on Sundays when he went to church

he threw the edges of his sheepskin coat wide open, so that everybody could see the medals.

One day when he happened to pass the village Soviet chairman
the official told Gavrila:

"Take those dangles off, old man. They're not allowed now."

Gavrila flashed up like gunpowder:

"Did you pin them on me, for you to order me to take them off?"

"I expect those who hung them on you have long been feeding
the worms."

"And let them. But I'm not taking them off. Would you tear
them off the dead?"

"That's a fine thing to say. I'm giving you advice because I'm
sorry for you. You can sleep in them for all I care. . . . But the
dogs . . . the dogs'll go for your trousers. They're no longer used
to seeing such things, they wouldn't recognize them."

That insult was as bitter as wormwood in flower. He took off
his medals; but his feeling of injury grew, it blossomed, and it
began to seem very much like spite.

His son was lost to knowledge; there was no one left to keep
things going for. The shed tumbled down, the cattle yard-fence
broke up, the rafters of the sheep shed began to rot under the
scrub roofing. In the stable, in the empty stalls, the mice went
about their domestic affairs; the mower went rusty under the overhang of the shed.

The cossacks had taken horses with them in their retreat; the
Reds removed whatever was left; and the last shaggy-legged and
long-eared animal, which the Reds had left in exchange, was
bought by the Makhno men at first sight in the autumn. In exchange they left the old man a pair of British puttees.

"We'll call them ours, now," the Makhno machine-gunner said
with a wink. "Grow rich on our goods, old man."

All Gavrila had accumulated over decades went to rack and ruin.
The work dropped from his hands. But in the spring, when the
baring steppe lay humble and exhausted underfoot, the earth called
to the old man, called him at night with a commanding though in-
audible call. He could not resist it; he harnessed bullocks into the
plough and drove off, to stripe the steppe with steel, to seed the
insatiable maw of the black earth with healthy, unbearded wheat.

The cossacks came back home from the sea and from overseas,

but not one of them had seen Piotr. They had served in different regiments from him, they had been in different parts—is Russia so small?—but the men who had been called up at the same time as Piotr had all fallen in a battle with a White detachment somewhere in the Kuban.

Gavrila hardly ever spoke to his wife about their son.

At night he heard her watering her pillow with tears, sniffing through her nose.

"What's the matter, old girl?" he would cough and ask.

For a moment or two she wouldn't answer, but then she'd reply : "The stove must be giving off fumes, my head seems to be swimming."

He did not reveal that he guessed what was really the trouble, but advised her :

"You should drink some of the water we've pickled the cucumbers in. Shall I go down into the cellar and get you some?"

"You get off to sleep. It'll pass anyway."

And once more silence spread an invisible, lacy web through the hut. The moon stared insolently through the window at their sorrow, and took pleasure in observing a mother's longing.

But they still waited and hoped their son would return. Gavrila put aside a sheepskin to be made up, and told his old woman :

"You and I'll get through somehow as we are; but if Piotr comes back what will he have to wear? Winter's coming on, I must get a sheepskin jacket made for him."

They had a sheepskin made up to Piotr's size and stowed it away in the family chest. They made working boots for him, for when he went to see to the cattle. The old man took great care of his own blue cloth uniform, and sprinkled it with tobacco to keep away the moths; but he slaughtered a lamb and stitched a cap of lamb's wool for his son, then hung it on a nail. He would come in from outside, glance at it, and get the feeling that at any moment Piotr might come smiling out of the best room and ask :

"Well, father, is it cold out?"

Two or three days later, as twilight was falling he went out to see to the animals. He threw hay into the manger, and was about to draw water from the well when he remembered he had left his woollen mittens in the house. He turned back, opened the door, and saw his old woman down on her knees by the bench, pressing the fur cap Piotr had never worn to her breast, and rocking it as one rocks a baby.

Everything went dark before his eyes; he rushed at her like an animal, threw her to the floor, and roared hoarsely, foaming at the mouth :

"Drop it, you good-for-nothing slut! Drop it. . . . What d'you think you're up to?"

He tore the cap out of her hands, flung it into the chest, and fastened the lid with the padlock. Not long after, he noticed that the old woman's left eye had developed a spasmodic twitch and her mouth was twisted.

The days and the weeks flowed past, the water flowed down the Don, in autumn translucently green and always rushing.

One day the edges of the river froze over, A gaggle of wild geese flew over the village. That evening the neighbour's lad ran to see Gavrila and said, hurriedly crossing himself before the ikon :

"Had a good day?"

"Praise be!"

"Have you heard the news, daddy? Prokhor Likhovidov's come back from Turkey. He served in the same regiment as your Piotr."

Gavrila hurried off down the alley, panting with coughing and his fast walk. He didn't find Prokhor at home : he had driven over to see his brother in a hamlet, and had promised to return by the next morning.

That night Gavrila couldn't sleep. He wore himself out on the stove with his sleeplessness.

He was up before the light, lit the floating wick, and sat down to sole a pair of felt boots.

The morning, pallidly impotent, spread a sickly light from the dove-grey east. The moon faded in the very zenith, she hadn't enough strength to get to the clouds and bury herself for the day.

*   *   *

Just before breakfast Gavrila happened to glance out of the window and said, for some reason speaking in a whisper :

"Here comes Prokhor."

Prokhor came in; he didn't look in the least like a cossack, he had quite a foreign appearance. English leather shoes were squeaking on his feet, and the coat of foreign cut, evidently taken from foreign shoulders, hung on him baggily.

"So you're still alive and well, Gavrila Vasilich?"

"Praise be to God, service-man! Come in and sit down."

Prokhor took off his cap, greeted Gavrila's wife and sat down on the bench beneath the ikons.

"Well, we've got some good weather, it's blown snow up, so much you can't get through it."

"Yes, it was snowing quite early this morning. In the old days the cattle would still be out to grass at this time of year."

For a minute there was an oppressive silence. Gavrila remarked in an ostensibly unconcerned and steady tone:

"You've aged in foreign lands, young man."

"There was nothing to make me younger, Gavrila Vasilich," Prokhor smiled.

Gavrila's wife opened her mouth and began to stammer:

"Our Piotr . . ."

"Shut up, woman!" Gavrila sternly shouted, "Let a man recover from the frost; you'll hear all in good time."

Turning to their visitor, he asked:

"Well, Prokhor Ignatich, what sort of life did you have?"

"Nothing to brag about. I dragged home like a cur with a broken back, and thank God even for so much."

"So-o-o! So you had a bad time with the Turk?"

"We had to use force to make ends meet." Prokhor began to drum on the table with his fingers. "All the same you've got older too, Gavrila Vasilich, your hair's sprinkled with grey. How do you find things under the Soviet régime?"

"Well, I'm waiting for my son . . . to provide food for us old people."

Prokhor hastily turned his eyes away. Gavrila noticed the movement, and asked straight out in a sharp voice:

"Tell us: where's Piotr?"

"Why, haven't you heard then?"

"We've heard all sorts of things," Gavrila snapped back.

Prokror kneaded the dirty fringe of the tablecloth with his fingers, and didn't answer at once.

"It was in January, I think. . . . Well, yes, it was January. Our company was quartered not far from Novorossisk. There's a town of that name down on the coast. . . . Well, we were just quartered there as usual. . . ."

"Tell me, was he killed?" Gavrila asked in a low whisper, leaning forward.

Prokhor didn't raise his eyes, and didn't reply; perhaps he didn't hear the question.

"We were quartered there, but the Reds broke through to the hills, to join up with the Greens. Our company commander sent your Piotr out in charge of a reconnaissance. Our commander was a Lieutenant Senin. . . . And something happened . . . you understand?"

At the stove an iron pot fell with a ringing crash. Stretching out her hands, the old woman went over to the bed; a cry tore from her breast.

"Don't howl!" Gavrila barked in a threatening tone and, leaning his elbows on the table, looking Prokhor straight in the eyes, slowly and wearily got out the words: "Well, tell us the rest."

"They sabred him," Prokhor cried, turning pale. He stood up and groped over the table for his cap. "They sabred him to death. The reconnaissance halted close to a forest to give the horses a breather, he loosened the saddle girth, and the Reds came out of the forest. . . ." The words were choking Prokhor, he crumpled his cap with trembling fingers. "Piotr caught hold of the saddle bow, but the saddle slipped under the horse's belly. . . . It was a fiery horse, it couldn't stand it, and he was left behind. . . . And that's all there is to tell."

"But supposing I don't believe it?" Gavrila said, distinctly articulating every syllable.

Prokhor went hurriedly to the door, and said without looking back:

"As you like, Gavrila Vasilich; but I'm telling the truth. . . . By the true God. . . . The naked truth. . . . I saw it happen with my own eyes. . . ."

"But supposing I don't wish to believe it?" Gavrila hoarsely croaked, going livid. His eyes flushed with blood and tears. Tearing his shirt open at the collar, he advanced towards Prokhor with his bare, hairy chest exposed, and groaned, thrusting forward his sweating head: "My only son killed? Our breadwinner? My little

Piotr? You're lying, you son of a bitch. D'you hear. You're lying. I don't believe a word you say."

But that night, throwing his sheepskin jacket round his shoulders, he went out into the yard. His felt boots scrunching and squeaking in the snow, he strode to the threshing-floor and stood by a stack.

The wind blew in from the steppe, sprinkling snow down. Darkness, black and stern, gathered in the naked cherry trees.

"Little son!" Gavrila called under his breath. He waited a moment, then, without moving, not even turning his head, he called again : "Piotr! My dear little son!"

Then he stretched himself out on the snow trampled down around the stack and heavily closed his eyes.

*　　　　*　　　　*

In the village there was talk of food requisitioning, and of bandits who were advancing from the lower reaches of the Don. At the village meetings in the Executive Committee house the news was passed around in whispers. But old Gavrila never set foot on the rickety veranda of the Executive Committee house, he had no need to; and so there was a great deal he never heard, a great deal he didn't know. It seemed wildly incredible to him when after mass one Sunday the village Soviet chairman called, and with him three men in short chrome-yellow jerkins, who were carrying rifles.

The chairman shook hands with Gavrila and shot out at once, like a smack on the nape :

"Now, admit it, old man, you've got grain stored away, haven't you?"

"Why, what did you think : we're fed by the Holy Spirit?"

"Don't snap like that, but tell us straight out : where's your grain?"

"In the granary, of course."

"Show us it."

"Allow me to ask what interest you have in my grain?"

A hefty, flaxen-haired man, evidently the chief of the three armed men, tapped his heels in the frosty snow, and answered :

"We're taking all the surplus grain for the benefit of the state. Food requisitioning. Ever heard of it, daddy?"

"But supposing I don't hand it over?" Gavrila said hoarsely, swelling up with fury.

"If you don't. . . . We'll take it ourselves."

The three armed men whispered together with the chairman, then went to the granary and climbed into the bins, dropping clumps of snow from their boots into the clean, darkly golden wheat. As he lit a cigarette the fair-haired man decided:

"Leave enough for seed and food, and take the rest." With a husbandman's appraising eye he estimated the quantity of grain in the bins and turned to Gavrila:

"How many acres do you intend to sow?"

"I'll sow the devil's bald patch," Gavrila hissed, coughing and grimacing horribly. "Take it, damn the lot of you. Steal it. It's all yours."

"What's the matter, losing your wits, or what? Come to your senses, daddy Gavrila," the chairman pleaded, waving his woollen mitten at the old man.

"May you choke with other people's property. May you burst!"

The fair-haired man tore a half-melted icicle from his whisker, shot an intelligent, humorous glance sidelong at Gavrila, and said with a quiet smile:

"You needn't dance like that, father. Shouting won't help. What are you screeching for? Has someone trodden on your tail?" Frowning, he suddenly changed his tone: "Don't let your tongue wag. If it's so long you'd better tie it to your teeth. For this sort of propaganda . . ." He didn't finish his sentence, but slapped his hand down on the yellow pistol holster stuck into his belt, and said more gently: "Take your grain to the collection point this very day."

Possibly the old man was frightened, certainly at the sharp and confident tone of the flaxen-haired man he softened up, and realized that shouting really was of no use. He waved his hand in despair and went towards the veranda. But he was hardly halfway across the yard when a savagely hoarse shout made him start:

"Where's the food detachment commander?"

Gavrila swung round. A horseman was reining in his prancing horse on the other side of the fence. A presentiment that something unusual was about to happen made the old man's legs tremble below the knees. Before he could open his mouth, the horseman noticed the group still standing by the granary, violently checked his prancing horse, and with an almost imperceptible movement of the hand slung the rifle off his back.

There was a ringing shot, and, in the silence which descended on the yard immediately after that shot, Gavrila distinctly heard the rifle bolt pulled back; the cartridge case flew out with a buzzing hum.

The moment of stupefaction passed: pressing close to the door post the fair-haired man drew his revolver slowly, almost casually from its holster; the chairman, squatting down like a hare in its form, rushed through the yard into the threshing-floor; one of the requisitioning detachment dropped to one knee, sending a bullet from his carbine into the black fur cap swaying on the farther side of the fence. The yard was lashed with the sound of firing. Gavrila tore his reluctant feet with difficulty out of the snow and heavily trotted to the veranda. Looking back, he saw the three men in leather jackets scattering, running towards the threshing-floor, getting stuck in the snow drifts, while horsemen poured through the gate which someone had flung wide open.

The foremost rider, on a bay stallion and wearing a Kuban fur cap, bent low over his saddle bow and whirled his sword above his head. The ends of his white cowl flickered before Gavrila's eyes like swan's wings, and snow flung up by the horse's hoofs sprinkled into his face.

He leaned impotently against the fretted veranda rail and watched as the bay stallion gathered itself up and flew across the wattle fence; then it swung round on its hind hoofs by the patched rick of barley straw. The man in the Kuban cap, hanging right out of the saddle, slashed with his sword from right to left and from left to right at the food detachment officer as he crawled along.

From the threshing-floor came a broken, indistinct hubbub, scuffling; someone gave a prolonged, sobbing cry. A minute later a single shot sounded heavily in the air. The pigeons, which had been frightened by the firing but had settled again on the roof of the granary, started up in a violent shower. The horsemen dismounted in the threshing-floor.

The crimson sound of church bells jangled incessantly over the village. The village idiot had climbed up into the belfry and, acting on his own stupid reasoning, had seized the clapper ropes of all the bells, so that instead of sounding the alarm he was ringing out a merry Eastertide dance.

The Kuban came up to Gavrila. His white cowl was flung back over his shoulder, his hot, sweaty face was twitching, the corners of his lips dribbled with spittle.

"Any oats?"

Crushed by all he had witnessed, unable to control his petrified tongue, Gavrila shifted with difficulty away from the veranda rail.

"Gone deaf, you devil? Any oats, I asked you. Bring a sack out."

Before they had time to lead their horses up to the trough filled with fodder yet another man galloped into the yard.

"To horse! Infantry coming down the hill!"

With an oath the Kuban bridled his still-steaming and sweating stallion, clawed up a handful of snow and with it rubbed hard at the cuff of his right sleeve, which was thickly smeared with a purplish red patch.

All five of them rode out of the yard. As the last man went out Gavrila recognized the fair-haired food detachment commander's yellow, bloodstained jerkin rolled in the rider's saddlestraps.

*   *   *

Until the oncoming of evening shots rattled and rolled in the Thorny Ravine over the hill. In the village, a whipped cur, silence had settled humbly. The shadows were turning blue when Gavrila forced himself to go out to the threshing-floor. He passed through the wide open wicket gate, and on the threshing-floor drying rack saw the chairman hanging with head downward, caught by a bullet. His hanging arms seemed to be reaching after his cap, which had fallen on the farther side of the rack.

Not far from the rick the three men of the food detachment lay side by side, stripped to their underwear, on the snow amid scraps of food and rubbish. As he looked at them Gavrila no longer felt the fury he had nursed since morning in his now quivering, horrified heart. It seemed unbelievable, a dream, that in his threshing-floor, where the neighbour's goats regularly played robbers, tugging out great tufts of straw, three sabred men were now lying; and that the scent of decay was already rising from them, from the pools of half-frozen, bubbly blood.

The fair-haired man lay with his head twisted unnaturally to one side; and but for that head pressed hard against the snow one would have thought he was lying there to rest, so carefree was the expression conveyed by his legs flung out one behind the other.

The second man, gap-toothed and black whiskered, was bent down with his head huddled between his shoulders, baring his teeth adamantly and furiously. The third, his head buried in the straw of the stack, seemed to be floating motionless over the snow : so much strength and tension were conveyed in the dead sweep of his arms.

Gavrila bent down over the fair-haired man, glanced into the darkened face, and was shaken with pity : below him was lying not the angry, prickly-eyed food commissar, but a lad some nineteen years old. Under the yellowish fluff of the whiskers around his lips the hoar-frost had frozen a mournful smile; but a little frown showed darkly, deep and stern, across the brow.

The old man aimlessly touched the bare chest with his hand and started back in astonishment : through the superficial chill his palm was conscious of a fading but perceptible warmth.

His old woman moaned and, crossing herself, fell back to the stove when Gavrila, grunting and groaning, brought in the rigid, bloodstained body on his back.

He laid the form on the bench, washed it with cold water, and rubbed the legs, the arms, the chest with a prickly woollen sock until he was tired and sweating. He put his ear down to the repellently cold chest and, straining his hearing, caught the faint, irregular beating of the heart.

*   *   *

Four days the lad lay in the best room, his colour a saffron yellow, like a corpse. The wound crossing his brow and cheek with congealed blood showed up livid; the blanket rose and fell as, with a wheezing and gurgling, the tightly-bound chest drew in breath.

Every day Gavrila put his gnarled, cracked finger into the man's lips, cautiously forced the clenched teeth open with the end of a knife, and the old woman poured warmed milk and a broth of sheep's bones down through a reed.

In the morning of the fourth day a flush spread over the fair-haired man's cheeks; by mid-day his face was flaming like a hawthorn bush caught by the frost, a violent trembling shook his body, and under his shirt a cold, clammy sweat larded the skin.

From that moment he began to talk quietly and incoherently in delirium, and tried to jump out of the bed. Day and night Gavrila and his wife watched beside him, turn by turn.

During the long winter nights, when the east wind, blowing from the Don basin, troubled the darkened sky and chilly clouds spread low over the village, Gavrila sat on and on beside the wounded man, his head resting on his hands, listening to the delirious babble in a strange, open-vowelled dialect; he stared long and long at the swarthy triangle of sunburn on the chest, at the azure lids of the closed eyes ringed with blue horseshoes. And when prolonged groans flowed from the faded lips, followed by a hoarse command and hideous oaths, and when the face was contorted with pain and anger, the tears grew hot in Gavrila's chest. At such times pity came uninvited.

Gavrila saw his wife going pale and more withered with every day, with every sleepless night by the bed; he noticed, too, the tears on her furrowed cheeks, and realized, or rather felt with his heart, that her unwept love for Piotr, her dead son, had flung itself like a flame on this motionless, death-kissed son of another mother. . . .

One day the commander of a regiment passing through the village turned into their yard. He left his horse with an orderly at the gate, and ran up the steps on to the veranda, his sabre and spurs clattering. In the best room he took off his cap and stood a long time silent by the bed. Pallid shadows wandered over the wounded man's face; from the lips, burning with fire, a little blood was oozing. The commander shook his prematurely grizzled head, his eyes clouded with sorrow. Gazing past Gavrila, he said:

"Look after the comrade, old man."

"We'll look after him," Gavrila said firmly.

The days and the weeks flowed past. Christmas came and went. On the sixteenth day the fair-haired youngster opened his eyes for the first time, and Gavrila heard a voice, a spidery creaking:

"Is it you, old man?"

"Yes, it's me."

"Have they given me a good carving up?"

"Christ forbid."

Gavrila thought he saw a sneer, though spitelessly simple, in his transparent gaze.

"But how about my lads?"

"Those others . . . they buried them on the square."

He silently ran his fingers over the blanket and shifted his gaze to the unpainted boards of the ceiling.

"What are we to call you?" Gavrila asked.

The eyelids, finely blue veined, dropped wearily :

"Nikolai."

"Well, but we shall call you Piotr. We had a son . . . Piotr. . . ." Gavrila explained.

He sat thinking, and was about to ask something else; but he heard an even, nasal breathing and, throwing out his arms to balance himself, tiptoed away from the bed.

*   *   *

Life returned to the lad slowly, as though reluctant. Two months later he still had difficulty in raising his head from the pillow. Bedsores appeared on his back.

As each day passed, Gavrila realized with a feeling of horror that he was growing intimately attached to this new Piotr, while the picture of the first, the son of his loins, was fading, growing dim, like the reflection of the setting sun on the mica window of the hut. He tried to call back his former yearning and pain; but those other features drew farther and farther away, so much so that he felt ashamed and awkward. He went out into the yard and fidgeted about for hours; but then, remembering that his old woman was sitting constantly by Piotr's bed, he had a feeling of jealousy. He went into the hut, silently shifted from foot to foot at the head of the bed, with rigid fingers awkwardly adjusted the pillow and, catching his wife's angry glance, humbly sat down on the bench and was still.

The old woman fed Piotr on marmot fat and an infusion of healing herbs picked in the spring, in their May blossoming.

Whether this was the cause, or youth overcame his infirmity, the wounds healed into scars, the blood flushed his filling cheeks; only the right hand, with the bone mutilated at the forearm, mended badly : evidently it had finished its work for life.

Even so, during the second week of Lent, Piotr sat up in bed for the first time without assistance and, amazed at his own strength, smiled long and distrustfully.

That night, in the kitchen there was a fit of coughing on the stove, and then a whispered:

"Are you asleep, old lady?"

"Why, what d'you want?"

"Our lad's getting on to his feet. You take Piotr's trousers out of the chest tomorrow. Have everything ready. He's got nothing to wear."

"I don't need you to tell me that. I got them out the other day."

"Why, you're smart. And did you take out the sheepskin jacket?"

"Of course; is the lad to go around in his underwear?"

Gavrila fidgeted about a bit on the stove, and almost dozed off. But he remembered something else, and exultantly raised his head.

"But how about the fur cap? I suppose you forgot the fur cap, you old gander?"

"Get away! You've passed it forty times and haven't noticed it. It's been hanging on the nail ever since yesterday."

The discomfited Gavrila coughed and said no more.

The precipitate spring was already ruffling the Don. The ice turned back, as though worm-eaten, and swelled spongily. The hill was bared of snow. The snow retreated from the steppe into the ravines and hollows. The Don basin melted out and was flooded with sunlit floodwater. The wind plentifully spread the scent of bitter wormwood from the steppe.

It was the end of March.

*   *   *

"I shall get up today, father."

Although all the Red Army men who crossed Gavrila's threshold invariably called him father after one look at his hair neatly sprinkled with grey, Gavrila now detected a warmer note in the voice. Maybe he imagined it, but maybe Piotr did really say the word with a filial caress in his tone. Anyway, Gavrila flushed deeply, began to cough, and muttered, concealing his embarrassed joy:

"Time you did, Piotr. You've been lying there three months."

Piotr went out on to the veranda, moving his legs as if they were stilts, and almost choked with the excess of air which the wind forced into his lungs. Gavrila supported him from the back, while the old woman fussed around the veranda, wiping away her customary tears with her apron.

As he walked pass the serrated roof of the granary, the chosen son, Piotr, asked:

"Did they take the grain that time?"

"They did," Gavrila reluctantly snorted.

"Well, but they did the right thing, father."

And again Gavrila felt a warmth around his heart at the word 'father'.

Every day now Piotr crawled outside, limping and leaning on a stick. And from everywhere—from the threshing-floor, from under the shed pent-roof, wherever he happened to be—Gavrila watched his new son with a restless, searching gaze. As though afraid he might stumble and fall.

They didn't talk much to each other, but their relationships grew simple and affectionate.

Some days after Piotr's first walk out of doors, as Gavrila was making up his bed on the stove he turned and asked:

"Where do you come from, sonny?"

"The Urals."

"Son of a peasant?"

"No, working class."

"But what sort? Did you work at some trade, such as a cobbler or cooper?"

"No, father, I worked in a factory, an iron foundry. Ever since I was a kid."

"But this grain-collecting job, how did you come to be in that?"

"I was sent from the army."

"Why, were you a commander with them?"

"Yes, I was."

Gavrila found it difficult to ask the next question, but it was what he had been leading up to:

"So you're a party man?"

"A communist," Piotr replied with a frank smile.

And because of that simple smile the strange word no longer had any terror for Gavrila.

The old woman, who had been biding her time, asked interestedly:

"But have you got a family, Piotr, my dear?"

"Not even the smell of powder! I'm as alone as the moon in the sky."

"I suppose your parents are dead then?"

"When I was quite small, seven years old. . . . My father was killed in a drunken brawl, but my mother's dragging around somewhere."

"What a bitch! So she abandoned you, you poor little one?"

"She went off with some contractor or other, and I grew up in the works."

Gavrila let his feet hang down from the stove, and was a long time silent. Then he began to say, distinctly and slowly:

"Why, then, sonny, if you haven't any family, you stay with us. We had a son, we've called you Piotr after him. We had him and he grew up in the old days; but now the two of us, me and my old woman, we're just playing blind man's buff. During all these months we've known so much sorrow because of you, you must have come to be fond of us. Though your blood isn't ours, our souls sorrow over you as if you were our own flesh and blood. Stay with us. We and you will get our food from the land; our land along the Don is fruitful, it's bountiful. We'll set you up, we'll find you a wife. I've had my day, the farm will be yours for you to run. After me, so long as you show respect for our age and don't refuse us a bite of food before we die. Don't go away and leave us, Piotr."

A cricket trilled behind the stove, grating and boring.

Under the wind the shutters groaned yearningly.

"And my old woman and I have already started to look for a bride for you," Gavrila winked with forced cheerfulness. But his quivering lips were twisted into a miserable smile.

Piotr gazed stubbornly down at his feet planted on the scoured floor, he drummed drily on the bench with his left hand. The resulting noise was sharp and disturbing: tuk-tik-tak; took-tik-tak. . . .

He was obviously thinking over his reply. Having decided, he stopped the tapping and shook his head.

"I'll remain with you with pleasure, father; only, as you can see for yourself, I'll be a poor sort of worker. My hand, my food-giver, will not grow properly, the blighter. All the same I'll work as well as I can. I'll stay through the summer, and then we'll see."

"And then, maybe, you'll remain for good," Gavrila ended.

The spinning wheel, worked by the treadle under the old woman's foot, hummed merrily; it purred away as it wound the fibrous wool on to the spindle.

Whether it sang a lullaby, whether it promised a plentiful life with its measured, soporific rattle I wouldn't know.

*   *   *

The spring was followed by days scorched with sunlight, days curly and grey with the rich steppe dust. The fine weather set in for a long spell. The Don, as boisterous as youth, was ridged with bridling rollers. The flood water brought drink to the huts on the outskirts of the village. The Don basin showed greenish white; the wind was saturated with the honeyed scent of flowering poplars; in the meadowland a lake glowed with rosy dawns and sunsets; its surface was sprinkled with the fallen petals of crab-apple blossom. Of a night the summer lightnings winked to one another like maidens; and the nights were as short as the fiery reflections of the lightning. The bullocks were given no time for rest from the long working day. Emaciated cattle, their ribs sticking through their skin, grazed in the pasturage.

Gavrila and Piotr lived for weeks on end in the steppe. They ploughed, they harrowed, they sowed, they spent the nights under their waggon, lying covered with the one great sheepskin coat; but Gavrila never revealed to the lad how strongly he was attached by invisible strings to his new son. Fairhaired, cheerful, hardworking, the new Piotr eclipsed the image of the dead. Gavrila's memory recalled him more and more rarely. He never had time to recall him when working.

The days passed stealthily, with an imperceptible tread. The time of haymow drew near.

One morning Piotr set to work on the mower. To Gavrila's astonishment he set and sharpened the blades in the smithy. and made new flails in place of the old, broken ones. He was busy over the mower from early morning; but when dust fell he went off to the Executive Committee : he had been summoned to some conference. Meanwhile Gavrila's wife, who had gone to draw water, brought a letter back from the post. It was stained and old, and addressed to Gavrila to be handed to comrade Nikolai Kosikh.

Tormented by a vague anxiety, Gavrila turned the letter with its sprawling writing, written in a sweeping hand with a copying ink pencil, over and over in his hands.

He held it up and looked at it by the light. But the envelope jealously preserved its secret, and he involuntarily began to feel a feeling of spite for this message which had come to disturb his normal peace of mind.

For a moment he thought of tearing it up; but, after thinking it over, he decided to give it to Piotr. He met him at the door with the news :

"There's a letter come for you from somewhere or other, son."

"For me?" Piotr was astonished.

"Yes. Go and read it."

Lighting the light in the hut, with a keen, searching gaze Gavrila watched Piotr's face; it lit up as he read the letter. The old man could not control his impatience, and had to ask :

"Where's it from?"

"The Urals."

"Who wrote it?" the old woman asked inquisitively.

"My comrades in the foundry."

Gavrila felt anxious.

"What are they writing about?"

Piotr's eyes darkened and faded; he answered reluctantly :

"They're calling me back to the foundry. They're planning to put it into operation again. It's been standing idle ever since 1917."

"Well, then? I suppose you'll go?" Gavrila asked huskily.

"I don't know. . . ."

*   *   *

Piotr's face went peaked, sunken and yellow. Gavrila heard him sighing and tossing on his bed of a night. After long meditation, the old man realized that Piotr could not make his life in the village; he couldn't turn over the virgin black earth of the steppe with the ploughshare. The foundry which had brought him up would take him away sooner or later, and once more the joyless, unsociable days would hobble past in mournful succession. Gavrila would gladly have scattered the hateful foundry brick by brick and laid it level with the ground, so that nettles grew over it and scrub flourished.

Three days later, during the haymow, when they met by the waggon to have a drink, Piotr spoke out:

"I can't stay here, father. I shall go back to the foundry. It calls me, it's troubling my mind. . . ."

"Are you having such a bad life then?"

"That's not the point. When Kolchak advanced we defended our works for ten days. The Kolchak men hanged nine of us the moment they occupied the settlement. But now the workers who've returned from the army are putting the foundry on its feet again. They're half starving, and their families too, but they're working. So how can I go on living here? What of my conscience?"

"How will you manage? With one hand that's useless?"

"That's strange talk from you, father. There every hand is valuable."

"I won't keep you back. You go," Gavrila replied, plucking up his courage. "But take my old woman in, tell her you'll come back. Say you'll spend a little time there and then you'll came back; otherwise she'll start grieving and that'll be the end of her. . . . You're all we have."

Clinging to his last hope, he added in a whisper, breathing spasmodically and hoarsely:

"But perhaps you will come back in very truth? Well? Won't you have pity on our old age, eh?"

*   *   *

The waggon creaked, the oxen paced along out of step, a crumbling, floury powder flew up from under the wheels with a swishing sound. The road wound along by the Don, and turned leftward by a shrine. From the turn they could see the churches of the district town and the green, intricate embroidery of gardens and orchards.

All along the road Gavrila chattered without stopping. He tried to smile.

"Near this spot three years back some girls were drowned in the Don. That's why the shrine was put here." He pointed his whip towards the despondent top of the shrine. "This is where we say goodbye. There's no road further on, the hill has caved in. It's less than a mile from here to the town, you'll get there taking it gently."

Piotr adjusted the strap of his wallet of food and slipped down from the waggon. Choking back his sobs, Gavrila flung the knout to the ground and held out two shaking arms.

"Goodbye, my own lad. Without you the bright sun will fade for us." His face distorted with pain and wet with tears, he raised his voice to a shout: "You haven't forgotten the cakes for the road, have you, sonny? The old woman baked them for you. . . . You haven't forgotten them? Well, goodbye. . . . Goodbye, my dear, my only little son."

Piotr limped away, almost running along the narrow verge of the road.

"Come back!" Gavrila cried, clinging to the waggon.

"He'll never come back," the unwept words choked in his chest.

The dear, fairhaired head showed clearly for a last time at a turn in the road; for a last time Piotr waved his cap; and in the spot where he had set his feet the wind idiotically blew up the whitish, smoky dust and sent it spinning.

1926.

A MORTAL ENEMY

THE cold, orange-coloured sun had not yet disappeared beyond the sharply outlined horizon. But the moon, flooded with gold in the deep azure of the sunset sky, was already confidently slipping up from the east and decorating the fresh snow with shadowy, dove-grey hues.

The smoke rose from the chimneys in curling, melting columns; the hamlet was redolent of burning scrub and ash. The cry of the ravens was dry and distinct. Night came on from the steppe, intensifying the colours, and the sun had hardly set when a little twinkling star, shy and embarrassed like a bride under her first scrutiny by a prospective bridegroom's parents, hung over the well-crane.

After supper Yefim went out, drew his shabby greatcoat closer round him, turned up the collar and, bristling with the cold, strode swiftly down the street. Just before he reached the old school building he turned into an alley and entered the last yard. He opened the door into the passage and listened : he heard talk and laughter in the hut. The conversation stopped the moment he threw open the door. Tobacco smoke was swirling round by the stove; a calf in the middle of the kitchen sent a fine stream on to the earthen floor, reluctantly turned its lop-eared head at the sound of the creaking door, and lowed brokenly.

"Hallo, everybody."

"Praise be !" Two voices answered separately.

Yefim cautiously stepped across the pool flowing from under the calf, and sat down on a bench. Turning to the stove, where the men were smoking, squatting on their haunches, he asked :

"Won't we be having the meeting soon?"

"Well, you can see how they're turning up. There's not many arrived yet," the master of the hut replied. He smacked the straddling calf and sprinkled sand over the wet floor.

Ignat Borshchov, who was squatting by the stove, put out his cigarette and, sending a greenish spittle through his teeth, came across and sat down beside Yefim.

"Well, Yefim, you're to be chairman. We'd been sorting it all out before you arrived," he smiled and stroked his beard.

"I shall wait a little longer."

"What's that?"

"I'm afraid we won't manage it."

"Somehow or other. . . . You're just the right lad: you were in the Red Army, you come from the poorer class. . . ."

"You need one of your own men. . . ."

"And what d'you mean by that?"

"Why, someone who'd hold up your arms. Someone who'd gaze into the eyes of prosperous people like you and would dance to your pipe."

Ignat coughed, and his eyes flashed under his fur cap. He winked at the men squatting by the stove.

"That's almost right. . . . Men like you aren't needed by us even as a gift. Who's the man that's always fighting the village assembly? Yefim. Who is it sticks in the people's throats like a bone? Yefim. Who is earning promotion by his services to the poor? Again and again, Yefim."

"I shan't do any service to the kulaks."

"We're not asking you to."

Vlas Timofeevich, who was by the stove, blew out a cloud of smoke and began to speak in measured tones:

"We haven't any kulaks in our village, but we have got people who're naked and barefoot. But as for you, Yefim, we shall elect you to another position. Minding the cattle in the spring, for instance, or looking after the vegetable plots."

Ignat choked with laughter, waving his mitten; the men by the stove laughed in raucous unison. When the laughter stopped, Ignat wiped away the spittle dribbling over his beard. Yefim's face had turned pale. Clapping him on his back, Ignat told him:

"That's quite right, Yefim; we're kulaks, we're this and we're that. But when spring comes all your poor people, all the proletariat will be taking off their caps and coming to me, the old this and that, with a low bow: 'Ignat Mikhailich, plough an acre for us. Ignat Mikhailich, for the love of Christ lend me a measure of millet till harvest time. . . .' And why should we? That's just the point. You do him a good turn, the son of a bitch, and instead of being grateful he sends in a complaint about you: 'you've concealed the amount you've sowed to avoid taxation.' But what am I bound to pay your state for? If it's got nothing in its purse let it come and beg under the window : maybe someone will throw it something."

"Did you give Dunia Vorobiova a measure of millet last spring?" Yefim asked, his mouth working convulsively.

"I did."

"And how much work did she do for you in return?"

"That's nothing to do with you," Ignat burst out sharply.

"All through the summer she bowed her back over your meadow. And her girls watered your garden," Yefim cried.

"But who was it handed in a complaint about my concealing my sowings in front of all the village assembly?" Vlas roared from his position by the stove.

"And if you try to cover it up again I'll do it again."

"We'll close your mouth for you. You won't talk too much."

"Remember, Yefim, the man who doesn't serve the community is the enemy of God himself."

"For you, for the poor, the sleeves; but for us the sheepskin coat."

Gazing at them from under lowering brows, Yefim rolled a cigarette with trembling hands and smiled sarcastically.

"No, respected elders of the village, you've had your day. You've finished flowering. We've set up a Soviet government now, and we're not going to allow anyone to set their foot on the throats of the poor. It won't be like it was last year : then you managed to get all the black earth for yourselves and left us with the sandy soil. But now it's not your dance that will be danced. Under the Soviet government we're no longer stepsons."

Ignat was livid and terrible, his brows were knitted, his features twisted with a malevolent look. He raised his hand.

"Take care you don't stumble, Yefim. Don't stand in our way. As we have lived, so we shall live. But you step back."

"I won't."

"If you don't, we'll make you. We'll tear you up by the roots, like filthy weeds. You're no friend and no fellow villager of ours; you're a mortal enemy, you're a mad dog.

The door was flung open and a dozen or so people pushed their way in through clouds of steam. The women crossed themselves before the ikons and drew to one side; the cossacks took off their fur caps, grunting as they pulled the frozen icicles from their whiskers. Half an hour later, when the kitchen and best room were packed with people, the chairman of the electoral commission stood up behind the table and said in a matter-of-fact tone :

"I declare the general meeting of the citizens of Podgornoe hamlet open. Would you please elect a committee to carry on the main meeting."

* * *

At midnight, when it was almost impossible to breathe for tobacco smoke, the women were choking with coughs, and the lamp was winking and guttering, the secretary of the meeting stared with bleary eyes at a paper, and exclaimed :

"I have to announce the list of those elected as members of our Soviet. The following have been elected by a majority of votes : first, Prokhor Rvachev; second, Yefim Oziorov. . . ."

* * *

Yefim went to the stable and put down hay for the mare. He came back, and had hardly set foot on the boards of the veranda, which squeaked with frost under his boots, when the cock in the shed began to crow. Yellow sprinkles of stars danced over the black floor of heaven. Right overhead the Great Bear was fading. "Midnight", Yefim thought, as he put his hand to the latch. Someone came along the passage to the door, shuffling in felt boots, and called :

"Who's there?"

"It's me, Masha. Open the door, quick."

Yefim shut the door firmly behind him and struck a match. The wick floating in a saucer of sheep fat spluttered smokily. Taking off his greatcoat, he bent over the cradle hanging by the bed, and his forehead smoothed out, a gentle fold appeared around his mouth; his lips, blue with the cold, whispered their usual caress. His six-month-old firstborn, rosy with sleep, lay wrapped in rags, its chest bare to the waist, its chubby little arms thrown out. On the pillow beside its head was a bottle tightly packed with masticated bread.

Gently pushing one hand under the hot little back, Yefim called to his wife in a whisper:

"Come and change his bed, the dirty kid's wetted himself."

While she was taking down a dry napkin from the stove, Yefim said in an undertone:

"Masha, they've gone and elected me secretary."

"Well, but how about Ignat and the others?"

"They were dead against me. But the poor are with me to the last man."

"Watch out, Yefim, that you don't bring sorrow on us."

"The sorrow won't be on me but on them. Now they'll start trying to put me down. And Ignat's son-in-law's been made chairman."

*   *   *

From the day of the new elections, life in Podgornoe was as though someone had ploughed a furrow right through the village and divided the people into two hostile groups. In the one group were Yefim and the village poor, in the other Ignat with his son-in-law Vlas, the village chairman, together with the owner of the watermill, four or five rich cossacks and some of the medium well-off peasants.

"They'll tread us into the mud," Ignat stormed during the Sunday sit-arounds. "I know what Yefim's after. He wants to level us all down. Have you heard the song he sang to Fiodka, the cobbler? He said they're going to start communal ploughing, we shall all work the land together, and maybe we'll buy a tractor. Oh, no! First, you work and get four pairs of bullocks, and then you can be my equal; but as things are now you own nothing but lice in your trousers. In my view, we can spit on their tractor. Our grandfathers managed well without it."

One late Sunday afternoon there was a little gathering of people in Ignat's yard. The talk turned to the reallocation of the land which was to take place in the spring. Ignat, who had had a little to drink in celebration of the holiday, shook his head and, belching with illicit home-distilled vodka, circled and hovered round Ivan Donskov.

"Look, Ivan, you think it over like a good neighbour. For instance, what d'you need land by the Perenosny pond for? Why, for

God's sake! It's very rich soil there, it has to be ploughed and tilled properly. But what sort of mess will you plough with your one yoke of oxen? The Soviets regard you as a medium cossack, that means you stand between Yefim and me. So you think it over, whom will it be better for you to be on good terms with? I'm talking to you for your own good, as a neighbour. What d'you want land by the pond for?"

Ivan thrust one finger behind his faded waistband and asked frankly and sternly:

"What are you getting at?"

"I'm talking about the land. . . . You judge for yourself, the land's so rich and heavy. . . ."

"So in your view we can do our sowing on the white clay?"

"There you go again! Talking about the clay. . . . Why on the clay? It can be taken into consideration. . . ."

"The soil by the pond is rich. . . . You watch out, old Ignat, or you'll choke yourself with your rich soil." Ivan turned sharply on his heel and walked away.

For some time there was an awkward silence among those left in Ignat's yard.

But on the outskirts of the hamlet, in Fiodka, the cobbler's hut, that very same evening, Yefim, sweating and crimson, tossing his hair, waved his hands furiously.

"Today it isn't a question of writing, but of acting. These village correspondents have multiplied just like flies. They push their way into the papers with facts and fairy tales, until sometimes it makes you sick to read them. But I ask you, how many of them have achieved anything? Instead of snivelling and running under the government's skirts, like children to their mother, you show the kulaks your fist. What? To the devil's dam with them! Under the Soviet régime the poor shouldn't be sucking at the titties for ever, it's time they went about the world for themselves. Without help, that's the point. I've been elected a member of the Soviet, and now we'll see who beats whom."

*   *   *

The night gathered awkwardly in the darkness of the alleyways, in the orchards, over the steppe. With a brigand whistle the wind tore along the streets, toussled the bare, frost-bound trees, insolently peered under the eaves of the buildings, ruffled up the feathers of the sleeping sparrows and set them in their sleep recalling the sultry heat of June, ripe, dew-washed cherries, dung maggots and other tasty things which we human beings never dream of in the winter nights.

By the school enclosure the fires of cigarettes glowed in the darkness. At times the wind snatched the ash away with a shower of sparks and diligently carried them upward until they faded, and again the darkness and silence, the silence and darkness trembled over the deeply violet snow.

One man silently smoked, leaning against the palisade, his sheepskin jacket thrown open. The other stood beside him, his head drawn down between his shoulders.

"Well, what do you think?"

"He's in the way. His father-in-law has a single daughter who works for us, and the other day he started intriguing. 'Have they concluded an agreement with her?' he asks. 'I don't know,' I told him. But he turns and says: 'Well, you as the chairman ought to know; they don't pat you on the head for not knowing.'"

"Shall we clear him out of the road?"

"We'll have to."

"But supposing they find out?"

"We'll have to cover our tracks."

"So when then?"

"Come along to my place, and we'll talk it over."

"The devil knows! It's rather frightening. Killing a man isn't like chewing and spitting."

"You idiot, it can't be done any other way. Don't you see, he may ruin the whole village. If you report your sowings correctly they'll strip your hide off you with taxes, and then the land. . . . He's at the bottom of all the agitation among the poor. . . . With him out of the way we'll squeeze the ragged arses like this!"

There was the sound of fingers cracking in the darkness as they were clenched into a fist. The wind caught up a savage curse.

"Well, will you come in with us, or won't you?"

"I don't know. . . . Maybe I will. . . . Yes, I'll come in with you."

*   *   *

After breakfast, Yefim was about to set off for the Executive Committee when, glancing through the window, he saw Ignat outside.

"Ignat's coming here : what's he up to now?"

"He's not alone; Vlas the miller's with him," his wife added.

The two cossacks came into the hut and, removing their caps, sedately crossed themselves.

"Had a good breakfast?"

"Good morning," Yefim answered.

"With fine weather, Yefim Nikolaich. And it really is a fine day; the snow is fresh, it's just the day for hunting hares."

"But what have you come for?" Yefim asked, perplexed by this unusual visit.

"But how could I go?" Ignat continued, taking a seat. "Now you can : it's a young's man's game. Come along to my place and collect the dogs, and then off into the steppe. The other day the dogs themselves took a fox down by the orchards."

Throwing open his long sheepskin, Vlas sat down on the bed, began to rock the cradle, and cleared his throat.

"We've come to see you, Yefim. We've got business to discuss with you."

"Go on."

"We've heard you're thinking of moving out of our village and living in the district centre. Is that right?"

"I'm not planning to move anywhere. Who sang you that song?" Yefim asked in astonishment.

"Various people have heard it," Vlas answered evasively, "and that's what we've come about. What point is there in your moving to the district when you can buy a little house with all the farm buildings and everything to hand, and quite cheap too."

"And where is it?"

"In Kalinovka. It's going at a low price. If you'd like to move, we can help with a loan. And we'll help you to move."

Yefim smiled.

"You would like to have me off your hands, wouldn't you?"

"The things you think of!" Ignat waved the remark aside.

"This is what I have to say to you." Yefim went right up to Ignat. "I'm not moving out of the village anywhere, and you can drop the whole idea. I know what's behind it all. But you can't buy me with money nor with promises." Flushing deeply, panting for breath, he spat and shouted into Ignat's bearded, sneering face :

"Get out of my house, you old dog. And you too, miller. Get out, you reptiles. And quick, before I knock the guts out of you."

In the passage Ignat slowly turned up his sheepskin collar and, standing with his back to Yefim, said distinctly :

"This'll be remembered against you, Yefim. So you don't want to go with good will? No matter. You'll be carried out of this hut feet first."

Losing control of himself, Yefim clutched Ignat's collar with both hands and, shaking him madly, flung him down the veranda steps. Entangled in the ends of his long sheepskin, Ignat fell heavily to the ground. But he jumped up nimbly, youthfully and, wiping the blood from his lips, which had been split in his fall, rushed at Yefim. Vlas restrained him, spreading out his arms.

"Drop it, Ignat. Not now. There's plenty of time."

Leaning all his body forward from the hips, Ignat stared hard at Yefim with an unwinking, sullen gaze, writhing his lips, then turned and went off without another word. Vlas followed him, brushing the clinging snow from his sheepskin, and occasionally looking back at Yefim on the veranda.

*   *   *

Just before Christmas, Dunia, Yefim's young sister-in-law who worked for Ignat, came running into the yard, streaming with tears.

"What's the matter, Dunia, my girl? What's happened?" Yefim asked. He thrust his pitchfork into a pile of straw and hurried out of the threshing-floor. "What's the matter?" he asked again, going up to her.

The girl's face was wet and swollen with crying; she blew her nose into her apron and, wiping away her tears with the ends of her kerchief, hoarsely vociferated :

"Yefim, have pity on my wretched head. Oh, oh, oh ! What shall I do, orphan that I am?"

"Now, stop howling. Tell me clearly," Yefim shouted.

"My master's turned me out. 'You go,' he said. 'I don't need you any more.' And now where shall I go? On St. Philip's day I started my third year with them. I asked them at least to give me a little money for all I'd done. 'Not a kopek for you,' he says. 'I'd pick them up myself, but money doesn't lie around on the road.' "

"Come into the house," Yefim said curtly.

Unhurriedly removing his outdoor clothes, he hung his great-coat on a nail, sat down at the table, and seated the sobbing girl opposite him.

"On what basis did you live with them : on a contract?"

"I don't know. I've lived with him ever since the famine year."

"And you didn't sign an agreement, or any sort of paper?"

"No. I can't read or write, I can hardly even sign my name."

Yefim sat silent for a moment, then he took a sheet of wrapping paper from a shelf and wrote clearly in a lame hand :

"To the People's Court of the Eighth Section :
Report."

*   *   *

Ever since the spring of the previous year, when Yefim had sent a report to the District Executive Committee saying the kulaks were concealing the amount they had sown and so avoiding taxation, Ignat, who formerly had domineered over all the village, had nursed a grudge against him. He never gave expression to it openly, but he slandered him behind his back. During the haymow he got across Yefim over some hay. One night, after Yefim had returned to the village, Ignat drove up with two waggons and carried off almost half of Yefim's freshly mown grass. Yefim said nothing, though he noticed that the wheel tracks led from his hayfield straight to Ignat's threshing-floor.

Some two weeks later Ignat's borzois came upon a wolf's lair in the Steep Ravine. The she wolf got away, but Ignat drew two shaggy, helpless wolf cubs out of the lair and put them in a sack. Tying the sack behind his saddle, he mounted his horse and rode home at a spanking speed.

The horse snorted and timorously set back its ears, arching its back as though preparing to take a jump: the borzois fussed and fidgeted right under its hoofs, sniffing, raising their short muzzles, and quietly whimpering. Ignat swayed in the saddle, and stroked his horse's neck, smirking into his beard.

The short summer twilight was yielding to the night when he

rode down the hill into the village. The stones gave off sparks as they flew up from under his horse's hoofs; behind him the wolf cubs silently fidgeted in the sack.

Just before reaching Yefim's yard Ignat reined in his horse and, making the saddle creak, sprang to the ground. Untying the sack, he drew out the first cub he could feel, groped for the thin wind-pipe under the warm fur and, frowning squeamishly, gripped it with his first and second fingers. A sudden crunch. The wolf, with a broken windpipe, flew across the wattle fence into Yefim's yard and fell noiselessly into a clump of thorns. A moment later the second fell with a thud two paces from the first.

Ignat wiped his hand fastidiously, leaped into his saddle and cracked his whip. The horse snorted and dashed down the alley, with the scraggy borzois hurrying after it.

During the night the she wolf came to the village and stood for a long time by the windmill, a black, motionless shadow. The wind was blowing from the south, bringing hostile smells, strange sounds to the mill. . . . Pointing with her muzzle, crouching in the grass, the wolf crawled along into the alley and came to a halt by Yefim's yard, sniffing at the scent. Without taking a run she sprang over the five-foot fence and wriggled her way on her belly through the thorns.

Yefim was aroused by the bellowing of cattle. He lit his lantern and ran outside. Hurrying to the sheep pen, he saw the gate was slightly open. Sending a glimmer of light through it, he noticed a sheep huddled against the trough; between its widely straddled legs the intestines ripped out of its bowels were giving off a bluish smoke. A second sheep was lying in the middle of the pen; the blood had already stopped flowing from its lacerated throat.

In the morning he came across the dead wolf cubs lying in the thorns, and guessed whose hand was responsible. Picking up the cubs on a spade, he carried them into the steppe and flung them down some distance from the road. But the she wolf visited his yard a second time. The next night, breaking through the reed roof of the cow shed, it silently slaughtered a cow and then fled.

Yefim carried the savaged cow to the clay pit where the villagers flung carrion, then went straight to Ignat's house. Ignat was work-ing under the hanging roof of a shed, adzing the ribs for new waggon sides. Seeing Yefim coming, he laid aside his axe, smiled and sat down expectantly on the shaft of a carriage standing beneath the roof.

"Come into the cool, Yefim."

Keeping tight control of himself, Yefim went and sat down beside him.

"You've good dogs, daddy Ignat."

"Yes, brother; my dogs are valuable. . . . Hey, Bandit, come here."

A broad-chested, long-legged hound started up from the veranda and, wagging its short tail, trotted up to its master.

"I gave a cossack a cow with calf for my Bandit." Smiling at the corners of his mouth, Ignat added : "He's a good dog. . . . He'll take a wolf. . . ."

Yefim stretched out his hand for Ignat's axe. Then, scratching the dog behind the ears, he asked again :

"A cow, you say?"

"With a calf. Why, d'you think I gave too much? He's worth more than that."

Swinging the axe with a short arm swing, Yefim split the dog's skull in two. Blood and clots of hot brain spurted over Ignat.

Going livid in the face, Yefim rose heavily from the carriage shaft and, throwing down the axe, got out the words in a whisper :

"Did you see that?"

Ignat sat panting, staring with goggling eyes at the dog's doubled up legs.

"Have you gone mad?" he hissed.

"Yes, I've gone mad," Yefim whispered, all his body gently trembling. "It's your head that ought to be split, you rat, and not the dog's. Who killed the wolf cubs in my yard? That was your work. You've got eight cows; if you lose one it doesn't mean much to you. But the she wolf slaughtered my only cow, and my child is left without milk."

He went towards the gate, taking long strides. Ignat overtook him at the wicket.

"You'll pay for that dog, you son of a bitch," he shouted, barring the way.

Yefim went right up to him and, breathing into his unkempt beard, told him :

"Don't you lay hands on me, Ignat. I'm not one of your sort, I won't stand any nonsense from you. I'll repay evil with evil. The days are past when people bowed their backs before you. Stand out of my way. . . ."

Ignat stood aside and let him pass. Then he slammed the wicket gate and swore and swore, shaking his fist at Yefim's retreating back.

*   *   *

After the incident with the dog, Ignat stopped persecuting Yefim. When they met he bowed and turned his eyes away. This state of affairs continued until the court sentenced Ignat to pay sixty roubles to his worker, Dunia. From then on Yefim felt that danger threatened him from Ignat's direction. Something was brewing. Ignat's little foxy eyes smiled mysteriously when he looked at Yefim.

One day, in the Executive Committee the chairman asked in a shifty tone:

"Yefim, have you heard that my father-in-law's been sentenced to pay sixty roubles?"

"Yes, I have."

"Who could have put that idiot Dunia up to it?"

Yefim smiled and looked straight into the chairman's eyes.

"It was necessity. Your father-in-law turned her out and didn't even give her a crust of bread for the road, though Dunia had worked for him two years."

"But we gave her her food."

"And made her work from dawn till night."

"You know yourself that in the country work isn't regulated by the clock."

"I can see you're curious to know who sent the complaint to the court."

"That's just it, who could have done it?"

"I did," Yefim answered. And the chairman's expression left no doubt that this confession didn't come as any surprise to him.

Late in the afternoon Yefim collected some documents and resolutions of the district Executive Committee to take home.

"I'll copy them out after supper," he thought.

He had his supper, closed the shutters from outside and sat down at the table to copy out the resolutions. His gaze happened to fall on the bare window-frame.

"Masha, what's all this? Didn't you buy some material to make up into curtains?"

"I bought two yards. . . . But we haven't got any napkins. . . . I'm having to wrap baby in rags. . . . So I made the curtain material into napkins."

"Well, that's all right. But all the same buy some more tomorrow. It's a bit awkward : anyone could open the shutters from outside and look right in."

Outside the windows, festooned with lacy frost, a ground wind was blowing. Shapeless, heavy clouds covered the sky. On the outskirts of the hamlet, where a beetling hill drops to the yards down a scrubby slope, the dogs were barking. Along by the stream the willows grumbled indignantly, complaining to the wind of the cold, the foul weather. The creak of their swaying branches and the noise of the wind were blended into a unisonous bass roar.

As he dipped his pen into the home-made inkpot filled with ink made from oak galls, Yefim glanced from time to time at the window, which in its mute black square concealed a silent threat. He had a queer, apprehensive feeling. He had been working for a couple of hours when the shutter creaked and was gently opened a little from outside. He didn't hear the creak, but, aimlessly glancing at the window, went cold with horror : through the tracery of hoarfrost a pair of well-known, grey eyes gazed at him fixedly, half screwed up, through the narrow slits. A second later, behind the window pane the black round hole of a rifle barrel appeared, dead level with his head. He pressed all his body against the wall, and sat motionless, white of face. The frame was a single one, and he clearly heard the click of the trigger. Then above the grey eyes the brows were knitted in astonishment. No shot followed. For a moment the little black circle vanished from behind the glass, Yefim distinctly heard the rattle of a rifle bolt. Then, recovering his wits, he blew out the lamp; he hardly had time to duck before a shot rang out, shattering the glass, and a bullet smacked juicily into the opposite wall, sprinkling bits of plaster over him.

The wind burst in through the shattered window, scattering

snow over the bench. The baby began to scream in the cradle, the shutter clattered.

Yefim noiselessly dropped on all fours and crawled over to the window.

"Yefim dearest! My dear! Oh, God! Yefim darling!" His wife wailed as she lay in bed, but he gritted his teeth and didn't answer. His body was shaking all over. Rising to his feet, he glanced through the broken window, and saw someone enveloped in a cloud of snow running along the street. Resting his hands on the bench, Yefim drew himself up to his full height, then dropped precipitately to the floor again: a rifle barrel appeared round the half open shutter, a shot rang out. The pungent smell of burnt gunpowder filled the hut.

*   *   *

Yefim's face was sunken and yellow when he went out on to the veranda next morning. The sun was shining, the chimneys were smoking, the cattle driven down to water were bellowing by the stream. The fresh tracks of sledge runners showed in the street, the newly-fallen snow dazzled the eye with its immaculate whiteness. Everything was so ordinary, everyday, intimate, the past night seemed like a vaporous dream. In the snow by the hut ledge, below the broken window, Yefim found two empty cartridge cases and a rifle bullet with a small black dent on the cap. He turned over the rusted bullet in his hands for a long time, meditating: "If it hadn't been for the misfire, if this bullet hadn't been damp, you'd have been done for, Yefim."

The Soviet chairman was already in the Executive Committee when Yefim arrived. As the door scraped he gave Yefim a swift glance and bent over his newspaper again.

"Rvachev," Yefim called.

"Well?" he replied without looking up.

"Rvachev! Look at me!"

The chairman reluctantly raised his head, and from under the steep line of his brows two widely set grey eyes looked at Yefim.

"So it was you, you scum, who shot at me last night?" Yefim asked hoarsely.

The chairman went livid and laughed forcedly:

"What on earth's the matter with you? Gone crazy?"

Yefim recalled the past night : the heavy, unwinking gaze behind the window pane, the black hole of the rifle barrel, his wife's cry. . . . Wearily waving his hand, he sat down on the bench and smiled.

"But it didn't come off. The cartridges were damp. . . . Where had you been keeping them? In the ground I should think."

The chairman had completely recovered his sang-froid, and answered coldly :

"I don't know what you're talking about. I think you've had too much to drink."

By mid-day the rumour that Yefim had been shot at during the night had gone all round the village. A crowd of inquisitive villagers swarmed round his hut. Ivan Donskov called him out of the Executive Committee, and asked :

"Have you informed the militia?"

"There's time enough for that."

"Well, brother, don't be afraid, we won't let you down. Ignat's only got five or so left supporting him now, and we've seen through them. Nobody will follow the kulaks any more now, everybody's turned against them, and they're finished."

That evening the young people of the village gathered in Fiodka the cobbler's hut, and a fiery conversation began, as always, to the sound of his hammer. Vaska Obnizov, who was the same age as Yefim, sat down beside him and whispered enthusiastically :

"Remember, Yefim, if they kill you there'll be twenty other Yefims in your place. Get that? I'm telling you the truth. You know the fairy story of the heroes : they kill one, and two more rise up in his place. Only here it won't be two, it'll be twenty."

*   *   *

Early one morning Yefim went off to the district centre. He called at the District Executive Committee office, at the Agricultural Loan Society, and spent some time in the militia, waiting to see the commander. By the time he had settled all his affairs dusk was falling.

He strode out of the village and made his way homeward over the smooth, slippery ice of the river. Evening came on. His cheeks burned a little with the frost. The night turned a chilly blue in the west. Round a turn he saw the dark lines of the buildings of his village. He quickened his steps. Then, happening to look back, he noticed a group of three men following some two hundred paces behind him.

He measured the distance to the village with his eyes, and stepped out more briskly. But, when he looked round again a minute later, he saw that the men behind him had not fallen back; on the contrary, they seemed to have drawn closer. Suddenly anxious, he broke into a trot. He ran as though on a training course, his elbows pressed close to his sides, breathing in the frosty air through his nostrils. He thought of turning on to the bank, but remembered that the snow lay deep there, and went on running along the frozen river.

It so happened that in his headlong flight he started to slide, failed to recover his balance, and fell over. As he picked himself up he glanced back : now they were overtaking him. The foremost man was running springily and easily, waving a crowbar as he came on.

Terror all but forced a cry for help from Yefim's throat, but it was a good mile to the village, and no one would have heard his shout. He realized this in a flash, pressed his lips together, and silently tore on, trying to make up the time he had lost through falling. The several minutes of space between him and the leader of the pursuit had hardly been reduced at all, and yet, glancing back, he saw that the man was overtaking him. He summoned up all his strength and put on a spurt, but now his ears caught a new sound : the crowbar was sliding precipitately over the ice, ringing dully. Its blow against his feet sent him flying. He jumped up and ran on again. For one moment he recalled that he had run just like this at Tsaritsin, when they had beaten back the Whites in an attack; then, too, he had had this burning, choking feeling in his chest.

The crowbar, sent skidding over the ice by a strong hand, again bowled him over. This time he didn't get up. Someone from behind knocked him sideways with a terrible blow on the head. Gathering all his will power into iron resolution he crawled along on all fours, swaying. But once more he was stretched out full length.

"Why is the ice so hot?" the thought passed through his mind. Glancing sideways, by the bank he saw a broken reed. "They've broken me too." But at once the words burned out in his fading consciousness : "Remember, Yefim, if they kill you there'll be twenty other Yefims in your place. Like in the fairy story of the heroes."

Somewhere in the hedges there was a prolonged, unbroken howl. . . . He did not feel the crowbar being forced into his mouth, breaking his teeth, crushing the gums as it thrust deeper and deeper. He did not feel the pitchfork piercing his chest and the prongs slipping as they came up against his backbone.

*   *   *

Three men, with lighted cigarettes, walked swiftly off to the village : one of them was followed by a borzoi. A blizzard blew up; snow began to fall over Yefim's face; but it did not melt on his cold cheeks, where two tears of unbearable pain and terror were frozen.

1926.

THE FARM LABOURERS

THE little houses of Danilovka settlement huddle at the foot of beetling brown hills, among willows which grow densely on each side of the river, as though sheltering from the pestering gaze of the passers-by, whether on foot or on horse.

The settlement numbers a hundred or so houses. The houses and yards of the more prosperous peasants are scattered widely and rarely along the main street running past the stream. You ride along the street and notice at once that good farmers are living here: the houses are roofed with sheet iron and tiles, the cornices are decorated with intricate serrated fretwork, the blue-painted shutters creak self-satisfiedly in the wind, as though telling of their owners' well-fed and carefree life. The main gates in this street are close-boarded, they're reliable; the wattle fences are new, there are granaries in the yards, healthy-looking dogs bark as you go by.

There is a second street, crooked and narrow, which runs along the hillside; the hill is overgrown with willows, and the street seems to flow under the green roofs of the trees. The wind drives clouds of dust along it, and sends the ashes scattered under the wattle fences whirling up in a fine cloud. This second street is lined not with houses, but with huts. Unconcealed poverty stares at you from every window, from every rickety fence with its widely-spaced boards.

Five years ago a fire burnt every building in the second street down to the ground. In place of the former timber houses the peasants ran up clay huts, and managed to organize their lives somehow. But ever since the fire need had come to live permanently with its victims, and need took stronger and stronger hold of their lives.

In the fire they lost all their agricultural possessions. During the following spring they found ways and means of tilling the soil; but the harvest was a failure, and that shattered the peasants' hopes, bowed their backs, and scattered to the winds all their dreams of managing somehow to get on to their feet, to scramble out of their misery. From that time on the victims of the fire went roving through the world, going on 'begging pilgrimages', or moving to the Kuban, where food was easier to come by. But their native soil called them home imperatively : they returned to Danilovka and went once more, cap in hand, to the prosperous peasants.

"Take me on as a labourer, master. I'll do anything for a crust of bread."

2

Early one morning, at first light, Father Alexander's man came along to see Naum Boitsov. Naum was harnessing the horse he had borrowed from a neighbour into a cart, and didn't hear the workman's footsteps. He was thinking of his own affairs, and started at the unexpectedly loud greeting : "Hallo, daddy Naum."

Naum looked up and, after tightening the horse's collar straps, touched his cap with his free left hand.

"Hallo ! What do you want?"

Delighted at the husbandman's mark of recognition, the workman sat down on a wretched-looking, overturned harrow and, drawing his shirt sleeve down over his palm, wiped the sweat from his brow.

"I've got a job for you," he began deliberately, obviously intending to have a long and circumstantial chat.

"What job?" Naum asked as he dealt with a broken rein.

"Well, you see, it's like this : I told the Father long ago : Father, if you want to geld your young stallion, you should . . ."

"Don't make such heavy weather of it," Naum snapped. "There's a stallion to be gelded, is that it? Then say so, for I haven't a lot of time : I'm just going off to the fields. . . ."

"Well, yes, a stallion," the workman ended his story reluctantly.

"Tell him I'll be along at once."

The workman slowly got up, brushed off a fresh shaving clinging to his trousers and, gazing down at his feet, said unconcernedly :

"People praise you all over the district : he's a good farrier, everybody says. That's true enough, but you're an old curmudgeon, nobody can ever have a pleasant chat with you. You're rough and blunt."

"Well, you must forgive me, brother; but that's how my mother bore me."

"Of course. . . . Of course, it's insulting, for I can talk with anyone you like."

"All right then, you go and talk with someone else," Naum said, his eyes smiling. Deliberately, planting his broad, bare feet down firmly and heavily, he went into his hut.

The workman picked up the fresh shaving which the wind had blown into the yard from somewhere, rolled it into a tube, sighed, and went off along the street, rolling sideways and waggling his buttocks like a woman. He walked as though the wind were driving him along willy nilly.

Naum went into the hut and took a bunch of stout cords from a nail. As he untangled the knot he turned to the stove and smiled at his wife, who was busily cooking.

"I told you something was going to happen from somewhere. Father Alexander wants his stallion gelded; he's sent his workman along for me. I won't take less than twenty pounds of ground corn."

"You say the Father sent him?" his wife asked in delighted tones.

"He's only just gone."

"Now we'll have bread. And here was I worrying because you were going off to plough and we'd no dumplings or any food for you to take."

Naum smiled, and with his smile the ruddy wedge of his beard slipped to one side, revealing his blackened, fleshy teeth. The smile made him look younger, and his stern face more friendly looking.

"You get ready too, Fiodor; you can help. But let the mare stand, don't unharness her," he told his son.

Fiodor, a boy of some sixteen years, and extraordinarily like his father in his features and big-boned, broad-shouldered body, belted his ragged shirt with a new thong and followed him. Like his father, he set his bare feet firmly on the ground and, like him, he stooped as he walked, and swung his arms, powerful for his age.

The priest met them close to his house. There was blood on his full, flabby cheeks, his forehead was bound with a clean towel. Under the bandage his slanting eyes darted like little grey mice.

"You can't get near him," he said after greeting them. "What an animal! He's a perfect demon!" His voice was thick and deep, quite out of keeping with his short, slender figure. "I went to bridle him and he snapped at me with his teeth just like a dog. He tore a piece of skin off my forehead, by the true God!"

The risible Fiodor went livid and swelled in his efforts to avoid laughing. But his father gave him a stern look and went through the wicket gate.

"Where is he?"

"In the stable."

"Get me another thong, Father."

"You've got to know how to handle him," the priest said irresolutely.

"We'll soothe him somehow. I've handled worse!" Naum answered rather boastfully, and neatly tied an intricate loop in one end of a cord.

Fiodor, the priest, and the workman stood at the stable door, while Naum threw the cords over his left arm and clutched a short, raw oak cudgel in his right hand.

"Look out, daddy Naum, or he'll scorch you," the workman said sarcastically.

Naum did not reply. He drew back the door bolt and, half closing his eyes to see better in the darkness, strode inside.

For a good couple of minutes those outside heard scuffling. His heart thumping rapidly, Fiodor waited for the shout: "Come and hold him. Quick!" But suddenly they heard a crash, the stallion snorted, there was a dull, heavy bang, then a groan. Hoofs sounded a rapid dance over the wooden floor, the door flew open as though carried away by a storm, and the stallion leaped out of the darkness, his head flung up wildly. In a couple of bounds he reached the dung heap, stood for a second with his sweaty flanks heaving, waved his tail and, jumping the fence, disappeared, sending up a translucent dust from the road as he went.

Naum came staggering out of the stable. He was pressing his mouth with both hands, the broken cord was still dangling from the left hand. He took a score or so quick strides through the yard, his legs entangling in each other drunkenly, ran his chest up against the fence and fell flat, tucking his knees up to his belly. Fiodor cried out, dropped the cord he was holding, and ran to him.

"Father! What's happened?"

In a terrible, snoring whisper, choking over the words, Naum got out :

"In my chest. . . . He kicked me in my chest. . . . He's broken the bone. . . . I'm finished. In my chest, right under the heart." He gave a whistling sigh and, rolling glazing eyes in his agony, burst into tears, hiccuping and choking with blood.

They picked him up and carried him into the shelter of the shed overhang. As they carried him across the yard a crimson trail of blood was left behind. Bent double like a bow, Naum groaned and tore his shirt into ribbons. With every breath he took the shattered chest collapsed horribly, and shook and rocked unevenly.

After ten minutes or so he felt a little better, the blood stopped gushing from his mouth, only a rosy spittle bubbled on his lips. The terrified priest brought out a carafe of home-made vodka, forced Naum to drink three glasses and, stuttering, whispered :

"I'll pay you. . . . I'll pay. . . . Only do go now. . . . Your son will take you. Oh, dear, what a sin ! But was it my fault? Go Naum, for Christ's sake go. . . . You'll die surrounded by your family. . . . Please go. I've no intention of being responsible for you."

"If I die . . . pay . . . my wife," Naum whistled out the words between attacks of choking.

"Don't worry. . . . I'll give you the sacrament, I'll go into the church and get the sacrament. . . . Fiodor, help your father to get up."

Supported by the priest, Naum let his legs drop; but he cried out thickly :

"Oh . . . I can't. Ooooh ! It's death. I shall die. . . ." He suddenly cried in a wild, piercing voice.

Fiodor's face worked hideously, he burst into tears; the workman drew aside and dug up the sand with his foot, smiling idiotically.

Taking great gulps of air with his gaping mouth, Naum got up. Leaning all the weight of his body on Fiodor's shoulder, he walked along, falling over his feet.

"Take me home . . . the Father ordered that. . . . Let's go," he said curtly.

As he walked he stumbled and got his feet entangled; but he bit his lips hard, uttered not one groan, only his eyebrows quivered and his face was wet with tears. When he was about a hundred yards away from home he tore himself out of Fiodor's hands, cried out, and strode to the fence. As Fiodor caught him under the arms he felt the body sag and go heavy, and he no longer had strength enough to hold him up. From under the half-closed eyelids of his father's head as it hung sideways two eyes stared fixedly at him with the sternness of death.

People came running up. Someone touched Naum's hand, someone else said half in fear, half in amazement:

"He's dead! Well, what do you say to that?"

3

On the third or fourth day after the funeral, Fiodor's mother said to him:

"Well, Fiodya, how are you and I going to live now?"

Fiodor himself had no idea how they were going to live or what they ought to do now his father was dead.

The house had had a master, their lives had flowed past in an orderly and stable succession, like a waggon with a heavy load. Sometimes it was difficult to get out of a hole, but somehow Naum was able to arrange things so that even in the famine year his family had not really known what it meant to go hungry, and in other years things had been quite easy and good. They may not have had enough and to spare, like the wealthy peasants of the other street, but they had not suffered the need which their neighbours had known, those who lived with them in the second street. But now that the house was deprived of its master not only Fiodor was perplexed, but his mother too. They managed somehow to plough an acre of land for sowing with wheat; their neighbour, Prokhor, did the sowing for them; but the shoots were not promising, they were thin and weak.

"Go and hire yourself out to some kind folk as a workman, sonny, and I'll wander about the world," his mother said to Fiodor one day. "Maybe we'll rove around for a year or two, get enough money together to buy a horse, and then we'll win a living from our own farm. What d'you think?"

"There's nothing to say," Fiodor answered gloomily. "Look at it how you like, I've got to find work with someone."

That very same evening Fiodor went to the house of Zakhar, the wealthiest peasant in the neighbouring Krenovsky settlement, stood below the veranda, crumpling his father's worn and shiny cap in his hands, and said, getting the reluctant words out with difficulty :

"I'll work conscientiously. . . . I'm not afraid of work. Pay me whatever you think right."

Zakhar Denisovich, a rather feeble individual who was bowed almost double with some internal complaint, was sitting on the veranda steps. He scrutinized Fiodor at point-blank range with dim, bleary eyes.

"I do need a workman, that's true. Only you're young, my lad; you haven't got a man's strength, and you'll never earn a peasant's wage. that's certain. But what pay d'you expect from me?"

"Whatever you give."

"But all the same?"

Fiodor started to sweat, he shook his cap in his embarrassment and raised his eyes.

"Pay me so that neither you nor I will be done wrong to."

"Half a rouble a month : that's my price. My food, but your clothing and boots. Well?" he looked questioningly at Fiodor. "Agreed?"

Fiodor screwed up his eyes, making mental calculations, rapidly wriggling the fingers of his free hand. "Half a rouble in a month, a whole rouble in two months. That's six roubles a year." He recalled that eighty roubles were asked in the market for the scrawniest of nags, and was horrified to find that he would have to work over thirteen years to earn so much.

"What are you wriggling your lips for? Speak up, d'you agree or don't you?" Zakhar Denisovich asked hoarsely, frowning with the colic troubling his stomach.

"But daddy. . . . That's almost working for nothing."

"For nothing? How about your food, how much is that going to cost me? Judge for yourself. . . ." Zakhar began to cough, and dismissed the question with a wave of the hand.

Firmly recalling his mother's advice, Fiodor decided not to hire himself out for less than a rouble a month. Meanwhile, Zakhar, his eyes goggling with his fit of coughing, was spasmodically thinking: "I simply mustn't let go of this half idiot. He's a treasure.

He's healthy enough, he'll work like a bullock for me. Such a bloodhound would snap the horn of the devil himself, not to mention. . . . A workman knowing his price won't hire himself out in the summer season even for five roubles, but I can get this fellow for a miserable rouble. . . ."

"Well, what's your final figure?" he said aloud.

"I'd like at least a rouble a month."

"A rouble? What on earth? Are you crazy, young man? No, brother, that's rather a lot."

Fiodor turned to go, but Zakhar Denisovich twittered like a sparrow as he sat on the steps, and seized him by the sleeve.

"Stop. Wait a bit, you're hot blooded, brother. Where are you off to?"

"We haven't agreed, and that's the end of it."

"Oh, all right. We'll leave it at that. Let it be as you say : I'll make it a rouble a month. You're swindling me, but we'll call it a day. Only watch out : a contract is more precious than money, so work properly."

"I shall work and look after the cattle as if they were my own," Fiodor said in his delight.

"Go back in the cool this very day to Danilovka, bring over your bits and pieces, and tomorrow at dawn we'll go out and mow. That's that."

4

A cock was fussing about under the shed. Before crowing to announce the oncoming of the dawn it flapped its wings, and Fiodor heard every flap clearly and distinctly as he lay under the overhang of the shed. He couldn't sleep. Peering out from under his sheepskin greatcoat, he saw the sky above the serrated granary roof go a muddy grey; clouds were crawling up from the east, faintly tinged with a crimson flush at their edges; and on the flails of the mower standing by the shed little heavy peas of dew were hanging.

A minute later Zakhar Denisovich came out on to the veranda in his canvas drawers. He scratched himself, pulling his shirt high up over his swollen yellow belly, and shouted :

"Fiodka !"

Fiodor threw off the sheepskin and came out from under the overhang.

"Drive the bullocks down to the river to drink, and be quick. Then harness the dappled oxen into the mower."

Fiodor hurriedly unfastened the little gate of the cattle yard, wiped his hands, wet with dew, on his trousers, and shouted at the bullocks:

"Come on, out with you!"

The bullocks lumbered reluctantly into the main yard. The leader opened the wicket gate with its horns and made off down the street to the river; the others dragged along behind it.

As they came back Fiodor saw his master doing something to a waggon, unfastening a nut with a wrench. He went up and helped him remove the wheel and oil the axle. Zakhar Denisovich watched out of the corner of his eye, noting the boy's expert, efficient movements, and sniffed.

By the time they had finished and were driving out of the village dawn had come. On the mounds along the wayside the faded brown, lubberly marmots were whistling; in the greenery, little bustards were fighting; the sun had peeled out from behind the hills, and, like a fool, was profligately pouring its burning light over the steppe. The dew rose above the gulleys in a dense, icy mist.

The wheels of the mower squeaked, the waggon rattled thunderously behind; in the back, water gurgled noisily and merrily in a large wooden pitcher. Having got warm in the sun, Zakhar Denisovich felt inclined for a pleasant chat.

"You be obedient, Fiodka, and I shan't do you any wrong. You're a healthy lad, and strong, and you'll be as much in demand as if you were a real workman."

"I told you I'd work as if it was my own farm."

"Well, we'll see. You must understand, brother, that I'm your benefactor, and you're my servant. And you're in duty bound to submit without questioning to your master and benefactor. I've saved you from death by starvation, as you might say, so remember my goodness to you. Understand?"

Bowing his head, Fiodor meditated on his master's goodness and was astonished: what kindness had he shown him so far?

Fiodor worked alone on the mowing. The master sat on a comfortable iron stool at the front of the mower, waved his whip, and urged on the oxen, while Fiodor, armed with a short pitchfork, threw off the heavy sheaves of green grass, panting with the strain. He had hardly thrown off one long swathe with strain and effort when the flails of the mower were aiming at a further line of grass with their dry, niggling rattle. Occasionally the oxen stopped to rest. Then his master stretched himself out under a stook and, pulling his shirt open, stroked his grumbling yellow belly with his hands and gazed stupidly at the white, floating lumps of cloud.

At their first halt Fiodor shook the prickly dust and grassy awns out of his shirt and also went to sit down by the mower. But Zakhar Denisovich ran his eyes over him from head to foot with a look of astonishment, and drawled:

"What are you up to? Don't you watch me, brother. I'm your benefactor and master, get that into your head. I needn't work at all unless I like, because of my internal complaint. But you take the pitchfork and go and stook the grass. Over the other side of the hollow the grass is already dry."

Fiodor followed the direction of the hairy finger, took the pitchfork, and went off to stook the swathes. Some half hour later his master, who was snoring pleasantly in the shelter of the stook, woke up because a grasshopper had crawled under his shirt. Swearing juicily, he tore the unfortunate creature to little bits and, shielding his swollen eyes with his palm, looked to see how Fiodor was getting on.

"Fiodka!"

Fiodor came back to him.

"How many stooks have you piled?"

"Nine."

"Only nine? Well, get on the mower."

The oxen set off, chewing the cud as they went; the mower shook, the flails clattered, sweeping the grass to the back platform. Zakhar Denisovich, who was extremely greedy, set the blades low, right to the roots of the grass. The blades clashed drily as they cut into the thick bottom growth, everything seemed to be going perfectly. But at the turn the mower suddenly came up against a hummock of earth thrown up by a mole, and stopped with its teeth dug into the ground, quivering with the strain. Fiodor jumped down from his seat to see whether anything was broken, but all was well.

They stopped work only as darkness came on. Fiodor carried some dry bullock dung to their encampment, tore up some old grass of last year's growth, and scrub, and lit a fire. His master poured a little millet out of a bag and told Fiodor to clean three miserable potatoes.

After dinner he was in a good mood, and even gave Fiodor a slap on the back. But just before supper the lad spoilt it all by cutting off too large a piece of fat to put into the millet gruel. Pulling a discontented face, Zakhar Denisovich gave him a long lecture, turned morose, and lay down to sleep, sighing and muttering to himself.

5

Fiodor often recalled his master's words : 'You remember my kindness.' He had lived with him for three weeks, but hadn't experienced any kindness at all. Only one thing he knew definitely : Zakhar Denisovich was a thorough peasant and would work a man till he drew the tendons out of him. The lad was running about from early morning till late at night, but his master never stopped shouting at him, writhing his lips and pulling discontented faces.

On the first Sunday after starting work Fiodor intended to go home to see his mother; but on the Saturday evening Zakhar Denisovich announced :

"Early in the morning you go and hoe the potatoes. The women say it's terrible to see how overgrown they are with weeds." After a moment or two he added : "Don't imagine that because tomorrow's Sunday you can lie about and do nothing but eat. This is our busy season : one day feeds a whole year. It's in the winter time you'll be able to live like a lodger."

Fiodor kept his mouth shut. A nagging fear of losing his job made him humble and submissive. Next morning he took a hunk of bread, picked up a hoe, and set off to hoe the potatoes. During the morning he used the hoe so vigorously that by mid-day he had a headache and felt sick. He had difficulty in straightening his back; he sat down on a hummock and spat out : in front of him the still unhoed grass showed a green, gleaming velvet for some sixty yards.

In the early evening, lifting his feet with difficulty, all his body howling with pain, he staggered back to the yard. His master called out to him the moment he entered the gate. Without rising from the hut ledge he asked:

"Hoed it all?"

"Just a small section left."

"Ah, you, brother! I suppose you've been idling or sleeping," he barked in a tone of vexation.

"I haven't been sleeping," Fiodor answered glumly. "It isn't possible to hoe the lot in one day."

"Go away, don't answer back. If you work like that again you won't get anything to eat. You drone!" he shouted after the re-treating lad.

6

The days and weeks passed in dreary, joyless succession. Fiodor worked from morn till night without stopping. On Sundays and holidays his master deliberately thought up some job to keep him busy and to ensure that his labourer was not without work.

Two months went by. The boy's shirt was never dry of sweat. He fawned on his master, thinking that by the end of the second month he would be paid for the time he had worked. But Zakhar said nothing about payment, and Fiodor didn't like to ask.

One evening at the end of the second month he did go up to Zakhar Denisovich as he was sitting on the veranda, and asked:

"I'd be glad if you'd let me have some money. To send to my mother. . . ."

Zakhar waved his hands in alarm.

"What money can you be given now? Are you mad, brother? When we've threshed the corn and paid the taxes, then maybe there'll be money to spare. But you earn it first."

"I've worn my clothes out, my boots are falling to pieces. Look!" Fiodor lifted his foot in its worn-out boot: his toes, split with toil and the heat, were poking through the broken toecap.

Zakhar Denisovich smirked as he stared down at the boy's feet, then turned away.

"It's warm now, you can go barefoot."

"You can't walk barefoot through nettles and over the stubble."

"Well, you're a tender sort, I must say. You don't happen to have blue blood in you, do you? You haven't come of the gentry?"

Fiodor turned away without replying and, crimson with humiliation, went off to his place under the shed, while his master roared with laughter.

During all these two months he had not once seen his mother. He never had time to walk across to Danilovka, his master wouldn't let him go; and to tell the truth he had no idea whether his mother was still at home, or whether she had thrown a sack over her back and gone begging about the hamlets and villages.

The harvest season drew to a close. A steam thresher drove into Zakhar Denisovich's yard. Workmen turned up. The master danced and fidgeted around them, urging them to get the threshing finished quickly.

"You work hard, boys, for the love of Christ. Get it done while the weather holds. God forbid that rain should come: the grain would be spoilt."

A youngster in a military tunic badly creased at the back came up, contemptuously studied the master's bloated features, and, rocking on his heels, mimicked him:

"You work hard, for the love of Christ! Why should we have to whine like beggars? Put out a bucket of home-made vodka for the whole team and the work will go with a swing. You know yourself a dry spoon tickles the throat."

"Why, of course, with the greatest of pleasure. I was just thinking of having a drink myself."

"There's no need to think about it. While you're thinking it over we shall be moving on to your neighbour's threshing-floor. He's been trying to get us for a long time."

Zakhar Denisovich dashed off into the village, and within half an hour, waddling from side to side, he brought back a bucket of home-made vodka covered with the dirty end of a woman's skirt. The team sat drinking till midnight in the threshing-floor, among the untouched stooks of wheat. The mechanic, an oil-stained Ukrainian no longer young, drank till he was drunk, and then went off to sleep under a stook with some loose woman; the day labourers bawled out songs incoherently and swore. Fiodor sat a little way off, watching his master drunkenly embracing the youngster in the military tunic, weeping and dribbling spittle. Through his sobs he exclaimed in a snuffling, effeminate voice:

"I've sunk capital in you, so to speak: a whole bucket of vodka. That costs money. And you still don't want to work, do you?"

Cocking his head up like a duck, the youngster shouted back:

"I don't care a damn. If I feel like it I won't work tomorrow either."

"But I've lost money already."

"I don't care a damn."

"Brothers!" Zakhar turned to the vague half circle of men in the yard. "Brothers! You'll upset me for the rest of my life. I may even die as the result of this."

"I don't care a damn," the youngster in the tunic thundered.

"I'm a sick man," Zakhar Denisovich groaned, streaming with tears. "This is where I've got my complaint." He knocked his fist against his swollen belly.

The youngster spat contemptuously on to the bottom of the master's cotton shirt and staggered to his feet. He walked away, his feet getting entangled in each other like a horse who has over-eaten of rye. He went straight across to where Fiodor was sitting by the fence.

7

He stopped a couple of paces away, set forward one leg in a proud attitude, tossed his workman's straw hat to the back of his head with a jerk.

"Who are you?" he asked, pronouncing his words deliberately, as drunken men do.

"Daddy Hoo-hoo!" Fiodor answered morosely.

"Idiot. I ask you, who are you?"

"A labourer."

"Living here?"

"Yes."

"Pah, you rotten sod. I suppose you're sucking your master's blood like a parasitic louse. Isn't that the truth? Ah?"

"What have you picked on me for? Get away!"

"Get away! On the contrary, this is what I'm going to do: I'm going to sit myself down here."

The youngster flopped down like a sack at Fiodor's side and breathed the stink of home-made vodka and onion into his face.

"I'm Frol Kucherenko. And that's that. But who are you?"

"I'm from Danilovka. Naum Boitsov's son."

"So-o-o! And what do you earn?"

"A rouble a month."

"A rou-ouble?" Frol whistled and hiccuped: "Why, I get a rouble a day. What d'you think of that, ah?"

The blood rushed to Fiodor's heart, and he asked, taking a long breath:

"A rouble?"

"Well, what did you think? And treating on top of it. My little berry, you were born a fool. Who on earth is going to work a whole month for one rouble? Listen! Leave your exploiter and come and work with us. You'll earn real money then!"

Fiodor got up and went to the overhanging roof of the shed, where he had slept ever since the spring. He lay down on boards covered with old straw, drew his sheepskin over his feet and, putting his hands under his head, lay a long time without stirring, thinking it all out.

Through the broken overhang of the shed a sprinkle of stars shed a yellowish light, like an ikon lamp; a bullfrog sang tenderly and quietly in the reeds, the sparrows under the eaves fidgeted in their sleep.

The night, moonless but bright, drew to its end. From the threshing-floor still came bursts of laughter and Zakhar's lachrymose voice. Sighing and tossing, Fiodor lay on and on without closing his eyes. He dropped off only as dawn was coming.

Next morning he waited in the kitchen to see his master. Unwashed, swollen, and bad-tempered, Zakhar came out from the bedroom. When he saw the boy he shouted:

"Playing the lazybones, you son of a bitch? I'll teach you. You're a full-grown peasant for eating, but a child when it comes to work. Didn't I tell you to bring in the corn from the farthest stack?"

"I'm not going to stay with you any longer. Pay me for my two months."

"Wha-a-at?" Zakhar jumped a good foot into the air and shook with fury. "Thinking of leaving me, are you? They've got you away from me, have they? Why, you scoundrel! You mongrel! Do you know I can have you put in prison for this sort of thing? For leaving your master in the height of the season? Ah? You'll get penal servitude for such insolence. Go! God be with you. But I won't give you a farthing of your wages. And I won't allow you to take your bits and pieces with you." He swore till he choked, began to cough and, goggling his crayfish eyes, stroked and kneaded his quivering belly with his hands. "That's all the gratitude I get for looking after you. So you've forgotten I'm your benefactor, and provided for you in your need? I've been in place of a father to you, and now . . ."

Zakhar Denisovich stared at Fiodor through narrowed slits of eyes. The moment the lad announced his intention of leaving he realized that his husbandry would suffer considerable loss: to begin with he would lose a labourer who worked like a bullock for him, and all for a scrap of bread; secondly, he would have to hire another man for a much higher wage, would have to shoe and clothe him, and, to make matters worse (if he got hold of some cunning rogue who knew what he was about) would have to sign a written contract with lots of binding paragraphs. Or, if he didn't hire someone he would have to set to work himself, to harness himself into the accursed yoke when it was far more pleasant to sleep in the sun and grow fat with doing nothing.

His first move had been to try and frighten Fiodor. Now, seeing that he had made some impression, he decided to appeal to the lad's conscience:

"And aren't you ashamed? Aren't you ashamed to look me in the face? I've given you food and drink, but you . . . Ah, Fiodor, Fiodor, that's not the way Christians behave. Why, you aren't a Young Communist, are you? It's they, the Judases, who cause all the trouble; may they be damned to hell! They're the sort that do that sort of thing."

He shook his head reproachfully, looking at Fiodor out of the corner of his eye.

The boy stood with his head hanging, kneading his cap in his hands. He realized only one thing: that all the plans he had worked out during the night—how to get the money for a horse more quickly—had gone with the wind. Something crushing had fallen on him, and he could not find any way of throwing off the burden.

He silently turned and went off to the threshing-floor. There the work was already going like one o'clock : the sheaves were being brought in from the distant stacks, the engine was puffing, Frol was bawling as he thrust bundles of scented, large-grained ears into the thresher's insatiable maw, the women were squealing as they scraped away the straw, and the golden dust rose in a swaying orange column.

8

All that day Fiodor went about in a daze. Everything went wrong for him.

"Hey, you devil's stepson, where are you driving to? Where are you driving to?" his master roared, knitting his brows.

Pulling himself together, Fiodor tugged at the rein tied to the bullocks' horns, and looked with unseeing eyes at the pile of chaff into which he had backed the hind wheels of his waggon.

They ate a hurried mid-day meal in the threshing-floor, and then set to work again, at first with obvious reluctance, but then more and more cheerfully, more and more persistently. The mechanic, shining with lubricating oil, fussed around the thresher, Frol fed it more and more swiftly with swathes of corn, and the workmen rushed about like mad, sneezing with the pungent dust, frequently changing places with one another, thirstily lapping up water like dogs from the buckets and flinging themselves down anywhere to rest.

Late in the afternoon Fiodor was called out into the yard.

"Some beggar woman's asking for you there; she's waiting at the gate," his mistress shouted to him as she ran past.

Wiping the dirt off his sweaty face with his hands, Fiodor ran out. His mother was standing by the fence.

His heart quivered and clenched painfully with sorrow and pity : during the past two months she had grown ten years older. Her greying hair had straggled from under her ragged yellow kerchief; the corners of her lips were drooping with suffering, her eyes were rheumy and shifted restlessly and wretchedly; a stout, patched bag hung over her shoulder; behind her she concealed a long stick which dogs had chewed at.

She ran up to Fiodor and fell on his shoulder. She broke into dry sobbing, which was more like an attack of coughing.

"So this is the way we have to see each other, sonny!"

Her stick got in her way, she laid it down and wiped her eyes with her sleeve. She tried to smile as she indicated the bag with her eyes. But instead of a smile her lips were twisted hideously, and the copious tears rolled down the furrows of her cheeks and dropped on to the dirty ends of her kerchief.

Shame, pity, love for his mother, all mingled in one feeling and prevented Fiodor from speaking; he spasmodically opened and closed his mouth and wriggled his shoulders.

"Are you working?" she asked, breaking the oppressive silence.

"Yes," he forced out the word.

"What's your master like? Decent?"

"Let's go inside the house. We'll have a talk this evening."

"What, just as I am?" She started back in alarm.

"Yes, just as you are."

On the veranda Zakhar's wife met them.

"Where are you taking her? We've got nothing to give you, my dear. Depart in peace."

"This is my mother," Fiodor said thickly.

Laughing shamelessly, the mistress surveyed the shrinking woman from head to foot and went back into the house without saying another word.

"Maria Fiodorovna, give my mother something to eat. She's been on the road," Fiodor asked her in an ingratiating tone.

The woman thrust her indignant face through the doorway.

"I've got twenty dinners to prepare, haven't I? I don't suppose she'll die before the evening. She can have supper with the workmen."

The door was slammed. Her indignant voice floated through the open window :

"They've hung themselves round my neck, the devils. He's got a yard full of parents out there. May you die, damn you! You've taken on a parasite to your own sin."

"Come under the shed where I sleep," Fiodor whispered to his mother, going crimson.

9

Dusk came on. The threshing-floor was silent at last. The work-men went off to their supper in the house. Three tables were laid in the kitchen. The master and mistress, the engineer, and certain of the workmen sat at one, with Fiodor and his mother at the very end of the table.

Zakhar Denisovich sluggishly sipped the thin gruel, and frowned as he looked round the room : these workmen ate an awful lot, a good thirty-six pounds of baked bread every day; they devoured it as though they were at a funeral repast.

The engineer ate in glum silence; he wasn't feeling well, Frol chewed away enjoyably, his ears working up and down, and talked without stopping :

"Well, dear master, are you satisfied with our work?"

"Satisfied, yes I'm satisfied. But why am I satisfied?" Zakhar Denisovich sniffed. "There's a lot of threshing to be done, and the workers this year aren't at all like they were before the war. There's no enthusiasm for work, that's the trouble. Take my Fiodka, for instance : he can eat as much as a man, but he works like a kid. Everything's left to be done by the master, and God knows why I have to pay him money."

Fiodor took a stealthy glance at his mother; she smiled in-gratiatingly, miserably. The mistress had deliberately set the pot of gruel as far away from her as possible, and had shifted the bread to the far end of the table. Fiodor saw that his mother was not eating any bread and had to get up from the table every time she put her spoon into the pot.

"They're kids for work," the master repeated with a titter (he evidently liked the phrase). "But they eat just like full-grown men."

Frol took a glance at Fiodor's pale face, and his lips quivered.

"Who are you talking about?" he asked curtly.

"I'm just talking generally."

"What d'you mean by 'generally'." Frol put down his spoon and leaned across the table. Half closing his eyes, he stared fixedly at the bridge of the master's nose and clenched and unclenched his fists.

"About workers generally," Zakhar Denisovich said self-satisfiedly, not noticing the quarrelsome tone in Frol's voice.

Sensing that a row was developing, the workmen at the other tables stopped talking and eating and began to listen.

"But supposing I give you one in your castanets for making such a remark?" Frol asked in a loud voice.

The master drew in his horns: goggling his eyes, he gazed without speaking at Frol's sweating, angry face.

"What do you mean?" he coughed out at last.

"Would you like me to try? I can, you know."

"You look out, brother; they run you straight to the militia for that sort of talk."

"Wha-a-at?"

Frol strode round the table. But the mechanic caught him by the arm and forced him back to his seat on the bench.

"There's no need to take offence," Zakhar Denisovich stammered, suddenly realizing what was happening.

"There's no need to take offence, but I'll disfigure your claypot physiog till it looks like a bee's honeycomb, that's all," Frol roared in his rage. "Don't you forget, you scum, that the old laws no longer apply. I don't care a damn for you. And don't you dare sneer at workmen. I'm not in your Fiodor's place, or I'd have wrung the soul out of you long ago. You're delighted to have got hold of such a lad, but you don't like to admit it, do you? We know the likes of you. What, bitten your tongue, have you? Shut up. These days you can't go complaining to the local chief of police. I shed my blood in the Red Army; but you dare to sneer at workers, do you?"

"Shut up, Frol, I ask you; do shut up!" the mechanic shook the sleeve of his friend's creased tunic.

"I can't. My soul's on fire."

Zakhar calmed down and turned the talk to the harvest and the autumn ploughing. To soften the impression caused by this scene, the mechanic readily joined in the conversation. Zakhar Denisovich unexpectedly turned amiable and prudent to the point of hypocrisy. He plied the workmen with food and drink in abundance, and called along the table to Fiodor:

"What's the matter, brother Fiodor? Why aren't you eating any bread? Wife, cut him off a crust. Thank God we've got enough bread now."

Fiodor pushed the dry crust away and, when the master looked at him in bewilderment, he answered with a curl of his lips :

"Your bread's bitter."

"That's right," Frol banged his fist on to the table and got up to go after Fiodor.

The other workmen rose and followed him with alacrity.

Zakhar Denisovich turned crimson and blinked; he went running from table to table, squealing in a piercing voice :

"What's all this for, brothers? There's some porridge made with milk to come. Wife, bring it to the table quick."

"Thank you very much for your hospitality," someone said sarcastically.

10

Next morning Fiodor's mother made ready to go without waiting to have any breakfast.

"Perhaps you could stay for the day?" he asked reluctantly.

For some reason he felt an unconquerable shame for himself, his master, his mother, for all his life, so joyless and maimed. He didn't care whether his mother stayed the day or not, even though he had felt such great, sunny joy when he had first seen her the previous day.

After all that had happened, he felt it would be better for him to be left alone with his thoughts, with his indignation and fury with all the world, where there was no one to whom he could turn for protection, no one he could ask for advice, and no one from whom he could expect a kindly word of sympathy.

His mother, too, was in a hurry to go. It was hard for her to look at her son, and still harder to sit at the table under the hateful, currish, greedy eyes of the master and mistress, who watched every little bit of food as it was carried to the mouth.

"No, sonny, I'll go now. . . . We'll see each other again some time."

"All right then, you go," he said indifferently through set teeth.

They said their last goodbyes. Then Fiodor remembered that his mother had no food for the journey.

"Wait a bit, mother; I'll go and ask the mistress, she may give me a measure of corn. My master doesn't pay me any wages, I'll take the corn instead of money. You can sell it. . . ."

At his request the mistress took the key to the granary and went off without a word. Unlocking the padlock, she asked:

"Got a bag?"

"Yes."

Fiodor opened his mother's sack and looked away at the grain-bin wall festooned with intricate cobwebs. The mistress niggardly poured out a measure, by no means full, of uncleaned wheat mixed with chaff and dust.

The door creaked. Zakhar Denisovich pushed his way in, belly foremost, and nodded to his wife.

"Go back to the house." He trotted over to Fiodor.

Carefully setting the sack down on the floor, the lad leaned against the wall of the bin, and waited.

"What's all this?" Zakhar hissed, pulling a face. "Have you been given grain?"

"I have."

"You're stirring up the workmen. You're causing trouble. The master of the house has his face all but punched in in his own house because of you, and now you're taking my grain. . . . My grain. Ah?"

Fiodor said nothing. Zakhar's expression changed, he drew closer and closer to the lad and suddenly, stuttering, shouted in a piercing descant:

"Clear out of my place. Clear out, you son of a bitch. . . ."

Fiodor picked up the sack in his left hand and strode to the door. Zakhar flew at him like a cock, tore the sack out of his hand and gave him a swinging, resounding smack on the face.

Little yellow spots danced before Fiodor's eyes. In his fury he lost all sense of prudence and his hands seemed filled with molten lead. Staggering, with one hand he clutched his master's throat with its folds of fat, with his other fist he struck out at his head as he flung it back.

Inside of three seconds Zakhar was lying on the floor beneath Fiodor, writhing like a fat snake under the boy's blows, trying to bite his face. Biting his lips till the blood came, Fiodor beat away at his fat, baggy neck, at the teeth clicking right up against his face. Zakhar brought into play all a woman's tricks: he scratched, he bit, he tore at Fiodor's hair; but after a few moments, thoroughly beaten up, panting hard, he burst into tears, smeared his lips with snot and lay groaning helplessly, his belly shaking.

Fiodor got up, wiped the blood from his scratched face, and waited for a second attack. But Zakhar nimbly turned over on his belly and crawled like a crab to the door, bellowing as he went.

"That's for everything. Everything. Everything!" the thought beat in Fiodor's brain. He tidied his clothes, picked up the sack and was about to lift the door latch when he heard a heartrending cry:

"Help! Murder! Help, good people!"

An unexpected gust of laughter rose in his throat. Leaning against the door post, he laughed as he had not laughed since his father's death. He laughed till he could laugh no more, then went outside. There he saw Zakhar Denisovich standing with legs astraddle in the middle of the yard, paying no heed to the anxious questions of the workmen surrounding him, but shouting with his mouth gaping like a round black hole:

"Murder!"

II

After seeing his mother off, before he himself left, Fiodor resolved to ask his master:

"So you're not going to pay me?"

"Pay you. . . . ? You ought to have your neck broken, and even that. . . . Well, but I'm not done with you yet. I'm sending a complaint about you to the People's Court; they don't make pets of the likes of you, you ragged-arse."

"All right, grow rich to your own good, Zakhar Denisovich. I don't suppose I shall die without your pay."

"You needn't stand snivelling here. Get out, I tell you."

Fiodor stood for a moment, thinking; then he walked out of the gate without saying goodbye. The wicket gate creaked. The hound under the granary rattled its chain.

When he got outside he stopped again. The evening fires were being extinguished all over the settlement. On the outskirts an accordion was wheezing, the words of a song came indistinctly to his ears. Occasionally the song was drowned under a roar of laughter, so hearty and powerful that he felt like forgetting all his own troubles and even the world's very existence. He aimlessly made his way along the street, and was about to turn down an alley to reach a distant threshing-floor where he proposed to spend the night in the straw, when someone called after him :

"Is that you, Fiodor?"

"Yes, it's me."

"Well, float along here."

He went across and saw Frol lying under a fence, his straw hat thrust to the back of his head, which signified that its owner was not yet completely drunk. He had his dirty handkerchief spread out in front of him on the sunburnt grass; on the handkerchief was a long-necked bottle giving off the smell of home-made vodka, a half-eaten cucumber, and some fine white bread.

"Sit down."

Glad of the meeting, Fiodor sat down beside him.

"So you're off?"

"I am."

"Did you give your master's mug a good bashing?"

"Oh no. Not all that much."

"A great pity. You should have given him more. How long have you been working for him?"

"Two months."

"For two months' work he owes you fifteen roubles at the very least. It's the working season now, and for fifteen roubles even I would agree to someone rolling me on the floor. Believe my words, it's pure profit."

Fiodor did not comment. Frol tucked his legs under him, pushed his hat off, and throwing back his head, thrust the neck of the bottle into his mouth. There was a long bubbling and gurgling, then the bottle described an arc and was thrust into Fiodor's hand.

"Drink."

"I don't drink."

"You don't drink? Then you needn't. I praise your abstinence."

The throat of the bottle disappeared once more into his mouth. Fiodor gazed silently at the golden sprinkle over the azure sky.

When the bottle was emptied, Frol flashed his eyes merrily, laughed aimlessly, and with nods of his head brought his hat back from his nape over his eyes, and worked it back again.

"Will you take him to court?"

"What for?"

"You idiot's favourite! Why, because you've received a hare's tail for two months' work. Are you taking him to court?"

"I don't know," Fiodar answered irresolutely.

"I tell you what," Frol began, as he crunched the cucumber between his teeth. "You go straight to Dubovka hamlet; there's a Young Communist Group there. You go to them, they'll take up your case. I've served in the Red Army myself, brother, and I welcome the new life; but I can't go in for it myself, because of my hereditary weakness. I've got my father's blood. I drink vodka, and under Soviet socialism that sort of thing oughtn't to be. So there you are. . . . Otherwise I . . ." He looked mysterious. "I'd get educated and join the party unanimously. And then I'd twist the tails of such kind friends as your master."

But a moment or two later all his animation had faded out. Wearily scrutinizing the bottle from its neck to its bottom, he stroked it lovingly and repeated in an indifferent tone :

"You go to the Young Communists. They won't let you be done wrong to. That's where your kith and kin are. They're naked lads like you and me."

Soon afterwards he fell asleep where he lay under the fence. Fiodor sat lost in thought, his head between his hands, and didn't even notice a dog run up, sniff at the drunken Frol, raise one hind leg and piss over him, then trot on.

The first cocks crowed. By the pond outside the settlement a duck quaked in the reeds; somewhere among the houses the drum of a winnower rattled away drily, then was silent, only to start again. Someone was taking advantage of the fine weather to spend all night winnowing his grain. Fiodor got up, looked at the snoring Frol and wanted to wake him up. But he thought better of it, waved the matter off with his hand, and unhurriedly walked away to the threshing-floor.

12

By noon next day he was drawing near to Dubovka hamlet. He had covered some fifteen miles and more during the morning.

Towards the end he grew tired, his legs seemed loaded with iron, and his soles and calves ached terribly.

From the hilltop he saw the hamlet as though stretched out on his palm : a square with a little white church with peeling stucco, the white cubes of houses and sheds, the green shaggy locks of gardens, and the smokily grey little streams of streets.

He dropped down the hill. The dogs in the outlying yards greeted him with a sluggish barking. He made his way to the square. Next to the neat-looking school the walls of the People's House gleamed with velvety whitewash. He asked a boy who ran past :

"Where can I find your Young Communist Group?"

"Over there, in the People's House."

He went shyly up the steps and entered the wide open door. From somewhere in the heart of the house came a quiet buzz of conversation. His footsteps clattered hollowly under the lofty white-washed ceiling. At the far end of the corridor he heard voices coming through a door. He went in. Some half dozen lads sitting on the window-sills turned their heads as the door creaked and, seeing a strange face, stared at him without speaking.

"Is this the Young Communist Group?"

"It is."

"But who's your head?"

"I'm the secretary," a freckled youngster answered.

"I'd like to speak to you," Fiodor said, still feeling embarrassed.

"Sit down, comrade, and tell us what you want."

They thoughtfully offered him a stool and stood in a ring round him. At first he felt awkward under the concentric gaze of these strange youngsters; but as he looked at their open, friendly faces he recalled Frol's words : "They're your kith and kin." He recalled those words, and poured out all his story, stammering and getting worked up; he told of his life with Zakhar Denisovich. As he spoke of all the wrongs he had suffered the tears came uninvited to his throat, his voice broke, and he had difficulty in breathing. He glanced from time to time at the others, afraid he would detect an insulting sneer in their eyes. But their faces were clouded gloomily, they expressed their sympathy, and an indignant look twisted the freckled lad's lips. He ended quite suddenly, as though cut off. The others exchanged glances without speaking.

"Take him to court?" one of them asked at last, breaking the silence.

"Of course. What else?" the secretary exclaimed fierily; he turned to Fiodor:

"But where have you fixed yourself up now?"

"Nowhere."

"Got anywhere to go to?"

"Before this I lived in Danilovka; but my father died, my mother has to go begging, and I've got nowhere to live."

"What are you thinking of doing then?"

"I haven't any idea," he answered uncertainly. "Find work somewhere or other. . . ."

"Don't you worry about that, we'll find you work."

"That we will!"

"Come and stay with me for the time being," one of them proposed.

After asking a few further questions, the secretary, Rybnikov, said to Fiodor:

"Listen, comrade! You hand in a complaint to the People's Court, and our group will support it. One of us will go with you to your former master to collect your things, and for the time being you'll stay with Yegor, that's this fellow here." He pointed to Yegor. "But as for his threat to take you to court, don't worry about that. We're not going to let the labourer lose his copeks. And we'll call him to account for exploiting you without concluding a labourer's hire contract with you."

They all went in a bunch to the door. Fiodor no longer felt tired. These rough-looking, sunburnt lads seemed amazingly near and dear to him. He felt he would like to show his gratitude in some way, but was ashamed to do anything, and walked without speaking, occasionally glancing with a quiet smile at Yegor's thin, hook-nosed face.

As he walked along the passage of Yegor's hut he again recalled the words "kith and kin", and smiled at the picture they conjured up of the drunken Frol. That phrase conveyed it all so perfectly. That was just it: they were his kith and kin.

13

Yegor lived at home with his mother and little sister. The mother welcomed Fiodor as if he were her own son; she made a fuss of him at dinner, washed his underwear, and made no difference between him and Yegor.

To begin with he helped Yegor on the farm : together they ploughed, drove out to cut wood, collected the cattle, and during their spare time began to enclose the yard with a new and high willow wattle fence.

Autumn came on imperceptibly. Dry, windless weather set in. There was a slight nip in the air of an early morning, the poplar in the yard lost more and more of its yellow leaves every day, the orchards were stripped bare, and on the horizon the distant forest beyond the river looked like the unshaven scrub on a sick man's cheeks.

Every evening Yegor and Fiodor went off to the club. Fiodor listened intently to new thoughts and words he had not come across before; with an avidly inquisitive mind he drank in all he heard during the long Saturday political readings and discussions with the agronomists on such close and intimate subjects as farming. But he found it difficult to catch up with the other lads : they had their political education off by heart, they read the newspapers, had listened for a good twelve months to the local agronomist's talks and could answer every question clearly and to the point. (Rybnikov, the secretary, even read Marx, with his fists thrust into his freckled cheeks.) But Fiodor had had hardly any education.

And besides, it was one thing to hold the rough handles of a plough and feel its hot, living rattle in his hands as he worked, and quite another to hold in his hand such a fragile and gentle thing as a pencil. His fingers at once began to tremble, his forearm went numb, and it wasn't long before the malevolent pencil had broken. His hands were far more inured to the first task; when undertaking his training his father had never thought Fiodor would be any good at books, and so he had given him grainsowers' hands, broad in the bones, hairy and unshapely, but with an iron strength. All the same, little by little he imbibed the wisdom of books : somehow, crookedly and criss-cross, like a waddling sledge sliding all over a hummocky and rutted road, he could explain what 'class' and 'party' meant, and what tasks the bolsheviks were pursuing, and the difference between bolsheviks and mensheviks.

His words, like his walk, were awkward and solid; but the other lads regarded him with approving seriousness; they may have smiled sometimes, but there was nothing insulting in their smiles Fiodor realized that, and didn't take offence.

In December, the day before the general meeting, Rybnikov said to him :

"I tell you what, hand in your application for membership. We'll consider it in the District Committee, we'll confirm it, and then in the spring you can go off and become a labourer. We're running a campaign now to get as many of the young labourers as possible into the union. Our group was asleep at one time, the secretary was the son of a kulak, and many of the members were unsatisfactory . . . they disintegrated like carrion on a hot day. We cleared them all out just a month before you arrived, and now we've got to work. We've got to win respect for the Dubovka group in the eyes of the people. Formerly, the only thing our Young Communists knew was how to gulp down vodka and push their hands down inside the girls' blouses during the Saturday evening fun and games. But we've stopped all that. We'll make the work go so that it's known about all over the Don province. When you get a job we'll give you tasks to tackle, and you'll get all the labourers into the Communist group. We'll all be scattered among the villages."

"But what do you think : will I be up to it? I'm not all that good at my books. . . ."

"Stop talking rot. What you don't know now you'll learn during the winter. We ourselves aren't all that educated. The District Committee tried to treat us high-handedly : no help, no good advice, only instructions to do this, that, and the other. We, brother, will manage everything with our own strength. So there !"

Rybnikov's idea of gathering in the young labourers of the surrounding hamlets and settlements dropped into Fiodor's mind like a grain of wheat into rich, black earth. He recalled his life with Zakhar Denisovich and burned with impatience to get to work. He scribbled out his application for membership that very evening. But when he gave his reason for wanting to join the Young Communists he didn't write down the one Yegor instructed him to give. Yegor had said : write that you wish to get political education; but Fiodor thought it over a little and wrote in black on white, without commas or stops :

"I wish to join because I'm a worker so as to grow very expert and to draw all the working labourers into the young communists because the young communists are the labourers' kith and kin."

When Rybnikov read it through he knitted his brows.

"That's quite right, but you've made rather a song of it. But it doesn't matter, it'll do."

The meeting began late in the evening. A hum of many voices echoed through the club. The meeting elected its presiding committee, Rybnikov made a report on the international situation, then they turned to current business.

With a sinking heart Fiodor waited for his application to be read out.

At last, Rybnikov, coughing and looking round the meeting, announced in a loud voice :

"An application has been received from Fiodor Boitsov, whom we all know."

He read it out slowly and, smoothing the paper flat on the table, asked :

"Who's in favour and who's against?"

Yegor rose from the back bench and, wrinkling his hook nose, declared :

"What is there to discuss? The lad comes of the labourer class, he's the son of a poor peasant in Danilovka. Now he's getting his political orientation he'll do. Let's cut the cackle : I propose we accept him."

"Anyone against?"

No one was against. The vote was taken. Hands were raised in a close palisade. Twenty-six for, the entire group. As Rybnikov counted the votes he looked with a smile at Fiodor's pale, beaming face.

"Accepted unanimously."

Fiodor found it difficult to sit on till the end of the meeting. He did not follow very well what was going on around him. Rybnikov opened a fiery attack on Yerofei Chornov because he took part in the Saturday evening junketings; Yerofei defended himself, declaring that others did too. Their voices reached Fiodor's ears as though through a dead wall, while his tangled thoughts pursued their course through his mind : "Now I'm one of their family, and no longer like a stepson. . . . These are my kith and kin; it's good to be with them, shoulder to shoulder, in a solid wall. . . ."

At last a voice cried :

"Silence. I declare the meeting closed. Vanya, will you take on writing out the minutes?"

The clatter of their feet sounded like a rattling padlock. Everybody went towards the door, lighting cigarettes and bristling with the piercing cold which penetrated into the corridor from outside. Fiodor, Yegor, and Rybnikov left together. They went down the frozen steps of the veranda and at once fell into a healthy snowdrift which the wind had blown up during the meeting. Grunting and puffing, Yegor was the first to crawl through the drift, Fiodor behind him. At a street corner Rybnikov said goodbye to them, and gave Fiodor's frozen hand a firm grip, saying as he looked into his eyes :

"You watch out, Fiodka, don't let us down. You're our hope. Now you've become a Young Communist more responsibility for your behaviour rests on you than when you were a non-party lad. Well, but you know all that. So long, friend."

Fiodor silently shook his hand and wanted to say something in reply, but he began to choke with his feelings. He hurried to catch up with Yegor and, still feeling that weightily joyous lump of tears in his throat, whispered to himself :

"I've become an old woman, I've gone quite soft. I've got to be stronger, not so flabby, but I can't. I'm too happy. . . . And only a little while ago I thought there was nothing but sorrow in the world and all people were strangers."

14

Next morning he was summoned to go to the Executive Committee.

"Summons to appear at court. Sign," the secretary said.

He signed the receipt and went over to the window to read the summons. He was to attend the court on the 21st. He glanced at the wall calendar and was alarmed : under the portrait of Lenin was the figure 20 in red.

He hurried home and began to get ready.

"Where are you off to?" Yegor asked.

"To the district, to attend the case against my old master. I only got the summons today, and I'm to be there tomorrow. . . . There's a fine thing! D'you think I'll manage to get there in time?"

Yegor glanced through the little window, which was smeared with frost as though with dough, found the yellow speck of sun in the azure sky, and said thoughtfully :

"Well, it's twenty miles and more . . . if you go at four miles an hour, a good pace, it's over five hours. You'll get there by nightfall if all goes well."

"Then I'm off."

"Have you got some food to take with you?"

"Yes."

Yegor went out to see him go, and shouted after him :

"Step it out, or you'll never get there before dark. Remember the wolves."

Fiodor adjusted his sack on his shoulder, drew the strap tighter round his padded sheepskin, and went with long strides down the middle of the street, over the road polished and slippery from sledge runners. He climbed the hill. He looked back at the hamlet sprinkled with white snow, and then, shrugging his shoulders, feeling a sweaty heat on his back, swiftly took the road to the district centre.

Down hill and up hill. Down hill and up hill again. The bluish bands of forests and copses sprinkled with snow floated evenly along the horizon. The snow glittered with dazzling bluish sparkles, the rays of the sun struck against the drifts and arched the road with rainbows.

He strode along swiftly, tapping with his stick, inhaling the smoke of his home-grown tobacco, which had a sweetish taste in the frost. He covered thirteen miles or so, looked up at the sun rolling towards the thin, wavy, spidery line of the earth, and took a piece of bread and lard cut into thin hunks out of his sack. He squatted down on his haunches at the wayside, had a bite, and went on again, trying to keep warm by walking fast.

The evening spread lilac tints over the snow. The road glittered with a bluish, steely gleam. In the west, darkness erased the line dividing the earth from the sky. When he entered the village, errant glows of stars were already twinkling in the clear sky. At the first little house he came to, poverty stricken and far from imposing, he asked to be allowed to stay for the night. The master, a friendly bearded peasant, let him in readily:

"You can stop the night, you won't overstay your welcome."

After chewing a piece of frozen fat for supper he spread out his sheepskin coat by the stove, put his cap under his head, and fell asleep.

As usual, he awoke at dawn. He washed, and the housewife offered to fry his piece of frozen fat. He had some food, then went off to the square in the centre of the village. Close by the building of the District Soviet he read a sign board over a gate: "The People's Court of the Fifth Sector of the Upper Don Region."

He went through the wicket gate. The first person he saw in the yard was Zakhar Denisovich. He was wearing a blue cloth coat lined with sheepskin, had a cowl tied round his neck, and was unharnessing his sweating horse. As he threw a horsecloth over the animal he happened to notice Fiodor and turned away, pulling a face and not saying a word of greeting.

The time dragged past terribly slowly. The clerk to the court arrived just before nine o'clock. He didn't remove his outer clothes but, snuffling through his nose, slapped a pile of documents down on a table and surveyed the crowd in the passage with sleepy, swollen eyes. The judge arrived an hour later, squeezing sideways through the door and noisily slamming it behind him.

"Fiodor Boitsov and Zakhar Blagurodov," the clerk called, half opening the door.

Zakhar Denisovich went in, his leather-soled felt boots squeaked as he walked.

"Ha, he stinks of vodka, he can hardly keep his feet. You can see he stinks all through with it," an elderly cossack in a soldier's ragged greatcoat laughed sarcastically after him.

Fiodor took off his cap and went in boldly. There followed a good ten minutes of questions asked by the judge and the two people's representatives. Zakhar Denisovich began to stammer; he was obviously getting the wind up.

"Did you pay him?" the judge asked, tapping with his pencil.

"Yes, of course . . . I paid him. . . ."

"How did you pay him, in kind or in cash?"

"In cash."

"How much?"

"Eight roubles, and I gave him his food in addition."

"How d'you get that? In your depositions you have stated that you hired Boitsov for half a rouble a month."

"Out of kindness. . . . Because he was an orphan. . . . I was his benefactor . . . in place of his own father," Zakhar Denisovich stammered, going crimson.

"So . . ." the judge smiled almost imperceptibly.

After several more questions the court asked them both to go out. Five or six other cases were heard. Fiodor stood waiting in the passage. Zakhar Denisovich gathered seven or eight cossacks around himself and declared, gesticulating furiously:

"They ask why I didn't enter into any contract. But you try getting a workman that way. . . . He came and pleaded for work in the name of Christ, and then he turns out to be a Young Communist and declares: 'I'm not going to work for you.'"

"The court's reopened."

The crowd rushed into the room. The judge read out the first sentence in a rapid patter. Fiodor could feel his heart beating violently under his sheepskin. The blood rushed to his head, then ebbed away to his heart. He was hardly able to distinguish the words of the sentence. The judge raised his voice:

"In accordance with para.— of the law . . . Zakhar Denisovich Blagurodov is sentenced to pay Fiodor Boitsov twelve roubles for two months' work. For not concluding a contract, and for exploiting a juvenile . . . he is fined thirty roubles or is sentenced to forced labour for a period. . . . Costs: so much. Sentence irrevocable," Fiodor caught the words.

He ran down the steps and, not stopping to button up his sheepskin, smiling happily to himself, walked swiftly out of the village. He hardly noticed that he covered several miles, he was so absorbed in thinking over the court decision, in working out plans, in reckoning that by the autumn of the next year he would have earned enough money to buy a horse and live off his own small holding, so saving his mother from want.

Then he thought of the work he was going to do among the labourers during the coming summer, and felt warmer as he considered it. The wind blew into his face and sprinkled him with snow; the fine, prickly dust filmed his eyes. Suddenly his ears caught the hardily audible squeak of sledge runners and the click-clack of horse hoofs behind him. He turned round sharply, and just as he did so he was struck a terrible blow in the chest with a shaft pole and went flying. As he fell he saw above him the foaming muzzle of a raven horse and behind it, amid a cloud of dusty snow, Zakhar Denisovich's purplish blue face.

The blow from the shaft was followed by the whistle of a knout over his head; snatching his cap off, the thong cut diagonally right across his face.

In his fury he didn't feel any pain; he jumped to his feet and in a mad frenzy tore capless after the sledge. Zakhar reined the horses back hard in full flight with his left hand, raised the knout in his right hand high above his head and, turning round to face Fiodor, roared with all the power of his lungs:

"I'll give you something to remember me by. I'll see you put where . . . by hell . . . where the crayfish spend the winter."

The wind tore his words to shreds and choked Fiodor as he ran behind the sledge. Suddenly he lost all his strength and halted in the middle of the road. Only then did he feel a lacerating pain in his chest, and the scalding, salty blood streaming from his face.

15

Here and there the ploughed land showed in black, thawed patches in the snow, and from these patches the spring advanced. A warm and moist wind blew at night, clouds hung over the hamlet, towards morning rain lashed down, and the snow, already half melted underneath, floated away in torrents of water. On the steppe the earth was laid bare; only the flakes of ice held on in places on the road and in the hollows, clinging firmly to the last-year grass and tussocks, and huddling as though pleading for protection.

Just before the season for field work began again, Fiodor said goodbye to his friends and, packing his belongings and the pamphlets Rybnikov had given him, went off in search of wages.

"Watch out, Fiodka, get them organized," Rybnikov said at their parting.

"All right, I will. I'll get them all gathered in a single pile," Fiodor smiled.

Half a dozen of the youngsters accompanied him out of the hamlet and stood waiting on the outskirts until he emerged on the highroad. As he crossed the first rise he looked back: his friends were standing in a little group on the track to the pasturage; Rybnikov and Yegor were waving their caps.

When the hamlet was lost to his sight he felt rather depressed. Once more he was alone, like that plant of last year's gypsophila which was growing all alone at the wayside.

He suppressed his feelings and pondered on the route he should take. The neighbouring hamlets were all poor, and the inhabitants had no need to hire labour; in this area there were no peasants as rich as those of Krenovsky in his native district. After thinking it over he turned on to the side road running to Krenovsky.

There he hired himself out to a neighbour of Zakhar Denisovich, a peasant named Pantelei Miroshnikov. Old Pantelei was tall, with skin shrivelled to his bones; he was a taciturn old fellow. He had lost three sons in the war, and carried on the farm with the aid of his wife and two daughters-in-law.

"Why did you leave Zakhar, my handsome fellow-me-lad?" he asked Fiodor, his grey eyebrows rising and falling on his forehead.

"The master paid me off."

"But how do you propose to hire yourself out?"

"On contract."

"What are you saying? My price for the summer season is three roubles, and in the winter I don't want you even as a gift. If you're thinking of a twelve-month contract I don't need you."

"I can make it till the autumn if you like."

"In a word, till the end of the season. When we've finished the autumn ploughing you can go to the four winds, my handsome young fellow-me-lad. Is it agreed, three roubles a month?"

"I agree, only there's got to be a contract. I'm not working without it."

"It's all one to me. . . . I'm not educated, anyway. . . . I suppose we've got to sign something, my handsome young fellow-me-lad? All right, my daughter-in-law Stepanida will sign for me."

They signed the contract in the local Farm Labourers' Union Committee, and Fiodor started work joyfully. For a couple of weeks old Pantelei stealthily watched his new workman. Fiodor often caught his testing, piercing gaze fixed on him. And in the end, towards the close of the second week, when Fiodor ploughed up the field vegetable allotment outside the village in a single day and drove home the weary, sweating oxen, the old man went up to him and said:

"Have you ploughed all the allotment?"

"I have."

"Without fault?"

"Yes."

"How deep did you drive the plough?"

"To the depth you said, daddy."

"Did you water the oxen in the pond?"

"I did."

"But how old are you, young man?"

"Seventeen."

The old fellow walked right up to Fiodor, seized him painfully by the hair, and, pulling his head down against his own shrivelled, bony chest, squeezed it hard with his hairy hand, and stroked the lad's muscular, springy back.

"You're a good workman, my handsome young fellow-me-lad. Remain for the winter if you'd like to. By God, I mean it."

He pushed Fiodor off and stared at him hard, smiling broadly and cheerfully. Fiodor was moved by the old man's kindly and parental attitude to him. When he had first taken on the lad he had asked:

"You're not one of those . . . what d'you call it . . . Young Communists, are you?" And when Fiodor confirmed that he was, the old man dismissed the matter with a wave of the hand. "It's nothing to do with me. You'll eat separately; I can't put you with myself, can I? I suppose you don't cross yourself, do you?"

"No."

"Oh, well. I'm an old man, and don't take offence if I keep you separate. You and I are fruit from two different beds."

He treated the lad well, gave him plenty to eat, let him have some of his own home-woven clothing and did not overtax him

with work beyond his strength. At first Fiodor thought he would
have to do all the work himself, as he had for Zakhar Denisovich;
but when just before Easter they drove out to plough he saw that,
despite old Pantelei's scraggy body, he could put any youngster to
shame. He followed the plough without wearying, ploughed
cleanly and with affection, and took turns with Fiodor to see to
the oxen at night. The old fellow was devout, he never used bad
language, and he ruled his family with a firm hand. Fiodor liked
his pet phrase, 'my handsome young fellow-me-lad', and liked the
old man too, for, though he was brusque and harsh outwardly, he
was genuinely kindhearted.

On Easter Sunday evening Fiodor ran into a stocky, freckled
youngster coming along the alley. He looked about twenty, and
came out of Zakhar's yard. From some remark old Pantelei had
made he guessed that this was Zakhar's new labourer. The young
man drew level, and Fiodor struck up a conversation with
him :

"Hallo, comrade."

"Good evening," the youngster answered rather reluctantly.

"You're not working for Zakhar Denisovich, are you?"

"Aha."

Fiodor went closer, and asked :

"Been with him long?"

"Four months, since the winter."

"How much is he paying you?"

"A rouble and my food." The lad grew more animated and his
eyes glittered. "They say your old man agreed to pay you three
roubles and you're working for him. Is that true?"

"Yes."

"That Zakhar's tricked me." He began to tell his story in a
bitter tone. "He promised to raise my wages, but now he never
says anything about it. He makes me work like the devil." In his
indignation he was beginning to get worked up. "It's just the same
in regard to holidays. . . . And I've worn out my own clothes, but
he doesn't give me any money or clothes. Look at my Easter
finery!" He turned round and showed his back; through the shirt,
with its rents running from top to bottom, Fiodor saw a swarthy
triangle of flesh.

"What's your name?" he asked.

"Mitry. And yours?"

"Fiodor."

Zakhar's snuffling voice called from the yard:

"Mitka! Why haven't you fastened the cattle yard gate, you scum? Go and drive in the bullocks."

Mitka shied across the fence like a frightened goat and, gazing out from a clump of nettles, beckoned to Fiodor. Fiodor climbed over the fence, chose a quiet, remote spot in the orchard, and, sitting down beside Mitka, began to do some propaganda.

16

Every Sunday evening Fiodor went off to the square to join in the regular fun. There he made the acquaintance of other lads working as labourers for the wealthy peasants of Krenovsky. Altogether there were eighteen labourers in the settlement, fifteen of them being youngsters. He got these fifteen together and laid the foundations for a local branch of the Labourers' Union.

At first they treated his talk with derisive mistrust.

"It's all right for you," the round-shouldered Kola declared furiously, "you've got a master like an apostle. But if I went in for Young Communism and a contract my master would twist my head off."

"I doubt it," another objected.

"Of course he would if you were all on your own," Fiodor retorted. "But that's not my idea. For instance, you can take one of my fingers and bend it till the knuckles crack, but if I put all my fingers up in a bunch or close them into a fist, can you bend them? No, brother; then I can knock out your ivories with this very same fist." There was a roar of laughter. "And we've got to close up in a fist just like that. We've worked enough like a lot of fools for the masters. Every one of you gets a rouble or even half a rouble; but I get three, and I don't work as hard as you do."

"That's true," they answered in chorus.

They usually met at night, behind the threshing-floors, and they sat talking till the first cocks crowed.

On the fifth Sunday Fiodor put forward a proposal:

"I tell you what, brothers. They shared out the grasslands yesterday, the mowing will start tomorrow or the day after. I propose that tomorrow we tell our masters they're to raise our wages and sign contracts with us, or if they won't we'll stop work."

"You can't do that. It's going too far."

"They'll turn us out."

"We'll be left without a bite to eat."

"They won't turn us out," Fiodor cried, flushing heavily. "They won't just because the haymow is right on top of us now. They'll be losing their centrepin, they'll be left without working hands. We can't go on living like this. The Labourers' Union Committee asks: What are your terms of labour? And one says: You see, I'm related to the master; another: I happen to know him. But as for you, nobody will take any trouble over you if you don't yourselves."

After long arguments they agreed to his proposal.

Next morning the entire settlement was agitated and buzzing like a disturbed flight of clegs. Any day now they could start mowing the hay, but the labourers working for the richest farmers had declared a strike!

During the morning Fiodor heard shouting, and ran out of the gate to see what it was all about.

He found Zakhar Denisovich throwing Mitka's belongings out into the street, shouting the while. Mitry, with a resolute air, was gathering them in a heap and darkly muttering:

"You wait, you wait. You'll ask me to come back before long, but I shan't come."

"You can go to hell before I ask you to come back."

Seeing Fiodor, Zakhar turned to a group of rich peasants standing around and fierily harangued them. The veins swelled on his forehead as he bawled:

"Christians! There's the mischief-maker. There's the one who's leading them. Beat him up, the son of a bitch; that's what ought . . ."

Fiodor clenched his fists and ran towards him. But he dived through his gateway like a mouse and whined fearfully:

"Don't come near me, if you value your life. I'll smash you."

17

"You can do as you wish, but I'm not going to turn out my labourer. For all I care he can be a party member, so long as he does his job. Nor am I concerned about the contract. I fling him three roubles a month and everything's fine; but if he leaves me my losses will be reckoned in hundreds."

"That's true, cousin. And now my wife's fallen ill, and how am I going to manage?"

"That's just how I see it."

"I tell you what, brothers. We'll sign contracts with them, increase their wages, all according to the law, and give them one day's holiday a week. You shut up, Zakhar. The court made you pay thirty roubles. That's just it! Sooner or later we'd have to fork out too."

"Why waste breath further. As things have come to this pass we've got to put up with it. We refuse them three roubles, and we lose hundreds. . . . That's downright stupid."

"You try to hire a man now. . . ."

"You'd burn your fingers.'

"All right, then."

"But we've got to teach that scum who gave them the belly ache a lesson. They've got this educated fellow among them, and he's a pest."

"You mean Fiodka? Why, he's a Young Communist. When he was living with me he spewed up all his real soul. He chased me round my yard with a knife, and thank you . . . the other workmen wouldn't stay with him around, God's truth. But now let him come my way. . . ."

"My son tells me they gather by the threshing-floors every Sunday night. And there he gets them all worked up."

"Supposing two or three of us were to meet him somewhere with good stout cudgels. . . ."

"He needs a lesson. So long as it doesn't smell of dirty work. . . ."

"Zakhar Denisovich, would you come in with us on this?"

"Lord! With all my heart. I'd like to have something heavier than a cudgel, that's all. . . ."

"We won't beat him to death."

"We'll see about that. So there'll be three of us? Well, come along."

18

That evening, noticing that Fiodor was getting ready to go out, Pantelei said with a smile:

"You know, my handsome young fellow-me-lad, if I was you I'd stay at home. You've cooked the gruel, so don't let it scald you."

"Why, what's up?"

"Well, they may do you some harm."

"I should say!" Fiodor laughed, and went off, making his way through the back streets to the threshing-floors.

That night the lads were slow in gathering. Then a good couple of hours were spent in talking. They were all filled with a brave and cheerful spirit. When they had discussed the situation thoroughly they retailed titbits of news. Then they decided to break up.

"Go off in different directions, to avoid people talking," Fiodor warned them.

The night hung pitch black over the steppe; the clouds clashed and jostled against one another like ice in flood water; there was a rumble of thunder; beyond the forest jagged lightning slashed the sky. Fiodor left with the last of the group, but parted from them and returned home the way he had come. At first he thought of approaching the house by the back way; then he changed his mind and turned into the alley. Squatting down by the wattle fence, he tried to light a cigarette; but a gust of dry, hot wind blew out the match. He put his cigarette into his pocket and went to the gate. He had no foreboding whatever and did not see the two forms creeping along behind him while a third stood on guard at the crossroads.

He had hardly set his hand to the gate latch when someone behind him swung a stake, grunting with the effort. The blow caught Fiodor on the nape. With a hollow groan he flung out his hands and dropped by the gate, losing consciousness at once.

*   *   *

The fleas were biting old Pantelei mercilessly. He tossed and turned again and again, grunted, flung his sheepskin on the floor, and was at last about to go off to sleep when suddenly, outside, he heard a groan, the clatter of feet and a stifled whistle. Letting his legs hang from the bed, he listened. "They've caught Fiodka," was his first thought. The whistle was repeated. Jumping out of bed, he snatched from its nail on the wall an ancient muzzle-loading gun which he used to scare the rooks in the vegetable allotment, and ran out on to the veranda. Someone was groaning by the gate, he caught the noise of running feet, the sounds of heavy blows. Pulling back the cock, the old man ran out through the gate, roaring :

"Who's that?"

Three dark figures started away from one another.

Pointing the barrel at the nearest of the three, Pantelei pulled the trigger. A shot thundered out, a stream of fire spurted from the muzzle, the pellets with which the gun was loaded whistled through the air. One of the men started to howl and fell flat on the ground. Panting, the old man threw away his gun and bent over the dark outline of a human body lying by the gate. He groped over the head with both hands and felt something thick and sticky. Turning the head round, he vainly stared into the face : the darkness prevented his seeing anything. Then a flash of lightning scudded across the sky like a lizard, and the old man recognized Fiodor's blood-stained face. Picking up the inert body, trembling and stumbling, he dragged him to the veranda and ran back out of the gate to collect his gun. Lightning lit up the sky again, and he saw a man squatting on his heels a hundred yards or so along the road. Clutching his gun by the barrel, Pantelei tore up to the man, sent him flying in the darkness, and, falling on him with all the weight of his body, roared :

"Who are you?"

"Let me go, for Christ's sake. All my bottom and back have been shot through. Aren't you afraid of committing a sin, neighbour, firing at people with grapeshot? Oi, how it hurts. . . ."

Pantelei recognized Zakhar's voice. Losing control of himself he brought the butt down on Zakhar's head and, seizing him by the hair, dragged him to the veranda.

19

"Our dear comrade Fiodya. I don't suppose you've heard how the trial ended. Zakhar Denisovich got seven years with loss of civil rights for three; the other two, Mikhail Dergachov and Kuzka, a Khrenovsky speculator, got five years. And now I'm glad to tell you that a Young Communist Group has been organized in Khrenovsky. All your labourer comrades, fifteen all told, and six other youngsters from poor families have joined. The District Committee is transferring me there to work, but we're all waiting impatiently for you to get well and come back to us. In Danilovsky settlement Yegor has organized a group of eleven. All our lads are on the job in various places. And I must tell you, too, that I saw old Pantelei the other day, and he's thinking of driving over to see you in hospital and bring you some food. Get well quickly and come back, there's still a lot of work to do, and time's flying like a horse which has broken its hobble.

"With Young Communist greetings to you from the Young Communist Group and from all the boys.

"Rybnikov."

1926.

DRY ROT

Yakov Alexeevich was a man of the old temper. Broad in the bone, with a stoop, and a beard like a millet besom—quite disgustingly like the kulak whom our bright artists depict on the last page of the newspapers. But in one respect he wasn't like them : in his dress. Because of the position he occupies, a kulak is invariably depicted with a waistcoat and high boots with a creak. But, in summer, Yakov Alexeevich goes about in a canvas shirt, unbelted, and barefoot. Three years ago the lists of the District Soviet gave his position as kulak, but then he paid off his labourers, sold his surplus yoke of oxen, keeping only two yokes and a mare. And so in the Soviet lists he was transferred to the next column : that of the medium-rich peasants. This did not cause him to lose his former bearing : he still walked with a sedate waddle, he carried his head like a cock, and, as before, he spoke slowly, rather hoarsely and ponderously at meetings.

Though he had disposed of his husbandry he carried on business on a broad scale. In the spring he sowed forty acres and more of wheat; with the corn he had saved from the previous year's harvest he bought a light plough, two iron harrows, and a winnowing machine. Every one knows who sells a winnowing machine in the spring : people who haven't any grain left to eat.

You could search all through the village and not find another husbandman like Yakov Alexeevich. He was an enterprising cossack, who knew what he was about. None the less, dry rot set in with him too : his younger son, Stepka, joined the Young Communists. Just like that, without permission and without asking advice he took it into his head to join. If such a disaster were to come upon a stupid man it would lead to arguments in the family, and fights. But Yakov Alexeevich didn't think that way. Why instruct the lad with an oaken cudgel? Let him make his own way to the shore. Day after day Yakov sneered at the new régime, the new customs, the laws, larding his remarks with jaundiced oaths, stinging like a fly in autumn. He felt sure the lad's eyes would be opened, and they were : Stepan stopped crossing himself, gave his father unsociable looks, and didn't talk at meals.

One day before dinner the family all stood up for prayers. Yakov Alexeevich tugged at his beard and crossed himself with great sweeps of his hand, as though wielding a scythe in a meadow; Stepka's mother bent double in her obeisances, like a folding rule; all the family swept their hands across their chests in unison : only Stepka stood by the door, fidgeting from foot to foot, keeping his hands behind him.

"Are you a man?" Yakov asked him when they had ended their prayers.

"You ought to know best. . . ."

"Well, if you're a man and you're sitting with people at the table, cross yourself, ugly mug. That's the difference between you and an ox. An ox chews from the manger, then he turns and pisses into the same spot."

Stepka turned to go to the door, but thought better of it, came back and, crossing himself as he went, slipped into his seat at the table.

For several days Yakov Alexeevich went about with a jaundiced look; as he walked about the yard he frowned; his family knew he was chewing over some idea, it wasn't for nothing that he lay groaning and grunting at night, fidgeting, falling asleep only as dawn was coming on. Stepka's mother whispered to her son :

"I don't know, Stepka dear, what our Alexeevich has got into his head. . . . He's either planning some trouble for you or he wants to trip someone up."

Stepka already knew his father was planning some step against him, and he kept himself to himself, simply wondering where he would go if his father ordered him out of the house and home.

Certainly Yakov Alexeevich had something to think about : If Stepka had been fifteen and not twenty he could have dealt with him easily enough. It wouldn't have been a couple of minutes' work to take the leather reins out of the store-room and wind them tightly round his hand. But when a lad's twenty any reins are thin, you instruct such idiots with a shaftpole. But in these new days they flay you so hard for such things that it would be hot and unpleasant for Yakov. So the old man had good reason to grunt and groan at night and to frown in the darkness.

As he sat carving wooden spoons, Maxim, Stepan's elder brother, a sinewy and strong cossack, asked Stepan one evening:

"Tell me, brother, what plague possessed you to join this Young Communist affair?"

"Mind your own business," Stepan snapped.

"No, you tell me," Maxim refused to be put off. "I've lived twenty-nine years, I've seen more than you, and I know and tell you it's all a lot of bosh. It's all right for the worker: when he's done his eight hours' work he goes off to the club, to the Young Communists. But that isn't for us who have to grow the grain. You'll go dragging around at night during the summer working season, and then what sort of work will you be good for during the day? Tell me frankly: are you after getting some sort of official post, is that why you've joined?" Maxim asked with a sneer.

Stepan turned pale but said nothing, though his lips quivered under the insult.

"It's a humbugging government. And positively harmful for us cossacks. Good living for the communists, but you can go and piss. That sort of government can't hang on for long. Though your Young Communists and such like have got their teeth firmly into the food growers' necks, when the time comes the devil will take the lot of them."

A wet strand of hair danced up and down on Maxim's sweaty forehead. The knife carving the block of wood angrily peeled off shavings. Stepan, who was aimlessly turning over the pages of a book, snorted sullenly; he was not anxious to be drawn into an argument, for his father was listening with silent approval to Maxim's words and obviously waiting for Stepan to speak.

"Well, and supposing there's another overthrow, which God forbid, what will you do then?" Maxim bared his teeth in a rapacious snarl.

"Your teeth will fall out before you see any overthrow."

"Look out, Stepan. You're no longer a child. The game's knock for knock now, and if you miss you'll be sent flying. If a war comes along or something of that sort I'll be the first to fight you. There's no point in killing off such whelps as you, but I'll give you a good hiding with a whip. Till the blood comes."

"And he'll deserve it," Yakov Alexeevich added his voice.

"I'll whip you, I swear it by the cross," Maxim thundered, his nostrils quivering. "I remember during the German war our squadron was driven to some factory near Moscow, because the workers there were mutinying. We arrived late in the afternoon and rode in through the gates, and the people were like a cloud round the office. "Brothers, cossacks!" they shouted, "come and join us." Our squadron commander, Bokov, ordered: "Give them the whip, the sons of bitches."

Maxim choked with his laughter and went crimson, neighing away in great rolling gusts.

"My whip was of raw hide, and it had a piece of lead stitched into the end of its lash. I ride in front, and shout to these strikers: 'Arise, arise you working people. The cossacks have come to lash your backs.' Right in front of the lot of them stood a very old, little man in a peaked cap, greyhaired and skinny. I gave him one swipe with my whip, and he kicked and fell under our horses' hoofs. The things we did!" Maxim went on, narrowing his eyes. "Our horses trampled over the women among them too, there was a good twenty of them. Our boys went mad and began to draw their sabres. . . ."

"But what did you do?" Stepan asked hoarsely.

"I gave some of them something to remember."

Stepan huddled with his back to the stove. He pressed against it hard, very hard, and said thickly:

"Pity they didn't finish you off, a snake like you. . . ."

"Who's a snake?"

"You are."

"Who's a snake?" Maxim asked again. Flinging the unfinished spoon on the floor, he got up from the bench.

Stepan's palms were wet with hot sweat. Clenching his fists till the nails pierced the flesh, he said firmly:

"You're a cur! A Cain!"

Maxim stretched out his hand and took hold of a bunch of Stepan's shirt at the chest, tore him away from the stove and flung him on the bed. A wave of hatred swept over the younger man. He flung himself to one side, leaving his shirt collar in Maxim's hands, and swung his fist. A hard blow on the cheek sent him flying. With his left hand Maxim clutched and unclutched his brother's throat, with the other he beat rhythmically on his cheek. Stepan felt his brother's rapid breathing on him from above; he saw

a cold, quite unnecessary smile on his lips. Every blow robbed him
of breath, a ringing nagged in his ears, tears streamed from his
eyes. A cry of affront for his involuntary tears, for Maxim's smile,
was stranded in his tightly-gripped throat. Blood flowed from his
split lips. Rolling his bulging eyes, he spat blood into his brother's
face; but Maxim turned his head aside, revealing his sinewy, clean-
shaven neck, and went on rhythmically, silently bringing his hairy
hand down on Stepan's swollen cheek.

Yakov Alexeevich waited for some time, then he separated them.
Still with the same smile on his lips Maxim picked up the spoon
from the floor and sat down by the window. Stepan wiped his
bloody lips with his sleeve, put on his cap and went out, quietly
closing the door behind him.

"That'll do him some good. Make sure he doesn't try that game
too much, or he'll be going for father next," Maxim remarked.

Yakov Alexeevich thoughtfully tugged at his beard, and his brow
furrowed as he looked at his wife's tear-stained face.

*   *   *

Next morning, Maxim was the first to strike up a conversation
with his brother.

"Are you going to the Soviet to make a complaint?" he asked.
"I am."

"And is that the way to treat your family?"

Stepan glanced at the grey face of Maxim's wife, at his mother
wiping her eyes on her apron, and said nothing. He mentally decided to endure the shame, to keep quiet about it.

Now a boring silence settled in the home. The women talked in
whispers. Yakov Alexeevich went about taciturn, and as clouded
as a November dawn. One day, Maxim, smiling guiltily, said to
Stepan :

"Brother, you mustn't take all I said word for word as I said
it. All sorts of things occur in a family. . . . But it's all through
your Young Communist business. Let it all go to hell. We've lived
without it in the past, and we'll get through now too. What d'you
want to go pushing in there for? The neighbours are throwing it
up in your father's face: 'What's this about Stepka becoming a
Young Communist?' It's an absolute disgrace for the old man. And

when it's time to marry you off what girl will take you without a church wedding? Take some draggle-skirt, will you?"

Stepan made no answer; he went off to the cattle yard. Every evening he made his way to the club in the square. He thought gloomy thoughts to the wheezing of the priest's requisitioned harmonium.

But all through the village the spring pushed its way insistently. Freckles appeared in the girls' faces, buds on the willows. The spring-flood waters tinkled as they rippled along the streets. The snow slipped away imperceptibly, no one knew whither; under the heat of the sun a steam haze arose; the turquoise steppe melted into an azure mist. In the steppe gulleys, in the ravines, along the edges of the slopes snow still lay, sullying the earth with its stale, wind-tousled whiteness; but over the rises, over the shaggy barrows the sheep were already kicking up their heels, the cows walked along sedately, and the green shoots of grass forcing its way through the last year faded greenery had an intoxicating and tender scent.

They drove out to do the ploughing in the middle of March. Yakov Alexeevich began to make preparations earlier than anyone else in the village. From Shrovetide onward he fed the oxen on maize, giving them an abundance, with the husbandman's thrifty prodigality.

The sun had not yet dried out the greasy scent of the spring mouldiness from the ground when he had his sons all fitted out. One Thursday, as soon as dawn began to break they drove off into the steppe. Stepan urged on the oxen, Maxim followed with the plough. For two days they lived in the steppe some five miles from home. The frosts fettered the steppe at night, the grass was overgrown with hoar-frost, the earth escaped from the icy fetters only towards noonday, and after ploughing two or three rows the two yoke of oxen came to a halt; the steam foamed in clouds above their wet backs, their sides heaved painfully. Cleaning the clinging mud from his boots, Maxim took a sidelong glance at his father, and said in a hoarse, chilled voice :

"You know, father, I think. . . . Well, is this what you call ploughing? It isn't work, it's purgatory. We'll do the cattle in completely. You can look all around you and you won't find a single soul ploughing except us."

Yakov Alexeevich scraped the ploughshare with a piece of stick and said through his nose:

"The early bird cleans its beak, but the late one rubs its eyes. So the old people say; but you get the meaning of it, my boy."

"What's the point of talking about birds?" Maxim began to boil. "May it be thrice accursed, that bird of yours; it doesn't sow and it doesn't reap and doesn't go out to plough in weather like this. But you, father. . . . Oh, well, what of it. . . . ?"

"Well, we've had a rest, so off we go again, sonny, with God's help."

"What's the point of starting off again? Let's make it a good left-about turn, and quick march home."

"Get a move on, Stepan," said the father.

Stepan brought his long stockwhip down over both the teams. The plough creaked, and seemed to cling to the ground; it quivered shudderingly and slipped along, sluggishly turning over thin rolls of mud.

*   *   *

From the day Stepan became a Young Communist the rest of his family held aloof from him. They drew apart and became strangers, as though he were a leper. Yakov Alexeevich said openly:

"Things now won't be as they were any more, Stepan. You've kind of become a stranger to us. You don't pray to God, you don't observe the fasts, the priest came to say a prayer but you didn't bow before the holy cross. Is that the way to behave? And then in regard to the farm, we're afraid to say too much in front of you. Once the rot has taken hold of a tree it's done for; if it isn't cured in time it'll turn to spunk. But it has to be treated firmly, cutting out the ailing branch without mercy. That's what the Scriptures say. . . ."

"I haven't anywhere else to go," Stepan said. "But this year I shall be going to do my military service, and that'll set you free of me."

"We shan't drive you out of the house; but do stop your stupid conduct. There's no point in your hanging around meetings, the milk isn't dry on your lips yet, but you go off there with your mouth gaping. The people are making me a laughing stock because of you, you heathen."

As he talked the old man went purple, hardly able to control his agitation. But as Stepan gazed into his father's cold eyes, at the cruel, bestially twisted lips, he recalled the reproaches of his Young Communist comrades: "You put a bridle on your father, Stepka. He's ruining poor people, buying up agricultural implements before the spring at dirt cheap prices. It's a disgrace."

And, recalling this, Stepan went red with burning shame; he felt that he no longer had any intimate love in his heart, nor pity for this ruthless brute who was called his father.

It was as though a mute stone wall had been raised between him and the rest of the family. And there was no climbing over that wall, no knocking to make the others hear.

The estrangement gradually changed to petty spite, and the spite to hatred. At the dinner table, happening to raise his eyes, Stepan met Maxim's icy gaze; he shifted his glance to his father and saw angry little sparks burning under Yakov Alexeevich's baggy eyelids. And the spoon began to tremble in his hand. Even his mother was giving him indifferent, hateful looks. A lump stuck in his throat, uninvited tears scalded his eyes, a mute sob rose in a wave. Taking a firmer grip on himself he hurriedly finished his dinner and went out.

Night after night he dreamed the same dream : he was being buried somewhere out in the steppe, under a sandy slope. He was surrounded by strangers, people he didn't know; scrub with dry stalks grew over the slope, and needle-leafed wild onion. He saw every little twig, every little leaf as clearly as if he were awake.

Then they flung his dead body into a hole, and heaped clay on him with spades. One cold, heavy clod fell on his chest, then another, a third. . . . He woke up; his teeth were chattering, his chest felt tight, and when fully awake he took in deep, rapid breaths, as though short of air.

*   *   *

The field work came to an end for the time being. The steppe without human beings was empty; the only colour was conferred by the kerchiefs of the women working in the plots. Of an evening the village, gently enfolded in twilight shadows, dozed on the withered breast of earth, whose green tresses of gardens and orchards were scattered round the edges. The sounds of accordions were to be heard from a spot outside the village where the steppe ends in a scar and the swollen blue of the sky begins. The time of haymow was approaching. The grass was up to a man's waist in height. Awns were showing on the sharp little heads of the couch-grass, the blades went yellow and rolled up, the rape was filled with juice, the horsetails grew curly in the hollows.

Yakov Alexeevich was the first of all the peasants to mow his allocation of grassland. One night he harnessed up the oxen and drove with Maxim out of the camp beyond the boundaries, to the free lands of the village communal fund. The stars faded, the sky went ashy grey, a quail welcomed the dawn with its rattle; as Stepan woke up where he was sleeping under the waggon, he heard the mower slipping over the dew, mowing someone else's grass.

Yakov harvested enough hay for two winters. He was a good husbandman and he knew that in the early spring, when the poorer peasants' animals would be dying of hunger, he would be able to get a good price for a load of hay. And if they hadn't any money a yearling calf could always be transferred from their cattle yard to his. And so Yakov Alexeevich raised his rick to a height of over twenty feet. Spiteful people said he had mown other people's hay too by night; but, after all, you're not a thief till you're caught, and anyway there are always plenty of folk prepared to make such un-just charges.

*   *   *

After dark one Saturday, Prokhor Tokin dropped in. He stood fidgeting for some time by the door, turning his shabby green Budionny cap over and over in his hands, smiling anxiously, im-ploringly. "He's come to ask father to lend him oxen," Stepan thought. The man's skinny body showed through his ragged sack-ing trousers, his bare feet were bleeding, his slightly slanting black eyes glowed faintly, like coals under ash, in the deep caverns of his eye-sockets. Their gaze was bitterly hungry and imploring.

"Yakov Alexeevich, help me, for God's sake. I'll work it all off to pay you back."

"Why, what's your trouble?" Yakov asked without getting off the bed.

"You might lend me your oxen for a day. . . . To bring in my hay. Tomorrow's Sunday, but I'd bring it in all the same. . . . People are stealing my hay."

"I'm not lending you my oxen."

"For Christ's sake!"

"Don't ask, Prokhor; I can't. The cattle are worn out."

"Do please listen to me, Yakov Alexeevich. You know very well I've got a family. . . . How shall I get my cow through the winter? I've struggled and struggled; I haven't mowed, I've torn up the grass blade by blade."

"Let him have the oxen, father," Stepan intervened.

Prokhor gave him a grateful glance, blinking rapidly, and fixed his eyes on Yakov Alexeevich again. Stepan suddenly noticed that his knees were trembling a little, and in the attempt to conceal this involuntary quiver Prokhor was shifting from foot to foot like a horse set to a limber. Feeling a loathsome nausea coming over him, Stepan turned pale and almost howled:

"Give him the oxen. What are you pulling his tendons for?"

His father knitted his brows.

"Don't order me what to do. But if you're so keen you go to-morrow and help bring in the hay. I don't trust my oxen in strange hands."

"And I will too."

"Well, go then."

"Thank you; oh, thank you, Yakov Alexeevich," Prokhor bent his body double in his obeisance.

"Thanks is all very well, but when threshing time comes along you come and do a week's work to repay me."

"I'll come."

"Then make sure you do."

*   *   *

Dawn had hardly broken next morning when there was the sound of the militia-man's stick rattling under the windows of the houses and huts. Yakov Alexeevich went out, and found a messenger standing by the veranda.

"The sun's already rising. You're to come to a meeting in the school. . . ." The man unwrapped his tobacco pouch and muttered unintelligibly as he licked a strip of newspaper to make a cigarette: "An official's arrived to take the details of everybody's sowings. For taxation purposes. . . . That's the business. See you later."

He went to the wicket gate, his raw-hide boots clattering; he struck a match as he went. Yakov Alexeevich tugged thoughtfully at his beard and, turning to Maxim, who was driving the oxen back from watering, shouted:

"Wait a bit before handing the oxen over to Prokhor. There's a meeting this morning about the taxes. An official's arrived. I'll go along and take Stepka with me. He's a Young Communist, maybe they'll allow me a bit for him. Is he to be allowed to go around in his father's boots and go off to the club and do nothing in return?"

Maxim hurriedly left the oxen and strode across to his father:

"Look out, don't make a fool of yourself in your old age. Tell them to put down twelve or fourteen acres to your account instead of forty."

"Think you can teach me?" his father laughed sarcastically.

Over breakfast Yakov Alexeevich said to Stepan in an unusually gentle tone:

"You'll go with Prokhor tonight to bring in the hay; you can put on your Sunday trousers now and come with me to the meeting."

Stepan made no comment. He had his breakfast and followed his father without asking questions. In the school the people were packed like ears of corn to the acre in a fruitful year. At last, it was the turn of Yakov Alexeevich. The statistical official, going green with tobacco smoke, asked as he stroked his ginger beard:

"How many acres sown?"

After a moment Yakov Alexeevich narrowed his eyes in a businesslike manner:

"Four acres of rye"; he bent one finger of his left hand back to the palm. "Two acres of millet"; he bent a second finger back. "Eight acres of wheat. . . ."

He turned down a third finger and turned his eyes up to the ceiling, as though making mental calculations. Someone in the crowd began to titter; to cover the laugh someone coughed violently.

"Fourteen acres?" the official asked, nervously tapping with his pencil.

"Fourteen," Yakov Alexeevich answered firmly.

Clearing a way for himself with his elbows, Stepan pushed through the crowd to the table.

"Comrade!" His voice sounded dry and hoarsely strained:

"Comrade official, there's a mistake somewhere . . . father's forgotten. . . ."

"What has he forgotten?" Yakov Alexeevich shouted, turning white.

" . . . he's overlooked another field of wheat. . . . That makes the total forty acres sown."

A dull muttering came from the crowd; they began to whisper among themselves. From the back rows several voices cried in chorus :

"That's true; that's right. Yakov's telling lies. . . . He's got three lots of fourteen sown."

"Does this mean, citizen, that you're tricking us?" the official knitted his brows sluggishly.

"Who's to know? . . . The devil got me muddled up. . . . It's quite true there are forty. Forty exactly. Well, for goodness' sake! Who ever would have thought I'd overlook them?"

His lips began to quiver with embarrassment; the knobs worked up and down in his bluish cheeks. There was an awkward silence. The chairman whispered something into the official's ear, and the official struck out the figure fourteen with his red pencil and wrote above it in thick strokes : 'forty'.

*　　　*　　　*

Stepan hurried off to Prokhor's hut, and they rushed through the orchards to Yakov Alexeevich's house.

"You'd better hurry, brother," Stepan said, "for when father comes back from the meeting you can go to the devil before he'll let you have a single ox."

They hastily rolled the waggons out from under the overhang of the shed and harnessed up the oxen. Maxim called from the veranda :

"Have they taken down the details of the sowing?"

"Yes."

"And did they allow any discount for you?"

Stepan didn't understand the question, and he left it unanswered. They drove out through the gate. At that moment Yakov Alexeevich came almost at a run down the alley leading from the square.

"Gee up!" Stepan shouted.

The knout sent the oxen off at a quicker pace. Gently clattering, the two oxen with their ladder sides lowered rolled off into the steppe.

At the gate the panting Yakov Alexeevich waved his cap.

"Come back!" the wind carried his hoarse shout along in gusts.

"Don't look round," Stepan cried to Prokhor, and he laid on the whip still more energetically.

The waggons bounced as though diving into a gulley; while behind them from the village, from Yakov Alexeevich's fine house, the protracted roar still floated:

"Come back, you son of a bitch!"

*   *   *

They reached Prokhor's plot of mown grass after dark. Unharnessing the oxen, they turned them loose to graze on the stubble of the mown field. They loaded the waggons high with hay and then decided to spend the night in the steppe, and to drive home before dawn.

After treading down the second load of hay firmly, Prokhor rolled himself into a ball on top, tucked up his legs, and went off to sleep. Stepan stretched himself out on the ground. Throwing his sheepskin over himself to give protection from the dew, he lay gazing up at the beaded sky, at the dark outlines of the oxen nibbling the grass. The steamy darkness raised unfamiliar grassy scents, the crickets trilled away deafeningly; somewhere in the ravines an owl screeched yearningly.

Imperceptibly Stepan dropped off to sleep.

Prokhor was the first to wake up. He fell like a sack from the hay, and squatted on the ground, looking about him for the oxen. A darkness, dense and violet, enveloped his eyes in a spidery web. A mist was smoking above the hollow. The shaft of the Great Bear was pointing towards the west.

Prokhor found Stepan fast asleep some ten paces away.

He touched the sheepskin with his hand: the wool, soaked with icy dew, freshened his palm pleasantly.

"Stepan, get up. The oxen have gone."

They searched for the lost oxen all day. They ranged the steppe for a radius of seven miles around, searched in all the ravines, trod down the luxuriant colours of the unmown hay in the hollows and gulleys.

The oxen appeared to have fallen through the earth.

In the late afternoon they came together again by the lonely waggons, and Prokhor, black and haggard of face, asked Stepan:

"What are we to do?"

His voice sounded hollow. His anxious, slanting eyes blinked tearfully.

"I don't know," Stepan answered with glum indifference.

*   *   *

Yakov Alexeevich looked up at the sun, sneezed, and called to Maxim:

"They must have had a breakdown in a ravine. Here's evening coming on and they're still not back. When he does come, blast him, I'll teach him, and good and proper. I've still got to give him my thanks for the sowing figures. . . . He helped his father all right. I've brought up a degenerate serpent. . . ." He turned crimson, and roared:

"Harness the mare. We'll go and meet them."

They were still some distance away when Maxim descried Stepan and Prokhor sitting idly by the loaded waggons.

"Father! Look at that! The oxen are missing," he whispered in a sinking voice.

Yakov Alexeevich shielded his eyes with his palm and gazed: after a good look he touched up the mare with his knout. The light cart bounced over the hummocky virgin soil. Maxim waved the reins to urge the mare on faster.

"Where are the oxen?" he thundered above the rattle of the wheels.

The light cart drew up beside the foremost waggon. Maxim jumped out before it stopped, recovered his footing, and ran scowling up to Stepan.

"The oxen: where are they?"

"They're lost. . . ."

Terrible in his bestial fury, Maxim turned to his father as the old man ran up, and roared in a frenzy:

"The oxen are lost, father. Your dear son. . . . He's ruined us. Send him packing."

Yakov ran up to the whitefaced Stepan and sent him with one blow to the ground.

"I'll kill you. I'll tear your throat out. Confess, damn you: you've sold the oxen, haven't you? I expect you had merchants waiting here. . . . And that's why you were so anxious to drive out to fetch in the hay. Tell me!"

Maxim sent Prokhor rolling over the ground, kicking him with his boots in the belly, the chest, the head. Prokhor covered his face with his hands and bellowed hollowly.

Snatching a pitchfork from the waggon Maxim jabbed the prongs into Prokhor's legs, and said plainly but quietly:

"Confess! You and Stepan have sold the oxen, haven't you? It was all a put up job between you."

"Brother! Don't sin!" Prokhor raised his hands, and the blood, thick and bluish black, oozed from his split lips over his shirt.

"So you won't say?" Maxim asked in a hissing whisper.

Prokhor burst into tears, hiccuping and twitching his head. . . . The fork prongs entered his chest below his left nipple, easily, as if into a stook of hay. The blood did not start to flow at once. . . .

Stepan struggled beneath his father, arching his body and trying to bite Yakov's hands, aiming at their swollen veins and the ruddy brush of hair. . . .

"Strike under his heart," Yakov Alexeevich said hoarsely, spread-eagling his son on the wet, dewy ground. . . .

*　　　　*　　　　*

Maxim and his father arrived home after dark. All the way back Yakov Alexeevich lay face downward in the cart. As it bounced over the furrows his head banged hollowly on the bottom board. Maxim dropped the reins and brushed invisible dust off his trousers. Just before they reached the village he asked in a rapid patter:

"So we've arrived, but they're lying out there beaten up. It looks as though we've finished them off over the oxen. But they took the oxen. . . ."

Yakov Alexeevich made no reply. At the gate they were met by Aksinia, Maxim's wife. Scratching her large, hanging belly under her home-woven skirt (she was with child), she said in a sluggishly compassionate tone:

"You've driven the mare like that for no reason. The oxen . . . there they are, they've come home, damn them. And I suppose Stepka's stayed behind to look for them?"

Without waiting for an answer, covering her mouth to hide her gaping yawn, she went with a heavy, waddling gait into the house.

1926.

THE END

SILVER'S CITY

Maurice Leitch
Winner of the 1981 Whitbread Prize

It is a desolate city, a ruined landscape carved into sectors by slogan-covered walls, barbed wire barricades and khaki checkpoints. Ten years ago when Silver was put away for firing the first historic shot in the bloody sectarian war, Belfast was bitter and brutal. But violent as it was, it was still a real city, a city a man could rule. It was Silver's city.

Silver is a hero, his name a household name spelled out on gabled walls and carved forever in the unforgiving chronicles of the Loyalist movement. Sprung from behind the wire by the cold, professional new breed of gunmen, Silver is thrown into an utterly changed city ruled by assassins who kill not for the cause but for the thrill of killing. Silver turns against the tide of blood he loosed on Belfast, but it is a city ruled by mercenaries – it is no longer Silver's city.

Fiction   0 349 12179 6   £2.50

WHEN THE EMPEROR DIES

Mason McCann Smith

In 1868 Queen Victoria's empire was at the height of its worldly power. But one nation stood against British dominion: in Ethiopia the mystical Emperor Theodore held a handful of Crown subjects captive. His courage had delivered his people from the rule of the Turks but the heroic arrogance of the Lion of Judah was about to bring the full strength of a British expeditionary force crashing down on his kingdon. As General Sir Robert Napier led 12,000 troops to the fortress at Magdala, the Emperor prepared for the death he had grown to love. WHEN THE EMPEROR DIES is both a remarkable novel and a brilliant depiction of the war between earthly and spiritual powers.

FICTION   0 349 13232 1   £3.95

Just some of the titles
available in ABACUS paperback

FICTION

TIME & THE HUNTER	Italo Calvino	£2.50 ☐
THE SAFETY NET	Heinrich Böll	£2.95 ☐
NOBLE DESCENTS	Gerald Hanley	£2.95 ☐
THE ROAD TO BALLYSHANNON	David Martin	£1.95 ☐
THE TRIAL OF FATHER DILLINGHAM	John Broderick	£2.50 ☐
GOOD BEHAVIOUR	Molly Keane	£2.95 ☐
SILVER'S CITY	Maurice Leitch	£2.50 ☐
SOUR SWEET	Timothy Mo	£2.95 ☐
SUNDAY BEST	Bernice Rubens	£2.50 ☐

NON-FICTION

KAFKA – A BIOGRAPHY	Ronald Hayman	£3.25 ☐
ROBERT GRAVES	Martin Seymour-Smith	£4.95 ☐
AN ANTHOLOGY OF EROTIC PROSE	Derek Parker (Ed.)	£2.95 ☐
SECRET POLICE	Thomas Plate & Andrea Darvi	£3.50 ☐
SCHUMACHER ON ENERGY	Geoffrey Kirk (Ed.)	£2.95 ☐
THE BAROQUE ARSENAL	Mary Kaldor	£2.95 ☐
THE SECOND STAGE	Betty Friedan	£2.95 ☐
THE DRAGON AND THE BEAR	Philip Short	£4.95 ☐

All Abacus books are available at your local bookshop or newsagent, or can be ordered direct from the publisher. Just tick the titles you want and fill in the form below.

Name _____

Address _____

_____

Write to Abacus Books, Cash Sales Department, P.O. Box 11, Falmouth, Cornwall TR10 9EN

Please enclose cheque or postal order to the value of the cover price plus:

UK: 45p for the first book plus 20p for the second book and 14p for each additional book ordered to a maximum charge of £1.63.

OVERSEAS: 75p for the first book plus 21p per copy for each additional book.

BFPO & EIRE: 45p for the first book, 20p for the second book plus 14p per copy for the next 7 books, thereafter 8p per book.

Abacus Books reserve the right to show new retail prices on covers which may differ from those previously advertised in the text or elsewhere, and to increase postal rates in accordance with the PO.